Death or Glory

PART IV

Code of Combat

MICHAEL ASHER

PENGUIN BOOKS

PENGUIN BOOKS

Published by the Penguin Group
Penguin Books Ltd, 80 Strand, London WC2R 0RL, England
Penguin Group (USA) Inc., 375 Hudson Street, New York, New York 10014, USA
Penguin Group (Canada), 90 Eglinton Avenue East, Suite 700, Toronto, Ontario, Canada M4P 2Y3
(a division of Pearson Penguin Canada Inc.)
Penguin Ireland, 25 St Stephen's Green, Dublin 2, Ireland (a division of Penguin Books Ltd)
Penguin Group (Australia), 707 Collins Street, Melbourne, Victoria 3008, Australia
(a division of Pearson Australia Group Pty Ltd)
Penguin Books India Pvt Ltd, 11 Community Centre, Panchsheel Park, New Delhi – 110 017, India
Penguin Group (NZ), 67 Apollo Drive, Rosedale, Auckland 0632, New Zealand
(a division of Pearson New Zealand Ltd)
Penguin Books (South Africa) (Pty) Ltd, Block D, Rosebank Office Park,
181 Jan Smuts Avenue, Parktown North, Gauteng 2193, South Africa

Penguin Books Ltd, Registered Offices: 80 Strand, London WC2R 0RL, England

www.penguin.com

First published 2014
001

ISBN: 978–0–141–04722–5

www.greenpenguin.co.uk

Penguin Books is committed to a sustainable future for our business, our readers and our planet. This book is made from Forest Stewardship Council™ certified paper.

To Marianonietta, Burton and Jake

They are the only people on earth to whose covetousness both riches and poverty are equally tempting. To robbery, butchery and rapine, they give the lying name of *government*. They create a desolation and call it peace.

From the *Germania* by Cornelius Tacitus
(AD 56–120)

Thus shall we begin again, or at least some amongst us.

Heinrich Himmler, *Reichsführer SS*
(From his diary, 1924)

I

Constantine, Algeria
11 November 1943

'You want to watch your step with this chap, love,' the MP sergeant said. 'Went over to the Hun, see. 'Angin's too good for 'im, I reckon.'

He was facing Lieutenant Celia Blaney outside a heavy wooden door that might have belonged to a medieval dungeon: the tunnel it stood in smelt of dry rot and rats' urine. The cells lay in the basement-complex of a half-ruined Algerian citadel that had once been bombed by the Allies, reached by a maze of stairs, walkways and corridors.

Blaney's rose-and-ivory cheeks flushed almost the shade of her flame-red hair. The sergeant was a spit-and-polish tyrant, she thought: razor-scraped cheeks, gleaming cap-badge, shiny brass buckles, mirror-like toecaps on his boots. She'd let him get away with ignoring her rank, addressing her as *love*, eyeing her boobs and crotch brazenly, all the way down here. Denigrating Tom Caine, though, was the last straw.

The whole thing – the insolent treatment, this oppressive place, the creak of iron gates, the moans of prisoners, the stink of the stairways and tunnels and, most of all, her anxiety for Caine, riled her in a way she hadn't been riled for a long time. She felt the urge to lash out, knock the MP's cap off.

'Captain Caine is one of the most highly decorated officers in the Eighth Army,' she told him curtly. 'So kindly keep your opinions to yourself.'

The sergeant's mouth fell open. He'd had Blaney down as the meek-and-mild type: the kind of bint who'd giggle if you pinched her bum and drop her knickers if you cooed in her ear. She was a cracker, all right, with that fiery hair, the pert lips, the knockers made for squeezing, the firm buttocks cradled in her BD. You didn't often see crumpet like that in Algeria: in fact, you hardly saw any crumpet at all.

He winked at her. 'I know, love,' he said. 'It's *supposed* to be innocent till proved guilty. But they reckon . . .

'I don't care what they *reckon*, Sergeant. And don't wink at me, call me *love*, or eye me up. I'm an Intelligence Corps officer, and as far as you're concerned, my name is *Ma'am*.'

The MP was so flabbergasted he took a step backwards. 'I'm sorry . . . *Ma'am* . . . I . . .'

'Thank you, Sergeant. That will be all.'

Tom Caine was standing in his cell, gazing into a broken mirror they hadn't bothered to remove when they turned the place into a temporary prison: the quartz goat-eyes of a stranger stared back vacantly at him from dark hollows.

'You ain't Captain Caine, you're the devil.'

He thought of Corporal Mitch Mitcheson curled up in a huddle under the cemetery wall after the battle at Capo Murro di Porco, ranting to himself. He'd tried to help, found Mitch hadn't got a scratch on him: the chap stared at him with eyes like saucers.

'Stay away. Don't touch me. I seen you on the battlefield. I know what you are. You ain't Captain Caine, you're the devil.'

The medics hadn't wanted to take Mitcheson to the aid post. They said he wasn't wounded. 'He's wounded all right,' Caine told them. 'You just can't see some wounds, that's all.'

Caine had lost count of the number of times he'd been wounded: the history of the war was written in his scars – on his legs, on his back, on his arms, chest, face: but the scars you couldn't see went deeper. Betty Nolan lying in a coma with a bullet in her head; the demon faces of men infected with a germ-warfare agent; the Senussi boy shot in front of him; the men who'd died because of his orders, because of his mistakes, because of his impulses; the Germans, the Italians, the Senussi and others he himself had shot, maimed, stabbed, cut to pieces.

'You ain't Captain Caine, you're the devil.'

Then I must be in hell, he thought. He'd done all that killing, and maiming and mutilating: he'd caused the death, and torture and disfigurement of his own men, as well as the enemy, and if he was in hell, he deserved it. The war had changed him into something he hadn't wanted to be – a killing machine, a monster. *But maybe I was that to start with. Maybe the war just gave it the chance to come out.* At sixteen, he'd broken both his stepfather's arms. *If it wasn't in my nature, would I have done that?* Yet hadn't it taken years of beatings, of trying to like his stepfather, of enduring the sight of his sister and mother being molested, tormented, humiliated, before he'd gone berserk? Surely he'd never been like that when his real father was alive? He remembered happier days, casting horseshoes in the forge, trotting behind his dad's bicycle down the Fen, dyking, haymaking, picking potatoes, laying trails for the foxhounds, and those precious occasions when they'd taken the old 4.10 shotgun wildfowling. Those things belonged to another world, a world stopped by the war, a world that could never come back.

Caine heard the lock tumble, heard the door creak: he turned and stared into the face of Celia Blaney.

For a moment he thought he must be dreaming. He hadn't seen her in three months, and nobody had warned him she was coming. Now here she was, standing at his cell door in her man's BD, with a flush on her cheeks, and her chip-bag cap perched on her red curls.

He didn't know whether to shake hands or kiss her.

Blaney paused to watch the MP close the door, turned back to him. Then, without either knowing who'd made the first move, they were in each other's arms. Caine pressed her tightly to him, felt her thigh between his legs, felt the thrust of her pelvis, felt soft breasts through his shirt. He caressed her shoulders, touched her neck. He felt her quiver, saw her close her eyes, part her lips. He kissed her, sucked in the softness of her mouth. The kiss went on until Blaney pulled away.

She took a step backwards, panting slightly, as if shocked by what she'd just done. They eyed each other, embarrassed, neither of them sure what had happened. Blaney guessed Caine was thinking about Betty Nolan, the girl who'd been wounded in Alexandria. As far as she knew, Nolan had never regained consciousness.

Blaney and Caine had been friends in Egypt: she'd helped to nurse him back to health after the *Nighthawk* op. They'd never been lovers, though: she knew Caine was fond of her, but he'd been too devastated by the loss of Nolan to commit himself. She didn't know if that had changed.

A lot had happened since he'd left Cairo three months earlier. He'd served with Paddy Mayne's Special Raiding Squadron in Italy, had been captured after the Termoli landing. He'd escaped, but something had gone wrong: he'd ended up being accused of treason. Blaney had read the Butterfield report, but whatever they'd accused him of, she knew it was impossible. Tom Caine was the most honest, most courageous man she'd ever known.

She put out a hand: Caine took it, but didn't pull her to him.

'You're looking good,' he said.

'You too. Considering you're up for court-martial.'

Caine flinched. He saw her flush deepen, noticed pricks of tears in her eyes. '*Treason*, Tom? Not *you*. I don't believe it.'

He frowned. 'Funny things happen in war.'

Blaney glanced around the cell, took in the small cot, the slop bucket in a corner, the washbasin, the crude wooden table with chairs, the broken mirror. The thought that Captain Thomas Caine, DCM, DSO, 1st SAS Regiment, who'd survived so many scrapes, seen so much death, struggled so hard, should end up in a place like this made her sick. She had to choke back tears. *This isn't right. It isn't right at all.*

She resisted the urge to hold him again. 'What funny things?'

'It's a long story, Celia.'

Blaney moved over to the table, brought out a packet of Gold Flake cigarettes from a blouse-pocket, laid it on the top. She drew out a box of matches and a silver hip flask, set them next to the fags, unpinned her cap, put it down, then pulled back one of the chairs. She nodded at Caine.

'Come on, Tom. I want to hear it.'

Her voice was business-like: Caine studied her profile, the mass of fiery curls, the small, shapely ears, the way fine strands of bronze hair fell across the nape of her white neck. He realized suddenly that he'd missed her.

He still didn't know why she was here, though. Had she made a special visit to Algeria to see him? To wish him goodbye? He glanced at her cap on the table, noted the rose-and-laurel badge of the Intelligence Corps, with the Latin motto '*Manui dat cognito vires*' – 'Knowledge gives strength to the arm'. She was still with Field Security, then.

'You shouldn't have come,' he said with sudden ferocity. 'I don't have anything to say, all right?'

Blaney stiffened. 'Tom, you're facing a court-martial tomorrow. If you're convicted, it could mean a death sentence.'

'I've been under a death sentence for a long time. Someone down there must have been saving me for this.'

Blaney drew a long breath. She sat down in the chair, pressed both hands on the table, locked eyes with Caine.

'I must know what happened, Tom.'

'Why?'

'Because I'm your appointed defence counsel. Major Mayne asked me to do it. All right, you deserve better. I'm not a qualified barrister or anything, but I was half a lawyer before the war. Mayne wanted to help you, and I want to help you, and I'm afraid I'm the best we could manage.'

Caine paced over to the table, gripped the spare chair, leaned towards her. 'I *deserve* a death sentence,

Celia. I've betrayed Betty Nolan, betrayed my friends, my regiment, my country. I've even betrayed *you*.'

Blaney swallowed, stared back at him unblinking. 'I don't believe it. You've been under a lot of pressure, Tom. *Nighthawk* was beastly, and you'd only just got over that when they sent you to Italy.'

Caine said nothing: his face was drawn, his eyes heavy, uncertain. Blaney sniffed, brushed tears away, opened the pack of cigarettes. She took one, pointed it at the other chair.

'Tom, sit down there. Have a drink, smoke this packet of fags. Tell me what went on in Italy. I'm not leaving till I know.'

He hesitated. Slowly, he shifted the chair, sat down. He took a cigarette from the pack, stuck it in his mouth, lit both their fags, sat back. Blaney exhaled smoke, unscrewed the hip flask, offered it to him. 'Scotch,' she said. 'Cairo's finest.'

Caine took it, gulped whisky.

'Damn' good stuff,' he said.

2

Termoli, Puglia, Italy
4 October 1943

They landed at Termoli shortly before sunrise: it had rained all night, but the rain stopped just as they went ashore. Caine was leading 'A' Section, No. 1 Troop: he was first off the boat. He stepped straight into six feet of seawater, carrying a ton of kit, took a mighty lungful before Harry Copeland pulled him out, spluttering. Caine no longer trusted water: it brought back disturbing memories.

The Navy had landed them too late and too far out, but they struggled to the beach anyway, sodden through, but thankful that Fritz wasn't shooting at them. The squadron assembled in troops and sections: Paddy Mayne was there, cool as a bayonet, the only man wearing an SAS beret. The rest of them were togged up in soup-bowl helmets, but Mayne wore his beret everywhere, even when the bullets were flying. *Perhaps it* is *bulletproof*, Caine thought.

The landing was part of a bigger scheme – 3 Commando and 40 Royal Marine Commando were being put ashore to the south of them, to assault Termoli town. Paddy's men were still part of 1st SAS Regiment, but for the invasion of Italy they'd been designated 1st Special Raiding Squadron, and deployed with the Commando Brigade. They still had their *Who Dares Wins* badges and wings, but for now their parachuting role had been nabbed by the Johnny-come-lately 2nd SAS, under Bill Stirling – David Stirling's brother.

Caine dropped his rucksack in the sand, mustered his 'A' Section lads, told them to clean weapons. His gunner, Trooper Spike Slocum, a titchy Cockney with a chest like an oildrum and bulldog features, stripped down the Bren on an empty sandbag: he and his No. 2, Trooper Lofty Wade, drained the seawater from the barrel and chamber, oiled the mechanism. Like many of Caine's section, these men were desert vets: Wade, a fifteen-stone ex-Fusilier from Leeds, with a wash-leather face, dense-cropped hair, and slow, rheumy eyes, had won the MM on the Berka raid in Libya. Slocum had come through some of the worst desert fighting without a scratch: '*If Spike was a horse, you'd have bet money on him*,' they used to say. He was so hot on the Bren that Caine was glad he was on their side. He was gobby about it, though, and sometimes Caine couldn't help ribbing him.

'What's a short-arse like you doing with that pea-shooter, Spike? Shouldn't it have gone to Lofty?'

'*Lofty?*' The scowl was indignant. 'That clown couldn't hit a belly-dancer's bum with a ten-round burst, skipper.

Not even if she was spreadin' 'er cheeks in front of 'im, 'e couldn't.'

''*Ere*.' Wade squared his deep gorilla chest. 'I'll 'ave you know I was a champ shooter at Bisley.'

'With what unit, the Brownies? Don't bust me britches, mate. Now *me*, I'm a *real* marksman. I've bin known to put in a three-inch group at a thousand paces.'

Wade snorted. 'The only three inches you've put in anywhere is your flamin' plonker, an' *that* was prob'ly a knot in a pine tree.'

The other men guffawed. 'Save it for the Krauts,' Ron Hardman said. 'If we get through this, you *can* blow your trumpet.'

Hardman was Caine's sergeant – a grizzled ex-Gunner from Brum who'd survived the Rommel Raid: solemn, six foot two, granite jaw and head like a chopping-block. Not a lot to say, but solid as a boulder. Next to him, medical orderly Lance-Jack Sam Smith was oiling the barrel of his carbine with a pull-through. He was a cherub-faced, curly-haired youth from Manchester, who swore he was twenty-one when Caine knew he was only seventeen. That was all right by Caine: he'd lied about his age too. Corporal Ted Dangerfield, the wireless op – a bean-pole, specky fellow from Brighton with teeth like pegs and wire-framed glasses – was shaking his head over the No. 19 set.

'U/S, skipper,' he said. 'Got half the flamin' Adriatic in it.'

'Just dump it.'

'Can't do it, sir. When it dries out it'll probably be OK.'

That was Caine's HQ group: Hardman, Slocum, Wade, Dangerfield and Smith. There were three other sub-sections – about twenty men in all, plus a three-inch mortar team, attached to them from the support troop. There was also Harry Copeland, now a full lieutenant, who was Acting Squadron Adjutant. Mayne objected to having HQ staff in the field, so Cope had volunteered to tag along with Caine's section.

Caine was glad to have him: Copeland was bright and steady. He'd been with Caine in almost every scrap since he'd joined the commandos back in '41. He was a world champion know-it-all, too, of course: six weeks out of OCTU, and sometimes you'd have thought he'd written the bloody manual. Glancing at Cope – cornstubble hair, sea-blue eyes, that ropy, runner's build which always reminded Caine of a Fenland wading-bird – brought back memories of Fred Wallace and Taff Trubman, the mates they'd had to dump in Tunisia. That was six months previously, and they were still missing in action, presumed dead.

Mayne pointed out 'A' Section's objective to Caine on the map – a bridge on the Senarca river, slightly inland, and on the Termoli–Pescara road. 'And try and hold on to it this time,' he chuckled.

Caine knew his CO meant it as a compliment: he was referring to the action at the el-Fayya bridge in

Tunisia, when Caine's seven-man patrol had fought off an entire SS Totenkopf battalion. But Caine had lost almost the whole section on that scheme, holding a position that didn't need to be held, chasing a black box and a germ-warfare agent nobody believed existed: it wasn't something he cared to boast about.

3

They moved off in sub-sections, Caine on point, patrolled across the headland in file, in full battle-order, carrying rucksacks. It was getting light: the sun was a burnished sprawl along a wave of magenta mist, forging a bright path across the fish-coloured sea, bleaching darkness out of the sky, lighting up whale-humps of cloud with undersides of bleeding fire.

It was rolling land: hills and ridges, low clefts filled with shadowy woods, a quilt of penny-packet fields, orchards, olive groves, grapevines in tight ranks, thickets of bramble-scrub and pawpaw cactus, ragged hedgerows around farmsteads that looked like white shoe-boxes in the new light.

There was no sign of the Hun: all the action seemed to be happening around Termoli to the south of them – visible as a huddle of roofs and church-towers, peeking over a high sea-wall on the beach. They could see dark blobs on the landscape – commandos skirmishing towards the town – could hear the crackle of small-arms, the occasional deeper *bomp* of ordnance, could make out gashes of fire, blue smoke in slowly rising spires.

The fields were soggy from the rain: they followed lanes and cart-tracks, moving five yards apart, weapons at the ready. They had two Brens with them, but most of the lads had M1 carbines: Caine had his trusty Tommy-gun, Copeland the SMLE .303 sniper-rifle that not even his promotion to full looey had parted him from.

The track led into a wood of Aleppo pines, umbrella shapes that dappled the way ahead with light in paisley patterns. They'd only been in its shade a few minutes when Caine heard the rumble of motors. He hopped behind a tree, scanned the track with his binos: at the other end of the wood, a good half-mile away, a small convoy was moving towards them at a snail's pace. Caine leaned out of cover, signalled *enemy approaching*. He checked to see that his whole section had melted into the trees on both sides of the road. No further order was needed: the boys would wait for his shot, then let hellfire rip.

He squinted over his sights: saw an odd-looking vehicle leading the convoy. It was the kind of weird hybrid contraption only the Jerries could have come up with: an open trolley with tank-type tracks and a motorcycle front wheel hauling a field-gun on a wheeled carriage. It was the first time Caine had seen one of these trolley things close up, but it gave him a start. The only troops who had them were the Jerry Parachute Division – the same hard-hitters who'd done the famous drop on Crete. That meant they were up against the best.

Behind the half-track came two soft-skin lorries in

camouflage trim, trundling slightly ahead of a German infantry platoon in field-grey tunics and coalscuttle helmets carrying sub-machine guns and rifles. They looked alert, but were tabbing so slowly it might have been a funeral march.

Caine proned out in a firing-position, eased the butt of his trench-sweeper into his shoulder: he fixed his bayonet to the lug, slipped off the safety, gripped the forward stock. He sighted up on the half-track: there were two Germans riding her, one clutching the handlebars, the other peering over his back. Caine had that strange sense he sometimes got before a contact – that it was all unreal, a kind of performance, a show – people acting out roles like extras in a film, going through the motions, following instructions from a hidden director. He knew it *was* real, though: the journeys of all their lives had brought them here to this point, on this day, and in a few moments some of them – Krauts or Tommies, or both – were going to be dead.

The half-track seemed to approach with painful slowness, pulling the field-gun after her: Caine touched steel, held his breath, went cotton-mouthed: his heart banged. The vehicle crawled into effective range: the Krauts on board had the casual watchfulness of veterans: the driver had a cigarette dangling from his lower lip.

Caine let her move a little further: he heard her flywheels rattle, the slap of her tracks, the sewing-machine stitch of her motor. She was only twenty yards away when he took first pressure. *Fifteen. Ten.* He aimed at the driver with both eyes wide, pulled steel, felt the Tommy-gun jump, felt its muzzle blitz fire, felt it dole out taps that sounded like his heartbeat, *lub-dub*, *lub-dub*, *lub-dub*.

His rounds scored red groove-lines across the Jerry's chest, gouged open his throat, tore out a cheek: he saw shock on the man's face, saw his eyes flare, saw him pitch across the handlebars. He hammered another burst, snagged the passenger's neck, ripped open his gullet, saw him go airborne spraying spats of arterial blood. He crumped into the road, lay there with his knees up, twitching. The half-track slewed, bulldozed a tree, tipped up, hurled the driver out. The gun-carriage turned on its side. Copeland fired a rifle-grenade: Caine heard it pop, saw it hit the field-gun, saw it prang up with an ear-budding *thwoooommmmppppp* in a dark vortex of fumes and shredded steel.

The lorries screeched into reverse: Caine could see the faces of their crews through the windscreens. Behind them, Jerry footsloggers flopped down in the road: some scuttled for the trees. Schmeissers razzled, rifles racked: hot midges honed past Caine's ears. From his right, Bren-guns bludgeoned: tracer-lines flicked out like gecko-tongues. A dozen carbines crackled, cross-hatched wefts of fire: bullets sizzed, sprayed dirt-spouts, tweetered off stones.

The three-inch mortar dumpered: Caine saw the big shell hustle a smoke-parabola, saw it hit the cab of the first lorry, expand in a shimmering miasma, rupture into a douche of fire-vapour, saw charbroiled bodies tumble out of the flaming core. The second truck was reversing erratically: Caine's mortar-crew pitched another shell. Caine heard the bomb chafe air, heard the *pwwwuummmffffff* as it belted home.

Field-grey figures were advancing through the trees towards him, led by a big *Feldwebel* with a fighting-bull's face, making frantic hand-signals from point position. Caine saw him crouch ready to skirmish. He swivelled his muzzle: Cope fired first, over his shoulder, *bummffff, bummffff, bummffff*. Caine heard his slugs punch flesh, clocked rose mandalas splatter field-grey, saw the big Hun stagger: bloody divots dribbled from his gut.

Caine saw another Kraut toss a grenade, ducked, felt the kick, saw smoke-rags blow, felt shrapnel tunk his tin-hat. A giant, ash-faced Jerry loomed over him out of the smoke, eyes wide as a troll's, a gleaming blade on the end of his weapon. The rifle went *blampppphhh*: Caine felt the lam of heat on his face, scrambled to his knees. He lunged up just as the Jerry jumped him, felt his bayonet pivot into the man's groin, felt the Jerry's own momentum drive it in.

The soldier's body hit him like a bag of bricks. He reeled under the weight, let go his Tommy-gun, glimpsed glistening cheekbones, murky eyes, rictus-twisted mouth above the chinstrap. He punched the Jerry's face, knocked him sideways, wrenched his weapon out, saw blood spritz, felt warm slavers on his hands and up his sleeves. The Hun jerked: his eyes rolled.

Caine stuck the bayonet into his guts, kept sticking him till he lay still.

Two Jerries were haring towards him along the track, hefting rifles with bayonets fixed. Caine hardballed a burst, saw one keel over with his belly hot-pokered, saw the other stagger, saw his hip hose crimson squidges, saw his Kaiser helmet demolished by a long tantivvy from a Bren-gun behind him, saw the Kraut's head flacked to rissoles, smelt burnt hair, sour cordite, poached flesh.

He looked up, panting, saw Slocum advancing down the track, a squat little cannon-ball on legs, with his Bren slung from the shoulder: Wade towered over him, loping along with his carbine held loosely at the hip. Jerry dead lay around the blazing vehicles: wounded writhed and groaned. A dead German suddenly jumped to his feet and dashed for the bushes: Wade shot him from the hip without breaking stride, hit him spang between the shoulder-blades, brought him crashing down. Slocum squeezed iron, *rat-tat-tatted* rounds, fire-hosed the bushes, just to make sure.

4

The lorries were exhaling curdles of black smoke, crackling with acrid fire. Caine counted twelve Jerry dead – not bad for their first action. Cope called him over to look at the *Feldwebel* he'd shot: the long body was lolling in the trees, field-grey tunic splotched with crimson, mouth open, dead eyes staring at the sky. Copeland showed Caine the bronze para wings on the man's chest, the white-and-gold band on his sleeve. 'That's a commemoration band for the Jerry drop on Crete in '41, he said. 'Luftwaffe Airborne Division. I knew it the minute I clocked that *Kettenkrad*.'

'*Ketta* – what?'

Copeland nodded at the blackened skeleton of the motorcycle-thing.

'*Kettenkrad* special-purpose vehicle. Used by airborne troops.'

Smith shuffled up to report that a trooper from another sub-section had taken a wound in the shoulder: Caine was relieved that it was the extent of their casualties. 'We were lucky, skipper,' the medic said. 'If Billy Hill, the bookmaker, had been here, he'd have given it a hundred to one against.'

'Let's hope it stays that way.'

He left a sub-section and the mortar-crew to secure the wood, led the rest on through the trees. He was still feeling the adrenalin-burn: his battledress was soaked in Kraut blood. The success of their first contact made him buoyant, though: without the wireless he had no way of finding out how the rest of the squadron was doing, but if it was all like this, Termoli would be a pushover.

He halted the section near the edge of the wood, slunk forward for a recce, found a patch of scrub, scanned the landscape with his binos. The bridge was less than half a mile away – a stone hunchback spanning the narrow river. An image of the el-Fayya bridge popped into his head: that was where where he'd last seen Trubman and Wallace. This Itie bridge wasn't on that scale, though: it couldn't have been more than ten yards across. The road from the forest sloped down to it through green pastures dotted with wild olives, sparse bushes, yellow flowers: the fields were intersected by a network of dykes. On the far side of the bridge stood a dilapidated farmhouse of butter-coloured stucco in a sprawl of outbuildings and a crescent of poplars and prickly pear. He watched the buildings for a while.

He waved the section forward: they moved into the open, spread out five yards apart, with one Bren on the flanks, the other at the rear. Every twenty yards or so Caine went down on one knee, eased the strap of his rucksack, swept the area. The sun was a gold yolk squashed behind long skeins of cloud that layered the sky with gossamer draperies: far to his right, the sea lay like grey lead under glittering highlights of silver and pearl. It was eerily quiet: no birdsong, no cicadas, no buzzing bees. There was no movement anywhere, yet the day seemed pregnant with it.

'*Skipper!*'

Caine dekkoed over his shoulder, saw Lance-Corporal Sam Smith sliding towards him, bent forward: his big rucksack sat on his back like a turtle-shell. Smith crouched beside him, cradled his carbine, his Boy's Brigade features flushed.

'I thought I saw something move down there.'

Caine scanned the farm again, examined every window, every shutter, every decaying niche. He didn't see anything, but something felt wrong. This bridge was a strategic point: it seemed unlikely that the Jerries wouldn't defend it. There was a culvert in front of them, a dyke on both sides of the road; otherwise, hardly any cover at all.

He squinted backwards: Copeland was surveying the landscape through his telescopic sights. To his rear, the section was stretched out over fifty yards.

'Deploy the men in that ditch,' he told Cope. 'Me and Sam are going to advance to the bridge for a close recce.'

'Right. Watch it, though, skipper. It's wide open.'

Caine nodded, made a fist to bring his Bren group in. Slocum and Wade stalked up the middle of the track, set up the light machine-gun on the culvert, ready to cover the rest of the crew as they deployed in the dyke.

Once the boys had started moving in, Caine rose to

his feet, hefted his Thompson in both hands. They were going straight down the road: he didn't like it, but there was no other choice. He nodded at Smith. 'Come on,' he said.

The orderly eased himself up, took a few paces forward. Caine shuftied the bridge, the riverbank, the farm buildings. For a fleeting instant, he caught the ghost of a movement.

'Hang on,' he said. 'I . . .'

Smith had half turned to him when there was a blinding flash from the direction of the bridge: a bright ball of flame expanding. The deep-throat grump of a Kraut gun came only a split second before the shell pierced air, chomped the road in front of them with an ear-splitting *barrroooooommffff*, raked them with a foam of earth, smoke, twisted iron. Caine ducked: shrapnel twanged his helmet. He saw Smith's lower jaw knocked off by a whirling hunk of hot metal bigger than his hand, saw the gush of blood, teeth, bone jetsam, saw Smith hurled back, felt bone-shards stab his cheek, felt warm blood and tissue splatter his face.

Before Smith had even hit the deck, a Spandau tattooed out *rick-tick-tick-tick-tick* – orange tracer whizzed in like a sunflash, struck the frame of Caine's rucksack, spun him round. He fell flat on the track, saw men roll and scatter, saw a trooper behind him take the brunt of the burst, saw his chest wrenched apart in crimson tapes, saw another hit by a round smack between the eyes, saw his brains flushed out the back of his head in sticky strings.

Men piled into the dyke helter-skelter: Spandau bullets dopplered and shrieked, tracer seeded patterns, fireballs skittered air. The Jerry field-gun stonked again: a small-calibre shell yawed over them with a shrill whinny, hit the track behind Caine in horns of fire: a forest of dust-splashes sprouted along the road in front of him. Copeland fired a round, cocked, yelled: '*Watch my tracer!*' So calm and collected, he'd already pinpointed the target. He whaled a clip of .303 bullets, almost stove in Caine's eardrums: *blammm, blammm, blammm blammm.* Slocum spotted his strike, pulled in spasms: Wade's carbine kicked in, a descant in staccato whines.

Caine brought his Thompson up, fired bursts around Smith's body: the enemy weren't in the farm at all: they had dug in behind the riverbank. Hardman's gruff voice came from the dyke. '*Twelve o'clock. Enemy behind bank, to right of bridge. Two hundred yards. FIRE!*' Carbines clattered: the second Bren-gun ripped and truckled.

Most of the lads were in cover now: there were two dead on the track. Wade and Slocum were lying with their heads in the dirt, bullets popping all around them. Smith was sprawled face-down a yard away from him. Copeland helped Caine drag the orderly back by the webbing: they heaved him into the dyke. Spandau slugs hived off damp sods around them as they propped him up against the side. He was still alive, but his eyes were vacant: there was gaping red sphincter where his mouth should have been.

They dumped their rucksacks, removed Smith's kit.

Copeland jabbed him with morphia, slapped a shell-dressing on his lower face: bullets lumped in with squalling wallops: dirt-spouts rilled along the parapet. A ricochet skimmed Cope's arm, hit the back of Smith's skull with a taut slap. Smith tipped sideways, left a mush of brain-matter on the wall. Copeland dekkoed his own arm, clocked blood welling from above his wrist: he grimaced, swore, put aimed shots over the edge with Hardman and the others.

Caine had a quick shufti at Smith: he was dead, lying in a swamp of mud and gore. He noticed Dangerfield bending over the wireless a few yards along, with the headphones clamped over his ears, shiny eyes behind wire-rim specs. '*It's working, skipper. I think I can get . . .*'

A dropping round beamed through the top of his hat with a fly-swatter *thwooockkk*, plopped out through his throat in a swelter of bloody skin-shreds, hit the wireless with a metallic clunk. Dangerfield's hands went rigid: his eyes blanked out: he slumped over the wireless, dropped blood-gobs from his nostrils.

An iron claw squeezed Caine's chest: he ground his teeth, breathed in sulphur, cordite, scorched blood. He popped up on the parapet right of where Slocum and Wade had set up their Bren, took a breath, triggered a long burst, saw Wade switch mags, heard Slocum crackerjack fire.

An artillery round clamshelled in front of Hardman, shook the earth, split into a poke-shaped core of fire. The blast blew away half the sergeant's torso, plucked his right arm out of its socket: his carbine soared ten yards: its fractured muzzle stuck through another man's neck like a bayonet, came out the other side festooned with bits of bloody flesh.

Hardman's body flew backwards, hit the other side of the dyke, helmet gone, boulder head smoking: his eyes were still open, but he looked no more than surprised. A bloody flap of skin hung over his belly: Caine could see his heart pulse through yawning white ribs. To his right, the speared trooper was clawing at the rod stuck through his neck: he went down with his eyes rolling, battling for breath. Caine saw the trooper next to him try to pull the carbine out.

There was a lull in enemy fire: it felt ominously like a prelude. Caine looked sideways: the dyke was slopping with blood, smeared with filaments of gut and entrails: dead and maimed men seemed to be everywhere. Caine made a swift head-count. Only eight men standing, some of them hurt.

He touched Cope's arm. 'They're going to attack, Harry. Take every man who can walk – pull out.'

Copeland stared at him dumbly. His cornflower-blue eyes were wet gems in a face black with dirt and powder. He'd lost his helmet: his blonde bog-brush hair was smeared with mud, blood, body tissue; his forearm bulged from the dressing he'd slapped on. 'What're *you* going to do?'

'Stay here with the Bren group. Give covering fire.'

Cope's big Adam's apple quivered. 'Tom, I'm not going to . . .'

'Get them out, Harry. That's a fucking *order*.'

Copeland's eyes widened. They'd been in so many tight corners together, had covered each other so often, that even to Caine it seemed like a betrayal.

Cope looked livid: for a moment Caine thought he was going to argue. Instead, he blinked, said quietly, 'I'll stay. You go, mate.'

Caine wasn't surprised. Cope could be the most patronizing blighter in the world, yet his loyalty had never wavered, not even when Caine had gone against the brass, not even when his plans had been barking mad. It was the old code of combat: no one dipped out on his mate. Caine had never forgiven himself for Wallace and Trubman.

He lowered his voice. 'This is my damn' fault for being so cocky. I led us into it.'

'They shouldn't have deployed us like infantry, Tom. It's not SAS. Our role's strategic.'

Christ! Caine thought. *Here we are facing the big dark and he's talking strategy*.

'Make sure and tell Paddy that,' he said. 'Now bugger off. I'm going to put down smoke. The Bren group will stay with me till you're clear.'

A weave of fire-spurts danced along the dyke-edge. They heard a feral roar like a football-crowd: Caine peered over the brink, observed a horde of Kraut infantry moving towards them – field-grey matchstick-men in Kaiser hats hefting sub-machine guns, rifles with gleaming bayonets. They must have outnumbered his section four to one. Copeland shuftied the advancing horde through telescopic sights, clocked the pointman, a giant soldier in full battlekit, chamber-pot helmet pulled down over a face as raw as a pound of steak: broken nose, eyes like polished flint, wearing NCO's rank, bronze para wings, Crete band on his sleeve. He was about to squeeze the trigger when Caine nudged him again, thrust his Thompson at him. 'Take this. Leave me a carbine, Harry.'

Copeland took the weapon one-handed, glanced at it, tried to work out whether it was a memento or a promise. Then he slung it over his shoulder, gave Caine a long look, turned away. '*Prepare to withdraw!*' he bawled.

'Wait for my order,' Caine said.

He monkey-ran along the dyke through gore, viscera, spent cases: he grabbed the M1 the speared trooper had dropped, took a quick dekko at him. He was face-down with his head propped at an odd angle by the bent weapon, drooling brown mucus. *Alfred John Weaver from Bolton, twenty-one, tile fitter in Civvy Street, unmarried, dead as a fucking doornail.*

Caine slipped a couple of smoke-canisters from his webbing, took one in each hand, pinned them with his teeth. He tossed them over the parapet, waited five seconds until the smoke was wufting along the edge in thick billows.

'*Go!*' he yapped.

Copeland and the others scrambled over the rear parapet: Caine didn't watch them pull out. In a second he was back with Wade and Slocum, waiting for the smoke to clear, for the Krauts to come ramping through. He fired a couple of rounds blind just to keep their heads down: Wade's carbine snapped in his ears. Slocum kept up a trickle of edgy taps.

The smoke thinned: Caine peered over his sights, saw field-grey forms shunting towards them – maybe forty men – coming on with precision-drill determination: jogging, rolling, firing. Schmeissers razzled, rifles clacked, bullets whooped, thunked into the dyke-edge, squawked insanely past his ears.

Caine willed the tremor out of his fingers, zeroed in on a tall Jerry brandishing a rifle and bayonet like a spear. He fired, opened up the Kraut's chest in berry-red bursts. He clocked a coalscuttle pop up from behind a wild olive tree, swivelled, stilettoed a slim .30 needle *splack* through the Jerry's eye. Slocum raked double-taps – *rat-TAT*, *rat-TAT*, *rat-TAT*: Wade spliffed carbine rounds, directed the Bren. 'Right a bit, bit more. See yon Kraut by the tree, looks like a pig in a bonnet? Smoke 'im, mate.'

Rat-TAT, *rat-TAT*, *rat-TAT!*

'On'y winged 'im, you useless bugger.'

'You wanna do it?'

'No, I'm jus'sayin'.'

'Shut yer trap, then.'

'See that bloke there, eleven o'clock, rat-faced sod with a moustache? Get 'im . . .'

Rat-TAT, rat-TAT!

'Gawd, coulda done better blowin' peas out me arse.'

Kraut bullets wellied, droned, ground off stones: Caine didn't even hear them. He was in a cotton-wool fuzz, in a place where all actions were happening in slow-time and nothing seemed real except reaction. He saw helmets bob up, squeezed metal: saw Jerries lurch forward, spouted rounds. It didn't feel as if he was doing the shooting: he was somewhere above it all, looking down, and the weapon in his hands was doing it for him. A Jerry slug went *thwick* on his stock, brought him back to earth with a sting of pain. He yawped, let go of the carbine, saw blood oozing between his knuckles. He dekkoed his hand: a bullet had skinned his middle finger.

He gripped the weapon again, wiped blood off the stock, picked a Kraut, lined up his sights, hauled steel: the hammer clacked on an empty chamber. He swore, released the mag, checked it, found it empty. *You bloody great clot. Why didn't you get spare ammo when you had the chance?* He thought of pulling his pistol: the enemy weren't in pistol-range yet. He glanced sideways, spied Hardman's gore-soaked ammo pouches lying a few yards away by the mutilated wreck of his body. *There must be ammo in there.*

He ducked down, darted for the pouches, grabbed at

them, paused, realized Slocum had stopped firing. He glanced back at the Bren-group, saw Slocum flip the empty magazine sideways, saw Wade reach in his haversack, come up with a fresh one. 'This is the last,' he growled. 'Now, can yer try an' *hit* a Jerry this time, mate? Ain't that what we're being paid for?'

''Ere, my tally's nine so far. Now stick that flamin' mag on and stop rattlin'.'

Wade chuckled: as he leaned over to clip on the fresh mag, a rocket squealed out of the air like a harpy on a smoke-trail, chumped his helmet, detonated with a flash of heat, a blur of light, a gut-curdling *kavvvrrrroooooommmmppp*: Caine felt the air unzip, felt the ground go bow-shaped, clocked a five-point starburst of matter, dirt, shrapnel, saw Wade's head guillotined off his shoulders. His big body convulsed, became a spiral of scarlet tissue, shattered bone, scorched sinew: Caine saw his leg-sockets unhinge, saw the burning remnants of his frame blown across the dyke. At the same instant, Slocum pitched sideways, the skin blasted off his skull: his eyes popped, his battledress shredded, his body became a bag of burning skin and fractured bone: his left hand flipped in one direction, his right arm in another.

The shockwave knocked Caine off his feet, threw him on top of Hardman's body. He rolled over, sat up, felt his head pendulum, felt the world breathe him in and out like a bubble. He extended a hand to steady himself: getting to his feet was like climbing a mountain. He blinked, rubbed gore out of his eyes, stood there quivering with shock. He didn't even know the Jerries were watching him until a voice crouped.

'*Hände hoch!*'

There they were, in a huddle above him, pointing their weapons in his direction. They could have shot him then, but they didn't.

A walking block of a man in a Kaiser hat and full battle-rig jumped down, surveyed the carnage in the dyke, the crushed and smouldering bodies, the smelted tissue hanging off the sides, the severed limbs, the puddles of blood-slush. He levelled his Schmeisser at Caine, peered at him out of a pug-face riddled with old shrapnel-scars, a broken nose, glassy green eyes. He wore NCO's rank, and the Crete armband on his sleeve: Caine recognized him suddenly as the giant NCO who'd led the Hun charge. His gaze fell on the bronze parachute insignia on the man's chest. The Kraut's eyes narrowed, peered at the SAS wings still visible through the blood on Caine's battledress.

'*Such a pattle*,' the Jerry said in broken English. It sounded almost as if he'd enjoyed it. 'I *vas* going to shoot you, but I see you are one of our airborne brothers, so I vill not.'

He glanced at the smoking remains of the corpses that only moments ago had been Slocum and Wade, let out a bitter laugh.

'Put up your hands and gif me your weapons,' he said. 'You are now a prisoner of Chermany.'

5

Villa Montefalcone, Le Marche, Italy
2 October 1943

The Waffen-SS detachment moved in on the Villa Montefalcone an hour after first light: jackboots crunched along the gravel drive, the men broke up into squads, cleared the gardens, set up a Spandau near the steps leading to the front door. *Reichsgeschäftsführer* Wolfram Stengel stood by a gleaming Horsch staff-car, twirled his moustache, whistled the 'Radetzky March'.

Although equivalent in rank to SS colonel, Stengel never wore uniform: this morning, he was dressed in a black leather trench-coat and broad-brimmed hat. His only insignia was a lapel pin in the shape of a sword through an inverted omega – the logo of the Ahnenerbe.

The villa looked more like a fortress than a house: a central mass of stone oblongs with arched windows, external staircases, verandahs, walkways: a mosaic of roofs at various angles, a forest of stone towers, perforated by arrow-slits, capped by red-tiled roofs that looked like oddly shaped, exotic hats. Part of the ground floor was obscured by a ruined girdle-wall with crumbling stone buttresses which was obviously much older than the rest of the building. Set into the wall, on one side, was a stone chapel with a bell-tower and a low-pitched, ochre-tiled roof. He'd been told that the villa was constructed on the ruins of a medieval monastery, some of which had been incorporated into its structure. It had a neglected air, though: fallen edgings, decaying stonework, dark stains of rain-damage on its walls. Grass grew through cracks in the stones: the grounds were a gone-to-seed jungle, hemmed in by deep brakes of forest. Yet it was impressive: standing against the heroic backdrop of the Apennine mountains, it had the brooding Gothic feel of a castle out of the Brothers Grimm.

There was certainly German influence, Stengel thought. There was *always* German influence – you could find it as far afield as Tibet, Brazil and Iraq. In the past few years, expeditions the Ahnenerbe had sent out to such places had returned with irrefutable evidence of the worldwide diffusion of ancient German culture. Stengel had enjoyed those expeditions. Now, as Ahnenerbe director, he was burdened with more mundane matters, mainly the medical experiments being run in the Reich's concentration camps, and the 105 Bolshevik-Jew commissars he'd had liquidated to provide skeletons for the Anatomical Institute of Strasbourg.

From the window of her suite, Countess Emilia Falcone heard the voices, saw Krauts scatter through the grounds, saw the staff-car sweep round the bend in the drive, saw it pull up, saw the man who got out – bearded, wearing a black coat and hat. She bit her knuckles, hoped that this wasn't about Ettore. Her brother had been working with the *Giappisti* – the partisans: she'd heard rumours that he'd been involved in a bombing in Ancona. She wasn't against the Resistance, but Ettore was only sixteen, and he was all she had left.

Her father, Count Giuseppe Falcone, and her American mother had been killed in an air-crash before the war. The count had left instructions in his will charging Emilia with the care of the family estates, including the Villa Montefalcone and its treasures. She was to act as Ettore's legal guardian until he came of age. She'd been reluctant to give up her life in New York to return to an Italy under Mussolini, but the Falconi were one of the oldest families in the country, and family duty came first.

Now, she lived in the rambling villa alone but for her housekeeper, Angostina: there had been a girl called Lucia, who'd come up every day from a local farm, until the Hun had arrested her on suspicion of being a runner – a *staffetta* – for the partisans. Emilia's small suite stood like an island among the house's great galleries: the staircases that linked the labyrinth of rooms were dusty and uncared for: furniture lay under acres of sheeting, books and art-treasures had been moved to the warren of cellars.

She heard a commotion by the door, craned her neck, saw that the Krauts had seized Angostina – a dough-faced old lady in a dark shawl and a widow's black dress.

Emilia caught her breath, watched the bearded German as he strutted over to the group, saw the old woman struggle, saw the Kraut soldiers twist her arms. She saw the bearded man slap her across the jaw with an open hand, saw Angostina raise her chin, saw the man slap her again.

Emilia ran out of her quarters, dashed along the corridor, down the main stairs into the hall, along the passage to the open front door. She stepped into the sunlight, took in the tableau of figures below.

'Don't hurt her,' she said in English. 'Please let her go.'

Stengel looked up to see the girl coming slowly down the steps. She was young – twenty-one or -two perhaps – with a slender figure, slim hips and ample breasts. Her skin was milky brown, her hair jet-black, combed from a centre parting to fall over trim shoulders in lush, wayward tangles. She had a broad face, with high cheekbones and a proud nose: her amber-coloured eyes were very slightly slanted at the corners, giving her an almost oriental look. Her chin was strong and dimpled, her mouth wide, with full lips that held a hint of mockery. Her simple black dress, short enough to display smoothly tanned calves, emphasized an almost feline flexibility. Altogether, Stengel thought, she conveyed a thoroughbred assurance: she looked very Italian, though her US-accented English reminded him that she was half-Yank.

'Countess Emilia Falcone?'

‘Yes. Who are you?’

‘I am Dr Wolfram Stengel. I have come to collect the Codex.’

The countess blinked eyelashes as delicate as a butterfly-wing, ran elegant fingers through her wealth of dark hair: Stengel noted that her right eyelid drooped very slightly over the iris, so that only half of it showed: it gave her a hint of sleepiness, he thought.

‘Which Codex?’ she said. ‘I don’t know what you mean.’

‘I mean the *Codex Aesinias*, a manuscript of Tacitus’s *Germania* possessed by your family for generations. Herr Mussolini promised it to our Führer before the war: I am here to see that promise fulfilled.’

Emilia dropped her eyes, partly to hide her relief. *It’s not about Ettore. It’s about the Codex.* Ever since she’d been a schoolgirl the Nazis had made periodic demands for the book: they seemed to think it was rightfully theirs. Her father had refused to give it up, though: not only was the Codex a priceless heirloom, it was also an Italian national treasure. In the end, even Mussolini had baulked at the idea of allowing it out of the country. The Falconi had never been Mussolini supporters: Emilia would have been overjoyed to see the back of that Fascist *stronzo*, if it hadn’t been for the fact that the Codex was no longer under his protection.

She batted her eyelids: Stengel was a tall man in his thirties, rather handsome, she thought, in a clinical sort of way – high cheekbones, a firm chin, a thick, black beard and moustache. His nose was long and sharp, his mouth thin, his eyes coal-black, with a coldness that was disturbing.

At first she'd thought she might get away with it by acting the dumb brunette. *Not with this one, though.*

'Oh, you mean the *Germania*?' she said. 'It's not in the house. My father had it moved to another location.'

Stengel's eyes never seemed to look at her directly. '*Which* location?'

'I don't know.' She smiled. 'He never told me.'

It lies in a room with no doors or windows. I am the door. Another holds the key.

Stengel gripped her arm suddenly: his fingers dug into her bare flesh. She winced, held herself rigid. *Don't scream. Don't struggle. Now's not the time to do anything.*

Over his shoulder, she saw that the SS-men had let Angostina go: six or seven of them were standing expectantly behind Stengel. He snapped orders: the men filed in through the open door, tramped down the passage. 'You and I will have a talk,' he said, 'while my men search this house from top to bottom.'

He frogmarched her upstairs to her private quarters, pushed her down on the sofa. He surveyed the room: mountain views and seascapes on the walls, empty wine-bottles, framed photographs. He took off his hat, brushed it, laid it on the table, folded his coat, draped it over a chair. His head was broad and cat-shaped, his hair a dense black mat, his eyebrows topped the deadman's eyes with circumflex accents. He picked up a photo of a lean, pasty-faced youth, studied it.

'I am guessing that this is your brother,' he said. 'Where is he now?'

Emilia sensed a trap. *Could this be about Ettore after all?*

She swallowed. 'He's still in America, where I left him.'

Stengel nodded, put the photo down. He marched over to the door, locked it.

The sound made Emilia jump: her nipples went taut: her legs tremored. Stengel leaned over her, his face expressionless. 'I don't think we yet understand each other, Countess,' he said. 'But, of course, we will change that.'

He hit her across the face with an open hand. 'Where is the Codex?'

She touched her stinging cheek, glared at him. 'I don't know.'

He hit her again. She gasped, felt tears creeping down her face.

Stengel leaned further: she flinched, gagged at the smell of his eau de cologne. He grabbed her right breast, pinched it until the nipple stood up.

No. Please. Not this.

Her eyes fell on the wine-bottles. They were the only available weapons, but they were too far away. *Don't do anything. The house is full of Krauts. They'll kill you.*

He grasped her left hand, lifted it: his finger and

thumb closed on the ring she wore on her middle finger. 'What's this?'

My ring. He wants my ring.

It was a signet ring of the Falconi, bearing their crest: a shield with a double-headed hawk in a laurel wreath. 'It's one of an identical pair,' she said hoarsely. 'It's been in my family for generations.'

Stengel dropped her hand, jerked her to her feet, hustled her through the open door of the bedroom, halted her by a double bed with a carved headboard.

'*Take off your clothes.*'

She hung her head: felt a claw close on her throat, felt cold fingers creep across her belly. The word *please* formed on her tongue: she bit her lips, felt surging cramps in her stomach.

She brushed back strands of hair, took a deep breath, drew the dress over her head, dropped it on the carpet. She stood trembling before him in her underclothes, head bowed, hands over her breasts, thick tresses falling across her face.

'*Take off your underwear.*' His voice was husky, excited.

'*No.*' The word was out before she could stop it, followed with dizzying speed by a punch that crashed into her mouth, sent her sprawling. She found herself face-down on the bed, her lips bleeding, her head spinning, her senses fading. When she came round, she was naked, her face in a blood-streaked pillow, her hands tied to the headboard with strips torn from her own underwear.

She heard Stengel's heavy breathing behind her, tried to see what he was doing, found she couldn't budge.

His fingers were on her thighs, parting them roughly: one hand groped her crotch: his fingers shoved into her. She whimpered, heard a breathless snigger, felt movement on the bed, smelt the sickening eau de cologne, sensed him crouching over her.

'So you do not know where the Codex is, eh, Countess?' he chortled. 'Perhaps this will help you remember.'

She shrieked as something rigid and cold was thrust deep inside her.

Later, she realized that her ordeal had lasted under an hour: at the time, though, the pain and humiliation seemed to go on for ever. Stengel raped her with a wine-bottle, sodomized her, croaked in her ear, bit her, raked her flesh. After a short while he seemed to lose interest in the Codex: he gave himself over entirely to tormenting her. The agony became unbearable: as she began to slip away she heard someone whisper: '*What is sought lies in a room with no doors or windows. I am the door. Another holds the key.*'

With a start, she realized that the whisperer was herself.

Stengel slapped her buttocks. 'What was that? What are you saying?'

Emilia moaned, shook her head. Stengel drove the bottle inside her once more, furiously. He violated her again and again, sneered, slobbered, made a queer grunting sound in his throat. The assault was so violent this time that Emilia thought he was going to kill her. He cast the bottle aside, thrust himself into her, curled tough fingers around her throat, his face slicked in sweat, his eyes popping. He plunged into her harder and harder: she mewled, thrashed, tried to kick at him: just before she passed out she felt his body shudder.

When she came to again, he was untying her wrists from the bed-head. 'Still with us?' he sneered. 'Getting acquainted has been a great pleasure.'

Stengel left her sobbing on the bed, found the bathroom, halted in front of the washbasin. He stared into the mirror: *What is sought lies in a room with no doors or windows. I am the door. Another holds the key.*

Gibberish, he thought.

He caught a movement behind him in the mirror: a shadow flitting past, then, just for a fraction of a second, a face staring over his shoulder – a face like parchment drawn taut over a skull: a leering, vacant mouth, glittering jewels for eyes. Stengel froze, broke out in a cold sweat. *There's someone else here – standing right behind me.*

He spun round, saw movement from the corner of his eye, felt his heart bump. *There's nothing. It's this old house: full of creaks and shadows.* He glanced in the mirror again: he'd been certain he'd seen that skeletal face, but now there was just his reflection. He still felt disquieted, though. Ever since he'd had to oversee the preparation of those 105 specimens, he'd been seeing Jew-Bolshevik commissars everywhere – the hidden eyes, the uncanny sounds like dogs howling, the dark presences that stalked him at night, which, when he looked, were never there.

He picked up a bar of soap, turned on the brass tap, washed and rinsed his hands with surgeon-like precision. He washed them again and again, but they felt as unclean as they had done to start with. He shuddered: it wasn't just his hands that were filthy but his whole body. He would have to take a shower at Jesi, scrub himself with scouring-powder until he got rid of it.

Emilia heard running water, heard Stengel whistling, heard him mutter. It seemed hours before he strode back into the bedroom, stood over her. When she didn't stir, he turned away. 'I will go back to Jesi now,' he said, 'but the SS detachment will stay. If you attempt to leave this villa, you will be shot. I will return in a few days. Perhaps you will have remembered where the Codex is by then. If not, the . . . *entertainment* . . . will continue.'

Emilia closed her eyes, heard his vacant whistle recede down the passage, cried to herself, tried to deal with successive waves of agony, shock and nausea. *I'm alive*, she thought at last. *That's the biggest mistake you'll ever make, you Nazi cocksucker.*'

6

Near Montefalcone, Le Marche, Italy
1 October 1943

The lorry drew up at the edge of the forest: Sipo-SD troops herded the prisoners out at gunpoint: *SS-Sturmbannführer* Karl Grolsch ticked off their names on a clipboard. Trooper Fred Wallace, a head taller than any of the other POWs, took a dekko around him: it was just after first light, with a splodge of crimson peeking through the foliage: no birds sang.

Like the other half-dozen prisoners, Wallace was wearing shabby civvies and down-at-heel shoes: his hands were cuffed in front of him. Ever since Grolsch had made the SAS-men hand over their uniforms the previous evening, Wallace had smelt a rat. Grolsch's story that they were being taken to the Swiss border for a prisoner-exchange didn't add up. Why, in that case, were they wearing civilian togs? Why had the lorry stopped little more than an hour after they'd started?

When Grolsch ordered them to march along the forest track, Wallace's neck-hairs prickled. '*Where the flamin' 'ell you takin' us? This ain't no Swiss border.*'

A stoat-faced Jerry hit him with a rifle-butt on a shin

still tender from the wound he'd taken in Tunisia six months earlier. Wallace jumped. '*Owwww! You fuckin' Fritz bastard, I'll . . .*'

'*Now, now, settle down there.*' Grolsch sounded like an exasperated schoolmaster. 'Let's make this exchange orderly: very soon you'll be free.'

'A prisoner exchange *in a forest*?' Taff Trubman hissed in Wallace's ear. 'That's a good one, boy.' The stubby Welshman was hobbling from the injuries he'd copped on the Tunisia mission: since then, the Jerries had transferred him and Wallace here to Le Marche, where they'd spent months recuperating in the POW hospital-wing at Jesi. They'd only just been declared fit to work when this *prisoner-exchange* had come up.

The five other SAS-men with them had been captured a month earlier, on a drop near Ancona. Their DZ had been compromised: Fritz had been waiting for them. Their stick-leader, Lieutenant Johnny Howard, had been hit in the groin, lost a lot of blood: he'd spent the whole month in hospital. Now, a couple of Krauts were dragging him between them while the rest of his patrol – Morris, Seymour, Yates and Cameron – tramped on, ashen-faced and dull-eyed.

They arrived in a clearing in the woods: the light through the trees wove the leaf-mould ground into a net of claws, fangs, talons. Wallace saw that half a dozen troopers in Kaiser helmets were waiting for them, noticed with a jolt that they were carrying Sten sub-machine guns. A cold fingernail raked his spine.

Why would the Jerries be using British SMGs? *They're gonna smoke us. I knew it. They're gonna smoke us with our own weapons and make it look like friendly fire.*

Wallace stared at Trubman: the Welshman's eyes behind his thick lenses were dilated: sweat trickled down his pink cheeks. *Come on, Taffy, mate. We've got out of scrapes worse than this.*

The Jerries formed the prisoners into line, elbow to elbow, positioned themselves five or six yards away. Propped up by two of his own men now, Howard raised his head. 'What the Dickens *is* this?' he demanded.

He was an unshaven, dishevelled youth whose features had the outraged innocence of a new-hatched chick: he seemed to have difficulty keeping his head up.

An apologetic smile curled Grolsch's lips. He straightened his shoulders, slipped a piece of paper from his pocket, unfolded it with careful ostentation. Wallace tugged at his handcuffs, swivelled his stone-carved head, searched desperately for a way out. His hands were shackled but not his feet. He could still run. He felt fire seeping through his limbs, caught his breath, shivered. *No, I'm not takin' it. It ain't going to end this way.*

Grolsch cleared his throat: he looked like a priest in the pulpit, Wallace thought – dimpled chin, domed forehead, receding hair: he had the same earnest gravity, same sincerity of purpose.

Fuck you, mate. Fuck all Nazi bastards.

Grolsch began to read from the paper in a mournful

voice. Wallace felt tiny electric shocks spark through his body: he clenched his fists, felt his calf-muscles go taut. He caught Trubman's eye, gave him a slow, deliberate wink. The signaller flushed: he nodded tightly.

'On the orders of the Führer, all so-called commandos, whether armed or unarmed, in battle or in flight, whether dropped by parachute or other means, whether or not they surrender, are to be subject to special handling, according to the rules of warfare –'

'*Which rules of warfare?*' Howard's slurred voice piped up. 'I demand a fair trial.'

Grolsch looked up, irritated, nodded at his men: there came a metallic tattoo as the squad cocked weapons.

A banshee screamed in Wallace's head. *I'm going. I'm fucking going.*

'. . . according to the rules of warfare, all such commandos are to be slaughtered to the last man, and no pardon given . . .'

'My God, we're all going to be *shot*!' Howard cried.

On the word *shot*, Wallace let out a blood-curdling roar, bounded straight towards Grolsch in bear-sized leaps: Trubman followed close behind him. The giant reached the *Sturmbannführer* in two seconds, bulldozed him flat with his sheer cliff of a chest. For an instant the Jerries were too astonished to fire: Wallace and Trubman leapt over the fallen Grolsch, plunged into the dense undergrowth, heard SMGs palpitate behind them, felt 9mm rounds stutter, splice leaves, groove branches, go *pwwwhhhhiit* on trunks.

They heard screams: Trubman traileyed back, saw in a single glance Howard's chest split-ribboned, saw a

Kraut nail Seymour and Yates with red craters across the back and abdomen, saw Morris and Cameron running for it, saw Morris's head kick, burst into a pink floss, saw Cameron disembowelled, saw his intestines whip like jelly-legs around the shot that blipped from his gut.

Jesus Christ, they really did it.

Trubman tripped over a dry root, stumbled, hit deck, clocked Wallace crashing through the undergrowth, heard rounds go *vwwwwwipppp* on tree-wood, saw Jerries coming at him. It was too late to run: he curled up, played possum. The Jerries – two, three of them – went straight over him, cursing in Kraut. As soon as they'd gone, Trubman got up and ran in the opposite direction.

Wallace crashed through trees, panted: he didn't look behind, didn't know that Trubman was no longer with him. He could hear Jerry shouts, though: the enemy seemed to be gaining. The trees were thin, densely packed, interspersed with vines and brambles: he considered stopping, standing dead-still in the shadows. *No, they'll rake the place with SMG-fire. Keep bloody going.*

It was the hardest he'd exerted himself since he'd left the hospital: his heart jackhammered, his calf-muscle telegraphed jolts of agony. Branches whipped his face: thorns ripped at his clothing. Cornfield stubble glinted sun-gold through gaps in the foliage: he considered turning left or right, decided to chance the open. He ran into cornstalks, flopped on his belly, writhed forward using only his legs, realized it wasn't working. *My bloody hands. If only they were free I could find a weapon.*

He staggered to his feet, heard yells, heard the *clatterclack* of SMGs, heard rounds wheeze past, saw them stove up dirt, scythe grasses. He ran on, wove from side to side, headed for tree-thickets in front of him. Rounds fizzed and grated. Wallace's legs worked like hydraulics, took him out of the stubble, across an acre of grassland to a stile on a drystone wall. He bowed over the stile, vaulted across it, almost fell, righted himself, found himself on a dirt-track lined with thorn-trees and poplars.

Two young men were standing in the road, grinning at him: kids, really, still in their teens, one tall, stoop-shouldered, pale, the other dark-eyed and olive-skinned: they wore scuffed farm-boots, baggy corduroy trousers, waistcoats, cloth caps that looked too big for them. They had cigarettes in their mouths: they were holding sub-machine guns.

Wallace hesitated: at that moment there were shouts from behind him. *'Bleiben Sie, wo Sie sind!'* A pair of coal-scuttle helmets popped up over the wall. Wallace took two steps, tripped, crashed over in the road, so hard that the breath was knocked out of him. He saw Huns on the wall, saw the boys in civvies go down on their knees, let rip with their weapons, cool as sea-slugs. Machine-pistols went *tock-tock-tock-tock:* rounds blammed hot wind past Wallace's ears, kicked into field-grey bodies, opened throats, punctured chins, peppered chests with crimson acne. The first Kraut fell against the wall with a grunt: the second wobbled for an instant on top, somersaulted into the road next to his comrade. The boys in the cloth caps pumped a few singles into their bodies for good measure: one of them – the pasty-faced, stoop-shouldered youth – moved forward, hunkered down by Wallace: he was still smoking his cigarette.

'Briddish?'

Wallace nodded, noted the American accent.

'You American?'

'Half Itie, half Yank.' He drew the cigarette from his mouth, stuck it into Wallace's. 'My name is Ettore Falcone,' he said. '*Allora, benvenuto in Italia.*'

7

Le Marche, Italy
4 October 1943

The road north hugged the coast: from the back seat of the *Kubelwagen*, Caine glimpsed endless vistas of leaden sea and steel-grey sky, watched flotillas of silver cloud cruise like schooners, saw bands of garnet-coloured sunlight strobe through them in gently revolving shafts. His captors had dressed his wounds, given him smokes, even joked with him, but it hadn't stopped the blighters from nicking everything he had, including his precious Zippo lighter. Now, though, he'd withdrawn into a shell-shocked world of his own, overwhelmed by the prospect of becoming a POW. It wasn't fear so much as irritation – that feeling of being trapped, of not being able to move at will. He'd been captured twice before, and though he'd escaped both times, neither had been a pleasant experience: he still had the scars to prove it.

When he closed his eyes he saw a turmoil of images from the battle at the Senarca bridge, replayed scenes of bloody carnage, saw Wade and Slocum blown to bits over and over in his head. His finger was painful where the bullet had grazed it: his face was sore from the fragments of Smith's jaw. *Smith too. And Sarn't Hardman. I was so jacked up after the first contact, I led them straight into it. That's more good men I've killed through bad judgement and bad leadership.*

He felt exhausted, weighed down by the war – four years of bitter struggle, blood, sweat and bullshit: four years of seeing comrades, young men – and women too – with all the promise of their lives before them cut down like weeds. And the enemy – how many of them had he himself cut down?

'*You ain't Captain Caine, you're the devil.*'

How had he become like this – a reaper of men? Was it really just the war, or had he gravitated to the army because he was drawn to violence? Did he, in the end, get some sort of pleasure or satisfaction from killing? If that was the case, why had he joined a support-arm like the Sappers, rather than a combat unit? As a child he'd been more interested in making things, in tinkering with engines, in shaping iron at the forge, than in tearing things to pieces. Yet he'd ended up in the Middle East Commando, and as if that hadn't been enough, he'd gone on to join the sharpest of sharp-end mobs: the SAS. Surely that must say something?

He closed his eyes again, was transported far away from the hills of Italy, to the desolation of the Lincolnshire fens, to the small village where he'd grown up – a single main street with the church one side and red-brick cottages on the other, with the Black Bull pub, the sub-post office, the smithy's forge where he'd lived with his parents. The village school lay at the end of that street – an austere institutional building with high windows set in a yard with iron railings – just before you turned right to go down into the fens. The yard was small, but to young Tommy Caine it had seemed vast, empty and devoid of any hiding place. That yard had been his first field of combat: the site of his greatest humiliations, the place where he'd fought out the days of his early childhood. His schoolmates had teased him mercilessly about being a *dirty smithy*'s son, had pretended to hold their noses as he walked past, even though his mother made sure that he was turned out perfectly clean and tidy every day.

Mary Caine was a graceful, dark-haired woman with liquid green eyes and the kind of figure that drew admiring glances from the men she passed in the street. There were rumours about Mary which Tommy hadn't understood until he got older: that she was the illegitimate daughter of a prominent local landowner named James Weatherby, for whom his grandmother had worked as a housemaid. In the end, they said, she'd had no choice but to accept the *dirty smithy*: he was the only one who'd have her.

Even when Tommy had begun to grasp what this meant, he'd laughed or shrugged it off: he hadn't resorted to punching heads. Or had he? What about that day in the playground, that *one* day when Micky Smith – a boy with a narrow skull and a chin like a old boot – had drawn attention to the fact that Tommy and

Julia Weatherby – James Weatherby's grand-daughter – were as alike as peas in a pod: more alike, in fact, than Tommy and his own sister, Margery. This was something Tommy couldn't deny: instead, he'd punched Micky Smith in the face, sent him scuttling to the headmaster. When he'd come back saying the headmaster wanted to see him, Tommy had belted him again for good measure. The headmaster had called him a delinquent, given him five strokes of the stick, told him he was the nasty product of a nasty, dirty, blacksmith family.

The *Kubelwagen* had left the coast now: she was climbing up into the mountains on a twisting track like a tunnel through dappled brakes of evergreen. Caine's eyelids were heavy: he let them droop, fell into a deep sleep. Somewhere an owl hooted: a sickle moon lay above him like a thumbnail poked through the tar-black night. The forest was familiar: he recalled the colonnades of black oaks like pillars, forming the nave of a great cathedral, the arches of mullioned windows, backlit with undersea light.

Someone whispered his name. A girl was standing in front of him – a figure in a white dress, stained with blood. The girl had dark hair cascading like strands of black velvet from a central parting: her face was a dark triangle: prominent cheekbones, haughty, high-arched nose, smooth café-au-lait skin, amber-coloured eyes tilted slightly at the corners to give her a mysterious oriental look: one of her eyelids was a touch lazy. Her neck bore red-purple bruises: her hands were bound in front of her. She held them up, eyed him imploringly: her lips worked but her words seemed to be inside his head:

'*The man in the mirror is not himself. The five dandelion seeds are buried in the forest, at the place marked "B". What is sought lies in a room with no doors or windows. I am the door. Another holds the key.*'

Caine wanted to ask what she meant, but she was no longer there: instead he was in a graveyard, where five graves stood, crumbled, cracked, green with moss. There were names carved on the stones. Caine tried to read them: the carving was too worn and ancient to make out.

A priest in dark robes was gliding towards him, leading a solemn procession of five black-and-white birds – sacred ibises, with mutilated beaks and broken wings, tied neck to neck with string. The priest slid past Caine without seeing him. Another disembodied voice droned: '*Ashes to ashes, dust to dust.*' The birds trotted past dejectedly, curved beaks dragging dirt.

Caine felt a featherlike touch on his cheek, saw a rain of dandelion seeds floating down. He was in a dimly lit room, staring at a fish-tank on a pedestal. The severed head of an old woman was immersed inside the tank, amid a swirl of lank, grey hair that wafted in the water like sea-grass. Her skin was shrivelled, her mouth slack. Her eyes snapped open like trap doors: the toothless mouth gold-fished. '*Whoever kills a sacred ibis shall die.*'

Reeling back in shock, Caine staggered through an open door into another room: he found a butcher there, a black-bearded man in a leather apron working at a chopping-block, slicing the heads off live fowls. The man chortled to himself as the birds fluttered and squawked. He worked eagerly, his bare biceps flexing, flinging the lopped-off heads into a basket on one side, hurling the carcasses on to the floor. There were thousands of headless birds in the room, piled up in heaps, lying in serried ranks in a river of blood. The butcher fixed malevolent eyes on him, grinned through white teeth: a voice from nowhere said '*Special handling.*'

Caine blinked, found himself standing in a dark cavern, a pit of darkness with a floor covered in skulls and bones, rock walls like living matter, pressing inwards, and the light falling down an endless staircase that reached up into the darkness. A figure was descending the stairs with slow, ponderous steps: a man cowled in shadow, a corpulent, pork-hog shape, a head like a dark pumpkin, eyes like burning yellow coals on a face masked by a mummy's winding-cloth. Caine felt rigid with dread: the corpulent figure seemed to bring with him a chill that seeped into his bones, moving towards him endlessly, never seeming to get any closer.

'*Wake up. We are almost there.*'

Caine opened his eyes, saw a Kraut soldier staring at him over the seat. The car had stopped at a checkpoint: Jerries in battledress and chamber-pot helmets were chatting with the driver. Caine tried to recall his dream:

a dark forest, graves and dandelion seeds. A talking head in a fish-tank: a butcher decapitating fowls: a jumbo-shaped figure coming downstairs towards him. A procession of sacred ibises with broken wings: a girl in a bloodstained dress. *It lies in a room with no doors or windows.* What did? How was that even possible? And *special handling* – what was that about?

It hadn't been an ordinary dream: it had given him a different feeling, a sweet-sour taste that the future had happened already. Almost like the time back in Cairo when he'd dreamed about Betty Nolan and the spy Johann Eisner. He hadn't dreamed like that for months, not since the last op in Tunisia, probably not even when he'd been delirious in hospital. It might be that he'd just survived a bloody contact, of course, but it made him wonder about the disorienting agent Olzon-13 that the Abwehr-man, Rohde, had once given him. Rohde was dead now, but he'd claimed that he'd given Caine enough of the stuff to cause lasting nerve damage. It might have been a lie: the medical tests they'd given him had been inconclusive – but with things like that you couldn't be certain. *You just can't see some wounds, that's all.*

8

Near Orsini, Le Marche, Italy
2 October 1943

Stengel's car threaded down the switchback road through woods of ash and Aleppo pine, with the barren shelves of mountains behind, ranging out of a faded chiffon sky. Grapevines grew in staggered ranks along the scarps, blazing in bursts of flame-red and Italian pink: fields of yellow sunflowers tilted like beaming faces in a valley where meadows intermingled with wedges of woodland, and a collage of ploughed and fallow plots lay like a quilt on the skirts of scrub-covered hills. The hillsides were criss-crossed by pathways and cart-tracks, scattered with slate-roofed cottages, cut with gorges where stony drawers caught running water in silver light.

Stengel's detachment had searched the villa as thoroughly as possible: they'd found paintings and books, but not the one thing he wanted. The villa was vast and dilapidated – who knew how many tunnels, hidden chambers and underground passages it contained? A real search would take weeks: it would mean ripping the whole place apart. He hadn't been successful with the countess: she was just a girl, but her family had kept the whereabouts of the Codex a secret for generations: one of her forebears had even been a saint. He couldn't stop thinking about what she'd said as she slipped out of consciousness, though. '*What is sought lies in a room with no doors or windows. I am the door. Another holds the key.*'

Was there anything in it? *No*, it was psychopathic rambling: nothing could lie in a room without doors or windows. He shrugged: *childish nonsense*. But then, if he really thought so, why couldn't he stop thinking about it?

He forced himself to remember instead how *Reichsführer* Himmler had requested him personally to bring back the Codex, recalled the tea in delicate china cups, the rich aroma of fat German cigars in the SS chief's inner sanctum. The excitement in Himmler's eyes. *This is a project close to my heart,* Reichsgeschäftsführer. *I have dreamed of possessing this book for many years – ever since I first read the translation. The Codex will be the jewel in the crown of the new Germany. It will be an everlasting symbol of the honour, courage and purity of the German race. This is the task I am entrusting to you, Wolfram. Bring back this book and you will have performed a very special service for the Reich.*

Wolfram. Himmler had actually called him *Wolfram*. Even now, the singularity of the honour brought a flush to his face. For some reason, though, another vivid memory clashed with it: of the day he'd been hauled out in front of his class at school in Hildesheim, told by the headmaster that he was being expelled, *'because your pathetic piano-tinkler of a father can't pay the school fee. Poverty is the fault of the inadequate. You are unworthy of this school, unworthy even of life, unless you can pay.'* Nothing had ever compared with the humiliation he'd experienced at that moment: despite all the honours he'd been given since, he'd never quite managed to erase the jeers of the other boys from his mind.

That was before the Führer. Things are different now. There were great things to be done, a new Germany to be built: life had started for him the day he'd joined the SS. Now, as director of the Ahnenerbe – the SS division for racial and cultural purity – he was one of the elite. His expeditions had brought back evidence demonstrating the major part Germanic peoples had played in world history. The Codex, though, was the key to understanding why their race was superior – generous, loyal, brave, and pure, ready to die for *Blut und Boden* – blood and soil. The Codex would be no less than a blueprint for the new Reich. Himmler wouldn't rest till he had the original Latin text: that was the gift which he, Wolfram Stengel, was going to give him.

The hills levelled out, the road meandered through low, wooded ridges, hamlets of cottages, some falling into ruin, rolling green fields where dun-coloured cows and rag-coated sheep grazed: denuded grey trees, reed-edged streams, ploughed fields, small farms standing amid poplars and grapevines, and the light coming in long beams through fleets of cloud. The car passed ox-carts driven by old men with weather-pickled faces, in waistcoats and cloth caps: women in dour dresses and headscarves hefting firewood, boys on bicycles balancing milk-churns on their handlebars.

There were work-parties from the Jesi concentration camp on the road, too – Jews and Gypsies in pyjama-like prison-garb, Allied POWs in tattered uniforms – carting ballast, breaking ground with picks, shovelling soil. Sipo-SD guards with rifles stood over them. Stengel found himself counting the number of prisoners in each party, then the number of guards, then the number of pickaxes, spades and wheelbarrows.

At the junction leading up to the hill-top town of Orsini, Sipo-SD troops had erected a barrier of oil-drums. As the car approached the turnoff, a rat-faced *Feldwebel* waved them down.

Stengel wound down the window. 'What's going on up there?'

'You haven't heard, sir? Two of our men were shot dead by partisans near Montefalcone yesterday. Two British saboteurs escaped. *Sturmbannführer* Grolsch is up there carrying out reprisals.'

'That's Sipo-SD business, *Feldwebel*. I'm on my way to Jesi. Why did you stop me?'

'The *Sturmbannführer* asked me to look out for you, sir. He sent a message asking me to direct you up to the town – said you might find something of interest there.'

9

Orsini, Le Marche, Italy
2 October 1943

Orsini was an apricot-coloured sprawl that seemed to have sprouted organically around the skirts of the mountain: close-packed stone dwellings spread along steep alleys that branched out from a main street like a dark gorge, pink-tiled roofs arranged in overlapping tiers rising like shallow steps up to the cobbled square of San Giuseppe da Copertino. It was there, in front of the church, that Stengel found almost the entire male population of the town crowded together under the guns of a Sipo-SD platoon. Six youths, singled out from the crowd, were facing the church wall with their hands on their heads. A gunner in an open *Kubelwagen* had a Spandau trained on them.

The San Giuseppe church was remarkable, Stengel thought. Built of the same burnt-ochre stone as the rest of the town, it had two asymmetrical wings with circular windows and angled roofs, an ornate bell-tower on one side. Between the wings, a set of precipitous steps – he counted twelve of them – rose up to an unusual tiled portico, supported by slim arches, extending either side of the main door.

Stengel found *SS-Sturmbannführer* Grolsch inside the church, standing alone before the altar, contemplating what appeared to be a dark bundle slumped on the chequered flagstones. The interior was lit only by flickering candles: Stengel took in the holy-water stoup – a seashell held by cherubs – disordered wooden benches, fresco-covered walls, the altar with its white hangings, gold crucifixes, statues of saints and angels, the smell of incense. On the wall behind the altar was a triptych – a three-panelled painting centred around the Virgin Mary holding an infant.

Stengel advanced down the aisle: Grolsch saw him coming, snapped to attention, gave him a *Heil Hitler* salute. Stengel didn't return it: his gaze was held by the bundle on the floor. It was the body of a priest in a black cassock, lying with one leg drawn up and arms extended either side of his body, as if demonstrating the crucifixion. Where the head should have been there was a shapeless mess of gory tissue and grey-matter flecked with bone fragments: the body lay in a spreading pool of blood. An odd-looking iron bar with a head like three curving claws lay next to him.

Stengel glanced at Grolsch, registered the fact that his field-grey tunic was splashed with crimson. 'Killing priests now, *Sturmbannführer*?' he said. 'Surely you didn't bring me here to look at this?'

Grolsch tilted back his peaked cap: his hand was sticky with blood. 'He came at me with that iron claw thing,' he said, his tone flat. 'I had no choice but to tackle him. In the struggle –'

'– you *accidentally* smashed his skull to a pulp?'

Grolsch swallowed. 'It was self-defence, *Reichsgeschäftsführer*. Someone took a pot-shot at us from the church tower: an SS-man was killed. When I came to demand the name of the person responsible, the priest attacked me.'

Stengel shook his head, made a tut-tutting sound. 'This won't look good, *Sturmbannführer*. First you let two British saboteurs escape, now you beat a priest to death.'

'A priest who attacked a German officer.'

Stengel picked up the claw-like instrument, examined it. It was a fork of some kind: three prongs like crooked fingers, moulded to a long iron shaft. The claws were greasy with gore. *The murder-weapon*, Stengel thought wryly. He turned it over, examined it with interest. 'This, I would hazard a guess, is a tool used by Catholic priests for torturing heretics in medieval times – must be three or four hundred years old. Most appropriate, don't you think?'

Grolsch clamped his jaw.

Stengel gave a soulless laugh, turned to look at the Madonna triptych behind the altar. He realized with a shock that he'd been mistaken. The central panel didn't feature the Virgin Mary, as he'd thought: in fact, it wasn't a painting at all but a mirror. In the mirror stood a man in prison-garb, so emaciated that his face looked like a skull with paper-thin hide stretched over it: the head was shaven, the nose bulbous, the front teeth rabbit-like and protruding. The eyes, unnaturally bright and large, were fixed on Stengel: there was an amused expression on the death-like face. The *Reichsgeschäftsführer* stared back, unable to tear his eyes away: suddenly, the apparition winked at him with insinuating slowness: almost at the same time, a lisping voice whispered in his ear: '*Behold the ravishing beast.*'

A cold flush spread up Stengel's spine: he dropped the bar, heard it hit the stone flags with a clang. He lifted his fingers, saw there was blood on them, saw them twitch.

Grolsch was gaping at him. 'What's wrong?' he said.

Stengel jerked a trembling a finger at the mirror. '*One hundred and five Jew-Bolshevik commissars*,' he stammered.

Grolsch eyed the triptych, confused. 'It's a painting of the Virgin,' he said. 'Quite famous, actually – the *Madonna del Soccorso* of Niccolò Alunno, from the late fifteenth century. Lacks a certain finesse, perhaps, but beautiful in its way, and, of course, worth a fortune.'

Stengel followed his gaze: there *was* no mirror, he realized – it *was* a picture of the Virgin Mary, just as he'd thought in the first place. *It's a painting, of course it is. But I saw that Jew. I saw him wink at me.*

He glanced at the dead priest on the floor, then at Grolsch. 'You were a priest once, weren't you? Isn't it bad form to kill one of your own?'

Grolsch watched his superior warily.

Stengel swivelled round 'Better have the body brought outside. At least we can make an example of him.'

He walked back down the aisle: Grolsch paused for a last look at the dead priest. Don Michele had been an old man: he wouldn't have had much longer to live anyway. *But I didn't have to kill him*, he thought. *I could have just disarmed him. He was twice my age. Once I'd got the iron bar off him, I could have subdued him easily.*

The truth was that he wasn't sure why he'd killed the old man. True, he'd refused to give up the name of the person who'd taken that fatal pot-shot, but perhaps he didn't know it. No, it was something else – that infuriating, placid, sincere expression Don Michele had worn whenever Grolsch had had dealings with him – the look priests assumed in order to inspire trust and confidence. From bitter experience, Grolsch knew the falseness, the hypocrisy of that look.

It was five years since he'd been expelled from the church for disgracing himself with a girl, but somehow even he had never quite managed to get rid of that worthy expression: he saw it in the mirror every time he shaved. As a young ordinand he'd been full of religious fervour, full of enthusiasm for the Christian message. True, he'd been ambitious, determined to end up a cardinal, but he'd certainly *believed*. The doubts had started to accumulate during the early years, when he'd realized how many members of the church fell short of its ideals. It took some time for him to understand the full extent of the corruption, and in particular how many ordained priests, sworn to celibacy, regularly misbehaved themselves with both girls *and* boys.

He'd even thought of exposing the scandal, but it was impossible: they used the old-pals network, covered each other's backs. Since he couldn't beat them, he'd joined them: he'd had sex with a girl. The story had got out, though: her parents had complained to the authorities, and he'd been carpeted. The argument that almost everybody else was doing it hadn't cut much ice: the establishment looked after its own, but he wasn't one of them. When they'd told him he was being expelled, he'd stared at those tranquil, worthy, self-important faces and wanted to smash them. He'd sworn at them, called them two-faced swine. All right, so the girl had only been fourteen years old – but in the end, what difference did it make?

Now, though, he wished he hadn't killed the priest. He'd been irritated, perhaps, by the loss of another Sipo-SD soldier: casualties had been unacceptably high these past few weeks. He was also angry with himself for letting those two saboteurs get away. Shooting unarmed POWs in cold blood was bad enough, but having eyewitnesses escape was worse. It was enough to get him transferred to the Russian front: he guessed it would be only a matter of time before the axe fell. Unless he could make himself useful to Stengel, that was.

He watched the bearded *Reichsgeschäftsführer* stalk towards the door in his immaculate dark suit, white shirt, silk tie, broad-brimmed hat. He didn't like Stengel: they were fighting the same war, but the Ahnenerbe chief was a fanatic, a man obsessed – German mythology, the Jews, his blessed Codex – forever washing his hands, peering over his shoulder, counting things, costing things, adding things up. Most unsettling of all, he never looked you in the eye – seemed to look right through you instead. If it wasn't for the fact that he was an intimate of Himmler, Grolsch wouldn't have bothered with him. The escape of those two SAS-men wasn't going to be easily painted over, though.

He hurried after Stengel, caught up with him near the door. 'Did you find the Codex, *Reichsgeschäftsführer*?'

Stengel shook his head. 'The countess was stubborn, despite my best efforts, and the place is vast, just as you said it was. If the Codex is there, we need to know where to look.'

Stengel halted before the door: to his left there was a narrow iron grille set into the thick, plastered wall. The grille was padlocked: beyond it, a staircase spiralled down into shadow. He jerked his bearded chin at it. 'Where does that lead?'

'A crypt, *Reichsgeschäftsführer*. Some of these old churches have them.'

Stengel inched past him, strode towards the grille, peered down the dark staircase. 'Couldn't somebody be hiding down there?'

'Unlikely. The grille is locked from the outside. In any case, I've already found the men responsible for helping the escaped saboteurs. Didn't you see them outside?'

'The ones facing the church wall? They're only boys.'

'Boys capable of murder.' Grolsch scratched his dimpled chin. 'Sir, are you going to talk to the countess again?'

'Of course. She'll tell me in the long run.'

'What if you were holding her brother? Wouldn't that give you some extra leverage?'

Stengel looked puzzled. 'Her brother? Isn't he in America?'

'That was the story.'

They stepped out of the door, descended the steps: the prisoners herded in the square ogled them with hostility: no one called out.

Grolsch signalled to the subaltern in charge of the Sipo-SD platoon, had him march one of the youths up to the church door.

The boy was pale, gristly, stoop-shouldered: he had smooth white skin, a hawk nose, shrewd green eyes narrowed to slits. He looked about sixteen, though tall for his age: he was dressed as a labourer, in shabby work clothes and a ragged cloth cap.

'What is your name?' Grolsch demanded in German.

'I have already told you: my name is Marco Luchetti.' The youth's German was slow but correct: Stengel wondered where he'd learned it.

He glanced at the boy obliquely, realized he was terrified but making an effort to conceal it.

'As far as I can ascertain,' Grolsch said, 'there is no citizen in this town called Marco Luchetti. There is no Luchetti family. If this boy is really called that, then it seems he has no mother or father, brothers, sisters, aunts, uncles or cousins. He is alone in the world.'

He turned back to the youth. 'But that isn't your real name, is it, boy?'

The youth drew himself up: his hands were shaking.

'My name is Marco Luchetti.'

'Then why, *Signore Luchetti*, were you wearing this when you were arrested?'

Grolsch brought something out of his pocket, showed it to Stengel. It was a gold signet ring bearing a shield with a double-headed hawk in a laurel wreath. Stengel gasped, took the ring, weighed it in his hand. There was no doubt about it, he thought: it was the Falconi family crest. *One of an identical pair. Been in my family for generations.* This ring was, in fact, indistinguishable from the one he'd seen on the finger of Countess Emilia Falcone, only an hour before.

10

Jesi, Le Marche, Italy
4 October 1943

Jesi lay east of Orsini, another hill-top town standing on a granite panhandle, overlooking a patchwork of fields and forests inflamed with a blush of blood – red, copper and bronze. The prison-camp stood at the edge of an adjacent plateau a couple of miles distant, joined to the town by a cinder track lined with trees and telegraph poles. The camp itself was a set of rectangles bounded by fences of rusting barbed wire, dominated by watch-towers on stilts – a series of compounds containing regimented groups of wooden huts, and a few permanent buildings – cookhouse, messes, administration, punishment blocks.

When the car pulled up outside the gates, a squad of Sipo-SD troops sauntered out to take custody of him. Caine felt almost sorry to leave the Airborne Division men: these Gestapo troops looked an altogether more grim-faced, moodier lot. They handcuffed him, marched him through the gates, manhandled him up steps into a hut of bare boards furnished with only a table and a chair. A swag-bellied corporal sat at the table, armed with a clipboard and pencil. He had cropped platinum hair, skate's eyes, thick lips, a raw, hairless face. He smiled when Caine was brought before him. 'Welcome to Jesi holiday camp,' he said in smug English. 'We hope your stay here will be pleasant, and that you will leave us a different man.'

'Thank you, *Kamerad*,' said Caine. 'I can hardly wait.'

The corporal's smile vanished. '*Remove your clothes*,' he snapped.

Caine held up his handcuffs. 'I'd love to, mate, but I seem to be a bit handicapped.'

The corporal nodded grimly to the guards: one of them smashed a rifle-butt into Caine's kidneys. He felt a searing shock in his side, doubled over, gasped for breath, gritted his teeth, tried to stand up straight: another Sipo-SD man kicked him hard in the shins.

'That's enough,' the corporal purred. 'If you are insolent again you will find yourself in solitary confinement for twenty-eight days. Do you understand this?'

Caine was tempted to inform him that the mistreatment, humiliation or torture of POWs was illegal under the Geneva Convention: he felt the blood pound in his ears, nodded, kept his mouth shut.

One of the guards removed his handcuffs: others grabbed his arms, tore away his bloodstained battle-dress, yanked off his boots. When he was naked, the fat corporal stood up, snapped a rubber glove on his right hand, moved towards him grinning, flexing his middle finger. The guards behind him laughed.

Caine's arms were restrained, but not his legs: as soon as the corporal moved into range, he delivered a withering kick straight into the Jerry's groin. It was a barefoot kick, but it was sent with all the force Caine could muster – enough to make the corporal stagger back squealing and clutching at his balls with both hands. Caine ducked a swinging rifle-butt, took the blow on the shoulder, felt air explode from his lungs, tried to use the momentum to break the clutches of his guards. Half a dozen hands jerked him back: a fist slammed into his nose, filled his head with birdsong: a club cracked his skull, sent him reeling into the red-black folds of night.

When he came round he was lying on a palliasse in a cell about twenty feet square: light fell in a single shaft through a narrow window. He tried to sit up: for a moment the light-shaft was a gramophone needle: the cell revolved around it, scraping in his head like a broken record. He choked back vomit, realized that his hands were swollen: the bastards had stomped on them when he was down. His nostrils were plugged with dried blood: his head was an egg-shell trapped in a vice.

He was still naked, but a blue drill shirt and a pair of shorts lay next to him on the floor.

He groped for the shirt: putting it on was relatively easy – it was the shorts that were the problem: his hands were like softballs. He eased the garment painfully up his legs, closed the waistband, couldn't button the flies.

At that moment the door cracked: two Germans in

battledress shuffled into the cell bracing between them what looked like a sagging bundle on stumpy legs. Caine tried to focus, saw that the bundle was a man in khakis – a keg-shaped figure in a pair of ragged shorts and a British battledress tunic. He had major's crowns on his shoulder-straps, and, to Caine's astonishment, SAS wings on his sleeve. Caine had to blink to make sure he was seeing right.

The guards rammed the apparition hard against the wall, pinned him there. Caine saw a head like an enormous, grey-stubbled billiard ball lolling on a broad chest under a BD top that was smeared with blood-stains. The man's face was badly bruised, one eye so swollen it was almost closed: a thin dribble of blood ran down his chin. His legs quivered: Caine noticed that one knee was livid and melon-sized.

The fat major moaned: one of the guards punched him in the belly: the other cracked his legs with his rifle-butt. He spluttered, sank to his knees, drooled bile. The guards held him up by the arms. They were obviously about to kick him when a man in a suit entered – a man with fish-eyes, a pointed nose, a full set of dark whiskers. He waltzed through the door, delivered a sweeping kick into the kneeling man's midriff with a wedge-shaped toe. Caine heard a carpet-beater wallop, saw the major topple over slowly, saw his bulging body hit the floor with a low thump.

'You have three days to tell us where it is,' the bearded

man shouted in English. 'After that, I cannot guarantee your safety.'

It looked to Caine as if the major was out cold. The bearded man must have thought the same, because he turned, glanced at Caine. 'Ah, another saboteur. Don't imagine you will be spared. You will all be subject to special handling.'

Caine's hair stood on end. *Special handling? That was in my dream. Five sacred ibises with broken wings. Five graves in the forest.*

The man gave him a hard look, turned on his heels, stalked out. The two uniforms followed, snapped the door closed.

Caine crawled over to the major, slipped his swollen hands under the fat man's armpits, rolled him on to his back. It was darker now the door was closed, but the shaft of light showed Caine a figure like an overgrown cherub from an oil-painting – pot-belly, pole-like legs, short arms, tightwad hands. Caine examined the SAS wings on his sleeve. They seemed genuine, but the major didn't look like any SAS officer he'd ever seen. Without the uniform, Caine would have taken him for a bank manager – perhaps a pastry-cook.

The major's lids flickered: he opened his eyes wide, stared at Caine's face. '*Water!*' he gasped.

Caine shook his head, helped him sit up, propped him against the nearest wall. He used his shirt-tail to wipe blood off his face.

'*How about a smoke?*' the man croaked.

Caine shook his head again. 'Fritz took them.'

The officer lifted a hand so small and fat it was almost a child's. He fumbled wearily in his breast pocket, came out with a cigarette and a match. He stuck the cigarette between hamburger lips, handed the match to Caine. 'Be careful, old boy. It's the last one.'

Caine tried to strike it on the wall, found his fingers were too clumsy: he dropped it, picked it up, struck it on the floor, cradled the flame in his hands, lit the cigarette.

The major puffed smoke: his eyes didn't leave Caine's face. For a moment Caine felt self-conscious: then the major winked, and for an instant it seemed that the whole bloated mask of his face crumpled up like wrapping paper.

The wink put Caine on his guard. He'd been told the enemy used stool pigeons among POWs: the man's accent was cut-glass, but maybe it was too good to be true. *But what about the bruises, the blood, the swollen knee? Fritz really laid into him. They couldn't have faked that.*

'You're thinking I might be a stoolie, aren't you?' the major wheezed. He smoked, coughed, tried to catch his breath. 'Don't blame you, old sport. I *could* be, but, as it happens, I'm not.'

'How do I know that?'

'Look here – you don't have to tell me anything about your operations, how you were captured, what your objective was, all right?'

Caine nodded. 'Fair enough.'

The major passed him the cigarette with a tremulous hand. 'My name is Butterfield. Major, Int. Corps. You can call me Bunny. You don't know me, but I *do* know you. You're Captain Thomas Caine DCM, DSO, 1st SAS Regiment.'

Caine was so surprised he let the fag drop out of his hand: it landed on his knee, burned his skin. He grabbed at it, brushed burning ash off his leg.

'You're a well-known name, Caine – one of our most decorated officers, in fact. From what I've heard, you've brought off some remarkable stunts.'

Caine narrowed his eyes. 'Thanks, but it still doesn't explain how you recognized me.'

The major took the remains of the cigarette back. He sucked smoke greedily into his lungs without holding it in his mouth, blew it out in jets through his nostrils.

'You were pointed out to me once at Shepheard's Hotel, Cairo. I would have introduced myself, but they told me you were in recovery from a serious trauma, not to be disturbed. If I remember rightly, there was a rather nice-looking redhead with you – Int. Corps insignia, as it happens. *She* didn't seem to be disturbing you.'

Blaney. Caine smiled, thought of how Celia had cared for him following the *Nighthawk* op. *If he knows about Blaney, he must be telling the truth.*

'If you're Regiment,' he said, 'why haven't we met before?'

The major smirked. 'I'm *2nd* Regiment, dear chap.

You know, that *other* unit you desert boys don't think about. At least that's what your Major Mayne told me. *"Sure we never think about you at all,"* he said.'

Caine chortled. 'That sounds like Paddy.'

'We're based in Algeria, so our paths don't cross much. I was in Cairo to meet my counterpart in 1st Regiment. You see, I'm Assistant IO, 2nd SAS.'

'*IO?*' Caine raised an eyebrow. 'That's a headquarters job, isn't it, sir? If you don't mind my asking, what are you doing in the field?'

Butterfield stubbed out the fag. 'I was dropped in a month ago, with an officer and four other ranks. Jerry was waiting for us on the DZ. The officer, Howard, copped one in the goolies – wounded rather badly, poor fellow. They bagged us, brought us here, shoved Howard in the hospital wing, dumped me in this place – the punishment block. The men were in the ORs' compound until three days ago: I used to talk to them through the wire in the exercise-yard. Then they vanished – *poof* – just like that. Jerry carted them off – poor Howard as well, I was told. There were a couple of prisoners from 1st Regiment hauled off, too.'

Caine pricked up his ears. 'Who were the 1st Regiment boys?'

'Don't recall their names. This was all gleaned in a few moments of whispering across the wire, you understand. I remember my sergeant, Bob Cameron, telling me they'd been captured in Tunisia. Been here for months.'

Captured in Tunisia. Like Wallace and Trubman. But, no: Fred and Taff weren't captured, were they? Their names never turned up on any War Box list. Whoever these chaps were, they couldn't be Fred and Taff.

'Where were they taken?' he asked.

'No one knows, but I've got a damn' good idea where they *are* . . . Dead as dodos, old man, that's where. Krauts call it *special handling*.'

A cold hand brushed Caine's neck. *That phrase again.*

'You mean the Krauts *murdered* them? Prisoners of war? That's a war-crime, isn't it?'

'*Sshhh*, not so loud, old boy. Of course – it's against every rule in the blinking book. Doesn't mean it's not true, though. You heard what Stengel told me?'

'Stengel?'

'Fellow with the beard: eyes like a Moray eel. He gave me three days to tell him what he wants to know. If I don't spill my guts by then, I'm next in line for special handling.'

His voice remained casual: a knot of gristle in his cheek twitched.

Caine was about to ask another question when Butterfield raised his puppet-like hand. His good eye narrowed to the width of the bruised one. '*They're coming*,' he hissed.

The door sprang open: two Jerries in coalscuttle hats barged in, rifles first. Caine and Butterfield jumped: one of the Krauts elbowed the major aside, the other belted Caine in the stomach with his rifle-butt. Caine buckled: before he could stand they were hustling him by the arms out of the door, down the corridor. They used his head to ram through another door, sat him down on a chair facing a battered desk. A Nazi officer sat behind it.

11

The officer was smooth-faced, with a strong, dimpled chin, penetrating blue eyes and receding fair hair. He had the slightly amused, he's-a-jolly-good-chap expression of a country vicar.

The room was dimly lit, the windows blacked out with hessian: the place smelt of stale hemp and tobacco. There was another desk to Caine's right, where a blocky young woman with curly golden hair sat at a typewriter, smoking a cigarette, drinking coffee.

The officer shuffled a sheaf of papers, drew a pencil from an inside pocket, tapped it on the desk. 'I am *SS-Sturmbannführer* Karl Grolsch, Sipo-SD,' he said. 'Who are you?'

'Thomas Edward Caine, Captain 2566798, born 17 January 1920.'

The pencil scratched. 'And which is your unit, Captain?'

'I can't say.'

Grolsch looked up: laugh-lines crinkled round his eyes. 'Of course you can't, but I do not need your answer anyway.' He lifted something off the floor, threw it at Caine. It was his bloodstained battledress tunic with SAS wings above the breast pocket. 'You are a parachutist of the 1st Special Air Service Regiment, founded by Colonel David Stirling, now residing in our facility at Colditz.'

Caine had never heard of Colditz. He put on the battledress quickly, kept his mouth shut.

'Tell me, Captain. Why do some of you wear wings on the sleeve and others on the chest? Take Major Butterfield, for instance. He wears wings on the sleeve, not on the chest. He appears rather – how do you say? – *green*? Not at all what one would expect of a commando officer. Could it be that he was sent here for a special purpose?'

'I can't say.'

Grolsch sat back in his chair, contemplated Caine thoughtfully.

'You, however, are different. Your chest and shoulders are unusually well-developed. You have powerful hands: they are swollen, of course, but one can still see that the knuckles are scarred and pitted, as if you are accustomed to fist-fighting. Your arms and legs show scars of gunshot and shrapnel wounds, some of them serious. I would say, Captain, that you are a veteran fighter, that you have been wounded many times, and that you have killed many of our men. Would this be correct?'

Caine wondered where this was leading. Were the Nazis going to put him on trial for being a soldier? He remembered the three Brandenburgers he'd once butchered with a rusty knife, shivered inwardly.

'It's a war,' he said wearily. 'In wars you kill the enemy.'

'Ah, yes. Quite so. Quite so.' Grolsch crossed his legs, scratched the back of his head, as if he had something to say but didn't quite know how to say it. 'You see, my superiors are a nuisance, Captain. Now, I know, for instance, that you were captured by our Airborne Division at the Senarca bridge, near Termoli, after an action in which you and your men fought bravely. My superiors, however, will, I'm sure, be inclined to insist that you are a saboteur.'

He said the word with distaste, as if it were a curse.

'I'm an officer captured in uniform.'

'Yes, of course you are. But I don't believe that my superiors will accept this as an excuse. You are a commando and a saboteur, they will say, and you are therefore subject to special handling.'

An icy block liquefied in Caine's chest. *Five broken sacred ibises. Five tombstones in the forest.*

'They will say that you SAS-men are subject to the *Kommandobefehl* – the *Commando Order* – issued by the Führer himself, stating that British commandos or sabotage-troops, even if they are soldiers in uniform, are to be slaughtered.'

'*What?*' The word had escaped Caine before he could stop it.

The *Sturmbannführer* threw up his hands, shook his head despairingly.

'Yes, I know. *Slaughtered*. But there it is.' He scrabbled among the papers again, came up with a sheet stamped with a swastika crest typed in Gothic script. 'Here, in black and white.'

He put on a pair of wire-framed glasses, began reading. '"I will hold responsible under military law all commanders or officers who neglect this order, or question it when it is to be executed." Signed "Adolf Hitler."'

Caine stared at him: was the Kraut pronouncing his death sentence?

Butterfield was right. They must have murdered the five men who'd dropped with him, kept the major alive because they thought he might talk. Why was Grolsch telling him this, though? *You don't warn people if you're going to kill them. He's got to be after something.*

Grolsch laid the paper back on his desk, drummed his fingers on the wood. He turned to the young woman still drinking coffee behind the typewriter. 'Maria, please go and get Amray.'

The blonde girl nodded, scurried out of the room. Grolsch moved around his desk, sat on the front with his arms crossed.

'Have you ever thought,' he said at last, 'that the Bolshies – the Russians, I mean – are a far more dangerous threat to Britain than the Germans?'

'As far as I know, the Soviet Union is our ally.'

'The Bolshevik dream is world domination. I admit that this has been a bad year for us on the Russian front, what with Stalingrad and von Paulus's surrender. We are renewing our efforts, though, and we are trying to recruit a corps of British POWs to help. Several hundred of your countrymen are already with us. They are training to fight the . . . what is it you call it? . . . *the Red Peril*.'

For a moment, Caine thought it must be a joke. He'd met traitors and stool pigeons – Jerries like Eisner, who'd been brought up outside Germany and could pass as Brits. It had never occurred to him that a true-blooded Brit would actually fight for the Nazis.

He heard the door open: Grolsch stood up. 'You can hear it from . . . how do you say? . . . the *horse's mouth*.'

Caine turned to see a man in field-grey approaching.

'This is *SS-Hauptsturmführer* John Amray,' Grolsch said, 'of the British Free Corps. I shall leave you two to talk.'

Grolsch went out: the two guards with rifles came back in, hovered by the door. Caine stood, faced the newcomer, not quite believing what he was seeing. *An Englishman in Nazi uniform.*

Amray was taller than Caine – a knotty, wedge-shaped man with razor-hasp jaws, a fleshy nose and black, haunted eyes. His uniform was the standard Jerry battledress, with a peaked forage cap. On his sleeve, though, he wore a Union Jack flash in the shape of a shield, with three lions passant guardant in gold on his right collar.

Caine refused the proffered hand. 'You're not really British, are you? You're part Kraut?'

Amray grimaced, showed bad teeth. 'British as tea and crumpets, old bean. Born in London. Father was a rubber-planter in Malaya – went to work out there when I was eighteen.' The voice was cultivated. 'Joined the New Zealand army when the war started, ended up in Greece in '41. Got bagged by Jerry.'

Caine scowled. 'A lot of men get bagged. They don't all become traitors.'

'Sticks and stones, chummy. Sticks and stones.'

'Come on, man. This must be some sort of trick.'

Amray shook his head. 'It's no trick. Signed up with the Waffen SS, swore an oath of allegiance to the Führer, the lot. Only to fight the Bolshies, mind, not against our own chaps.'

Caine's fists tightened: he had to take a deep breath to control himself. Just being here, talking to a man who'd sold himself to the enemy, made his flesh creep. Amray leaned against the desk where Grolsch had just been sitting: he brought out a silver cigarette case, flipped the lid, offered one to Caine. Caine shook his head stiffly. Amray shrugged, took a fag, tapped it on the case twice, let it droop from his mouth, lit it with a silver lighter. He blew smoke in a long, cool stream.

'Now look, Caine, I'll make it short and sweet. I know what you're thinking. I felt like that at first. Natural, isn't it? But be honest with yourself. Haven't you ever felt that you were just a pawn in the game, being moved around by the brass? Haven't you ever felt that they were incompetent imbeciles who regarded you as mere cannon fodder?'

The question was so unexpected that Caine almost

answered *yes*. It was true. He'd felt like that, especially on these Italian operations. The SAS weren't supposed to be shock troops, yet that was how they'd been deployed: *cannon fodder – all those years of experience behind enemy lines wasted. And the shit they handed me on* Nighthawk: *lost almost my whole section, risked my life saving GHQ from a germ-warfare agent. Then the officer I proved was a traitor got away with it. You can betray your king and country, as long as you have friends in high places.*

It was all there, he realized: the years of bitterness, of being cheated, lied to, set up as an Aunt Sally as they slowly changed him from a man into a demon. '*You ain't Captain Caine, you're the devil.*'

'There's a war on,' he said. 'Someone's got to be the boss. Do you think Jerry'd be any better? Do you want to see Hitler running things back home?'

Amray let smoke waft through both nostrils. 'Bound to come, Caine, bound to come. And when it does, men like us in the Free Corps – we'll be sitting pretty. I'd expect to be a general, at least.'

Caine snorted. Amray stood up, jabbed his cigarette out in the ashtray, regarded Caine with condescension. 'You can scoff, old boy, but let me tell you, they can make life very hot for you SAS people. They say you're saboteurs and spies, you see, not real soldiers. And we all know what happens to saboteurs and spies.' He drew a finger across his throat. 'Seven of your SAS-men were taken away a few days ago – one of them was dragged out of the hospital wing. Nothing to do with me: all I know is that they refused my offer. There's your cell-mate, Major Butterfield. He hasn't been very cooperative. I shouldn't be at all surprised if the same fate awaited him.'

Caine's fists tightened: he had to press them to his sides to stop himself lashing out. 'Those are our own men you're talking about, you bastard.'

Amray looked annoyed. 'I was doing them a favour. I gave them a chance to avoid anything unpleasant. I mean, why let that happen when you could be fighting the Bolshies? Imagine *them* running round Blighty, shagging the women, eh? Perish the thought. All right, you have to wear a Jerry uniform, but killing Russkies can't really be called treason, can it?'

'I wouldn't bet on it.'

Amray shook his head pityingly. 'Think it over, Caine. You'll never escape: they've got this place sewn up tighter than a duck's arse. The moment you join the British Free Corps, though, you're free – women, booze, you name it. Better than spending the rest of the war in a prison-camp. *Much* better than ending up in a shallow grave with a bullet in the head.'

12

Villa Montefalcone, Le Marche, Italy
4 October 1943

From her apartment, Emilia could hear voices like far-away, snarling dogs: the Krauts were in the wine-cellar, getting through her family's best vintages. *Good luck to them. The more drunk they are, the better*, she thought.

She opened the door, peered down the shadowed corridor. The chair normally occupied by the guard was empty.

She closed the door, returned to her room, put on a blouse, sweater, slacks, soft-soled shoes, tied back her hair, paused to examine her bruised neck and face in the bathroom mirror. *The swine treated me like an animal. It wasn't just about the Codex. He enjoyed doing it to me. He's turned on by domination: a weak man trying to prove to himself that he's strong. If I get through this, I'll see that Nazi bastard burn in hell.*

It was the second day after Stengel's assault: she was still sore, but at least the bleeding had stopped. Her main worry was that she'd suffered some serious internal injury: she needed a medical examination, but she knew the Cabbage-Heads would never allow a doctor through the cordon.

Stengel hadn't told her when he'd be back. He might pop up any minute, and when he did, she didn't want to be there. Why had he left her at home when he could have had her taken to the prison-camp at Jesi? *Because he wants to do it to me again. He wants a slave he can abuse in private.*

For a moment her nostrils were filled with his smell: his sweat, the revolting eau de cologne: she heard his feral grunting. She gagged, let out a sob, held on tight to the sides of the basin. Then she forced herself to stand up straight. *No, I'm not going let that* stronzo *terrorize me. I'm going to get out.*

The frustrating thing was that, if she'd had the run of the house, escape wouldn't have been that difficult. The foundations of the villa were riddled with passages, stairways, tunnels, ancient catacombs, some of them older than the house itself. One of the tunnels led to a door hidden in the forest. If she could only slip out that way, she could find Ettore, take refuge with the partisans, live rough in the woods.

The problem was getting access to the cellars with the Krauts in the house. It was Angostina, her housekeeper, who'd suggested letting them into the wine-cellar. *There's more wine down there than they could drink in a lifetime. When they get legless they'll forget you're even here. Your father would turn in his grave, but let them have a party.*

It was risky, though. If she got caught, the boozed-up

pigs might do anything to her. '*Ma tira ti su*,' Angostina had said. *Remember Marco Pellati?*

She did remember. Out riding in the woods, thirteen years old: Marco Pellati, about her age, had shot her mare with a catapult. The horse threw her, galloped off: she sprained an ankle. The boy ran away: probably wanted to do more but didn't have the guts. Her ankle was swollen and painful but, instead of heading back home, she'd hobbled off in search of the mare. By the time she'd tracked her down, the ankle was the size of a football and she was sobbing in agony. She calmed the horse, rode her back home, refused to tell anyone but Angostina what had happened. When the ankle was right again, she found a stick, waited for Pellati as he walked home, thrashed the living daylights out of him.

Years later, the youth had apologized. He'd been madly in love with her: he'd just wanted to bring himself to the notice of the count's daughter.

She'd promised her father that she would protect Ettore, the villa and the Codex. Ettore was beyond her control now, but she'd done the best she could: she had always known she might have to abandon the house one day. The Allies were pushing up the Adriatic coast, but the Germans were still pouring troops into Italy: they wouldn't give up without a fight. They might occupy the villa, but they would never find the Codex.

It lies in a room with no doors or windows, she thought.

She paced down the landing, carrying an unlit torch,

a handbag slung over her shoulder. She cocked an ear for movement, heard tuneless singing rising from the cellar. *Have a good time, boys.* The landing passed the main staircase at right angles, continued into another wing of the house. She had only to make the small dressing-room on the other side, where a hidden stairway led down into the warren of cellars. It would bring her dangerously close to the boozing Jerries, but at least she wouldn't be bumping into any of them on the way.

She drew abreast of the stairhead, where the wooden handrail ended in an ornate spiral flourish: the staircase curved down sinuously: marble steps sheathed in purple pile, between wrought-iron banisters topped with polished wood. The hall had a domed ceiling from which dangled a crystal chandelier: the space beneath was lit by oblongs of moonlight through arched windows: it was austere and unfurnished except for a round table, carved upright chairs standing against the walls. The door leading to the cellars was directly opposite the foot of the stairs: it was in darkness, but Emilia heard unsteady footsteps coming from that direction, saw the red glow of a cigarette-end approaching. She froze, felt her heart bump, stifled a breath. *Is it the guard? What if he comes up?*

A figure emerged from the doorway into a block of light – a heavy soldier with a head like a wooden block. She caught a glint of gunmetal, heard an indistinct mutter. *He's talking to himself – the guy's loaded.* As she watched, the man dropped the cigarette on the stone flags, ground it out with a boot, turned and, with one hand on the banister, started to stagger upstairs.

Emilia ran. She heard the floorboards creak, heard the German yell: blood screamed in her ears. She raced down the landing, found the room she was looking for. She let herself in, locked the door behind her, leaned on it, tried to get her breath back. She heard unsteady footsteps, drunken shouts. *A dozen rooms open off this corridor: he'll never know which one I'm in.*

The room was wood-panelled, lined with massive Gothic armoires decorated with elaborate iron hinges and locks: a threadbare Persian rug lay on the floor: the wall was festooned with wine-coloured draperies. A fine cabinet on elegantly curved legs, set on casters, hid the secret entrance. Emilia rolled the piece aside, found the panel in the wall, slid it open, shone her torch down a narrow, dark stairwell. The soldier roared suddenly from outside: fists pounded on wood. Emilia squeezed through the opening. *He's knocking at random. He can't know I'm in here.* Emilia closed the panel behind her, began to make her way down the stairs.

The steps seemed to go on for ever, into the bowels of the earth. As she approached the bolted door at the foot, she heard singing. '*Lili Marlene*'. *Don't they ever get tired of that morbid dirge? At least the guard upstairs hasn't alerted them. Maybe he's passed out.*

She hesitated: the door opened into an underground

tunnel that led past the wine-cellar, into the maze of store-rooms and catacombs where other secret entrances were concealed. She had no choice but to pass the cellar. She suddenly wished she hadn't come this way: there were other hidden passages she could have used, but they involved crawling for miles through confined spaces in pitch darkness: she hadn't been in them since she was a child. *I'm here: there's no turning back.* She put away her torch, eased open the door: its creaking made her wince. She stared out into the darkness, heard the discordant resonance of male voices, took in the glow of lamplight from the cellar entrance. It was only a few yards away.

She steeled herself. *Come on. You've only got to get past that, and you'll be free.* She pressed herself against the wall, felt the cold comfort of stone, eased herself along it towards the block of light. *Four more paces. Three. Two.* She was just about to step across the light-spill when there came a piercing whistle from behind her, a cracked voice bawling German. The singing stopped. Emilia's blood turned cold: a soldier clad in a vest and trousers burst through the doorway, saw her, cocked his Schmeisser, scowled, '*Bewegen Sie sich nicht!*'

The man was heavy-set and muscular, with stuffed biceps, a globular head, bald as a bone. He stepped towards her: half a dozen more Jerries lurched out of the cellar, closed in on her. She backed against the wall. The bald man laid the muzzle of his sub-machine gun between her breasts: his eyes were phosphorescent marbles. '*Schauen Sie, Jungen!*' he said. '*Ve hev got now a little chicken to eat.*'

'*Don't touch me!*'

The bald Jerry hooted, let the muzzle of his weapon drop. He closed a big hand over her right breast, pushed his belly against her, lowered his bull head: she felt his hardness on her crotch, saw soapcurd eyes and thick lips, smelt sour wine-breath. '*Just one little kiss. I want to . . .*'

'*SS-Mann Stolbe. Lassen Sie sie!*'

The order cracked out like a lash: the bald man checked himself, let her go, retreated. The others snapped to attention. Emilia saw a young officer standing by the door with a pistol in his hand: he had the keen eyes and angular face of a fox: he was hatless but otherwise properly dressed. He marched forward, boots clicking on the stone flags, shoved the bald man out of the way, snarled something at him, eyed Emilia. 'I am *SS-Hauptsturmführer* Kaltenbraun. Where are you going, *Fräulein*?'

'I . . . I was looking for my housekeeper.'

'In the cellars? Your staff hev strange habits, no?'

He took a step closer, holstered his pistol. 'Herr Stengel gave orders that you were not to leave your rooms.' He looked round: a sloppily dressed soldier sidled into view, a whistle still stuck in his mouth: it was the blockheaded man Emilia had glimpsed on the stairs. '*SS-Mann* Karloff here left his post,' the fox-faced officer said. 'He will be punished.'

He directed a burst of harsh syllables at Karloff: the rifleman looked abashed, swayed on his feet. The officer turned back to Emilia.

'You vill return to your rooms, *Fräulein*. But first I hev a message for you. It was for the morning, but now you are here . . . It is your brother . . . Ettore? He has been arrested . . . as terrorist. Tomorrow, Herr Stengel vill visit you . . . to discuss his execution.'

13

Jesi, Le Marche, Italy
4 October 1943

Bunny Butterfield huddled in the corner of his cell, listened for footfalls in the corridor. It was about an hour since they'd marched Caine off. He wondered what they were doing to him, decided he didn't want to know.

He'd been in the punishment block a month, with only brief stints out in the exercise yard: it had become so monotonous that he almost looked forward to the interrogations, despite the routine knocking-about that went with them. Grolsch was better than Stengel, though. While Grolsch was ready to hurt people because it was part of his job, you could tell that Stengel enjoyed it. That, with his constant twitching, grunting, mumbling, and whistling, was enough to put the wind up anyone.

Stengel suspected he'd been sent to snatch the Codex. Butterfield was convinced that was why he'd been left when the others had been taken away. So far, he'd managed to keep the story under his hat, but how much longer he could do it, he wasn't certain. Now, Stengel had given him three days to admit that he was here for the manuscript and to reveal where it was hidden. If he didn't come up with answers by then, he'd go the way of the others.

He wondered if the operation had been worth it. *The whole team missing, presumed dead: myself on the condemned list? Is a book worth the lives of those men?* He decided it was. The Nazis had already gobbled up half of Europe's art treasures. Why should Hitler get away with the only extant manuscript of Tacitus's *Germania*?

Butterfield longed to get his hands on the Codex. He loved beautiful, old things: it gave him a thrill just to be near a medieval artwork, to caress a Greek amphora, to handle a book written before London even existed. As a child in prep school, ignored by his parents, he'd found solace in paintings, sculptures, carvings, leather-bound volumes, archaeological treasures – they gave him the satisfaction of knowing that material objects could outlast a few short lives. After school he'd pulled strings to get a job with Sotheby's: while working there he'd started to build up a small collection of his own.

As a Sotheby's insider, it hadn't been difficult to locate precious artefacts – a manuscript here, a miniature there, a statuette somewhere else: it had to be small and easy to conceal. Neither had it been hard to *case the joint* – protesting Sotheby's concern for the security of the objects they were to auction. It was remarkable how lax some clients were. He did sell a few items to keep his funds topped up, but he didn't do it for the money: he did it because he was a collector – and because he enjoyed the thrill.

When the war came along he'd signed up for the Int. Corps, expecting to get a cushy number. Instead they'd posted him as Assistant IO to 2nd SAS in Algeria. When he'd found out it was a special-service unit, he'd almost blown a gasket. He'd quickly stowed it, though, when they'd told him that part of his job would be collecting art treasures in Italy. It was as if a chest of bright wonders had just opened up. The parachute course had almost killed him, but luckily he'd been inducted into the unit without having to endure the rest of the blood, sweat and carry-on.

The Codex wasn't just any old book. It was regarded by SS-Chief Himmler as the German bible. The int. that the Nazis were about to grab it had galvanized Butterfield into overcoming his antipathy to combat: not that he was afraid – he just didn't see much point in risking one's life unless one got something out of it. He'd been in the Int. Corps two years and this was his first taste of action. *Well, the action didn't last long. Landed behind enemy lines: Jerry bagged me in the first minute.*

He hadn't given up the idea of snatching the Codex. *If I ever get out of here, that is.* The chances of that, though, were slim. He thought about Tom Caine. Could it be coincidence that an officer so renowned for his ability to get himself and others out of tight corners had dropped from the blue into his very cell? Hadn't Caine brought back that female SOE agent from behind enemy lines? Hadn't he survived an op in Libya where the Nazis had exposed him to a nerve toxin? And another in Tunisia, where his section had held a bridge against a Kraut advance? *Caine may not know it, but he's going to help me. If anyone can find a way out of this place, it's him.* He heard the creak of Jerry boots along the corridor outside.

The guards shoved Caine into the door of his cell, jerked him back, unlocked it. They kicked him inside, tripped him over for good measure. He headbutted the floor, felt blood spurt from his nose again. He rolled over on his back, groaned: the door slammed shut.

Butterfield crept over to him. 'You all right, old fellow?'

Caine sat up, pinched his nose between thumb and forefinger, peered at the blood on his hand. 'I've been better.'

'Who was it? What did they do?'

'Chap with a face like a vicar: Grolsch, I think his name was. Never touched me, though. Only showed me an order from Hitler saying that all captured British commandos are to be executed.'

Butterfield stiffened. '*What?* They never showed *me* that. It's official, then?'

'That's what he said: it might be a bluff.'

He wiped blood off his nose with the sleeve of his blouse.

'It's no bluff, I tell you.' Butterfield wobbled his bulbous head. 'Howard and the others are six feet under, and I'm next on the list.'

Caine remembered his dream: a girl in a white dress.

Five graves, five sacred ibises, five dandelion seeds buried in the forest.

'There was another bloke in the office with Grolsch,' he said. 'An Englishman in SS uniform. Name of Amray. Queerest thing I've ever seen. He actually tried to get me to join the Nazis – *British Free Corps* he called it.'

'Traitor bastard,' Butterfield said. 'Don't have anything to do with him.'

'Did he give you the same proposition?'

'Never met him, but I heard he had a go at my team.'

'He said that, if they'd accepted, he could have saved them.'

Butterfield stared at Caine, his sound eye gleaming. 'Saved them from *what*? That's as good as an admission that they *are* dead.' He examined his small hands. 'I've got three days to come up with the goods – you heard what Stengel said.' He searched Caine's face. 'Do you think there might be any way out of this, old man? I hear you're rather handy at that sort of thing. Didn't you once climb out of a hundred-foot well Fritz dropped you into and slaughter three of them with a rusty knife?'

'My finest hour,' Caine scoffed. 'I wasn't locked in a cell, though. The Jerries thought I was dead: they never expected me to get out.'

He sat up straight, pushed himself back until his spine touched the wall. He leaned against it, eyed the major's pudding-like face: the bulging neck, the drooping dewlaps. He couldn't get used to the idea that this was an SAS officer he was looking at. He didn't blame the fellow for being windy, but the continual harping on the fact that he was *next on the list* put Caine on his guard. It gave him the feeling that Butterfield was trying to manipulate him. For what? To help him escape, probably. Yet, looked at in another way, it could all be an act. Today he'd met an Englishman in Nazi uniform: if that was possible, anything was. True, Butterfield had known about Blaney, but then he might have got it from anywhere. And if he was being pumped for int., why not just spill it? Holding out might be heroic, but SAS operational procedure was to drop a cover story after the first forty-eight hours. Butterfield had been in here a month now.

He pressed himself against the wall, raised his shoulders, squeezed his nose. 'If this Stengel is threatening to have you shot, why not tell him what he wants to know? No point holding on if your life is in the balance. Any strategic stuff you can tell him will have been stale for weeks.'

Butterfield gave him a hunted look. 'That presupposes I know the answer to his question, old man. The fact is, I don't.'

Caine shook his head. 'Look here,' he said. 'You've just asked me to help you get out of this place. I might consider it, but first I want to know *what it is* you can't tell Jerry. Why is an Assistant IO working behind enemy lines? What are you doing here?'

14

Termoli, Puglia, Italy
6 October 1943

The streets of Termoli lay in smoking ruins: jagged holes in walls, roofs demolished, entire house-façades crumbled and strewn across the streets in fans of broken glass, matchwood and rubble. Smashed shutters were festooned with torn sheets and curtains, flapping like celebration flags. Some houses were still smouldering: children cried, families fussed around sticks of furniture they'd managed to pull out. On the way back from the defence, Harry Copeland clocked a knot of Tommies in a side-street trying to blow open a safe, saw another bunch gleefully carrying off a piano. It was looting pure and simple, but neither Paddy Mayne nor he had the energy to stop it.

The Commando Brigade had not only taken Termoli, they'd also defended the town all night against a savage Jerry counter-attack. *The boys played a blinder*, as Mayne put it. In three days, the SAS had sustained more casualties than they'd taken in the entire desert campaign. They'd done the job, though. You couldn't blame them for letting off steam.

The aid post was in the Franciscan monastery near the waterfront. After they'd checked the wounded there, they crossed the road to the *palazzo* where Mayne had set up his command post. They found a spontaneous frat-session in full swing: British commandos, town big-wigs, local belles in best party-frocks hugging, smooching, squeezing, back-slapping, babbling in incoherent voices. At least some of these Ities must have supported the Nazis, Copeland thought: now they were celebrating the British victory with gusto. Cigarette smoke danced along shafts of sunlight: flagons of vino went round: couples waltzed tipsily to the tune of a little man with a walrus moustache playing a piano-accordion.

When the noise became unbearable, Mayne and Copeland took mugs of wine through wide double doors into the salon, a room opulently furnished with Persian rugs, brocaded armchairs and settees, a gramophone, a long mirror and, to Mayne's delight, a full-sized billiard table.

'Who's for a wee game *nauy*?'

Copeland gaped at him: Mayne's enthusiasm for any kind of game or sport was legendary, and he wasn't the kind of person you turned down, not even if you were dropping on your feet after three days' combat. Right now, though, the last thing Cope wanted was to knock little balls into holes. He caught sight of himself in the mirror: gore-soiled battledress hanging from his lean shoulders, clawed hands, field-dressing on his wrist, face black with dirt, dried blood on his teeth. He shuddered.

Mayne set his mug on the mantelpiece, chose a snooker cue from the rack, gauged its straightness. He cocked an eye at Cope.

'All right, sir.'

Mayne unslung his M1 carbine, stood it against the wall. He moved to the table, scooped the red snooker balls together, set them in the triangular frame. Copeland put down his mug, leaned his sniper's weapon against the table, placed the coloured balls, chalked a cue. 'Go for the break, Major,' he said.

Mayne inclined his scrum-forward's torso, lined up the white ball with the wedge of reds: his hands moved with a delicacy Copeland always found startling in such a slab of a man. He watched fascinated as Mayne drew back the cue between his thumb and finger, paused for a split second, as if he were taking first pressure on a trigger. He hit the white in exactly the right spot, with exactly the right force: balls clacked: reds spun in all directions.

Cope didn't see snooker balls fly, though, he saw blinding streamers of flame flash from the muzzle of a Kraut gun, saw Smith's jaw come apart in scarlet rivets, saw red claws of fire that ripped Sergeant Hardman limb from limb, saw crimson gore spume out of a man with a carbine stuck through his neck. He shivered, gasped at the vividness of the images. He'd left Caine in that dyke with Wade and Slocum. All right, it was an order, and he'd got the boys back to Termoli, but still, he could have stayed. Now Caine was in the bag: a recce patrol had returned to the position later, accounted for everybody but him. What with the shelling of the town, and the all-night defensive action, he hadn't had much chance to think about it. Now it hit him that he might not see Caine again for the rest of the war, maybe never.

Mayne cradled the cue along the crook of his left elbow, sent him a quizzical glance. 'I thought we had a game, Harry?'

'Sorry, sir. I was just thinking about Tom Caine. The recce patrol didn't recover his body – must be in the bag.'

Mayne let out a long sigh. 'That's a third of the squadron lost since we landed in Italy, so it is.'

'We shouldn't have been used as storm-troopers, sir. Colonel Stirling said that the idea of the SAS was stealth if possible, force if necessary. He ruled out stand-up battles.'

Mayne's face screwed up. 'You're telling *me* about it? A *mon* out of OCTU six weeks?'

Cope flushed: for a moment he thought he'd overstepped the mark. *I opened my big trap again.* He knew Mayne could flip in an instant, lash out with big fists: Copeland got ready to duck. Then he saw the faraway look in Mayne's eyes, remembered that the hard-punching – bruiser legend was only half the story: the Ulsterman's loyalty to his men was a byword – no one took the losses more personally than he.

Mayne sighed again. 'You're right, Harry, but this was the last match of the season. It's back to Blighty and retraining for the invasion of Europe for us: the brass say we're going to be a brigade. *Nauy*, if ye've no more pearls of wisdom to impart, for Pete's sake play your –'

'*Excuse me, sir.*'

An elegant young captain in khaki drill trousers and shirt and an SAS beret marched smartly through the double doors carrying a Schmeisser sub-machine gun under his arm.

Mayne grimaced, sloped his cue over a ship's-mast shoulder.

'Sure, if it isn't Roy Cavanaugh. Make yourself at home, why don't ye, Roy? Harry, Roy here is with that *other* unit – the one we never talk about.'

Cavanaugh made a wry face. 'With due respect, sir, our lads fought beside yours at the cemetery last night. Of course, it was our first engagement as a unit, but I don't believe we were found wanting.'

'Och, you were found all right for greenhorns.'

'Thank you, sir. Personally, I've been wounded twice since Dunkirk.'

'Cavalry doesn't count,' Mayne grinned, holding out a broad hand, 'but since you're a fellow Irishman, I'll excuse ye. What's your parent mob?'

'Inniskillen Dragoons.'

'Sure, now you're talking. There's the boys who know how to fight.'

Cavanaugh had the look of an overgrown leprechaun, Cope thought – broad, flat Slavic cheeks, slitted eyes, slim-arched nose, a sardonic mouth that curled up at the corners, giving him an expression somewhere between mischievousness and arrogance. Despite the all-night battle, he was neatly dressed.

'Where's the famous Tom Caine?' Cavanaugh asked. 'I came to shake hands with him.'

'Bagged,' Copeland said morosely. 'Not long after the landing. We advanced to contact at the Senarca bridge, found the Krauts waiting for us. Luftwaffe Airborne – good fighters.'

'That's bad news. If we had any idea where he's been taken to, I might be able to help.'

Copeland raised his eyebrows. 'How's that?'

'I've got orders from Bill Stirling to take jeep-borne patrols behind enemy lines to look for escaped POWs. There are a lot of Allied soldiers wandering around – ex-POWs who took the chance to do a bunk when the Ities surrendered. If we had any idea where Caine might be, we could look for him.'

He slung the Schmeisser, drew a folded map from the patch pocket of his trousers, spread it out on a chair. Copeland squatted next to him, snooker cue across his knees. 'Here's Ancona, capital of Le Marche region.' Cavanaugh pointed a slim finger. 'This is Jesi, about fifteen miles due west. It has an airstrip and a prison camp. We've had int. from our "A" Force operator, Savarin, that SAS personnel are being held there, including a section we sent in by parachute a month ago. Our Assistant IO, Major Butterfield, is with them.'

'Butterfield?' Mayne chuckled. 'That fat desk-wallah with the cushy job collecting church paintings? If *he's* jumping behind the lines, you must be hard up.'

Cavanaugh narrowed his eyes. 'I'm not privy to his mission, sir. Anyway, he might be there and, if that's where Jerry's sending SAS-men, so might Caine.'

He tapped the map. 'There's a road from Termoli to Ancona: it follows the coast, then dips into the mountains. It's a fair way, but if I was Fritz, and I was going to take Caine anywhere, Jesi's where it would be.' He considered Copeland appraisingly. 'Why don't you come with us? I've got four jeeps. We're going to split up into pairs: with your experience, you could take charge of the Jesi party. It would be an honour to have you.'

'Hold ye horses, *navy*, Roy,' Mayne cut in indignantly. 'What makes you think you can poach my officers? Harry here is my adjutant. I need him.'

'Sorry, sir.' Cavanaugh's eyes glittered. 'I understood your mob was due back in Blighty.'

'So it is. But maybe Harry would prefer to ride back with the boys, rather than swanning around Italy on a wild-goose chase.'

Through the open doors, Copeland could see couples dancing in the smoky light of the next room: the accordion-man had been replaced by a gramophone, again playing 'Lili Marlene' – the German version. Two drunken subalterns were smooching with a couple of dark-haired, doe-eyed beauties.

He thought about his sweetheart, Angela Brunetto: the Italian girl he'd met in Libya. She would be waiting for him in Blighty. He felt a sudden craving for her, wondered if he'd ever see her, touch her, hold her again. He hadn't been home in four years. *I need a rest, for God's sake. I don't want to be gallivanting about behind Jerry lines, while the rest of the squadron leaves without me.* Apart from seeing Brunetto, he'd been looking forward to that first pint of English ale he and Caine had always promised themselves. Without Tom, though, it wouldn't be the same, not after all they'd been through. *I can't go back without trying to find him. Tom would do the same for me.*

He looked at Mayne. 'With your permission, sir, I'd like to go with Captain Cavanaugh.'

Mayne scratched his nose. 'Even if Caine and these other men *are* in the Jesi camp, how the bejaysus will you break them out? That's a job for a squadron, not a patrol.'

Cavanaugh and Copeland exchanged glances. Cavanaugh stood up, put the map away. 'We'll have to work it out when we get there, sir. *Improvization* – isn't that what it's called? Our intrep. suggests that POWs from Jesi are taken out in working parties every day, doing maintenance on the roads. That might be a better bet than trying to bump the prison-camp, but one can't really say until one's on the ground.'

In the next room, the gramophone music had

stopped: the crowd was thinning. The two drunken subalterns had been abandoned by their partners and were now supporting each other, singing 'When the Troop-Ship Leaves Bombay' in raucous voices.

Mayne let out a long breath. 'All right, Harry. I'm giving you *green on* for this. It's a long shot, but I admire your loyalty. There's one condition, though.'

'What's that, sir?'

'That you help me finish this sodding game.'

15

Jesi, Le Marche, Italy
4 October 1943

'A *book*?' Caine repeated. 'You dropped behind Jerry lines for a *book*? Wouldn't it have been easier to order it by post?'

Butterfield's bruised eye was closed, forming a 'C' shape in the puffy skin of his eyelids. He was sitting cross-legged on a palliasse: his head, transfixed by the beam of light from the single high window, looked like a wide oval topped by a smooth dome. His good eye blinked.

'Keep your voice down, will you, old boy. I don't think Jerry's got the place wired, but you never know.'

He shuffled nearer to Caine, spoke through teeth like corn niblets. 'This isn't *Mrs Beeton* we're talking about. This is the *Codex Aesinias*, the only extant manuscript of the *Germania*.'

Caine stared round the cell, took in the crumbling walls: lumps of plaster gouged out in pale craters, scratch-marks, the splatters of squashed insects, traces of what might have been blood. He pulled at the skin on his chin, winced at the sudden pain from his swollen hands and bandaged finger. He turned his gaze back on the major: Butterfield looked like a statue he'd once seen of the Buddha, he thought: boulder-headed, full-bellied – despite thirty days in a Jerry glasshouse.

'None the wiser, sir,' he said.

Butterfield drew air noisily through splayed nostrils. 'It's a manuscript written in medieval times. A copy of an ancient Roman text going back two thousand years. It contains the earliest known description of the Jerries – noble savages, honest, honourable, brave, handsome, generous – *blah*, *blah*, *blah*. Just the sort of blokes Himmler wants to think of as his ancestors. He's got his heart set on finding the Codex for the Führer: they want to use it as a model for the new German society they reckon they're going to create after the war.'

Caine sighed. 'But a *book*. Words on paper. Surely it can't be as important as all that.'

'Think of it like, say, the Crown Jewels. Can you imagine the brouhaha if Hitler were to appear in public with the British crown on, conducting the choir with the orb and the royal sceptre? Well, if he gets his hands on the Codex, it'll be something like that – a huge boost to German propaganda. What a coup for us if we get in there first.'

Caine thought about it. It was still hard to imagine that a book, no matter how old, could have a major effect on the war. But he could certainly picture Himmler's chagrin on discovering that the object of his desire had been snatched away. It would be worth grabbing this . . . Codex . . . just for that.

'So you were sent to nab it before the Nazis?'

'That's about the size of it. It wasn't my plan: it came down from "A" Force, the Deception Service.'

Caine nodded. 'Why did *you* have to go in, then? An assault-team would have been fine, wouldn't it?'

Butterfield drew up his sagging head. 'It wasn't my first choice, believe me. When I thought about it, though, I realized that the whole bally thing would come apart without someone who knew what we were looking for. As it happens, old books and *objets d'art* are what I do. My main job is collecting paintings, statues and manuscripts from Itie churches on behalf of the Vatican. To make sure they don't get looted, you see. Nazis are buggers for looting. Half the art treasures of Europe have already gone into their vaults.'

Caine mulled it over. 'So Stengel wants this Codex, but doesn't know where it is. He thinks you know, and is threatening to kill you if you don't talk?'

Butterfield nodded. 'There's only one person who knows where it is. I was supposed to contact her.'

'*Her?* A woman?'

'Countess Emilia Falcone. Lives at Villa Montefalcone – a castle in the mountains about twenty miles from here. Family goes back to the Ark – kept the Codex hidden for centuries. Our "A" Force bloke with the partisans was supposed to guide me to her: chap named Savarin. Then, of course, it all went for a burton when we found

Fritz waiting on the DZ. Stengel is on to the countess – he let that slip. That means she's in for some rough handling: it can only be a matter of time till she talks.'

'How do you know she hasn't already?'

'Stengel would hardly be bothering with me, would he? He'd already have the Codex. Problem is, if I tell him I don't know where it is, he'll think I'm stalling, and I'll be for the high-jump. I need to get out of here, find the countess, snaffle that manuscript.'

Caine was impressed. 'So you're not giving up on your mission?'

'I can't stand the thought of Himmler getting it.' He glared at Caine: his closed eye struggled to open. 'Of course, there may be no way out for me. Ironical, really – my first action is my last –'

'Steady on. You're not dead yet.'

'I reckon you'd have more chance of getting out of here alive than me: more chance than anyone, maybe, given your record. And you *have* to get out, Caine: they're not going to let you off the hook. If you can help me get out, spiffing. If not, do the best you can for yourself. But if you *do* escape, I want you to promise me one thing. That you'll find Countess Emilia and get the Codex.'

'Aren't you pushing the boat out a bit?' Caine said. 'The chances of escaping from this dump look about as good as those for winning the pools.'

Butterfield blew air. 'Maybe it's a long shot, but if the impossible happens, I want you to promise as an SAS officer that you'll do your best to carry out the mission. I'm in no position to give you an order, Caine, but I'd feel a lot happier going to the firing-squad if I knew that a man like yourself had undertaken the mission.'

Caine knew it was a request he couldn't refuse: he'd had a few of those in his career, and they'd usually turned out badly. But this amounted almost to a plea from a condemned man, a fellow officer, wearing the same cap-badge.

'If I see a chance, I'll get you out,' he said. 'If not, and I *do* manage to get out myself, I'll do my best to complete your mission. I'll find the countess and the Codex for you, if it's the last thing I do.'

16

Santa Lucia, Abruzzo, Italy
7 October 1943

They parted company an hour before dawn: Cavanaugh took two jeeps and headed north-west, while Copeland took the other two, drove north-east across the mountains: his orders were to recce the Jesi prison camp. He was to RV with Cavanaugh in three days.

Staying away from the main coast roads, hugging hills and forests, they drew no attention from the Hun: in the sleepy hamlets the locals hardly seemed to notice them. Copeland felt unexpectedly buoyant: it was good to be in action with his own patrol. That hadn't happened since the Western Desert, when Caine had copped a shrapnel wound, and Cope had taken over his troop. He'd been a sergeant then: Mayne had commissioned him in the field. Now he was a decorated lieutenant with a mission to liberate SAS prisoners. It was the stuff of legends: there might be another medal in it, certainly promotion. The rumour was that the SAS was due to be expanded for the invasion of Europe: Mayne would be looking for squadron commanders. If Copeland played his cards right he could end up a major – even a half-colonel. That depended on his surviving, though: and it wouldn't be worth much to him, anyway, unless he managed to snatch Tom Caine.

The road wound through woodland, emerged into a valley, descended to a crossroads. Copeland halted the patrol, dekkoed the map spread across his knees, stood up to scan the distant vista of blue hills, farmland rolling in waves around peaks and corries, patchwork-pattern lands with soil so rich it looked almost purple, interspersed with oblongs of the brightest green, white stucco homesteads wreathed in orchards, red-roofed villages in circlets of trees. He noticed a dense smudge of blue-black smoke hanging over a village about a mile away, smelt carbon and fire-ash. He waved the second jeep alongside: she was commanded by Sergeant Tony Griffen, ex-Royal Tank Regiment, a pugnacious Yorkshireman whose mouth seemed to be set in a permanent 'O' of objection.

Apart from Copeland and Griffen, there were two drivers: Trooper Bill Harris, a beet-faced, straw-haired youth from Maidstone, and Lance-Corporal Carlo Lombard, a swarthy, hook-nosed man from Cardiff who had an Itie father and spoke Italian. Lombard was at the wheel in Cope's jeep: Harris drove for Griffen. Both jeeps had twin Vickers mounted on the co-driver's side and on the back: they each carried a Bren, and between them enough carbines, pistols, grenades and ammunition to take on a small army.

Copeland pointed out the pall of smoke over the village. 'Something going on there, Sarn't,' he said.

Griffen stood up, peered through narrowed eye-slits. 'Ities prob'ly havin' a cook-up.'

There came a crude ruckle of gunfire.

'That ain't no cook-up,' Bill Harris said. 'That's Jerry.'

'Someone's comin',' warned Lombard. 'Old bat on a pushbike.'

Copeland sat down, tweaked the Vickers, peered over his sights, saw an old lady in a faded black dress and a headscarf pedalling a bicycle full tilt towards them. She stopped when she saw the jeeps: Lombard called to her in Italian, waved her over. She pushed the bike closer: Copeland saw tears streaking a wrinkled walnut face. Lombard jumped down from the driver's seat, went to talk to her. They chatted, gesticulating, then Lombard sauntered back. 'It's Jerry all right, sir. She says they've set fire to houses in her village. They're lining up the men to be shot.'

Copeland's forehead puckered. 'How many Jerries are there?'

'From what she says, there could be over a hundred. She's on her way to the local partisans to get help.'

'Good, let the Ities sort it out 'emselves,' Griffen said.

Lombard caught Copeland's eye. 'We ought to do something, sir. By the time the partisans get here, it'll be too late. All they'll find'll be burnt-out shells and dead bodies.'

Copeland swallowed. His first instinct was to agree with Griffen. He'd been in a situation like this once before, in Libya, when Tom Caine had insisted on rescuing the inhabitants of an Arab village from a Brandenburger company. He'd argued against it at the time: in the event, they'd suffered casualties, but it was through that intervention that he'd eventually met Angela Brunetto.

'Tony's right,' he said. 'It's not our concern. We're on a mission and we have orders. There are only four of us: that makes odds of twenty-five to one. If we get scragged, it won't look good.'

'Have a heart, sir,' Lombard pleaded. 'If we leave, those civvies'll be dead.'

The old lady shook her head sadly, spoke to Lombard.

'What'd she say?' Cope enquired.

'She said there's too many of 'em for the likes of us. They're Airborne, she reckons – special troops.'

'Special *what*?' Griffen gasped. 'She don't know who she's talkin' to. We're SAS, ain't we?'

It was the kind of thing Fred Wallace might have said, Copeland thought. And it was true. Liberating Itie villagers wasn't in their brief, perhaps, but Copeland knew which way Caine would jump. If he ever saw Caine again, and admitted that he'd dipped out, his mate would never forgive him. *These 2nd SAS boys consider me a decorated desert-vet. If I pull out of a fight now, it'll go back to the Regiment.* No, he wanted to be able to tell Caine that his crew had at least lived up to the motto *Who Dares Wins.*

'I mean, it's only twenty-five to one, *innit*?' Harris commented. 'You must of seen much worse in the desert, sir. Those ain't much odds for the SAS.'

Copeland's Adam's apple worked. 'We've got the element of surprise,' he said slowly, 'and we've got the firepower. We'll steam in there, hit 'em with all we've got, liberate the Ities, beat it before the Hun knows what's happened.' He only realized after he'd said it that he'd sounded exactly like Tom Caine.

Griffen stuck a cigarette in his mouth, lit it, took a long drag. He pulled it, blew smoke. 'All right, sir. You're the DSO, after all. Let's go for it.'

Lombard said something to the old lady: she smiled thinly. He sent her on her way. Copeland groped behind him in the jeep's bed, came up with a Union Jack furled on its pole. 'We go in with colours flying,' he said. 'Let them know who we are.'

He gave the flag to Lombard: the driver unfurled it, stuck it in the socket behind his seat. A breeze caught it, sent it fluttering – a blaze of red, white and blue against the olive-drab uniforms.

Two crisp rifle-shots rang out from the village.

'*Christ!*' Griffen said. 'They're killing the flamin' hostages.'

Copeland braced the twin Vickers, cocked the handles, rammed them forward with a metallic snap.

'Let's see the buggers off.'

Engines roared, wheels spun, rubber flayed, dust blew: the jeeps bounced down the track with Union Jack streaming. The village was an 'L'-shaped constellation of three-storey, red-tiled houses with balconies around a village square with a church on one side and an orchard on the other – thin trees behind a dry-stone wall. In the square were two 3-tonners and two *Kubelwagen*, a mob of Jerry soldiers milling around the burning houses, others herding Itie civvies in a cluster.

A lone figure stood at the entrance to the square – a barrel-chested officer in field-grey uniform wearing a peaked cap. Cope raised the elevation of the Vickers a tad, pressed himself back in the seat, saw the Jerry's eyes go wide, saw him fumble for his pistol, yanked iron, let rip with a burst, *klatta-klatta-klatta-klat*. He saw the Jerry snap back like a released spring, saw blood-spurts blister the field-grey chest, saw him hit the wall, saw his pistol skitter.

The jeeps screamed into the square with machine-guns whomping, bowling bright skeeters of fire, hacking down Huns, slamming into truck-bodies, bursting petrol-tanks. The lorries went up in waves of fire, shot out cones of molten steel: one *Kubelwagen* leapt up on a cushion of flame, flipped over on top of the other, exploded in a blinding fireball.

Cope traversed the Vickers, fingered iron, steamdrilled rounds, saw Jerries scatter, clutch at ruptured flesh, saw them twitch, jump, pitch, roll, dry-swim dust. Itie civvies ran in all directions: Krauts clawed out of the firestorm, staggered through smoke, wormed into doorways. Copeland clocked star-flash from the church portal, heard Schmeissers lawnmower, heard rounds blip, heard slugs spatter the bonnet like hail on a tin roof. The jeep was racing pell-mell at the church. '*Ease off the throttle, mate!*' Cope yodelled at Lombard. '*Put her in reverse!*' The vehicle swerved: Copeland traileyed the driver, saw him convulse at the wheel, saw him vomit blood in quick lurching throws, saw brain tissue ooze from his skull like black gravy. He made a grab for the steering wheel: the jeep stalled, rolled to a halt in the dead centre of the square.

Schmeisser rounds went *wheeeeeeeeuwww* past Cope's ear: he shoved Lombard's legs out of the way, smacked the starter. Not a whisper. *The engine's hit.* He clocked Huns on balconies to his right, skinched back in his seat, swung the Vickers, squeezed steel. Nothing happened. *Fucking jammed.* Kraut rounds spoinged off ammo-drums, heeched over his head, ripped the flag to tatters.

Copeland jumped into the back, grabbed the other Vickers, fired one-handed, heard it burp twice, die. *Jesus, another dud.* He heisted the Bren from its brace, levelled it from the shoulder, snatched the trigger, felt the gun jigger, saw the muzzle blear fire *rack-tack-tack*, felt the working parts stick. *I don't fucking believe it. Engine dead and three guns down.*

Rounds went *ka-chunk* on the jeep's body-work: Copeland gripped his SMLE by the forward stock, vaulted out of the vehicle, crouched behind it, breathed deep, worked the chamber. *Not you, please.* He aimed at the figures in the church doorway, fired, cocked, fired, cocked, saw field-grey bodies tipple, sprawl: he switched to the balconies, saw Krauts pop up, spray rounds, duck back down, saw Jerries hang out of windows, fire, dip back in. He scoped in on a window, waited for a coal-scuttle to pop up, spiked the Kraut with an AP round, saw his head burst apart like a red cantaloupe. He emptied his mag in a steady blitz, groped in his pouch for another, flashed a glance over his shoulder, clocked Griffen's jeep halted near the orchard. He saw Griffen's forward twin Vickers blazing, saw Harris yawing fire from the back.

He clicked the fresh mag in place, raced round to the other side of the jeep, dragged Lombard out of the driving-seat: he was sure the man was dead, but he wanted to get the body out. He slung his rifle, drew his Colt .45, hauled the driver by his webbing towards the other jeep. A Jerry ducked out of a doorway on his right, fired at him. Cope lobbed pistol rounds straight-armed, felt the .45 jump, *thunk*, *thunk*, *thunk*, saw the bullets kick into the Hun's gullet, gnash flesh, open his throat, saw him drift backwards, saw gore gush in thick rivers down his neck. He kept on lugging Lombard: Jerry fire pooped dust, punted spouts.

'*Watchit, sir!*' Griffen's voice cracked. 'Eleven o'clock.'

Huns were advancing through the orchard to his left, behind a raft of Schmeisser fire: Cope saw a Jerry jump over the wall, squibbed a low double-tap, ripped off the backend of his thigh, saw the Jerry go down on one knee, pumped two slugs into his chest. More Jerries were coming through the trees. *Keep bloody shooting.* Copeland raised the pistol, tugged iron, heard the chamber clack, heard a Jerry rifle go *spammfff*, felt a round skid his knuckles, felt the Colt whipped out of his hand.

Cope swore, heard rounds chirr, swung his rifle off his shoulder, eased the safety with a blood-slicked thumb. He drew a bead on the next Jerry over the wall, heard a jeep engine rev.

'*Get out of it, boss!*' Griffen's voice chimed. '*Leave Lombard.*'

Copeland hipfired, hit the Kraut in the guts at ten yards, clocked the red-mouthed entry wound, clocked the gore spray out behind, saw the Jerry's face crumple, saw him double over. He left Lombard's body, loped towards the jeep, legs going like pistons. Slugs bulled and snorted around him. He made the jeep, clocked Griffen bending over wide-legged in the bed, one hand on the rim, the other reaching out for him: he grasped the hand with his bloody fingers, hurdled into the bed, fell on top of Griffen, felt the jeep careen forward, heard the engine scream, felt the wheels spin.

A single figure stood in the middle of the road outside the square: a great pillar of a Jerry NCO in full battle-rig, with a face like raw steak and a Schmeisser in his hands. As he raised his weapon, Harris jabbed the throttle: the Jeep lurched forward, hit the Hun a glancing blow in the legs, sent him flying with his weapon zipping long splits of fire into the sky. '*Stop!*' Copeland yelled from the back. 'I want to snatch this chap.'

Harris exchanged a dubious glance with Griffen, slammed on the brakes. Copeland jumped out of the back, sprinted over to the big Kraut: the man lay face upwards in the road, great chest heaving, breath coming in rattling sobs. Cope crouched by him, saw tree-trunk legs twisted at odd angles, saw a trickle of blood from the gash of a mouth, set in a mottled, scarred, mutilated face. The NCO wore para wings on his chest, and a Crete wristband: his eyes were open and full of tarnished green steel. Copeland realized with a shock that he'd seen the man before – through his telescopic sights. It was the big buffalo of a Kraut who'd led the charge at the bridge – the one Cope had been a split second from whacking out. 'I saw you at the Senarca bridge,' he grunted.

The glass-green eyes blinked at him. 'Vas a *gute* pattle, no? Your men was very brave.' The voice was a rasping whisper, hoarse and faint.

'You captured an officer, a captain. Where is he?'

The big NCO gasped with pain, tried to move a chip-pan hand, gave up.

'*Caine*,' he whispered. 'He was a brave man: an Airborne brother: one of us.' His eyes drifted to Copeland's chest, took in the SAS wings over the breast pocket. 'Is wrong ve are on different sides, no?'

'Yes,' Cope said. 'What happened to him?'

A Hun bullet flipped lazily out of the sky, snicked past Cope's ear: he flinched.

'*Come on, boss!*' Griffen bawled. 'Snatch 'im or dump the bugger. 'Is mates'll 'ave us for dinner.'

'Feel . . . in my chest . . . pocket,' the big Kraut moaned.

Copeland hesitated an instant, dug into the Jerry's pocket, brought out something small and metallic. It was a scratched and battered Zippo lighter: the initials *TEC* were etched on the base. *TEC – Thomas Edward Caine. Tom's Zippo: the one that saved his life.*

Cope felt a frisson pass down his spine: the lighter seemed like a sacred object. He stuffed it into his battledress.

'Where is he?' he asked.

The NCO's lips worked soundlessly for a moment: bloody drool ran from the side of his mouth. 'We take him . . . take him . . . to Jesi prison-camp.' He tried to focus his glazed eyes on Copeland. 'Now you . . . shoot me . . . one Airborne brother . . . to another.'

A salvo of machine-gun rounds hit the road surface,

flicked up tiny parachutes of dust. Cope heard the jeep engine rev. '*We're goin', boss!*' Griffen roared.

Copeland stood up, swung the muzzle of his weapon at the wounded Hun. His thumb lingered on the safety catch: he cast a last glance at the bottle-glass eyes, the heaving chest, turned and ran for the jeep.

17

Jesi, Le Marche, Italy
7 October 1943

They came for Butterfield at midnight: the door crashed open, torch-beams strobed darkness, dark figures dragged the major from his palliasse. Caine heard a sharp whack: Butterfield yelled. '*Caine. Wake up. If I don't get out of this . . . Remember what you promised.*'

Caine didn't answer: he watched the play of light, the knot of dark bodies struggling through the doorway, waited for the door to close. It didn't. He tensed, listened to the scutter of boots receding down the corridor, saw the flame of a lamp leap up, saw the soft yellow glow press into the cell. The light was broken by two knotted shadows that seemed to worm silently into the room like snakes. Caine gazed up, saw Amray standing there holding an oil lamp. Next to him was a girl, slim and cute, with a dark fringe of hair framing a heart-shaped face: she was carrying an enamel tray with a bowl of soup and a hunk of bread. She knelt down gracefully, placed the tray on the floor in front of Caine. The soup was steaming and smelt good: Caine forced himself not to look at it.

Amray was still wearing his SS uniform: Caine saw lamplight reflected in the shine of his riding boots. The seams of his face were cross-hatched with dark rivets: the coal-tinctured eyes, switchblade jaws, prominent nose, weak chin and feminine smile lent him a quality that was almost clownishly sinister. The girl was dressed in a dark skirt and a white blouse: her hair was a rich and deep black, cut page-boy style: her features were even and demure. She was evidently nervous, though: she held her hands loosely by her sides: her fingers twitched.

'To what do I owe the honour?' Caine said. 'You didn't come just to bring me soup.'

Amray crouched in front of him, set the lamp down on the floor, changed the configuration of shadows: the girl remained standing.

Amray slipped out the same cigarette case Caine had seen earlier, opened it, offered it to Caine. 'Have a gasper, old man.'

Caine shook his head. 'No, thanks.'

'Still not ready to dance with the devil, eh? Well, I can understand that, but I think it's the wrong move. They're slamming Butterfield in solitary now: he's had three days to think about it and come up with the right answers. If he doesn't give Stengel what he wants by tomorrow, he'll be scragged.'

Caine balled his fists in the darkness, longed to punch Amray's lights out.

Amray stuck a cigarette in his mouth, left it unlit.

'Butterfield didn't quite come up to our standards, so we never invited him,' he said. 'You, however – we'd be proud to have a man like you with us.'

He lit the cigarette with his lighter; the sudden whoosh of fire chased the dark rivets from his face. Caine saw a naked intensity there. *He really believes all this*, he thought. Amray blew smoke, removed the cigarette, waved it around between two fingers.

'The British Free Corps is a volunteer unit, Caine. Conceived and created by British subjects from all parts of the empire. We have pledged our lives to the common European struggle against Soviet Russia.'

'Spare me the bullshit.'

Amray took a drag of his cigarette, watched Caine with moonish, bovine eyes. 'We'd like to have you on board, but the invitation won't last for ever. Just say you'll come over to us, you get out of this cell, get a shower, a good meal and a drink, a soft bed, and . . .' He glanced slyly up at the girl. 'You get Lucia here. She's a civilian prisoner, arrested for partisan activity, but she's agreed to become your companion in return for certain considerations. You can do what you like with her, old man. Shag her front and behind, all the way till morning.'

He took a toke of his cigarette, grinned at the girl. 'Isn't that right, Lucia? He can fuck you all the way through till morning, can't he?'

The girl nodded, smiled, joined her hands bashfully at the waist. Caine guessed that she'd understood, but was feigning ignorance to save face. He felt angry at the way Amray was humiliating her.

'No, thanks,' he said again. 'I've told you already. I'm not interested in betraying my country.'

Amray tittered. 'And I've told *you* already: fighting the Russians is not betraying your country.'

'Isn't it? What about swearing an oath of allegiance to Hitler and putting on an SS uniform?'

Amray took another puff of smoke: his eyes were boreholes in dark stone. 'Your country never loved you, Caine. Your country is a conspiracy run by the king and Winston Churchill, a mob of gangsters born with silver spoons – the bankers and the money-men, taking advantage of those like you and me for their own benefit. Blood-suckers who drain you dry and throw aside your empty husk. They've never done anything but used you. A means to an end, Caine – that's all you are. You're an object, a fighting-cock, whose life they are willing to throw away, as long as they stay on top.'

Caine swallowed. There was nothing in what Amray had just said that he hadn't told himself. But Britain was still his country, his home. Was he going to aid and abet people whose object was to help the enemy take it over?

'I've heard it before,' he said. 'Even if what you say were true –'

'Ah . . . so you admit it, then?'

'I said, *even* if it *were* true, we'll put it right after the war. For now, though, I'm not ready to risk my life for people who change sides for their own advantage. I'll stick it out with my own lot for better or for worse.'

Amray's face never lost its frowzy smile. He put the cigarette in his mouth, shifted the lamp, stood up. Diamond-patterns of light and shadow raced across the walls.

'That's what they all say at first. Then, when they think about it, they realize that the Nazis are no worse than those people – the *toffs* – who've been exploiting them and others for centuries, stealing land, stealing resources, massacring anyone who objects, controlling everything, turning everyone into zombies. You're here because of them.'

He paused for breath. 'Think about it, old man. Wouldn't it be better to be out there, fighting the Russians, than stuck here in a box? Or, worse still . . .' He gave a hollow chuckle. 'I'll tell you what, I'm not going to take your answer as a definite no. Why not sleep on it, consider your options? You're tired, mentally exhausted. Perhaps things will look different in the morning.'

Caine didn't answer. Amray turned to the girl. '*Andiamo!*' he said. He glanced back at Caine. 'Don't waste the soup, old chap. You might not get any more.'

Caine couldn't keep his eyes off the soup and bread: he fell on it ravenously the moment the door was closed.

The food made him feel drowsy: despite everything, a deep sense of ease and well-being flooded through him. He lay back on his palliasse, thinking about

Butterfield, about his dream – the girl in the white dress, the sad parade of sacred ibises. He didn't doubt that Butterfield's five SAS-men had been shot, nor that the plum-shaped major was next in line. He didn't doubt that he and his 2nd SAS team had come for the Codex, nor that the countess who knew of its whereabouts was in mortal danger. And he didn't doubt that the Nazis would eventually execute him, too. The only way to dodge it was to escape, but that would take time: he couldn't do it from this cell. He'd have to be outside, to learn the layout of the camp, the procedures, the routines. Yet escape was always easier within forty-eight hours of capture. After that, you got accustomed to imprisonment: the inertia set in.

He thought about Harry Copeland, wondered if he'd made it back to Termoli with the survivors of his section. The SRS would soon be sailing for Algeria en route for Blighty. He'd have given anything to be sailing with them: that wasn't going to happen now. He lay in the darkness for a long time, letting these gusts of thought spiral through him, and no matter how hard he tried to deflect them, they kept coming back and back to a single thought: *SS-Hauptsturmführer* John Amray, of the British Free Corps.

At last he fell asleep, and dreamed that he was facing a gigantic gilt-framed mirror that covered most of the cell wall. A dark figure was staring back at him. It was a Nazi, dressed in a field-grey serge tunic with three lions passant guardant in scarlet and gold on the lapel: there was a Union Jack armshield on the left sleeve and a Waffen-SS eagle and swastika above. He wore a leather belt with a shiny square buckle, a German field cap with a death's head badge on the crown. The man was unusually broad-shouldered and deep-chested, with a squarish head, a freckled, blunt face, a snub nose and the polished quartz eyes of a stranger. Caine strained to look more closely, realized that the face didn't belong to a stranger, after all. Its landmarks were familiar. '*You ain't Captain Caine, you're the devil.*' Caine felt a hoarse scream rising up from his gorge: the Nazi in the mirror was himself.

18

Jesi, Le Marche, Italy
8 October 1943

What had begun as a scream emerged as a chuckle. He peered into the mirror, grinned sardonically, tugged down the peak of the field cap, tilted it over his eyes at a more acute angle. He examined the death's head badge on the crown, recalled the insignia from the battle he and his section had fought against the Totenkopf battalion in Tunisia earlier that year. He'd lost almost the entire unit: good men, killed holding a bridge that need not have been held. That was the story of almost every mission he'd undertaken since he'd been recruited for the SAS: the brass had set him up, knocked him down every time.

He squinted in the mirror at the bed behind him where Lucia lay naked under white sheets, her slim brown shoulders and half-moon breasts with their broad nipples peeking out of the draperies, her swirl of black hair fanned out across the pillow. He wondered if she was awake.

He glanced around the hut: daylight came in splints

and pin-pricks through the curtains. Compared with the cell he'd been in before, this was luxury: clean sheets, windows, an armchair, a table, a stove, even a rug. On the wall was a poster showing an androgynous figure watching a parade of marching soldiers in German uniform, flying the black, red and white Nazi banner over a fluttering Union Jack. *Our flag is going forward too*, ran the caption.

Caine couldn't remember having moved into this hut. The events of the previous day were foggy: he had vague memories of shaving, taking a hot shower, of a medical orderly treating his face, his head, his bruised hands, dressing his wounded finger, of being brought a lunch of bully beef, pasta, potatoes, red wine, of being measured for his new uniform. From what he recalled, though, the uniform had turned up almost immediately, as if the measuring had been a mere ritual. He stared at the field-grey suit in the mirror for a long time, examined the Waffen-SS eagle, the lion passant guardant lapel-flash, the Union Jack armshield.

From what he remembered, he'd put on the uniform at Amray's prompting: he'd attended a swearing-in ceremony in Grolsch's office. Once again, the images were indistinct: he had a notion that the blonde woman, Maria, had been there, that Grolsch had delivered a speech of welcome, standing under a portrait of Hitler, that there'd been a lot of clicking of heels and *Heil Hitler* salutes, that everything had gone silent as he'd sworn allegiance to the Führer, that the blonde woman had clapped. Afterwards, he thought he recalled schnapps and cigars and slaps on the back.

The problem was that the events of the entire day felt remote, as if he'd been watching them from afar. He knew he'd donned the Nazi uniform, sworn fealty to Hitler; he recalled odd details, but when he tried to focus on the memories, he couldn't remember having actually *been* there. It was almost as if someone had described them to him second-hand. He gazed at his reflection in the mirror, realized he'd taken an irreversible step. Whatever happened now, he'd joined the Nazis: there was no turning back.

Lucia stirred, sat up, draped the sheet around her, posed on the side of the bed. '*Buongiorno*,' she said.

Caine turned to her: her eyes were sleepy, and when she drew her hand through the fringe of her hair, he found it so alluring that he had to fight the temptation to touch her.

'Morning,' he said. 'How do you feel?'

She shrugged. 'I did what the pigs wanted. Now I will be fine.'

Caine wondered if she included him in the category of pigs: he had only the dimmest memories of having spent the night with her: he knew that they must have had sex but, oddly, he couldn't remember it, couldn't recall having even kissed her.

A few moments after she'd left, Amray bustled in

carrying a pick-helve. He gave Caine a sly wink. 'Some pretty intense shagging going on last night then, eh? Heard it through the walls. Needn't ask if she was any good, need I?'

'I wouldn't tell you anyway,' Caine said.

'After *that* gala performance? Should think the whole camp heard it. Was she a fitting reward for your *conversion*?'

Caine smiled quietly. 'Thank you.'

'First of many, old man, first of many. We're not short of a bint or two in the BFC. Your life with us will be roses after the other side, I'll tell you.'

Caine pointed at the pick-helve. 'What's this?'

'This is your weapon. Have you forgotten you're on duty today? We have to escort our old pal Butterfield on his final journey.'

He studied the helve for a moment, handed it over. Caine hefted it in his scarred, fight-hardened hands: it was only a club, but it felt good. Amray watched him with a look of apprehension: Caine gripped the shaft, swung it with his right hand, fixed Amray with a stare so hard that the man took a step back.

'What about a *real* weapon?' Caine said. He nodded towards the Walther pistol holstered on Amray's belt. They've given *you* one: what about me?'

'Now, hold your horses, old man. Just because you swore an oath to Hitler doesn't mean they trust you. You've got to prove yourself. That's why they detailed you for the Butterfield escort. If you can do this without turning a hair, it'll go a long way to convincing them that you're in earnest.'

Caine pulled at his newly shaved chin. 'I'm not sure about this. I *know* Butterfield. He's from my regiment.'

'I get it, old boy.' Amray's mouth was a narrow slot between lean-bladed jaws. 'But that's why it's a test, you see. If you can do it, then they'll accept that you really are with us. If you refuse, they might think you joined us just to get better conditions for yourself, or even to escape.'

Caine set the helve down. 'So what do *you* think?'

'How do I know, old chap?' Amray made an effete gesture with a thin hand. 'Why *did* you change your mind?'

Caine thought about it for a moment, realized that he couldn't remember having changed his mind. He took a breath. 'I'm fed up with seeing men die thanks to the blundering of our command. I'm still loyal to my country, but not to commanders who are willing to sacrifice human beings for their own good. Russia is the real enemy, not the Germans. I'm a soldier: I'd rather be fighting the Russians than rotting in a prison-camp.'

Amray nodded approvingly: Caine was astonished at himself. The explanation had come out in a rush, like a rehearsed speech, yet he couldn't recall having learned it. *There's something going on, here*, he thought. *It's as if I spent the whole of yesterday half asleep*. He turned to Amray. 'What's the date?' he asked.

'Eighth of October 1943. Why?'

Caine shrugged to hide his disbelief. *Eighth of October? That's impossible. I arrived here on 4 October, the day we landed at Termoli. The day they took Butterfield away was 7 October: Stengel had given him three days to talk. So what happened to yesterday – the day I joined the Nazis? It's like I've got memories of a day that never was. I must have made a mistake somewhere.*

Amray picked up the helve, handed it back to him. 'Let's get to it, old boy,' he said.

19

Karl Grolsch was standing by his *Kubelwagen* outside the punishment block when Caine and Amray arrived. Parked along the wire Caine saw a 3-ton lorry without a cover, and a couple of motorcycle combinations. The crews were loafing about, smoking, nursing Schmeisser sub-machine guns. Caine gave the vehicles the once-over: neither the jeep nor the lorry appeared to be armed, but one of the motorcycle sidecars carried a Spandau machine-gun mounted on a tripod, bolted to its frame. It didn't look as if the Germans were expecting trouble: there was an air of jollity about the party, almost as if it were an outing – everyone but Grolsch seemed at ease.

Amray saluted Grolsch as they came up: he returned the compliment fluidly, eyed Caine's uniform with an amused air. 'I want you two to sit next to him in the lorry,' he said. 'He'll have some company, so to speak.' He glanced at his watch. 'What is keeping those people? We haven't got all day.'

It occurred to Caine that this might be a ruse: perhaps the whole BFC recruitment, the ceremony, everything, had been a trick to assure his compliance, to get him to the same place as Butterfield in the end. *But no, it couldn't be. Why go to all that trouble when they could have just overpowered me?*

They left the commandant, took up positions at the tailgate of the lorry, waited. The Sipo-SD guards glared at them with barely disguised hostility. *They hate us because we've betrayed the code of combat*, Caine thought. *If they had the chance, they'd kill us too.*

He gripped the helve in his right hand, swung it a little. It made him feel better. He examined the barbed-wire perimeter: the high fence was rusty in places, overgrown with bushes, grass and vines. He followed its line with his eye to where it passed the foot of a watch-tower – a tin-roofed hut on four big stilts, with access by ladder, and both a machine-gun and a spotlight set up in the guard's aperture. He glimpsed a face in there, the glint of a chamber-pot helmet in a stray band of light.

Amray nudged him: a squad of four Sipo-SD men were escorting Butterfield through the gate, moving with the slowness of a funeral march. Caine couldn't mistake the major's figure: the drooping jowls, the slack bagginess of his physique. Otherwise, though, this was a different Butterfield from the one he'd last seen: he was wearing a shapeless mufti suit of grey flannel, a ragged shirt and broken shoes. The suit was too loose and he walked hesitantly, stumbling, bow-backed, hanging his head. Caine thought of sacred ibises: he'd seen them in a dream, but somehow that dream seemed more real than the events of yesterday. How come he'd taken an oath to Hitler? He was wearing a Nazi collaborator's uniform, yet he felt no loyalty to the Hun. He was acting as a trustee, escorting Bunny Butterfield to what would probably be his execution: he felt no desire to do it, yet he was doing it, as if he were following the beat of an inaudible drum.

When the party reached the tailgate, the guards ordered Butterfield to halt. He glanced up with effort, saw Caine standing there with a pick-helve in his hand. His good eye glimmered as if from the far end of a distant tunnel: Caine noticed livid marks, burns and bloodstains on his face that hadn't been there before. He held Butterfield's glance, nodded at him. Butterfield said nothing: Caine couldn't tell if he'd even recognized him. It was only as the Jerries began hustling him up into the back of the lorry that he turned his head in Caine's direction. 'You betrayed your promise,' he said chokily. 'You, of all people, a traitor. You'll burn in hell for this, Caine.'

A guard elbowed him in the kidneys, cracked a joke that made the others hoot. Butterfield clung to the rope: two soldiers already on the lorry hauled him in like a big, flabby fish.

Caine's cheeks felt hot. *I'm a traitor. The first time I've been called that.* He noticed Amray watching him: he shrugged, gripped the rope, shimmied up into the lorry after Butterfield.

He was glad the vehicle was open: it enabled him to get his bearings. The lorry occupied mid-place on the convoy, with the motorcycle combination scouting ahead, Grolsch's car behind. They were heading west, Caine was sure of that: this road would eventually take them up into the Appenines. If they really were going to execute Butterfield – and all the evidence suggested it – they were likely to end up in a forest sooner or later. At first, the road crossed a plain of neatly manicured fields – flax yellow, rose madder, green – interspersed with long brakes of trees. Soon, the land dropped away and the road hugged the high ground of a ridge, arched gently around its contours on a trajectory lined with stark firs and thorny copses, and the hillside sloping steeply on both sides in olive-coloured meadows dotted with outcrops of rock. The day was overcast: cloud lay in thick wads across the dome-shaped sky, breaking up into ribs and puffball flurries, fraying at the edges into bristling swales of fibre, like unravelled basketwork.

There were hard benches on both sides of the lorry. Caine and Amray sat with Butterfield between them. The major ignored them, balanced his cuffed hands on his knees, sank into silence. Two Sipo-SD guards sat on the seat facing them, and one on Caine's right. The guards were armed with SMGs: they chatted, roared with laughter at wisecracks, pointed and nodded at Butterfield, drew fingers across their throats. The guard next to Caine was a rangy sergeant with a beak of a nose, bird eyes and a smug expression: his cheeks were puffed out by the tightness of his chinstrap. Caine gripped his pick-helve across his knees, realized he felt boxed in.

The truck rocked and wobbled down into the valley: Caine saw peaks and saddles of blue mountains along the skyline, saw sunlight glitter on cutstone cliffs like the facets of dull diamonds. The valley road ran through rippling hayfields, grassy patches hedged with trees, through spreads of forest so dense they looked like growths of fur. Sometimes they passed the junctions of dirt-roads that climbed steeply through the woods towards some unseen hill-top village: they passed a tiny redbrick church with fluted sides, standing amid poplars, and one-storey cottages with terracotta roof-tiles, pink stucco walls and shuttered windows. They passed squads of prisoners being marched to work by Jerry guards. Shortly, the convoy began to climb again, following a track that coiled through winding galleries of conifers: Caine was just quick enough to catch a signpost standing at the junction. *Villa Montefalcone*, it read.

At the top of the escarpment the road flattened out, undulated between evergreens lining a high bank on the left and forest falling away on the right: in the far distance, above the treetops, Caine could make out a striated cliff-face, stretching beneath a hogsback ridge topped with knuckles and peaks. The convoy rounded a bend into a stretch where the trees thinned. Almost at once, Caine felt the driver apply the brakes: the soldiers on board craned their necks to see what was happening.

Amray stood up to peer over the cab. 'An accident,' he said. 'Overturned wagon, by the look of it.'

Caine got up, glanced ahead, saw a big four-wheeled cart on its side in the middle of the road, with logs scattered everywhere, saw a grey carthorse lying in the shafts, saw it twitch: he saw red slashes of blood from its injuries on the gravel surface. There were a couple of people there – a dark man in a waistcoat and a battered hat and a petite woman in a calf-length dress, shawl and headscarf: they were trying ineffectually to raise the heavy cart.

There was no way around the obstacle. The motorcycle escort drove straight up to it: the NCO in charge began to berate the Ities furiously. The peasants stared back with cowlike eyes: there was a split-second standoff, as both parties faced each other. The lorry-driver slammed on the brakes: the lorry came to a halt. Grolsch had his car creep past the 3-tonner, draw up behind the escort: Caine saw him step out, strut around the accident-scene, examine the dying horse.

The motorcyclists parked up their machine: the NCO ordered the gunner to keep watch with the Spandau. He and the other two slung their SMGs, moved towards the cart. Grolsch drew his pistol, leaned over the horse's head: his driver, a rotund man bulging out of his field-grey, stood at his shoulder. The Italian couple lurked together a few yards away: the woman had the figure of a young girl, Caine saw, but the crows' feet around her eyes and mouth showed that she was older. The man held her arm as if to prevent her running away, his eyes heavy-lidded and watchful. He carried a shabby knapsack with a strap slung over over one shoulder.

Grolsch tucked the muzzle of his pistol behind the horse's ear, squeezed the trigger. The weapon cracked: the horse's great frame went rigid. In the same instant, the woman strode forward with neat, tripping steps – a small, upright figure, slim, solid under the shawl and the shapeless dress, her fine features framed by the headscarf, composed, still, hard as flint. She drew an automatic pistol from beneath the shawl in a graceful sweeping movement: without even breaking step, she shot Grolsch twice in the upper chest: *blammppp, blammppp.*

Grolsch's eyes went wide: his lips worked. He toppled over on the dead horse. The driver reeled away in horror: the woman shot him once in the back, turned and ran.

Caine saw the woman drift towards the trees as if floating, saw the Itie in the hat produce a short SMG from his knapsack, come up into a crouch, crackle a long burst at the three Sipo-SD men nearest the overturned wagon. The raw *tack-tack-tack* snapped at Caine's eardrums: he saw Jerries grab for slung weapons, saw the Itie's rounds punch black yawns in field-grey buttocks and chests, saw a Kraut go down, saw arterial blood spurt in gushes from his thigh. A machine-gun opened up: rounds heaved through the undergrowth in long spits. Caine saw Jerries kick and writhe, saw rounds gouge furrows across the pale dirt, heard the slow *bomp bomp bomp* of a second machine-gun, firing from another position, heard rounds go *pphhwaaaattt* against the body of the sidecar, saw patterns of redness crawl up the gunner's arm, clocked the look of anguish on his face. An improvised bomb in a canvas sack sailed out of the bushes, hit the combo, went off with a deep-gutted slap like the whip of a wet towel. The combo tore apart in a fission of rods and shards: the fuel-tank ballooned out like a squashed sun: yellow fire-talons snaggled through wreathed black smoke. Caine saw man and machine fly and separate, saw the bike crash in a tumble of flame, saw a smoking body roll and shriek.

Caine had no time to see what happened next: at that moment the lorry went into fast reverse: the standing soldiers were knocked sideways. Caine kept his balance, grasped Butterfield's wrist with his left hand, jerked him up. He turned to the beaky sergeant on his right, saw the birdlike eyes narrow, saw the Schmeisser quiver as he released the safety catch. Caine drew the pick-helve back across his left shoulder, hit the sergeant a crumpling smack at the base of the neck, felt the collar-bone give. Just then, the lorry-driver hit the brakes: the sergeant fell heavily against the tailgate.

The two Krauts opposite Caine were hurled on top of each other. Caine fought to stay upright on legs planted firmly apart: he dropped the pick-helve, snatched the sergeant's Schmeisser with his right hand. He saw the other Jerries pivot towards him, clutched the pistol-grip, tickled iron, felt the gun vibrate, heard the deafening *tack-tack-tacka-tack*, saw Huns twist and scream, saw one of them pitch clear over the side of the lorry. He dragged Butterfield to the tailgate, wrapped the SMG sling around his arm, grabbed the rope, swung down, heaved the major after him. Butterfield landed in a soft heap, let out a short *ooooffff*.

Caine pulled him to his feet: rounds clanged against the tailgate, squibbed off metal, roasted air. Caine ducked, saw Amray's haunted face glowering down from the tailgate, saw the Walther pistol in his hand. The weapon cracked: Butterfield staggered, fell in a heap with a bloody rut carved across his temple. Amray swung down from the lorry: Caine smashed him across the jaw with the muzzle of the SMG, sent him sprawling. He shuftied right, saw Itie civvies emerge from the trees, letting rip with rifles and pistols. His first impulse was to raise his hands and shout, '*Amico!*': then he became intensely aware that he was wearing Nazi uniform. These partisans had already killed Germans: they weren't about to debate his loyalties in the heat of battle. Caine took a last glance at Butterfield: the wound was a graze, but the major was out of it. *There's no way you're going to get him out of here,* a voice in his head screamed. *Beat it. Now.*

He pumped a burst into the air above the advancing partisans, hared off in the opposite direction, making sure he got the lorry between himself and them, only dimly aware of bullets twanging around him. It seemed for ever until he made the trees on the far side of the road, threw himself down on the slope. He rolled, crawled, peeked over the top, saw hard-faced men in ragged clothes gathered around Amray, jerking him to his feet. He saw them pinion his arms, snatch his pistol. He saw Amray struggle, saw his slim jaw-hasps work in furious protest, glimpsed the deep horror in the black eyes, just before one of the partisans cut his throat with a razor. Caine crawled a few yards down the slope, then, sure he couldn't be seen, rose to his feet, dashed down-hill through the trees.

20

Near Montefalcone, Le Marche, Italy
8 October 1943

When he awoke it was already dark: he was lying on a bed of pine needles in the forest. He sat up: his limbs ached, his head was sore, his mouth felt like plaster of Paris. A cheese-paring moon cruised above him, clinging on the smooth, glossy night. Caine recalled his dream, wondered if this were still a dream: the place seemed familiar, as if he'd been here before. Abruptly, he recalled Butterfield lying in a heap by the lorry with a red crease on his head: the terror in Amray's pit-bull eyes, just before the partisans had slit his throat. *Did that really happen?* He recalled standing in front of a mirror, looking at the face of a stranger. '*You ain't Captain Caine, you're the devil.*'

He scrabbled at his sleeves with crossed hands, found the BFC Union Jack armshield. *I'm still wearing it. It wasn't a dream: it was real.* For an instant he strained to remember why he'd put on that uniform: he couldn't believe he'd actually done it. Whatever his intentions had been, wearing the badge of the Waffen SS and swearing an oath of allegiance to Hitler were irrevocable acts of treason. He shuddered at the thought. *How did it happen?* He'd been looking in a mirror one minute, had found himself on the other side of it the next, in Nazi dress. He recalled the girl, Lucia, lying naked on his bed. '*Should think the whole camp heard it. Was she a fitting reward for your conversion?*' Strange that he couldn't remember having sex with Lucia, couldn't recall having touched her at all.

He began to focus. This wasn't a dream: he'd joined the Jerries, and now he'd escaped. Amray was dead, Butterfield wounded. He was on his own. The Jerries would soon be hunting him, but after what the partisans had done to Amray, he wasn't inclined to throw in his lot with them, either – at least, not until he'd got shot of the SS togs.

There was only one possible plan: head south to Allied lines. He didn't know how far that was. He had the Schmeisser with perhaps half a magazine of rounds: he had cigarettes and matches, but no food, and no equipment, not even a cup or a water-bottle. He probably wouldn't make it without help from the locals, but he would have to be cautious: not all Ities sympathized with the partisans, or supported the Allies. And who was going to trust him dressed like this? His first mission would be to beg, borrow or steal a civilian outfit. Steal, preferably. Begging or borrowing would mean revealing himself to someone, and that might be a problem.

He retrieved the Schmeisser, checked that it was

ready to fire, stood up, listened to the forest, heard leaf-rustle and the pulse of cicadas. *Which way's south?* The road from Jesi ran east–west, and he was on the north side of it: south was back the way he'd come, which meant retracing his steps to the area of the ambush. He must have run away from the road for a good sixty minutes, he thought: it had to be four or or five miles away. He slung the SMG over his shoulder, took a breath. *Better get going. It's a long walk back.*

He'd only taken a few steps when he heard someone whisper his name. He stopped, let the SMG drop into his hands, cocked his ears. Nothing stirred: the whisper didn't come again. *It was a girl's voice*, he thought. It reminded him of the girl in his dream – the figure in the bloodstained white dress, with the black velvet hair, the coffee-coloured skin, the Chinese eyes.

'The man in the mirror is not himself. The five dandelion seeds are buried in the forest, at the place marked "B". What is sought lies in a room with no doors or windows. I am the door. Another holds the key.'

He shivered. What had any of that rubbish got to do with him? He paused, swallowed, realized that he knew *exactly* what it had to do with him. *I'm the man in the mirror. I walked through a mirror and became a mirror-image of myself.* The dandelion seeds were parachutists. A five-man SAS team, carted off by the Hun and murdered. Buried in the forest, at the place marked 'B'. *'B' for Butterfield – Bunny's men?* But what was sought in a room with no doors or windows? Butterfield had come for the Codex: that was what *he* sought. And there was only one person who knew where it was: *Countess Emilia Falcone, who lives at the Villa Montefalcone – a castle in the mountains.* Caine remembered the signpost they had passed on the road just before the last climb. *Villa Montefalcone.* It must be near. He recalled guiltily what he had promised Butterfield: '*If I see a chance, I'll get you out. If not, I'll find the countess and the Codex, if it's the last thing I do.*'

He felt a sudden pang of rejection. *I got Butterfield out: I kept my word. I don't have any further duty to him. It's his task, not mine.*

He thought of the head-wound Butterfield had taken. *He won't be in any fit state to go after the Codex: even if he were, he'd never do it alone, not with all the Huns who are supposed to be guarding it. The partisans could do it, but why the hell should they? Why should I? Why should I risk my life carrying out someone else's mission? What has it got to do with me?*

He thought of Butterfield's determination to snatch the Codex, his stoical acceptance of his fate, his faithful attempt to pass the mission on. The major might not be his idea of a fighting soldier, but he had guts and he was SAS: whatever the real value of the Codex to the war, this was an SAS task. Caine might be wearing enemy insignia, but he was still Regiment, and he'd given his word. *You also gave your word to Hitler, remember? You promised to fight for the Nazis.*

On the other hand, Caine knew it wasn't only his

word that mattered: Countess Emilia Falcone was in danger of being tortured to death by Stengel. Caine didn't know the countess, but he couldn't help associating her with the woman in his dream – the girl in white, with the bruised neck and bound hands. *She's in for some rough handling*, Butterfield had said. *It can only be a matter of time till she talks.*

It wasn't just his honour, or the honour of the Regiment, but also the life of an innocent woman that was at stake. Caine couldn't turn his back on that. He had always blamed himself for his mother's suicide, convinced that he could have saved her had he been there. He'd struggled with every nerve and sinew to save Betty Nolan, and he'd failed. He'd never met the countess, but the thought of deserting her stuck in his craw. *You've got this thing about women and children first*, Harry Copeland would have told him. On the other hand, if Stengel murdered Emilia, that would be another sin of omission Caine would have to live with, and he was living with enough of those already.

How would he find the villa in this dense woodland? He would need a guide: he shied away from the idea of enlisting a local, though. He had to regard the natives as hostile until proved friendly: his best chance of success lay in remaining out of sight. In these forests and hills that was at least possible. His first priority was water: his mouth felt as if it had been scoured with a sander. Finding water in the forest at night wasn't going to be easy, but he reasoned that he could at least follow the slope into the valley: if a stream existed, it was likely to be down there.

He descended the gradient, pushed through spiky underbrush and hogweed until he found a narrow track leading downhill. There was just enough moonlight to allow him to see it. The path meandered around tree trunks, passed under foliage so low that Caine was forced to crawl on his hands and knees. It was hard going: his hands had swollen up again, and his wounded finger was becoming painful. At least, though, the earth under his palms was damp: there ought to be water nearby.

He crept down the path, watching, listening: every ten paces or so he halted, trying to catch any sound, any smell, that was out of place. The heartbeat of the forest had increased in intensity: there was a distinct in-out rhythm to it, a warm pulsation of energy in the heaving of leaves, the creak of branches, the insect-trill. It gave Caine the feeling the forest was *alive* – a sense that was menacing and comforting at the same time.

A nasal growl came from the underbrush ahead: his heart jolted: he heard twigs snap, heard a heavy body tumble through the thickets, heard a series of exasperated grunts like clipped explosions. It was an animal, and it was moving away from him. *Wild boar*, he thought. *I startled it.* He realized that he'd been smelling the rich, sour-dung odour of pig ever since he'd joined the track. He heard the scuffle of hoofs, then the unmistakable plop of a body hitting water. *There* is *a stream down there. My pig friend's just gone for a dip in it.*

He smelt moss and the odour of waterlogged leaves long before he saw moonlight streak the oil-black rivulet that tunnelled through the foliage. The trees were bigger here: huge grey trunks two men couldn't have joined hands around, with roots like dark tentacles that trailed into the water across a low bank. Caine hunkered by the edge near a nest of boulders half submerged in the stream: it was muddy, and he could clearly see the scuff-marks of boar in the moonlight: it was evidently a regular pig crossing-point. He felt an instinctive disquiet, but not because of the boars. At the stream's edge he was exposed, vulnerable to anyone with the nous to move silently through the woods. He knelt on both knees in the mud, took the Schmeisser in his left hand, held it like a pistol, balanced the long mag against his knee. He bent down, used his painful right hand to scoop liquid.

When he'd had enough, he wiped his mouth, wished he had some sort of vessel to carry water in. One thing he'd had learned in the desert was that water was life: he didn't intend to get that thirsty again.

He stood up, passed his weapon to his right hand: studied the place in the darkness. He could make out another path, running parallel with the stream, curling around clumps of trees and nests of reeds. His best guess was that the Villa Montefalcone lay on his left – the direction the vehicles had been going before the partisan ambush. He turned and began to move silently along the track: the undergrowth was denser here, and the going slow. He would never get to his destination in darkness: his best bet was to lie up till first light. The path widened out into a clearing, where he found a rickety wooden footbridge spanning the flow. He moved to examine it, saw that there were wide paths leading to it from both banks. In daylight, this would be a place frequented by locals. Not far from the bridge lay a patch of low grass with a drop of a few feet into the water. The stream seemed to run deep here: it looked as if it might be a bathing-place for local villagers. The grass was clean and comfortable-looking: Caine was tempted to lie down on it and go to sleep again. He nudged the thought out of his head: this was the last place he wanted to be found sleeping.

He forced himself on, realized suddenly how tired he was: a little downstream the bank grew higher and was topped with a thick tangle of bramble and stunted trees, like a solid mass in the darkness. Caine slung his SMG, took to his hands and knees, forced himself through rasping thorns, deep into the thicket. There was a convenient space inside, just large enough to accommodate him. He wriggled his body round until he was facing the direction of the bridge: it was too dark to see it from here, but he would be able to at first light.

He lay awake for a while, listening to the sounds of the forest. Despite his precarious position, he began to feel peaceful, almost safe. He was in enemy territory, yet the forest felt familiar, like home. It brought back vivid childhood memories: the smell of earth and trees, the sound of branches rustling in the wind, of birdsong, chittering fieldmice, foxes coughing in the thickets. No matter how bad things had become at home with his stepfather, he'd always been able to escape to the woods and fields: there, amongst the plants and wild creatures, he'd understood that he need never be alone.

He wasn't aware that he was asleep, or even that he'd closed his eyes, only that he could hear a plaintive sobbing, so clear and insistent that the sound felt like claws dragging down the inside of his skull. He knew what it was, remembered it from his childhood: the crying of a half-witted little Gypsy-girl named Anna-Maria, who, like him, had been a pupil at the village school. He'd been nine years old, the girl no more than seven, small for her age, with a brown face wrinkled like a little old lady's, and shiny black hair that fell almost to her waist. She wasn't really half-witted, he knew, just shy: the village children used to call her *monkey* and *nigger*, and insisted that she was filthy and smelt of rancid fat. Caine knew what it was like: ever since he'd started school, they'd been calling him *dirty smithy* because his dad was a blacksmith. People, even the adults, had seemed both to despise and fear his father.

It was worse for Anna-Maria, though: she didn't even live in a house but in a decrepit old caravan on Mr Weatherby's land: her father, an itinerant tinker, was frequently in trouble for poaching. *Tinkers and blacksmiths*, Caine had often thought: *why is it that folk are afraid of people who work metal? Because they think it's a kind of magical power, perhaps?*

That day he'd been walking back from school when he'd heard her sobs coming from behind the tall hedge that ran along Robertson's meadow. Caine recognized the sound – deep, urgent, like the wail of an injured animal. He had climbed over the stile, and found them there – Arthur Weatherby and two other big boys of twelve or thirteen, all farmer's sons. Anna-Maria was on her hands and knees, wearing only her underpants: the boys were gleefully engaged in smearing her small body with cow-dung.

Weatherby was a strapping youth with a head like a slab, and a shock of ginger hair. 'Well, if it isn't Tom Caine, the dirty smithy's kid,' he said, grinning, holding up a hand slathered in cowshit. 'Maybe you'd like some of this, too, eh, Tommy?'

Caine was scared but couldn't take his eyes off the girl: it was the most disgusting thing he'd ever seen. He wanted to run away, but found he couldn't move. '*Leave her alone*,' he'd said: to his surprise his voice hadn't sounded as shaky as he felt. 'She's just a little girl.'

The boys tittered nastily, nodded at each other, cruised towards Caine, towered over him – or so it had seemed at the time. They peered down at him, jeered with leering mouths: he'd never felt so terrified in his life.

'You're dead, Tommy,' Weatherby sneered, shaking a dung-daubed fist at him. 'I'm going to kill you.'

'Sergeant Tiverton will put you in prison,' Caine piped up. 'You'd better make sure I'm dead, because if I'm not, I'm going to tell him what you did to Anna-Maria . . . and I'm going to tell the vicar, and the headmaster too. I won't say anything if you let her go.'

Weatherby scowled, held his fist under Caine's nose, so near that he could smell the cowshit. 'I'm going to . . .'

One of the other boys elbowed him in the side. 'Come on, Artie, let's go.'

Weatherby's eyes narrowed: he raised his fist at Caine once more. 'If you ever –'

'Come on Artie, leave the little prick.'

Weatherby spat, lowered his fist. 'What is it, fancy her, do you, Tommy? Why don't you go and wallow in the shit with her? Pigs like wallowing in shit, don't they?'

Caine said nothing. He didn't take his eyes off Weatherby until the boys had climbed over the stile. For a long time afterwards he'd wondered why Weatherby and the others hadn't beaten him up. It was the first inkling in his life that it was possible to defeat bullies just by standing up to them, by showing courage and resolution. It wasn't till much later that he'd realized that Arthur Weatherby was actually his half-cousin: they had the same blood in their veins.

That day, though, he'd carried Anna-Maria back to her father's caravan on piggy-back. Her parents accepted his explanation but expressed no feelings about Caine's intervention. Anna-Maria hadn't returned to school: the caravan had vanished from Weatherby's field, and Caine never saw her again. Arthur Weatherby had joined the Gunners at the beginning of the war: he'd been killed in action at Dunkirk.

21

Near Montefalcone, Le Marche, Italy
9 October 1943

A girl was screaming in his head, but this time he wasn't dreaming. He woke with a start, found himself lying in the thorny thicket in bottle-green light, heard the wail of precocious birdsong at its high crescendo. But it wasn't the birdsong that had woken him: the girl's shriek came again, and for a moment Caine thought someone was being tortured. But no, these were shrieks of excitement: He peered through the foliage and saw a boy and a girl frolicking in the stream just below the bridge: he could make out their bobbing heads, their clothes and a basket left on the grassy bank. He guessed they were dipping naked: that would explain the excited shrieks and the early hour.

His eyes fell on the discarded clothes again. He had no idea whether they would fit him, but they were just what the doctor ordered. Providence, that goddess of good soldiers, had come up with what he most needed and handed it to him on a plate. He simply had to get out of his hide and take the garments without being seen. He didn't want the couple to raise the alarm, but he certainly didn't want to kill them. *Stealth if possible, force if necessary?* No, it was stealth or nothing this time: if they clocked him he'd have to make himself scarce.

The swelling in his hands had gone down and the throb in his injured finger was less insistent: he was ravenously hungry. He found his gaze drawn back to the basket on the stream-bank: surely there must be some rations in there? He hated to deprive people of their breakfast, but he was desperate: and, anyway, it was no worse than nicking someone's clothes and making them walk home in their birthday suit.

He crawled painfully out of his hiding place, kept his eyes on the couple in the water: their heads were close together now. Both had dark hair: the boy's short, the girl's hanging in long braids across one shoulder, the tousled ends straggling in the water. The boy had his back to Caine: the girl was facing him, but still too far away for him make out her features. The couple kissed: by the time their mouths had separated, Caine was near enough to hear the girl's groans: whatever the boy was doing to her under the water, she seemed be enjoying it. Caine banished the thought: his name might be Tom, but he wasn't a peeper. It was to his advantage that they were focused on each other, that was all – that way they wouldn't notice him. Who would they imagine had stolen the clothes? Probably a passing tramp.

It took him ten long minutes to crawl as far as the shelter of the bushes nearest the grassy bank. The couple had moved a little further on, almost under the bridge. They were engrossed in each other: the girl had thrown her head back, letting her hair float on the rippling surface. She was gasping shrilly, the boy snorting in a way that wouldn't have shamed last night's wild boar. Caine crouched behind the nearest bush, slung the Schmeisser: the girl's gasps were building up to a climax. Caine waited two more beats, sprang a couple of yards, grabbed the pile of men's clothes with one hand, the basket with the other: he turned and retreated fast. No shout of rage followed him, only the pants and moans of satisfaction.

He ran parallel with the stream until he was sure no one was following him. He left the path, found a large tree half fallen across a dense thicket by the water's edge. He crouched behind the trunk, examined his prizes, found they were a pair of faded brown corduroy trousers, a parchment-yellow shirt, a corduroy waistcoat. He'd inadvertently picked up a pair of lady's pink bloomers too, which he put down gingerly. In the basket he found fresh bread and a paper packet of white cheese and salami: there was also a bottle of red wine and a rubber condom. He decided to keep the condom. His stomach growled: he tore off a chunk of bread with his teeth, bit into the cheese: still chewing, he stripped off the Kraut field-grey, threw the garments down, pulled on his new attire.

The trousers were too slack, the shirt tight around the chest, but they would do, and he was grateful for them. If caught dressed in civvy clothes, he might be shot as a spy, but that chance was better than bearing the stigma of a Nazi stool pigeon. He wondered what to do with the uniform. He had matches, and could burn it, but that would only attract attention to the spot. Burying it would be better, although it would probably still be found, and it would take a lot of work anyway. He clocked a couple of loose boulders in the stream, decided to tie them up in the uniform and submerge the bundles. The water was muddy here: if he pitched them in the middle of the stream it was unlikely they'd be noticed.

He was about to dispatch the second bundle when he remembered the woman's bloomers. He wadded them up and stuffed them into the bundle reluctantly: it came over him that he'd done the young couple a bad turn. He didn't imagine their passionate encounter was something they'd want the world to know about: returning home without clothes would mean exposing their secret. Or maybe they'd be cunning enough to get away with it, in which case they wouldn't be very quick to inform anyone that there was a voracious tramp in the woods.

He sat down, ate bread, cheese and salami, drank sips of wine. Almost at once he felt his energy rise. He wrapped the rest of the food in the paper packet, stowed it away in an inside pocket of his waistcoat: he stuffed the bottle into the other. At least he had something to carry water in now. His final act was to lob the basket into the stream, weighted by another big stone.

He still had no idea where he was going: Providence had helped him once, and she favoured those who dared. He was more or less confident that he was going in the right direction: staying by the stream might be risky, but he needed access to water. He would tag along with it for a while.

He moved with deliberate slowness, all his senses open, taking in the insect drone and the chirp of birds, the babble of the brook, the smell of leaf-mould and humus. Total concentration on his surroundings was an art Caine had mastered in the desert: it was a matter of blocking out the chatter inside and letting your instincts work. It must be, he had sometimes reflected, how animals related to the world – they were *inside* it, not floating away on a current of thoughts and images to some far-off place and time.

The trees here were slim, tall beeches, close-packed through beds of dried leaves, low brambles, lichen-cushioned stones: their trunks, some bent and bow-shaped, others straight as ramrods, were a mottling of dark moss and silver bark, their branches festooned with autumn foliage like spun gold and beaten copper. Sunshine spilled through the canopy in fans and bursts of sheeny light, splayed dappled patterns across the forest floor.

The stream dipped through a rock cutting and turned north: Caine kept to his western path, striking out from the water, until the trees began to thin out around brown fields with grapevines and olive groves. Beyond them stood a small cottage – an oblong of flaking stucco under a pitched roof of fractured ochre tiles, with a weather-beaten door and a tiny shuttered window. The cottage was circled with rambling timber and chicken-wire outhouses: Caine saw two or three scrawny black chickens poking about in the dirt.

His immediate instinct was to give the place a wide berth, yet he was somehow drawn to it. He had resolved to avoid all contact with the Ities, but he also admitted to himself that he had no chance of snatching the countess without help. He didn't even know how to get to the Villa Montefalcone from here. Intelligence was the key to operations like this and, before he proceeded, he needed as much as he could get.

Caine left the shelter of the trees, crept along an avenue between the vines with his SMG in the crook of his elbow. Suddenly, a dog began to bark: Caine swore, knowing he should have expected it. He stopped crawling, brought the Schmeisser slowly to bear, cursed the long magazine that made the weapon awkward to fire from the prone position. He peered through the vines: he couldn't see the dog, but he saw the door of the cottage open and a man come out – a lean peasant with a weathered face and keen eyes. He was clad in a garb similar to Caine's: corduroy trousers and waistcoat, farm-boots: a collarless grey-white shirt and a cloth cap. Caine saw that he was carrying a hunting rifle: he looked as if he knew how to use it.

Caine considered the situation. If he revealed himself,

he would be at the man's mercy: he had no way of knowing whether the chap would help him or sell him to the Hun. He could shoot the chap: he was armed, after all. But he was also a civilian, and Caine had no more desire to kill him than the couple he'd encountered that morning. The man's alert posture suggested he was quite aware that another human was present: even if Caine managed to get away, he might inform the Jerries. On the other hand, if Caine exposed himself without intending to fire, the chap might put a bullet through his head before he could even explain himself.

He thought of trying to get behind him, take him by surprise, but he discounted the idea: it might cause complications and, anyway, it was time to take a chance. It might be a fatal one, but trusting anyone, especially here, was always going to be a leap of faith.

He laid his weapon aside, concealed it under a grapevine. '*Don't shoot!*' he yelled.

The man's eyes sought out the place the voice had come from: he raised his rifle, his rawhide, grey-stubbled features drawn in concentration.

'*Amico!*' Caine shouted. 'I'm a friend. I'm going to get up. I'm not armed.'

Whether the Itie had understood him, he didn't know: the man let his rifle-muzzle drop a tad, though. Taking it as his cue, Caine rose ponderously, with his hands up. The Itie was no more than ten paces away: he raised his weapon again, scanned Caine's peasant attire and raised hands. Time stilled: Caine realized that his fate would be decided by this man's readiness or otherwise to shoot a stranger in cold blood. It all depended on how scared he was. The peasant stared at Caine's face: Caine saw the end of his mouth twitch, saw the rifle drop, let out a long breath.

The man's name was Cesare: he spoke some fragments of English he'd learned in the navy before the war. He didn't invite Caine into the cottage but made him sit behind a clump of bushes outside. Caine decided to tell him as much of the truth as he dared: he explained by gestures and in short phrases that he had escaped from a convoy carrying prisoners from the Jesi prison camp. He didn't mention his trustee status, nor the BFC uniform, now submerged in the stream.

Cesare nodded gravely. '*Si, ho capito*. There is partisan attack on road yesterday. Some people are escape. The *tedeschi* search for them.'

Caine stowed away the information: *enemy behind me, enemy ahead.*

'You have been at the Jesi camp?' Cesare enquired.

'Yes.'

The man's eyes dropped: his features grew heavy. For a moment Caine thought he was about to burst into tears.

'They take *mia figlia* to that place,' Cesare said. '*Hanno detto che lei è una staffetta*. They say she is with the partisans.'

'I'm sorry,' Caine said. 'And *was* she? With the partisans, I mean.'

Cesare shrugged narrow shoulders. '*È molta coraggiosa, mia figlia.* She is too brave. I tell her no do it. The *tedeschi* shoot you, I say. But she not listen to her father.' He sniffed. '*Non so se possa vederla ancora.* I don't know if I see her again.'

There were tears in his eyes: Caine couldn't help but feel the man's distress: what must it be like to have a daughter arrested by the Nazis? Rage kindled inside him, helped cement his determination to carry out his mission.

'*Diciasette anni*,' Cesare went on. 'Seventeen years old. She is good girl, Lucia. She work at the Villa Montefalcone from the time she is small. The countess love her.' Caine's neck-hairs prickled. Surely it couldn't be the same Lucia he'd encountered at Jesi? The girl Amray had given him as a reward for joining the Nazis? Lucia must be a common name. *Seventeen years old.* It seemed too much of a coincidence.

Caine felt his cheeks flush. *The Nazis used an innocent young girl as a sex-slave, and I went along with it.* Or had he? He recalled Lucia lying naked in his bed at the Jesi camp, but as far as he remembered, he'd never touched her. She was still a child – he'd never have taken advantage of a child. Or was this denial: just his guilt making its case?

He became aware that Cesare was staring at him: he scratched his chin-stubble. Perhaps the man sensed he was holding out.

'There *was* a girl called Lucia . . . at Jesi,' Caine said.

He made the shape of her page-boy haircut with his hands. 'About seventeen. They said she'd been arrested carrying messages for the partisans.'

Cesare's eyes lit up: he nodded. '*Lucia?* You see her? You see her, yes?'

'Yes. She's . . . all right. They haven't hurt her.'

Cesare crossed himself. Caine felt a lump rise in his throat. *You can do what you like with her, old man. Shag her front and behind, all the way till morning.*

A child. How could he have taken advantage of a *child*?

For a moment he wished he could go back, break Lucia out, get her away from her captors. But that was beyond his capabilities. There was another woman in jeopardy, at the Villa Montefalcone. Better to stick to what was possible. *Was* it possible to rescue the countess, though? Was it any more than a madcap, kamikaze plan hatched in the half-demented mind of Bunny Butterfield? How was he going to take on a whole SS platoon with half a mag of rounds and no back-up?

He wadded his fists. 'I'm going to do it,' he said.

Cesare opened his eyes wide. 'You do what?'

Caine told him that he was heading for the Villa Montefalcone: his plan was to rescue the countess, he said. Spoken out loud like this, his words had a vacant feel: it sounded like a half-baked, hopeless quest.

Cesare looked impressed though. '*Sarà difficile*,' he said. 'The villa is guarded by many Cabbage-Heads.

Getting out will not be a problem. *Il problema principale* is to get in.'

Caine blinked, wondered what he meant.

'The villa is full of hidden passages,' Cesare said. 'One passage come out at door in woods. But door is strong. Is lock from inside. You escape that way, maybe: but how you get in? You don't have gun even.'

Caine had left the Schmeisser hidden in the vineyard: he'd wanted to avoid presenting a threat. He considered Cesare's words for a moment. 'I'll get in by stealth,' he said at last. 'Will you help me?'

Cesare narrowed his eyes, weighed it up for a moment. 'I help, but you get my daughter out.'

It was too steep a price, Caine thought. A fully armed SAS troop might liberate the prisoners from a camp as heavily defended as Jesi, but even that was uncertain.

'I can't do that on my own,' he said. 'I can only promise to report it to my command and urge them to take action.'

Cesare wrinkled his face in an effort to understand. 'Is all right,' he said finally. 'A man do his best.'

He gave Caine precise directions to the villa, telegraphing with his hands, drawing with a twig in the dust till Caine had memorized the details. He asked what Caine needed, offered him provisions, a rope, a knapsack, a poncho, even weapons. He told Caine to stay put while he went into the cottage to get things ready.

Caine watched Cesare go in through the cottage door, realized he had no way of knowing if there was an exit at the back. How could he be sure the man wasn't about to report him to the Nazis? He shifted tensely: if there was a flap, he was unarmed except for the half-empty wine-bottle inside his waistcoat: that wouldn't get him far. He itched to retrieve the SMG from the vineyard, longed to get out of there. He didn't have a watch: the minutes seemed to tick past endlessly. He stood poised on the balls of his feet. He was tempted to walk over to the door, wrench it open, peer inside: he was prevented only by the thought that the old man might see it as a breach of trust. *But am I behaving like an idiot? The chap could be taking advantage of my trust to turn me in? Fritz pays well for that kind of thing. Maybe he needs the money.*

He didn't move. Instead he scanned the brown fields, watched flies wheel, watched bees home in, took in the burnished colours of the vine-leaves, the olive trees with heads like matted hair, tilted away from the prevailing wind, the beeches on the forest purlieus where schools of rooks roosted. The skies were pale azure, laced with flimsy trimmings of cloud: he watched a falcon spin out of its spiral, drop towards the forest-edge, saw rooks take to the air in cawing squadrons.

He wasn't sure how long Cesare had been gone: it seemed a while, and he was feeling uneasy. Sometimes you had to rely on intuition, and his intuition had been to trust Cesare. But intuition could be wrong. *The chap wouldn't stab me in the back, surely? Not after the Nazis arrested his daughter.* But Caine hadn't been able to promise that he'd get her out: maybe that was the problem. *Maybe he thinks he can do a deal with the Nazis: Lucia's life for an escaped British saboteur.*

He stood up: he couldn't wait any longer. Assuming Cesare had told him the truth about the villa, he now knew how to get there. He would just pick up the Schmeisser, beat it, sharpish.

He was still wavering when the door creaked and Cesare toddled out. He'd brought Caine a much-patched rucksack of canvas and hide, with neat packets of bread, cheese, fresh olives and grapes, an oilskin poncho and a shepherd's knife that looked razor-sharp. He laid this bounty down, unslung two firearms from his thin shoulders, showed them to Caine – the hunting rifle he'd come out with previously, and a 12-bore shotgun.

'Which you want?'

Caine thought guiltily about the SMG hidden in the vines. A second ago he'd been half convinced that Cesare was about to trade him in for his daughter: now the man was offering him what must be his most treasured possessions.

He was reluctant to accept, but his mission was life or death and he couldn't afford to grope in a gift-horse's mouth. *A hunting rifle would be good for long shots.*

He took the rifle, hefted it, jacked the cocking-handle, checked the breech: a round popped out. He picked it up: it was small-calibre – .22. Ten-round magazine, he thought.

'You got more bullets?'

Minutes later he was crossing the fields with the 100-round box of .22 ammunition Cesare had given him stashed in a rucksack pouch. He came across the place where he'd left the Schmeisser, bent and scooped it up in a single movement, kept it tight to his chest. He was grateful for Cesare's gift – more than grateful – but at close quarters an SMG would come in handy, too.

When he reached the trees he paused and turned back. The old man was still standing motionless by the cottage: Caine waved: Cesare didn't return the salute.

22

The Villa Montefalcone, Le Marche, Italy
9 October 1943

The forest remained thick almost to the villa itself: there was no wall or fence, and Caine was able to move to the edge of the trees for a close target recce. The size of the place was stunning: it was like a country mansion set in the remnants of an old castle, an ornate central block under tilting tiled roofs and nests of towers: a crumbling girdle-wall of stone slabs with a chapel built into its structure on one side. The buildings seemed to shift endlessly into the background in a warren of high terraces, balustrades, alcoves, cupolas, windows, interlocking roofs. Caine wondered how he would ever find the countess in this labyrinth: she might be anywhere. And how the hell was he going to get in?

It would have to be a night-op, that was obvious. He spent the rest of daylight hours making a full reconnaissance, boxing around the building, lurking in the woods, sprinting across open patches, crawling from one bush to another. Sometimes he stood still among the brindles of sunlight, letting the chiaroscuro break up his body-outline. He watched SS prowler units stalking around the villa – fit-looking, apple-faced men, alert and efficient. On one occasion he was almost near enough to touch them.

There were eight guards on patrol at any one time: two pairs prowling around the villa in one direction, two in the other. They were staggered at intervals of roughly ten minutes: Caine counted the beats between their appearances from various positions, worked out the shortest interval he was likely to get in between. There were several doors around the rim of the place, but the only one that appeared to be functional was the front door, standing at the head of a short flight of stone steps on the eastern side. Fritz had mounted a deep-sandbagged machine-gun nest there, with a three-man crew.

Quartering the woods, he came upon the gravel drive leading to the front of the house, guessed it joined the main road from Jesi, along which his convoy had come. There was no gate: no guards were in sight. A limb of forest divided it from the house: he backtracked through the trees, found a grassy dell in undergrowth sparse enough for him to keep an eye on the front of the villa. He sat down, ate bread, cheese and olives, drank water. He was tempted to smoke a cigarette, rejected the idea: the SS guards would certainly smell the smoke. The results of his recce weren't encouraging, he thought. The prowler units were well-organized and the house was well-defended. The only way in was through the front door, and that meant getting past the Spandau team.

He'd had plenty of experience of slipping into enemy bases: it had been the bread-and-butter of SAS sabotage ops in the desert. He thought wryly of the el-Gala cock-up in Egypt the previous year, when they'd infiltrated an airfield only to discover that the enemy had been waiting for them. The aircraft were dummies: the Ities had bumped them on the way out.

But, unless they were sound asleep, slipping past that Spandau crew without being clocked would take a miracle. He was confident that he could get near enough to bump them, but that wouldn't do him any good: the gunshots would immediately forewarn the rest. He didn't know how many Krauts were billeted inside the house: alerting them would mean having to fight his way into the villa, and he didn't even know where the countess was being held.

Force wouldn't work: it had to be stealth or nothing: it all came back to that damn' M42 covering the door. He thought briefly of using the knife Cesare had given him to slit the crew's throats, dismissed it. It was hard enough to cut one guard's throat, let alone three. He was fast all right, but it only took one of them to start bawling, and his goose would be well and truly cooked.

Caine sensed movement at the front of the house, heard the drift of voices. He peered through the foliage, saw a woman walking away from the building towards the drive. She wore a long peasant's dress and a dark shawl: she seemed oldish, but Caine couldn't tell for certain, because her face was veiled in the folds of a black headscarf. This couldn't be the countess: she had to be a servant of some kind – someone who worked here and was allowed to come and go as she pleased.

The woman's arrival gave him an idea, reminded him of the *Runefish* op, in Libya, when he'd snatched Betty Nolan from behind Axis lines. On that mission, he and his oppo had gone in disguised as Senussi Arabs and, though they'd used force, the disguise had allowed them to get close to the enemy. The only way he was going to get through that door was by adopting a similar approach. Maybe the woman could help him: in any case, if she *was* a domestic, she'd be a vital source of inside information: she would certainly know where the countess was being held. Caine watched her, saw her vanish around the bend in the drive. He rose to his feet: at the very least, she'd be an ally. He had to talk to her.

He left everything except his rifle, passed briskly back through the forest, skulked in the trees at the edge of the drive. He could hear the woman's steps on the gravel: he slung his rifle, waited until she was a yard past him, sprang up behind her. His left hand closed over her mouth: he grasped her arm with his right, manoeuvred her back into the trees. She blubbered, squirmed, twisted, tried to throw him off. Caine kept hold of her, pushed her further into the forest, sat her down. Keeping his hand across her mouth, he leaned forward, whispered. 'I'm a friend. I'm here to help the countess. Nod if you understand me.'

The woman nodded.

'I'm going to let you go. Don't scream: don't call the Germans. I'm not going to hurt you. Nod if you understand.'

She nodded again: Caine was faced with yet another leap of faith. He readied himself to run, let go the woman's mouth. She spat on the ground: her eyes never left his face. He shifted, sat on his heels, faced her: she adjusted her headscarf. She had a square, mannish face: rosy cheeks, plump jowls criss-crossed with a grid of lines. Her lips were pursed in an expression of resistance: her stone-blue eyes were wary.

'You speak English?' Caine asked in a low voice.

The woman's head bobbed: her black headscarf fluttered. 'I learn from old *contessa* – *L'Americana*. When they are *bambini*, Emilia and Ettore try make me *pazza* by spik *Inglezi*, but I know what they say.'

Her name was Angostina: she'd worked at the villa most of her life and was currently housekeeper. She'd been married and had two grown-up sons: her husband had died before the war. One of her sons was a Fascist who had served with Mussolini's army in Ethiopia and been captured by the British: the other was a Marxist fighting with the partisans. Two brothers, devoted to each other as children, she said: God knew she loved them both, but how, in heaven's name would they get on together after the war?

When Caine was satisfied she wasn't going to sound the alarm, he moved her to the thicket where he'd left his gear, gave her bread, cheese, olives.

'You help my Emilia?' she enquired suspiciously through a mouthful. 'How?'

'I'm going to get her out.'

Angostina stopped chewing, studied him with a touch of disdain. 'How many you are?'

'Just me.'

She scoffed. 'The *tedeschi* are many, many.'

'*How* many . . . inside the house?'

Angostina shuddered. 'Twenty-five maybe. They sit in cellar, drink old count's wine like *acqua*. The old count he turn in his grave –'

'Who's in command?' Caine cut in.

'The *capitano* is called Kaltenbraun. Face look like a fox. Last night the countess she try to escape – in villa is many hidden ways, you understand. But Emilia pass wine-cellar where they are guzzle old count's wine like *acqua*, and they catch her and want to . . . you know . . . *do* things to her. Kaltenbraun he stop them.' Angostina eyed him dubiously. 'How you get her out? How you fight all Cabbage-Heads?'

'I won't fight them unless I have to. I'll go in silently, like a thief.'

He asked her about the secret passage Cesare had mentioned: the one that connected with a door hidden in the forest. It existed, she told him, but the door was strong, bolted from the inside.

'You go out that way,' she said. 'But how you get *in*?'

Caine enquired if any doors other than the front were being used: she shook her head – they were all sealed from the inside: the windows were barred, shuttered, locked.

'Then the front door is the only way?'

He made her describe the route from the door up to Emilia's apartment, with all its twists and turns. He closed his eyes, memorized it, then went over it again and again until he could visualize it perfectly. What about the Germans? Where were they billeted? Where were the sentries stationed? How many would be awake at any one time? Finally, he asked her to describe the countess: he didn't want to run the risk of snatching the wrong person, he said.

Angostina hesitated. Caine said, 'She's dark, with long black hair, isn't she? He eyes are a little slanted, like an oriental?'

Angostina's jaw dropped. 'You know the countess? You meet her before?'

Caine wondered how to explain that he'd met her in a dream. Instead, he said, 'She's been hurt, I think. She has bruises on her neck?'

The housekeeper's eyebrows arched. 'How you *know* that? Yes, is true. That *pazzo* Stengel, he come to ask her where is the *book*, the one they call Codex. Always the *tedeschi* want the *book*. Emilia say she don't know, so

Stengel do things to her, *mi hai capito? Terrible* things – things a woman does not tell a man.'

Caine felt suddenly livid. Stengel had molested the girl, maybe raped her. He couldn't abide the abuse of women: the idea had sickened him ever since his stepfather had done it to his mother and sister and even *boasted* about it. True, he had settled his stepfather's hash, but neither of his womenfolk had really survived the ordeal. His sister had run away, his mother had taken her own life.

He felt a suffocating tightness in his chest, felt his fists stiffen: he wanted to rush into the villa, pull the countess out right now. He drew a deep breath, made a conscious effort to control himself: ops like this one had to be carried out with cold detachment, not blind rage. He forced himself, instead, to think about the Codex.

'So Stengel never found out where the Codex is?' he asked.

Angostina shook her head. 'He say he come back today, but he don't come. He come tonight, maybe. *Non mi piace* to leave Emilia alone, but she *make* me go. If she don't tell him about the book this time, maybe he kill her.'

'But then he'd never find the Codex. '

Angostina lodged a finger against her grizzled temple. '*Non hai capito? Quest'uomo è proprio matto.* He is completely mad. Always looking behind as if there is ghost following him, jumping like he hear voices. That devil can do anything, anything.'

Caine fought to keep himself steady: he looked up to see Angostina staring at him.

'You get through fron' door how?' she demanded. 'Krauts shoot you.'

Caine grinned uncertainly. 'I'm going to need your help. I'm going to ask you to do something a gentleman should never ask a lady.'

'What is that?'

'Take off all your clothes and give them to me.'

23

Stengel's staff-car pulled up outside the villa just before last light. By then, Caine had shifted to another position, which gave him a better view of the villa's eastern façade. He watched the dark-bearded figure slip out of the vehicle, vanish into the shadows: his heart raced, he itched to get moving. What if Stengel murdered Emilia before he got there? Once again, he had to force himself to desist. He might be wearing a peasant-woman's clothes, but it was still too early to start the mission. Whether he liked it or not, he had to hang fire until it was fully dark.

The sun was a rim of liquid gold lying along the knuckle-bones of the distant hill-tops: massed clouds were collapsing steadily into a foaming whirlpool on fire with carmine and blood. The eastern side of the villa lay in a lake of darkness stretching almost as far as the forest, its lumpen outline punctuated by the elongated shadows of the cone-shaped towers. The last wild colours of the day burst through the upper foliage in brilliant asterisks of bronze and copper. The individual character of the trees faded: the forest reverted to a dark-caverned creature of the night.

It had taken him some time to persuade Angostina

to remove her clothes: it was an assault on her dignity, he understood that, but it was the only plan he had. Finally, he convinced her to accept the oilskin poncho Cesare had given him in exchange for her things: it would at least cover her modesty. She moved behind a bush, took off her garments with slow deliberation, donned the poncho, then, red-faced and giggling like a schoolgirl, handed them over to Caine.

She wouldn't consider returning home, though: she would wait by the hidden door in the forest for Caine and Emilia to emerge: she wouldn't budge until they did, not even if it took all night. Caine gave her his knapsack with the left-over provisions, escorted her part of the way, then returned to his observation point. The skirt tripped him: the clothes were like drapes, smelt of lavender. He felt awkward in female apparel but, again, it was better than wearing the Nazi stool-pigeon get-up he'd ditched in the stream. And at least he had his stolen shirt, trousers and waistcoat on underneath, as well as his prison-camp-issue boots.

He stripped down his firearms, inspected the working parts: the Schmeisser magazine held fifteen rounds, enough for three or four good bursts. The Beretta's ten-round mag was full: he thumbed out one cartridge to ease the spring, filled his waistcoat pockets with spare .22 rounds. There were no clips, he noted: loading a mag round by round wasn't a good idea in a close-combat situation.

He'd given some thought as to how he should carry

his weapons. The SMG was his best bet for close-quarter battle: it needed to be where he could bring it into action easily. He decided to carry it, folded, in his right hand, hidden under the shawl. As for the hunting rifle, he slung it muzzle-down over his left shoulder, with the stock under his armpit. The shawl concealed all but the last foot of the barrel: he would just have to hope that, if he was spotted, it wouldn't be noticed in the dark. Finally, he took out the shepherd's knife he'd got from Cesare, weighed it in his hand: it was sharp, well-balanced: it would throw well. He stowed it in the waistband of his trousers.

The redness in the west had dwindled to a ruby gleam: the sky had turned charcoal. The shadow of the villa had lost its distinct outline and almost merged with the forest. Caine was relieved to see that the Jerries hadn't erected spotlights: the prowler teams seemed to rely on their torches – a sure-fire way of getting blotted by a sniper. Not that Caine was intending to take any potshots tonight: he would rather see Fritz coming, though, than have them creep up on him from behind.

He waited until the darkness was almost full, then moved silently through the limb of the woods that separated him from the drive. His plan was to march boldly up to the front door as if he belonged there, relying on the night to hide his identity. He'd quizzed Angostina as to whether her arrival after dark would be remarked on: she'd done it before, she said. He tried to summon up Italian phrases he'd memorized, in case Fritz stopped him. Fritz would almost certainly be as ignorant of Italian as he was, so as long as he said *something*, it would do. He hoped it wouldn't come to that.

He stood up, readied himself for action: the full enormity of what he was attempting hit him. *This is suicide: one poorly armed man against a Waffen-SS platoon equipped with a heavy machine-gun and God knows what else.* He wished he had some grenades, sticky bombs, smoke-canisters. He wished Harry Copeland were here: Fred Wallace and Taffy Trubman, too. *Even Bunny Butterfield would have been better than nothing.* But they weren't here and he was, and this was the task that had fallen to him. His kit might be wanting, but he was going in regardless. What was it that the Spartan mother had told her son when he complained that his sword was too short? *Take a step forward.* In the end, it wasn't the kit that counted, nor how many of you there were. *It's having the guts to challenge things, even if the whole world is against you. It's not size but courage that makes a man.* He made final adjustments to his shawl and headscarf, gripped his weapons, stepped out of cover into the darkness.

Wolfram Stengel returned *SS-Mann* Karloff's salute with a nod, let himself into Emilia's apartment, unaware that he was whistling the 'Radetzky March' under his breath. The room was lit by a single hurricane lamp – a matrix of wan light and gloomy patches. The countess was sitting on the sofa: as he advanced towards her, an ogre's shadow seemed to leapfrog over his shoulders –

a grotesque, elastic human shape with elongated fingers and an impossibly long nose and chin. Stengel was startled: it took a moment before he realized that the shadow was his own.

The curtains were still open: outside, a tide of darkness was rolling in, overwhelming the last faint shards of bone-coloured light. Stengel changed course, went to look out of the window. The forecourt below him was diapered in darkness: he could make out the faintest reflection on the fender of his Horch staff-car down there. For a moment he had the impression of a furtive movement by the car: his cheek twitched: he drew the curtains, turned to Emilia.

She wore fawn slacks, a grey polo-necked sweater, soft-soled sneakers: her gleaming black hair was tied over one shoulder, emphasizing the high cheekbones, the oriental eyes with the sleepy lid. *Natural poise*, Stengel thought: *an aristocratic elegance. A woman like this has everything: birth, privilege, wealth. Normally, she wouldn't look at a man like me, wouldn't even know I existed. Well, now she* has *to look at me.*

Emilia didn't get up: despite Stengel's vicious assault, despite the bruises on her neck and mouth, she didn't seem afraid of him. It was as if she'd made peace with herself. This irritated Stengel: if he'd had her begging for mercy, he would have felt more certain. The partisan ambush on Grolsch's convoy yesterday had unsettled him: they'd done it with a certain cunning, blocked the track with an overturned cart and a dying horse. The Sipo-SD escort had been slaughtered, except for a couple of men who'd run away, and Grolsch, who'd been wounded in the upper chest. The great hope of the British Free Corps, John Amray, had ended up with his head almost severed. Butterfield had disappeared; so had the other SAS officer – the trustee, Caine. He might have guessed that Caine's recruitment to the BFC wouldn't work, despite Amray's hopes: the man had obviously seen it as a chance to get away. On the other hand, he'd been in SS uniform: in view of what the partisans had done to Amray, he couldn't entirely rule out the possibility that Caine had fled to avoid the same fate.

That aside, the fact was that four SAS saboteurs had got away in the past few days. Of course, special handling was a Gestapo matter, and the responsibility was Grolsch's but, as senior SS officer in the area, it wouldn't look good for Stengel, either. For the past twenty-four hours, Sipo-SD patrols had been scouring the forests and hills for partisans. The back-up squads had arrived too late, though: trails had gone cold. The question that kept coming back to him was: *how did the partisans know that the convoy would be there, at that time, at that place?* It had been a special-handling convoy, and secret. *They must have had inside knowledge*, he thought.

At least the incident hadn't affected his search for the Codex. Butterfield was gone, but he'd wasted too much time on that *Dummkopf*. He was sure the countess knew the location of the Codex, and now he had the means to prise the secret out of her: the imminent execution of her brother, Ettore.

He placed his hat on the table, smoothed his whiskers. 'So, my dear countess,' he said, 'Kaltenbraun tells me you were wandering about outside your room last night. Didn't I say that you were confined to your quarters?'

When Emilia didn't answer, he went on. 'The problem with wandering about is that these vulgar enlisted men might get the wrong idea. They may try to take advantage of you.'

'I'll take my chances with the vulgar enlisted men.'

Stengel picked up the photo of Ettore he'd examined on his previous visit. 'Please remind me of something. Where was it you said your brother was to be found?'

Emilia crossed her arms. 'In America.'

'Ah yes, in America. America is a very long way off, isn't it?'

The countess was eyeing him more calmly than he'd anticipated. He put down the photo, swung round on her. 'So how do you explain the fact that our troops arrested your brother two days ago at Orsini?'

She showed no surprise. *Of course, she knew already: Kaltenbraun told her.*

'It's not him,' she said. 'Ettore is a common name in Le Marche – so is Falcone, for that matter. You arrested the wrong man.'

Stengel smiled. 'Yet the youth we detained bears an

uncanny resemblance to the one in your photo: they might be twins.'

He paced over to her, grabbed the third finger of her left hand, forced it up so that the ring she wore there almost touched her nose. 'The Falconi family crest,' he sneered. '*One of an identical pair . . . been in the family for generations.* Isn't that what you told me?'

'Yes, but . . .'

Stengel slipped a shiny object into his hand, held it up between thumb and forefinger. It was a ring, bearing the double-falcon-and-laurel-wreath crest of the Falconi: it was a perfect match for the one on Emilia's finger.

'The youth we picked up not only *just happened* to look like your brother, he also *just happened* to be wearing a Falconi family signet ring, of which, you tell me, only two exist.'

Emilia tried to wrest her finger out of his clutch: he closed his hand round hers, squeezed it with a crushing grip. His eyes blazed. 'You lied to me, Countess. Your brother is not in America. He has been here all the time, with the partisans. He was involved in the murder of two of our men a week or so ago, while helping British saboteurs to escape. He will, of course, be shot. You are invited to his execution.'

He let go of her hand: he'd been hoping for a hysterical reaction. Instead, two large tears appeared in the corners of her eyes: her lips trembled.

'*He's only sixteen,*' she said.

That was all. Stengel was aware that Kaltenbraun had forewarned her, but still he felt disappointed.

'I agree he's young,' he said. 'If you tell me where the Codex is hidden, I may suggest he gets a reprieve.'

Emilia examined her fingers, sore from Stengel's crushing grip. She poked tears from her eyes, watched him steadily. 'I've already told you, I don't know where the Codex is.'

'Yes, you told me. How likely is it that the heiress of the Falcone estates doesn't know the whereabouts of one of the family's most precious heirlooms?'

'It's true. I can't tell you what I don't know.'

A tic quivered in Stengel's jaw. 'Suit yourself. I will make sure you have a ringside seat at your brother's execution.'

Emilia crossed herself. 'What's to be, will be,' she said.

Stengel gawked at her: there was a sinking, hollow feeling in his guts. He felt ill with frustration, incensed that his threat hadn't worked.

He shot out a hand, clutched her bruised neck, forced her up, pulled her towards him, mauled her breasts through her blouse. She bit her lip, didn't resist: Stengel jammed his right hand into her crotch, pinched her brutally. Emilia gasped: he groped for the buttons of her trousers, ripped them open, pulled them down, pushed his fingers hard into the cloven soft flesh between her legs, his breath coming in raking bursts. Emilia held herself rigid, clamped her mouth tight, gagged from the smell of his eau de cologne.

Stengel sensed her resolve, felt her passive resistance, felt the lust ebb away from him. He let go of her, stood there catching his breath. She hoisted up her slacks, glared at him defiantly.

'You're sick in the head,' she said. 'You mutter to yourself, hear voices, see things that aren't there. This isn't just about finding the Codex, is it? If it was, you'd have had me carted off to Jesi long ago. You kept me here because you wanted to hurt me, because that's the only thing that arouses you, the only thing that makes you feel you're a man. You belong in a madhouse, not the Nazi Party. Or maybe it's the same thing.'

Stengel's features turned puce: his eyes knobbed out. No one spoke to him like that: he was a full SS colonel, director of Ahnenerbe, a personal friend of *Reichsführer* Himmler. For an instant he couldn't believe she'd had the effrontery to say it. He clenched his teeth, blinked, groped under his jacket, brought out a Luger pistol, pointed it at her. 'I'm going to kill you,' he panted. 'I don't need a cunt like you to find the Codex – not you, not your pimp brother. I'll have this place torn apart stone by stone.'

Emilia saw white flecks of saliva on his lips, saw the gun-muzzle twitch in front of her like an unsteady black eye. She forced herself to meet his gaze: it was like looking down a tunnel into a soul in torment. She saw the bearded face, the shifty black pupils, the tremor in the pistol-barrel: she was tempted to shut her eyes and let the apartment come down. *I promised you I'd keep Ettore safe, Papa. If they're going to kill him, I don't deserve to live anyway.*

She forced the thought out of her mind. *No. Fight. Resist.* She'd prepared herself for his visit this time: above all, she must not let him tie her up. She'd concealed a wine-bottle under the covers of her bed: she was mentally prepared to attack him when he least expected it. There could be no compromise with an animal like Stengel: whatever she might or might not tell him, whatever he promised, she and Ettore were dead meat.

Stengel licked his lips, raised the pistol in line with her temples.

At that moment there came a splutter of automatic gunfire from below, startlingly loud in the silence of the evening. Stengel's eyebrows leapt skywards: he let his pistol-hand drop, took a step backwards. '*Guard!*' he bawled at the sentry outside. '*Go and see what the hell is happening down there!*'

24

Caine crouched in deep shadow at the place where the drive swept round the bend into the forecourt, watched the torchlights of two German patrols coalesce. He heard the low croup of Goth voices, saw cigarettes lit, saw the torches separate, saw the lights float off in opposite directions. He started counting: it would be ten minutes before the next relay of patrols came into view, but he couldn't move before the current ones were out of sight. He waited until the beams had been absorbed into the night, stood up, adjusted his weapons under the shawl, started towards the house.

He moved quietly but not furtively: if anyone did clock him, he wanted them to see a familiar old servant going about her business. The forecourt was dark, but there were shades in the darkness: he could make out some features of the house: the outline of windows, gable-ends, masonry protrusions. The only light came from a first-floor window: the dim yellow glow of an oil-lamp through open curtains. The room lay above, and to the right of, the main door: from Angostina's description, this was the suite of rooms where Emilia was being held. The fact that there was a light on there encouraged him.

He was so intent on the window that he almost

walked into the back of Stengel's staff-car: he checked himself, peered inside. The windows were fuzzed up: the driver must still be in there, probably asleep. This car was the Krauts' only motor-transport, he reasoned: it would give Stengel the advantage in a pursuit. He considered sabotaging it: slashing its four tyres with his knife would be effective. On the other hand, if he woke the driver, he could wave goodbye to his mission – it wasn't worth the risk.

He was about to set off again when he noticed a movement at the lighted window. For a moment a dark silhouette was framed there: Caine got the impression of cold, probing eyes, a keen, calculating presence. Whoever it was, it wasn't the countess. He knelt by the car's bumper, glanced up just in time to see the curtains drawn, the light all but extinguished. He took a slow breath, boxed away from the car, maintained his bearings carefully. The door was visible as a faint oblong: he could make out the shape of the sandbag-nest at the top of the steps, where the M42 crew were holed up. There was no sound, no glow of cigarette-ends, no movement: he hoped fervently that the Krauts were in the land of Nod.

He reached the foot of the steps, paused to listen. He thought he heard heavy breathing, couldn't tell if he was imagining it. Suddenly there was a snore: a distinctive rattling intake he knew he couldn't have imagined: he felt like laughing. *They're asleep. All I have to do is get up the steps and in through that door.*

He still had to pass the machine-gun nest, though: he decided to forfeit stealth for speed, to get past the danger-point as quickly as possible. He urged himself forward up the steps, climbed smoothly, avoided any jerky movements. He kept his breath under control: his heart was banging like a snare-drum – so loud he thought it must wake the enemy. He was at the top now, abreast of the gunpost: he was tempted to look inside, stopped himself. *Don't look into the dragon's mouth. Don't tempt fate.*

The doorframe towered above him, a massive eight-foot-high aperture: the door was open, giving him a glimpse of a long passage that seemed to be lit by lamp-light at the far end. He had to force himself not to rush. He'd taken three silent paces, almost reached the door, when a voice cracked. '*Halt! Wo gehen Sie hin?*'

Caine's blood ran cold. He'd been challenged: in the dark, though, he hoped the sentry would be seeing only the outline of an old peasant-woman.

'*Buonasera*,' Caine said, lifting his voice an octave.

He pinched the ends of the headscarf across his mouth with his right hand, turned very slowly, gripped the Schmeisser under the shawl. Not one but three shadows confronted him from behind the sandbags: Caine caught the faint blue glint of weapon-muzzles, the dull sheen of Kaiser hats.

'*Wer sind Sie? Was machen Sie hier?*'

Caine shook his head. '*Buonasera*,' he repeated.

'*Was verstecken Sie darunter?*'

He didn't grasp the words, but the Jerry's tone clanged *warning* as plainly as a fire-alarm: the snap of a Kraut cocking-handle came like a gunshot. Caine squeezed steel, pumped a burst from under the shawl, *tack-tack-tack-tack-tack-tack*. He felt the weapon kick and pull, felt cases bump his chest, smelt firegas, clocked Kraut silhouettes erupt into a giddy ghost-dance – flailing limbs, bobbing heads, shifting torsos: he heard snorts, felt blood spray. A shot sleared over his shoulder, fractured against the wall, spun off in fragments with a high-pitched *wheeeeeuuuwww*. He shifted the pistol-grip to his right hand, stepped closer, boosted another five-round spurt, traversed the barrel to make sure he'd got them all. A dark body lolled over the parapet. Caine put out a hand, felt bloodslick, raddled flesh: he found the Jerry's webbing, felt the cylindrical head of a spud-masher grenade, drew it out, backed away with the Schmeisser still trained. He heard a shout from far-off, saw torches blaze, realized a patrol was coming. He cursed his luck. *Three more steps and I'd have made it. Now there's hell to pay*. He wheeled round, dashed through the open door.

25

Karloff was sober: *SS-Hauptsturmführer* Kaltenbraun had bawled him out for leaving his post last night: he'd been banned from the booze-ups in the cellar, acquired extra sentry duty outside the countess's quarters. Karloff hailed from Feldberg in the Black Forest, where his father had run a lumber business before the war. Felling trees all his life had given him kite-shaped shoulders and pit-props for legs. If he'd wanted to, he could have crushed that city-boy Kaltenbraun, he thought. *Maybe one day I will.*

The *tack-tack-tack* of automatic fire cut through his thoughts, set his senses buzzing. He cocked his SMG, listened, heard nothing. '*Go and see what the hell is happening down there!*' Stengel's voice snapped from behind the door. After last night, nothing but a direct order would have budged him from his post: this was a direct order.

'*Jawohl, Reichsgeschäftsführer.*'

He inched towards the head of the staircase, peered down into the sallow lamplight of the hall: nothing moved. Suddenly, though, he heard the unmistakable snick of a door closing, heard the snap of bolts being shot. *There's someone down there. All those doors bolt from the inside.* He gripped his Schmeisser in both hands, descended the stairs, scanned the hall below. Four separate doors opened into it, one from the level of the cellars. *Didn't Kaltenbraun and those other boozers hear the gunshots? Why aren't they here?*

From the foot of the stairs, he saw that the door on his far left was closed and bolted: it was the door to the passage that led from the front entrance. *That door is never closed or bolted.* He took a breath, let his eyes roam the dark alcoves and recesses around the door, where, he guessed, paintings and tapestries had once hung. He heard running footsteps in the passage, heard raucous voices: fists began to bang and pummel on the door. It was two inches of solid oak with enormous iron bolts, top, bottom and middle: Karloff moved to let them in.

He'd taken a few steps past the stairwell when an arm gripped his neck with vice-like force. Karloff angled his head, shifted his body to dodge the knife-blade he knew would be dicing up his kidney any moment, felt the blade deflected on his thick webbing. He dropped his weapon, jerked down on the arm with all his strength: his assailant was powerful but evidently hadn't been expecting the swift reaction. The arm gave slightly: Karloff reached behind him, grasped the wrist of the hand that held the knife, pivoted abruptly, broke out of the stranglehold. He wheeled, still holding the wrist in an iron grip, wrenched the knife out of his opponent's hand, heard it clatter on the floor. It was then that he saw with astonishment that the person he was fighting was an old woman in widow's black, with a shawl and headscarf. His face dropped.

Caine clocked his surprise, slipped the hunting rifle from under his right arm, swung the butt at his head. Karloff twisted just too late, took a glancing blow on his left shoulder, stepped back quickly.

'*Ein Mann*,' he spat.

Caine hefted the rifle, lunged, found himself bear-hugged in the Jerry's massive arms. It was like being caught between two tar-barrels: he couldn't move, couldn't bring the rifle up, felt the air being crushed out of him. He clenched his fists, strained his biceps against the Jerry's solid limbs. He and Karloff were almost the same height, same build, same age. Except for the clothes, it was almost like looking in a mirror. Last time he'd looked in a mirror, a Nazi had walked out: now he was locked in a dance of death with his alter ego. He saw the strain in Karloff's eyes, felt it in his own, heard the German's heaving breath, heard his own, felt his enemy's whole being grapple against his. He gritted his teeth, held his biceps rigid, let out a roar of agony, felt Karloff's arms sag: he burst out of their grip with explosive force, squirmed backwards. He brought the rifle up, slewed the butt across Karloff's jaw, felt the jawbone crack. Karloff teetered, his eyes wolf-slits, his face white: Caine hefted the rifle like a cricket-bat, hammered Karloff's face again and again, went on slugging until he collapsed in a bloody heap and lay still. Caine spat phlegm, lowered the weapon, stood back, saw that his clothes – Angostina's clothes – were red with gore. The struggle with the sentry had lasted what seemed like hours but couldn't have been more than seconds.

Krauts were bellowing like beasts, bodies slamming against the door to his left: the wood was jumping in its frame. Caine heard more roars and thumps from behind a door to his right: he skipped over to it, made sure it was locked, rammed the bolts across. He ran back to where he'd set down his Schmeisser, changed his mind, retrieved Karloff's instead, checked the mag, found it was almost full. He helped himself to a couple of stick grenades from Karloff's belt, picked up his knife: he hitched up his skirt, adjusted his headscarf, scooted up the curving stairs.

He turned right at the top, where the banister ended in a spiral flourish, passed a couple of rooms, spotted the sentry's chair outside a flimsy-looking door that was obviously a modern addition. He paused there, listening. Barging in might be a mistake: he remembered the figure he'd seen at the window: whoever was in there would have heard the shots and would be prepared. If he went in with his SMG blazing, though, he might end up smoking the countess. He was keyed up after his fight with the sentry: he had to do something fast, or the rest of the Krauts would be on his back. '*Fuck it!*' he thought.

He laid the hunting rifle on the floor, readied himself, kicked the mid-section of the door with a crumpling punt from his right boot. The door flew open, Caine leapt to one side. *Boooompppbhh*, *Boooompppbhh*. Two pistol-shots whiplashed out: Caine dodged inside, found himself staring across one room into another, at a bearded man in a dark suit – Stengel – and, behind him, a black-haired girl in pullover and trousers, leaning over a bed, fumbling for something: Stengel was pointing a Luger at him. Caine hurled himself sideways: in that instant he saw the girl raise a wine-bottle, smash it down on Stengel's skull. The glass shattered, Stengel went boss-eyed, took several staggering steps forward: ribbles of blood coursed through his thick hair, trickled off his chin. Caine snatched the pistol out of his hand, delivered a sharp kick into his crotch, bowled him face-forward on to the carpet.

He searched Stengel's suit for hidden weapons, removed his tie, started to secure his wrists with it. The bottle had gashed a groove in the Nazi's head: the wound was welling blood, the broken flesh dotted with fragments of green glass. His face was glossy with gore and snot, but he was jerking breaths, his eyelids flickering. *He'll be round in a second*, Caine thought. He glanced at the girl: she was staring at Angostina's blood-draggled clothes with wide eyes.

'Angostina's all right,' he said. 'She's waiting for us. Come on, help me get him up.'

The girl gave Caine a probing glance: he stared back into soft amber eyes, took in Mongol cheekbones, ripe lips with a hint of mischief, even white teeth, a halo of wavy hair, saw the discolorations on her mouth and neck. He knew she was making a judgement about him, but something else was passing between them, some surge of energy, some ancient, eternal human message. It was over in a blink, but Caine felt changed by it: this was the girl in his dream.

She moved to his side, helped him pull Stengel to his feet. Now she was only inches away, Caine felt her physical presence like a distortion in space. 'You're Countess Falcone? Emilia?'

She met his gaze, dropped her eyes: Caine noticed that one of her eyelids was slightly lower than the other.

He told her to grab Stengel's arms. He stepped back, stripped off the shawl, dress and headscarf, kicked them away, stood up in his Itie peasant's togs and German army boots.

'Who *are* you?' Emilia demanded. She had a soft American accent, Caine noted.

'Captain Tom Caine, 1st SAS Regiment. I'm here to get you out.'

She hesitated. 'Why aren't you in uniform?'

'Long story: no time.' He nodded at the open door. 'We're going out through there: Stengel'll be our shield. If we're lucky he'll get us past the rest of them. We can't go back through the front entrance. Is there another way?'

Emilia nodded breathlessly. 'There's a way. I'll show you.'

'Good. Can you handle a rifle?'

'Yes, but I'm –'

'I left a hunting rifle outside. Pick it up as we go out.'

'All right. But don't go down the stairs. Go straight across the landing. I'll show you where from there.'

'Got it.'

Stengel made a retching sound: his eyes were narrow slits. Caine seized his wrists from the countess, unslung the Schmeisser, poked the muzzle hard into his spine. 'Don't give us any trouble and you might get through this. Come on, let's go.'

'Just a minute,' Emilia said. 'He's got something of mine.' She rifled through Stengel's jacket pockets, found the signet ring he'd taken from Ettore. As she held it up to Caine, Stengel's viscid eyeballs flashed.

'*Stupid bitch.* You'll never get out of here. I'll have it back, and I'll have *you.*'

Emilia slipped the ring into her pocket: she stood facing him for a long moment, head tilted pensively, drifts of black hair veiling her eyes. Then she spat right in his face.

26

Caine forced Stengel towards the stairhead, lodged the muzzle of his weapon at the base of the Nazi's blood-streaked neck: Emilia stalked behind him with the hunting rifle. Coarse voices rose from the hall beneath: the Jerries from the cellar must have gone back and around, Caine thought: they must have used another entrance: he cursed himself for not having taken the time to bolt all the doors. He reached the ornate balustrade at the stairhead, peered down into the hall, clocked SS-men clattering in the shadows, crouching over the dead sentry, rushing to let the others in. A top-heavy Jerry with broad arms and a head like a polished orb glanced up, clocked Caine hovering. The soldier leapt up the stairs, cocked his Schmeisser in mid-step. '*Bleiben Sie, wo Sie sind!*'

Bwommmfffff. The report came from behind Caine's left ear: he traileyed the countess, saw her crouched over rifle-sights, saw the puff of smoke around the muzzle of the weapon she'd just fired: he saw the bald-headed SS-man stiffen, saw the baffled look on his face, saw his eyes cross inwards as if trying to focus on the hole the .22 round had just punched in his forehead. For a moment it seemed that he would continue charging up the steps: then his legs jellied out on him. He pitched over face-forward, dropped his SMG, started to roll down the steps in spatters of blood. Other SS-men ran to replace him: Caine got a glimpse of tense faces, bared teeth, weapons pointed in his direction. He shoved Stengel into full view. '*Come on. Who's going to shoot the boss?*'

Nobody fired: for a split second there was pin-drop silence.

'*Schiessen Sie ihn, dann wird er mit uns tauschen.*'

It rolled out of Stengel's throat like a death-rattle. Caine didn't know what it meant, but he heard the contempt in it. He kept a grip on his captive with one hand, slid out two of the stick-grenades he'd salvaged, pulled the draw-strings. He kneed Stengel hard in the back, sent him sprawling downstairs, lobbed the two grenades as hard and as far as he could. '*Three – four – five,*' he counted.

Babbooooommmmffffff.

In the confined space, the twin-detonations seemed to come from deep down in the world's guts: Caine and Emilia were already pelting across the landing, past the dressing-room she'd used the previous day, to a door at the far end of the corridor. It was unlocked. They scrambled into the room, closed the door: Emilia lit her torch. Caine made out a king-sized bed with a brocaded cover, drapery hangings, a vast, square armoire with carved doors. Emilia moved to the armoire, opened it, balanced the rifle under her arm.

She turned: Caine saw half-moon eyes, saw the faint gleam of her teeth, saw a dark hand brush away darker strands of hair. 'I hope you don't have a problem with confined spaces,' she said.

She shone her torch into the cupboard, stepped in, pulled Caine after her, closed the door. Inside, it was as big as a small bedroom, empty except for a length of cloth covering the back wall. For a second Caine felt the compelling force of her presence, took in her pneumatic figure, the provocative curl of her lips, the mown-grass smell of her hair, the faint muskiness of her body. He watched her whip down the back-cloth, clocked behind it the circular mouth of a shaft no wider than a sewer pipe. 'This is where the villa abuts the walls of the old monastery,' she told him. 'The original walls are honeycombed with shafts like this – I guess they were bolt-holes in times of trouble. Don't start thinking you've gone deaf in there. The stone work is ten feet thick.'

'In *there*?' Caine repeated. He'd never thought of himself as claustrophobic: with his water-buffalo shoulders and deep chest, though, he wondered if he could possibly get through it.

'It's the only way,' she told him. 'Just follow me.'

'You've been in there before?'

'Not for ages. I was smaller then.' She nodded at the hunting rifle. 'I'll have to leave it here.' She laid the weapon on the floor. 'Come on,' she said.

She wriggled into the opening: in an instant the

darkness had swallowed her up. Caine paused, considered how to manage his weapons: the knife and the grenade in his waistband were all right – he moved them round to his back. He studied the Schmeisser for a second, then removed the magazine, folded the stock, stuffed the two parts inside his shirt. Finally, he took off his waistcoat with its heavy baggage of .22 ammunition, laid it next to Emilia's rifle.

'What are you waiting for?' came her voice, slightly muffled, from the shaft.

He wormed into the tunnel after her.

He'd expected it to run straight: instead it twisted and turned: in places it dropped so steeply that Caine had to stop himself from sliding into Emilia, using his hands and knees as brakes. Mostly, he had enough room to raise himself on his elbows, but often he had only an inch or two of clearance, obliging him to pull himself along, with his chin almost scraping the floor. *Walls ten feet thick*: it was like crawling across the seabed with the immense weight of water pressing down on him. The countess moved fast, squirming her legs, flashing her torch occasionally: in the flickers of light, Caine could see only the kicking soles of her feet: he struggled to keep up with them. The dismembered SMG was heavy: its hard metal stuck into his flesh under the shirt. He realized how hot it was: sweat dripped off his forehead, his hands were damp, a clammy layer enveloped his body.

Emilia's torch flicked on: Caine got a glimpse of her

feet and buttocks, grey stonework beyond. The shaft appeared to stop abruptly: he soon realized that it went into a ninety-degree twist, and he was grateful for it. It meant that the Jerries wouldn't be able to shoot down the shaft: even if they lobbed in a grenade, the blast would be deflected by the sudden turn.

On the other hand, he was finding it harder and harder to breathe: the air was as thick as soup: often he had to stop to ease his straining lungs. As they stumbled on and on in the darkness, he found himself getting anxious that the shaft might be blocked: the countess hadn't been down here for years – there could have been any number of cave-ins since then. The horror of trying to crawl backwards around those twists and up those slopes didn't bear thinking about.

The shaft was getting narrower, he was sure of it. In places now he could raise his head only slightly: the stonework was crushing his limbs, confining his elbows: each thrust forward required an excruciating effort. His hands were hot and swollen, chafed by the rough stone floor: his ironmongery was cutting into his chest. He felt his energy draining, felt himself slowing down. He tried to bring his arms forward for the next thrust, found he couldn't move. He realized with a start that he could no longer sense Emilia in front of him, that she hadn't lit the torch for a while.

He resisted the impulse to call out, gritted his teeth, tried to pull himself forward, found that he was wedged in the shaft: struggle as he might, he couldn't extend his arms. He gulped at the air: his whole body was soaked in sweat. It was pitch dark: the shaft here couldn't be more than a foot high, he thought – impossible for someone his size to get through. *I'm stuck. I'm never going to get out.*

Caine's nerve almost failed him. He'd brought off hazardous ops behind enemy lines, survived a crash in the Nile, escaped from a hundred-foot well: nothing had scared him like this. Even in that well he'd been able to see the sky. *Buried alive*, he thought. *This is what it must be like to wake up in a coffin and realize you're six feet under. No one to help you. No one to hear you scream.* He was trembling: his heart was pumping so fast he thought he was going to faint – or die. He was a hair's breadth from panic, from shrieking madly, from clawing at the stones until his fingers were stumps. He remembered stories of premature burials: how corpses had been found whose arms and legs had been fractured in their frantic attempts to escape their grave. He shuddered, closed his eyes, felt blackness steal over him. *Is this it? Am I going to die here like a rat in a drain?* The blackness was in his head: he was drifting.

'*Hi, you there? You all right?*'

Emilia's voice came to him from far away: it felt like a lifeline.

'I'm stuck,' he panted. 'Can't bloody move. Shaft's not more than a foot high.'

'That's just an illusion. If I got my big butt through, you can.'

An illusion. Caine choked back a comment. It might be true: in a situation like this your imagination could play tricks on you.

An image drifted into his mind, of his old friend Fred Wallace, the six-foot-seven giant, built like a Bren carrier: Fred would *really* have been in trouble here, he thought. Not only was he twice Caine's size, he was utterly terrified of enclosed spaces. *At least I'm better off than* he *would have been.*

The thought somehow raised his spirits. He scooped a breath, closed his eyes, lifted himself on his forearms, tried to force himself on. *It's no narrower here – that's just an illusion.* For an instant it seemed that the stones were snatching at him, holding him back: then the feeling faded, as if the shaft had decided to widen itself to allow him through. He willed his muscles to tense and release, tense and release, crab-walked through the shaft until the fear was forgotten, until he could feel only the pain of burning lungs, straining sinews, hands flayed raw from the stone floor. He kept going, working hands, knees, feet, pumping on and on through the darkness until he ran into the soles of Emelia's shoes.

'*You OK?*' she said.

'Yeah . . . just . . . lost my bearings there for a sec.'

They crawled on. Caine was convinced now that the shaft was getting wider: suddenly he sensed Emilia sliding away from him: he felt the floor tilt, slithered down a steep incline of polished stone, buffered himself with his knees and swollen hands. He bumped into Emilia's soft rump, heard a stiff intake of breath, realized that they had emerged from the shaft into a wider tunnel.

The air stank of dust and decay. Emilia flashed her torch around: Caine saw that the new shaft had a vaulted roof: it was easily tall enough to stand upright in. The walls were of smooth, red stone – it looked as if it had been carved through bedrock. In the instant before Emilia switched off the torch, he noticed that the walls were lined with shallow alcoves, like shelves: bleached bones glinted from them – human bones: skeletal fingers, ribcages, skulls, unarticulated, yawning jaws.

In the darkness he wondered if he'd really seen it. 'What the hell is this?' he demanded.

'The catacombs,' Emilia said. 'They used to bury the monks here.'

She flicked on the torch again: Caine saw piles of bones: bones of all shapes and sizes poking out of the alcoves, scattered on the tunnel floor: armbones, legbones, ribs, foot tarsals, white plates of clavicle. In one place six or seven crumbling skulls had been crushed together in a crude pyramid. After the awful descent of the shaft, Caine thought, it was as if they'd plunged into hell.

'We follow the catacombs a little way,' Emilia said, 'then drop down to another level.'

'All right. Let's take a breather here.'

They slid down against the wall: their thighs brushed in the darkness. Despite his unnerved state, Caine felt an electric tingle at her touch, sensed the magnetic warmth of her body, the wild musk of her scent. He felt an almost overwhelming desire to put his arms round her. Instead, he fumbled for cigarettes, then thought better of it: his mouth was like pasteboard. He drew the pieces of the Schmeisser from under his shirt, clicked the magazine into place. He reached inside the shirt, rubbed the sore patches where the SMG had dug into him.

'Thank God we don't have to go back up there,' Emilia sighed.

Caine suppressed a shudder. 'How far down are we?'

'On the level of the cellars. These catacombs go on for ever: you can get lost in them.'

She cut the torch: for a moment they sat silently in the pitch-darkness. 'That man I shot,' Emilia said. 'His name was Stolbe. He tried to . . . well, you know. He was a pig, like Stengel. I hope Stengel's dead. I hope you killed –'

'*Sshh. You hear that?*'

In the stillness, Caine's ears had picked up voices. He paused, listened, came up into a squat, shuffled forward, felt his feet crunch on brittle bones. He listened again. *Kraut voices. Coming down this tunnel.*

He gripped the Schmeisser across his knees, squinted along the tunnel, saw dim twinkles of light, heard footfalls: they were still some way off. *But not that far.*

Emilia was on her feet. 'They've found the way in,' she hissed. 'But how did they guess we were here?'

'Can't have. Just doing a thorough search. That means there'll only be a couple of them . . .'

He fingered the stick-grenade in his belt, considered laying an ambush: a spud-masher and a burst of nine milly would do the trick. He tugged the grenade out of his belt. 'Once I chuck this, we've got five seconds,' he said. 'You move: I'll cover you.'

They listened again: heard footfalls coming nearer. Emilia grabbed his hand. '*Forget it*,' she whispered. '*Run*.'

It was almost impossible to run in the darkness: instead they jogged at a slow trot. Emilia let the torch-beam wink at intervals: they wove around a series of tight zig-zags, came into a straight stretch where more alcoves pitted the walls, where bones crunched under their feet. At the end of that the tunnel turned sharply left: Caine followed Emilia into the turn, felt her stop abruptly.

'Is this it?' she said. 'I think it's here.'

She flashed her torch at the wall. Caine saw, among the bone-littered alcoves, a large framed tablet bearing a faded fresco and a Latin inscription. The fresco showed what looked like the severed head of a woman, with a thick array of stray locks floating around her. The eyes were full of horror, her mouth open in a terrifying grimace. For an instant Caine was reminded of the severed head he'd seen in his dream – a woman's head floating in a fishbowl. Then he realized that *this* woman's hair wasn't hair at all but a mass of writhing snakes.

'*Medusa*,' Emllia said. 'Come on, help me with this.'

She hooked the nails of her right hand under the frame of the tablet: Caine saw it move outwards. He ran to help her, got his fingertips behind the frame, pulled, felt it slip open. The tablet was a door, he realized – a stone door that couldn't be spotted from the outside, yet which had been so finely tooled and balanced that it opened as if it had been oiled.

Emilia shone the torch on the entrance to a shaft not much wider than the one they'd come down. Caine's jaw tightened.

'It's all right,' she said. 'This is only the entrance. The rest is fine.'

Caine wasn't listening: he'd picked up footsteps and muffled voices again: the Jerries were coming down the straight stretch just before the sharp-left turn. *Damn Fritz. He hasn't given up.*

'They're still here,' he said.

He rested the Schmeisser across the crook of his elbow, reached for the stick-grenade, felt Emilia's hand close on his wrist. 'They don't know we're here,' she whispered.

'How can you be sure of that?'

'Intuition. Come on.'

This time she made him enter the shaft feet first, so that he could close the concealed door by the stone knob on its rear-side. Caine pulled it to gently, lay still, listened. Despite the door, he could still hear the voices, the crunch of boots on the tunnel floor. The voices grew louder: he guessed they'd passed the turn: they were almost there. The footfalls stopped. Caine knew the Krauts were standing outside, probably looking at the Medusa fresco. His heart clumped: his breath sounded like bellows. The Jerries were debating something: Caine didn't know what it was and didn't care: he just wished they would go away.

The talk stopped: the men didn't move. Caine felt helpless: he'd had to break up the Schmeisser again to get into the shaft: if they opened the door, all he'd be able to do was spit at them. Suddenly, though, he heard footsteps again, moving cautiously away from him. He waited – it seemed for ever – until they had faded, let out a long breath. 'They've gone,' he said.

Emilia was right: the tunnel here was short. It ended only about four yards further on, in a vertical shaft, with an iron ladder running down its side. Caine fought his way backwards on to the ladder: Emilia helped him to place his feet on the rungs. They scrambled down in the darkness, dropped the last few feet on to the floor of another passage.

'This is the lowest level,' Emilia panted. 'It twists and turns a bit, but it'll take us to the forest door.'

By the light of the torch the tunnel looked more like a mineshaft – the walls had been shored up by galleries of pit-props: the roof was of stout timber. It was humid down here: the smell of earth and mould was overpowering: in places, tree-roots penetrated between the props: several times Caine almost tripped over giant coils that snaked across the tunnel from one side to the other. The way dipped and zig-zagged, then began to rise. The smells of dirt and humus became even stronger: Caine felt as if he were passing through the belly of Mother Earth. Emilia turned left abruptly, continued for another twenty yards, halted, shone her torch on a door of thick wooden beams strengthened with metal bands, studded with iron. The door was squat, with a lock the size of an ammunition box and sets of double iron bolts top and bottom.

Caine focused on the lock. 'The key,' he said. 'What about the key?'

Emilia cast around with her torch, found an alcove set in the wall: a large, ornate key hung there on a nail. She took the key, handed it to Caine. It fitted the lock perfectly: Caine turned it, heard the tumblers fall: Emilia worked on the lower bolts: Caine dealt with those on top.

Emilia was about to open the door when Caine stopped her.

'You never know,' he said.

He gripped the Schmeisser in both hands, took up a firing pose.

'Go on.'

Emilia opened the door warily, keeping out of Caine's line of fire. The wood creaked, swung wide to admit lush moonlight, a torrent of woodland scents, cool night air. The door stood in a short, cave-like tunnel whose entrance was half shrouded by foliage. Emilia scanned it with her torch: Caine moved up beside her. Suddenly a dark figure appeared at the mouth of the cave, moved steadily towards them. Emilia flinched: Caine's fingers tensed on the SMG. The figure stopped a couple of yards away: Caine got the impression of a body engulfed in an ankle-length cloak. '*Finalmente, siete arrivate*,' an old woman's voice croaked.

27

Angostina led them through the moonlit dapples of the trees, around the base of a gnarled black cliff where moonshine caught the inked-out waters of a brook, to a rock overhang concealed in a deep thorn thicket. It wasn't much of a shelter – just a shallow recess where fallen slabs of volcanic rock had poised themselves in precarious positions. The place smelt of goats: it had a smooth, sandy floor scattered with loose boulders, bone fragments and the black pearls of animal droppings. They sat on their heels, while Angostina gave them water and the leftovers of food from Caine's knapsack – bread, cheese and olives – washed down with slugs of wine from the bottle. Afterwards Caine handed Emilia a cigarette, took one himself: Angostina waved them away. He lit both cigarettes with a match, wondered how far away from the villa they were. It couldn't be more than half a mile, he guessed. Smoking wasn't tactical: the Germans would almost certainly be searching this area soon. Caine decided that morale required a cigarette, though: right now, morale was more important than tactics.

Emilia coughed, removed the cigarette from her mouth, studied it. Even in the overhang, there was enough moonlight to turn the place into a weft of silvery shadows. 'Do you think we're safe here?' she said.

Caine took a deep drag of his cigarette, held the smoke in his lungs, let it out slowly. 'For a while, maybe – unless they found that tunnel. Even then they'd have a problem getting through that door after we locked it from the outside.'

Emilia shook her head, took a tentative pull on her cigarette, coughed again, patted her chest. 'God, what do they put in these things – donkey crap?'

'Something like that.'

'Those catacombs are a maze. I wouldn't mind betting that the Krauts who followed us are already lost.'

'They'll start searching these woods come daylight, though. We'd better get moving soon.'

'*Ma dove sono i miei vestiti?*' Angostina wailed suddenly 'Where are my clothes? You say you bring them back.'

Caine noticed that the old woman was shivering under the poncho: he remembered guiltily that he'd sacrificed her garments for greater freedom of movement. 'I'm sorry, I had to leave them. They were covered in blood – Kraut blood. You wouldn't have wanted to wear them, believe me.'

'*Ma erano i miei vestiti?*' Angostina complained. 'How I go back home without my clothes? Now Cabbage-Heads find them and know I help you, no? They take me to Jesi and shoot me.'

'I'm sorry,' he said. 'We could leave you tied up so the Krauts think I stole them. I'm not sure they'd even believe it, though. And they'd know we came this way. You'll just have to go home like that.'

'Ma cosa dici? Non posso tornare a casa senza vestiti . . .'

She launched into a long and plaintive dialogue in Italian with Emilia. Caine drifted off for a moment, found himself wondering whether Stengel had been killed in the grenade attack, whether Bunny Butterfield had survived. He thought about the horrific *buried alive* experience he'd been through in the shaft: he shuddered.

Emilia broke off from her conversation with Angostina, sniffed the air. 'Can you smell burning?' she asked, holding the smoking cigarette away from her face. 'I'm worried about those grenades you threw in the hall. The whole villa might have gone up.'

Caine sniffed, smelt only tobacco smoke. 'Those chaps looking for us in the tunnels wouldn't have been so calm if the whole place was on fire. If there was a blaze, they'll have put it out.'

Emilia toked her cigarette, puffed smoke without inhaling it. 'Parts of that house go back to the twelfth century. God only knows what damage you might have done.'

Caine flushed. 'Well, I'm sorry: I was trying to get you out.'

'Yes, but if you'd arrived on time, none of this need have happened. Why were you so late?'

Caine glowered at her. '*Late?* I only escaped from Fritz yesterday. At least I *think* it was yesterday . . .'

Emilia blew a thin blue line of smoke from turned-down lips. 'You were supposed to be here a month ago. It was all arranged through Savarin. A party of British parachutists, he told me, in uniform, led by an officer who was meant to be an expert on antiquities. Instead I get a man in women's clothes who tries to burn my house down. I mean, I'm grateful and everything, but don't even know who you are . . .'

Caine pulled fiercely at the bristled skin on his jaw, bit back a caustic remark. He couldn't say that the countess hadn't worked her passage: she'd kayoed Stengel with that bottle right on cue: she'd shot the bald Nazi. She was certainly no wallflower: she'd led him through the tunnels without hesitation, even kept him going when he'd flagged. But what did she mean by saying he should have been here a month ago?

Then he got it: she was talking about Butterfield and his stick: the five-man 2nd SAS patrol who were now almost certainly pushing up daisies.

'You were supposed to tell them where the Codex is?' he asked.

'They were supposed to get me, *and* my brother, *and* the Codex, out of the country.'

Caine sighed. 'The scheme went cock-eyed. The Krauts were waiting for them on the drop-zone.'

'How come?'

'Either pure coincidence, or somebody let the cat out of the bag. I know which idea I'd favour.'

He wondered suddenly if the date of Butterfield's

drop had been known only to Emilia and Savarin, or if others had been in on the secret.

'What happened to the parachutists?' Emilia asked.

'Disappeared, probably shot. The only one left at Jesi was the officer you mentioned: the *expert.* I met him while I was a prisoner. He was afraid you were in danger from Stengel. I promised him that if I escaped I'd come and get you. I *did* manage to escape, and here I am.'

Emilia had let the ash build up on her cigarette: she stared at it for a moment, flicked it off. 'Angostina said there was a partisan ambush on the Jesi road yesterday. Is that how you escaped?'

Caine nodded.

'How come you aren't with the partisans?'

Caine stubbed out his cigarette in the dust, picked up the butt, put it in his pocket. He didn't want to go into the matter of his Nazi uniform, or to discuss Amray and his British Free Corps.

'I got separated from the others in the firefight. I decided to make my own way here.'

Emilia watched his face closely, her eyes dark pits in the moonlight. 'But did you come for me or for the Codex?'

'Both. I had to reach you before you talked, or before Stengel . . . did something to you.'

'It's a bit late for that.'

Caine saw the silver oozing of tears in the corners of her eyes, remembered what Angostina had told him, about how Emilia had been abused by Stengel. He felt awkward. Whatever Stengel had done to her, it wouldn't have happened if Butterfield's mob had got here on time. Caine had been helpless to prevent it: he hadn't even known her name until three days ago. Yet still he felt guilty. The fact that the 2nd SAS op had been compromised, too, had been beyond Butterfield's control. Someone had blabbed, and he found himself wondering again who it might have been. *If only Emilia and Savarin knew about it, there must be a chance . . . But, no. It couldn't have been her. It would have been against her interests.*

They sat in silence: Emilia stubbed out her half-smoked cigarette.

'It's too late for back-jobbing,' Caine said. 'We need to pick up the Codex and get out. Is it far from here?'

'What?'

'The Codex. Where is it hidden?'

'I don't know.'

Caine's first thought was that she was stonewalling him. 'What do you mean, *you don't know*? You *must* know.'

'That's what Stengel thought. I wasn't holding out, though: I was telling the truth. I couldn't have told him where the Codex is even if I'd wanted to: I simply don't know.'

28

Near Montefalcone, Le Marche, Italy
10 October 1943

Fred Wallace and Taffy Trubman laboured up the forest slope: Wallace was hefting two jerry cans in his saucepan-sized mitts: Trubman was toiling under the weight of a third, lagging way behind. Sherbet sunlight fell through the canopy, dropped in long elliptoids along the grassy path: there were white butterflies here, and starlings hovering in the foliage. Wallace laid the jerry cans by the roots of a big beech, sat down, waited for Trubman to catch up. He pulled a twist of tobacco from the pocket of his waistcoat, rolled cigarettes with squares of newspaper. He watched Trubman lurch over the brim of the slope, panting and sweating, suppressed a chuckle. The trout-faced, bespectacled Welshman hadn't put on weight since they'd been captured in Tunisia, but he hadn't recovered completely from his wounds either.

He watched as Trubman dumped his jerry can unceremoniously, sidled over to him, sat down in the grass, heaved a long sigh. 'Daft time to go for water, crack of dawn,' he wheezed. 'Should be a night job, see: no movement during the day.'

'Savarin doesn't know his arse from his elbow,' Wallace grunted. 'The all-singin', all dancin' "A" Force agent? Ain't got a bleedin' clue.'

He handed Trubman a roll-up: the signaller adjusted his glasses, studied it in the palm of his hand. 'Newspaper? That's not good for you, see. Mess your lungs up something chronic, that will, boy.'

'Shut up and smoke the bloody thing. Better than nowt, innit?'

Wallace lit his fag ostentatiously with a match, watched the end-paper flare, took a long, satisfying drag. Trubman shrugged rounded shoulders, set the roll in his mouth, held out his hand for a light. Wallace passed his own fag, took it back, smoked, massaged his left calf where he'd been wounded in Tunisia: it was still giving him trouble. Not surprising really, he thought, after that bastard of a *Totenkopf* warrant officer tortured him by sticking the twin-muzzles of his own weapon into the wound. Still, you had to give it to Fritz: by the time they'd got them to the field-hospital, Trubman had been on the way out: the Kraut MOs had saved his life. On the other hand, the Nazi bastards had also executed five of their SAS comrades in cold blood, damn' near scragged him, and Taffy too. He was no barrack-room lawyer, but bumping off soldiers captured in uniform wasn't cricket. Problem was, nobody seemed to believe them, not even Savarin.

Trubman coughed violently over his fag. 'Savarin's edgy after the convoy ambush,' he choked, 'and the

Kraut comb-out before that. They picked up six of his lads, after all.'

Wallace scratched in his shock of gypsy hair: he hadn't shaved in days, and his chunk of a chin was prickly with the makings of a stiff black beard. The Nazi arrest of half-a-dozen young partisans at Orsini over a week ago stank, he thought, especially as they'd included the youths who'd found Trubman wandering round the woods half delirious, and the two lads – including Ettore Falcone – who'd saved Wallace's bacon by slotting the Krauts.

'Don't tell me that comb-out weren't fishy. ''Ow did Fritz know them lads was in Orsini? Sounds like Savarin's got a problem with big ears.'

'Big mouths, you mean: someone singing lullabies to the Hun.'

'Wot about Howard's drop? Fritz was waitin' for them on the DZ, wasn't 'e? Somebody must 'ave tipped 'im off.'

'Makes you wonder if you're safe with the partisans.'

Wallace spat out a shred of tobacco. 'Don't trust nobody, mate. Don't tell 'em nothink.'

'I mean, why wouldn't Savarin let us take part in that convoy job? We've done more vehicle ambushes than he's had hot dinners.'

The giant gunner snickered. 'Prob'ly thought we'd show 'im up.'

'Good idea, that dying horse.'

'Poor thing,' Wallace grumped. 'Why the 'ell they 'ad

to use a dumb creature, I don't know. And talkin' of dumb creatures, that Major Butterfield ain't said a word yet.'

'Give him a chance, boy. He's still out of it, see.'

Wallace stubbed out his fag in the grass. He had once glimpsed Butterfield through the wire at the Jesi camp: the 2nd SAS lads had told him that he was their Assistant IO, on special assignment. He'd wondered why the major hadn't been with them in the execution party, put it down to senior-rank privilege. Now it occurred to him that the convoy the partisans had attacked must have been taking Butterfield to his own private execution.

'What about the one that got away?' Trubman said. 'Savarin reckons he was a traitor, a British chap gone over to the Hun. Can you believe that?'

'One of Amray's lot. You remember 'ow that creep came sniffin' round us at Jesi, offerin' us Itie girls to shag if we joined 'is . . . what were it called . . . *Free Corps*?'

'Yep, but I didn't believe anyone would really *join* it. He tried all the 2nd Regiment boys. They gave him the cold shoulder.'

'An' 'oo wouldn't? Can you imagine any sane Englishman . . . I mean, British person . . . puttin' on a Nazi uniform? Of his own free will? Makes you shudder. The *disgrace* of it. Anyone who'd betray his own country deserves to be hung, drawn and quartered.'

'Amray got his come-uppance anyway. The partisans

cut his throat, so they said. I didn't see the body myself, but they were sure it was him. Said he was wearing his Hun uniform with a Union Jack shield on it.'

'*Christ!*' Wallace spat. 'If I ever get me 'ands on that joker that ran away, I'll bleedin' throttle 'im, I will. Can you imagine what Tom Caine would of said?'

Trubman straightened his specs, focused on the remains of his cigarette. Wallace thought about Caine, wondered where he was now. His memory of events in that gunpit on hell's highroad, in the Matmata Hills, was dim. All he recalled was that Caine and Copeland had been there one minute, gone the next: he'd woken up a prisoner of the Nazis. Caine might be dead for all he knew. He doubted it, though: it would take a lot to kill Tom Caine. At Jesi, Wallace had pumped the 2nd SAS lads for news of him: they'd heard no report of his death.

Wallace heaved his colossal body up: at six feet seven he soared above the short, tubby Welshman. 'Come on, they'll be wantin' this water back at camp.'

29

The camp was sited in a deep vale in the forest, in dense thickets at the foot of a steep, grassy bank: the partisans had made rough tents by slinging canvas sheets and parachute-canopies under the spreading boughs, covering the floors with bracken. It was only a makeshift camp, but in the two days they had been there Savarin's crew had made it ship-shape, building a cookhouse of deadwood, digging refuse pits and supply caches. Wallace and Trubman approached the place cautiously: the security system was good: booby traps on the main approaches and watchers hidden in the bush.

The first thing that struck Wallace, though, was how quiet it was: when they'd left to get water at first light, the place had already been bustling with men and women boiling cans of water on open fires, frying eggs and sausages, cleaning teeth, darning socks, buffing weapons, wandering off with spades to dig their own latrines. Now there was an eerie silence: no chatter, no movement, not even the smoke of a cooking fire. Wallace set down his jerry cans, crouched in long grass among the tree dapples: when Trubman arrived he placed a finger the size of a candle across his lips, motioned him to ditch his burden, slipped out the

Webley .38 revolver the partisans had given him: it looked like a cap-gun in his giant hand.

Trubman checked his own weapon – a half-rusty Beretta pistol: they left the jerry cans and moved down the grassy bank. Wallace whistled tunelessly – the usual signal of approach. No one answered. The sun was still low and the thickets were a mass of shadows and alternating sequences of bronze light: the silence, though, was unsettling: not a branch rustled, not a blade of grass stirred. They moved unchallenged into the main camp-area, found a scene of disorder. The makeshift tents were gone, leaving only flattened bracken flooring: the cookhouse enclosure had been dismantled, store-pits had been dug up: haversacks, bits of equipment, cooking-cans, ration-bags lay scattered around the ashes of cold fires. Wallace called out softly: when no answer came, he shouted more loudly, heard nothing but a sudden flush of wind in the tallest trees.

They halted, confused: Trubman spotted an open box of chocolate bars among the debris, made towards it. Wallace stopped him with a tug of his massive hand. 'Too good to be true, mate,' he growled. 'Pound to a pinch of dog turd it's a booby trap. Don't touch it. Don't touch a damn' thing.'

Trubman squatted down, looked disconsolate. 'They've done a bunk,' he said. 'Just like that.'

'Fritz must have come callin'. Savarin prob'ly got tipped off at the last minute.'

'He knew where we were. He could have sent someone.'

'Yep, he could. I'm wonderin' why he didn't. Like you said, it was a queer time to send us on water-detail, anyway.'

'The whole thing stinks, boy.'

'Yep, an' if Fritz has been here, where is he now?'

'*Hey! You hear that?*'

Wallace cocked his ears, picked up a low moaning coming from the direction of the thickest trees. 'Somebody in there.'

Trubman tweaked his specs. 'Could be a trick. Could be *them*.'

The moaning came again, louder this time: Wallace thought he could make out the fading syllables of words among the groans. He swallowed hard. 'Cover me, Taff. I'm goin' for a dekko.'

'I'm coming too.'

The man was lying on the bracken under the tree where the hospital tent had once stood, surrounded by discarded medical packs and furls of soiled bandage. He was dressed in peasant clothes: they recognized him from the blood-soaked field-dressing, the Buddha head, the pudding-shaped torso: Major Bunny Butterfield, large as life.

Butterfield was dazed but conscious: they dragged him over to the tree, propped him against the trunk. Trubman gave him water from his canteen: Butterfield gulped it down so fast that Trubman had to stop him. He coughed: his eyelids fluttered. He tried to speak: his words came out as almost voiceless gasps.

'Don't overdo it, sir,' Trubman told him. 'Just tell us what happened here.'

'*Jerry . . . Jerry* came.'

'Where's Savarin and the partisans?'

'Struck camp . . . pulled out.'

Wallace and Trubman exchanged a glance. 'You mean they left you for the Hun?' Wallace demanded. 'After snatching you from that convoy yesterday? It don't make sense.'

'*Traitors*,' Butterfield mouthed: his lips curled up suddenly with anger. '*Like Caine. Traitors everywhere.*'

Wallace blinked, wondered if he'd heard right: Trubman was staring at him, eyes wide under his thick lenses. 'Did he say *Caine*?'

Wallace lowered his simian head, spoke in Butterfield's ear. 'What's this, sir? Who's Caine?'

Butterfield coughed again, struggled for an instant before he said, '*Caine . . . escaped from the convoy . . . in Nazi uniform. One of . . . Amray's . . . traitors.*'

'Caines are common as dishwater,' Trubman said.

'Was this Caine a POW in Jesi?' Wallace asked. 'I was in the camp six months: never come across anyone with that name.'

Butterfield whispered something unintelligible. Wallace leaned closer.

'*Caine's SAS. Decorated officer. Captain Tom Caine . . . DSO.*'

For a second Wallace and Trubman were thunderstruck.

'*Tom Caine?*' Wallace gasped. 'A *traitor*? It can't be *our* Tom Caine. That just ain't –'

'*Guten Morgen*,' a cold voice said.

A German soldier was standing upright among the trees: he was clad in a field-grey tunic with high boots and draped on his shoulder was a cylindrical ammunition-box. He was pointing a service rifle at them.

Wallace's *Würstel*-sized fingers twitched for the pistol stuffed into his belt.

'*Don't!*' another voice cracked out.

This time the Jerry was behind them. Wallace shifted his head slightly, clocked a German with a Schmeisser leering at them from behind a bush – a fresh-faced farmboy with an aggressive grin and startling blue eyes. There was a flurry of movement in the trees around them: a bunch of Krauts were getting up, moving in.

Wallace caught Trubman's gaze, saw he'd turned pasty. ''Ow daft can you get,' he sniffed. ''Ook, line and bleedin' sinker.'

He raised his hands slowly: Trubman did the same.

The fresh-faced Jerry moved out of cover, pushed his coalscuttle helmet back on his head, stood in front of them beaming.

'So, it is Fishface and the Giant,' he chuckled. 'You did not get far, my friends. Now you are once again prisoners of the Reich.'

Wallace glared at Trubman. 'Oh, bloody 'ell,' he said.

30

Near Montefalcone, Le Marche, Italy
10 October 1943

The woods were a tangle of trees with twisted limbs and torsos: leaves like burnished copper fractured the light into hazy colours, blazed a trail among gold shafts, through deeper seams of bronze and raw siena. At mid-morning, Caine and Emilia slithered down a carpet of leaves to the edge of a brook that gurgled shallow and clear over buffed stones. There were rocks padded with moss here, and green-velvet deadfall branches in knots like entwined pythons. They crouched in the black mud, ladled up water in their hands, lapped it thirstily: Emilia washed her face, smoothed back her hair. They sat in the grass: Caine watched red and blue dragonflies dive, hover, skim the surface of the water. Then he watched the countess as she stretched out on the ground, propped herself on her elbows: there was a feline fluidity to her body, he thought – she looked bendable, like a gymnast. She obviously found nothing awkward in lying on the earth, among the trees and grasses: it was almost as if she belonged here rather than in the castle. Her face had lost the severity he'd noticed earlier: now it was graced with a wry expression which, enhanced by the sleepy, half-narrowed eyelids, was almost sensuous.

'You seem to be at home here,' Caine said.

She picked a grass-blade, stuck it in her mouth, gave Caine a glimpse of pointed teeth. 'I spent a lot of my childhood riding and hiking in these forests. I also spent time in New York, though: I didn't really want to come back – it was only because I'd promised my father that I'd look after the villa. Now I *am* back, I know it's where I should be – in the midst of nature.'

'And yet you're leaving again.'

She shrugged. '*C'est la guerre.*'

She sat up abruptly, removed the grass, brushed hair out of her eyes, clasped her knees, stared at Caine with that frankly challenging, slightly mocking expression he'd noticed back in the villa: her face was so close he could feel her breath on his cheek.

'I'm sorry if I snapped at you about being late,' she said. 'I know it wasn't your fault.'

'Don't worry about it.' Caine felt mesmerized by the movement of her lips over her sharp white teeth, by the drowsy look in her eyes that seemed almost an invitation. Their eyes met: Caine felt the same magnetic power-surge he'd experienced when he'd first seen her – the feeling that he knew her, deep in his soul. She opened her mouth slightly: Caine was unable to draw his eyes away: he parted his lips, narrowed his eyes, moved his face towards hers.

'*What's that?*'

Caine opened his eyes fully, followed her gaze, clocked a set of scuff-marks in the mud by the stream-bank a few paces distant: they were human footprints, and they looked fresh. He got up, went to examine them. The marks had been made by civilian shoes, that was obvious, but there were also oblong impressions in the mud, of hard objects that had been set down: three of them. 'Jerry cans,' he concluded. 'Someone was here filling jerry cans. Not long back, either: in the past few hours.'

He returned to Emilia, hunched down by her: her look was distant now.

'Is it the partisans?'

'Two men, a big chap and a small chap, in civvie shoes. Big chap's a clodhopper – shoe size thirteen, at least. Unless locals use jerry cans, it's got to be partisans. Shouldn't be too difficult to follow their trail to the camp.'

He didn't add that he had no idea what he would do when they got there. *What if they recognize me as the Nazi stool pigeon who ran from the convoy? Will Butterfield be there? Will he back me up or condemn me as a traitor?* It was ironic, he thought, that he was risking his life to carry out a promise made to a man he couldn't trust to support him.

Caine tried to consider alternatives, but there was no plan B. They'd have to head for the partisans. He'd just have to use all his powers of persuasion when he met them. *Either that or run like hell.*

He sat down close to Emilia again, gave her a cigarette, lit it for her, then lit his own. He took a long drag, held smoke in his lungs, let it out.

'Look here,' he said. 'Before we find the partisans, I want to sort out something. You say you don't know where the Codex is and, frankly, that's hard to believe. I can't blame you for not trusting me: I appear with no warning, no uniform, dressed in women's clothes. I must look like a rank amateur.'

Emilia sniggered. 'Boy, you're no amateur. The way you demolished my centuries-old hall with those grenades was the work of a master. Don't worry, I've no doubt whose side you're on. I still don't know where the Codex is, though.'

Caine bristled. *She's not telling me the whole story. She arranged to have Butterfield snatch her and her brother,* and *the Codex. That must mean she knows where it is.*

Maybe it had all been a bluff, he thought, to get herself and her brother evacuated in style. Maybe there *was* no Codex. But then what had Stengel been after? That didn't add up either. And the countess had guts: she'd been abused by Stengel but she'd come up fighting: she was a girl, but she didn't seem the kind who'd give up easily.

He felt frustrated: he would have pulled Emilia out of the villa for her own sake, even without the Codex – he'd have been glad to get her out of danger, her brother, too. He paused, knew he'd missed something. *The brother. Where is he? He wasn't at the villa, but she hasn't mentioned him. Is that what this is about? The Codex for her brother?*

He took a deep breath: Emilia was lying back with her head against a moss-braided stone, her eyes narrowed, almost closed: she blew smoke coolly through pursed lips. Caine touched her ankle.

'Let's stop playing games,' he said. 'Is this some kind of tit-for-tat set-up? You won't tell me where the Codex is unless I get your brother out. Is that it?'

Emilia sat up, blew smoke, glared at him. 'Yes, we have to find my brother. But no, that's not it. Not really.'

'*Not really.*' Caine was so incensed he rose to his knees. 'Look here, a lot of people have risked their lives for this bloody manuscript: five SAS-men have been murdered for it. What about that? What about five dandelion seeds buried in the forest? What about the man in the mirror who's not himself? What about the thing that lies in a room with no doors or windows? What's all *that* about, eh?'

It came out in a rush: Caine was hardly aware of what he was saying. The effect was dramatic, though: Emilia went rigid, gazed at him with eyes like hub-caps. 'How did you *know* about that? Nobody knows but me and Ettore.'

Caine was confused. 'Know about what?'

'*What is sought lies in a room with no doors or windows.* How could you possibly know?'

Caine shifted, stuck for words. He was reluctant to admit that he'd dreamed it: on reflection, though, there didn't seem to be any other way he could explain it. *Another leap of faith*, he thought. He took a breath. 'I know this sounds crazy, but I heard it in a dream. In fact, I saw *you* in a dream. I didn't imagine it: I recognized you as soon as I saw you at the villa. There was a lot of other stuff, too, about dandelion seeds and a man in a mirror, but it was the room without doors and windows that stuck in my head.'

He sat down, embarrassed, searched her face again: her eyes were still riveted on him. 'In a *dream*?' she repeated.

'I know, it sounds nuts. But I *saw* you. You were wearing a white dress –'

'I *never* wear a white dress –'

'That's not important. But what does it *mean*? How could anything lie in a place with no doors or windows?'

Emilia watched him pensively, tugged at wayward strands of hair. She swallowed, stubbed out her cigarette, licked her lips.

'OK,' she said quickly. 'That verse is a mnemonic. It was something my father made up before he died, to remind me how to find the Codex.'

Caine's jaw dropped. 'But you say you don't know where it is.'

'Hold your horses, I'm coming to it. My father loved the Codex: he considered it a direct link to the Romans, a priceless national treasure. He knew the Nazis wanted it, and would kill to get it. He was the only one who knew where it was, but in case anything happened to him, he passed the secret on to me –'

'So you *do* know –'

'My father was a scientist – a physicist, actually. He had a friend in the scientific community called George Estabrooks – a professor of psychology at Columbia University who was an expert on hypnotism. Have you ever seen anyone in a hypnotic trance?'

Caine nodded. He recalled a hypnotism show they'd once put on at the barracks: a heavy-set man in a suit with glasses and a goatee: a lot of his Sapper mates joining hands over their heads and not being able to part them: soldiers on stage grunting like pigs, running around quacking like ducks: one of them made so rigid he could lie like a plank between two chairs while a staff-sergeant stood on his chest. Caine remembered being amused but not convinced. 'All that's fake, isn't it?' he said.

Emilia's eyes were grave. 'No, it's not. Estabrooks worked with military intelligence, on a technique called the *hypnotic messenger*, or *locking*. In one experiment, he hypnotized an officer codenamed Smith, in Washington DC, and gave him a message to take to another officer – *Brown* – in Tokyo. He conditioned Smith to forget the message: it could only be retrieved by Brown, using a signal-phrase that would put Smith into a trance and unlock the secret. Smith had no conscious memory of the message, so he couldn't give it away. And even if someone other than Brown gave him the signal-phrase, it wouldn't work: no-one else could hypnotize him.'

Caine felt completely at sea. 'I don't understand. What has this got to do with your father?'

'Papa used Estabrooks' method on me. He put me in a trance, told me the location of the Codex, locked it in my head. When I came out, I didn't even know I'd been hypnotized: Papa gave me the *no doors or windows* phrase so I'd remember that the secret was in my memory, even though I couldn't recall it.'

Caine was still confused. 'What use is it if you can't recall it?'

'I didn't say it can't *be* recalled. It can, but it requires a signal-phrase like the one Estabrooks gave Brown. That code is the key to the room with no doors and windows. I am the door, you see, and . . .'

'Another holds the key?'

'Exactly. Papa gave my brother, Ettore, the signal-phrase. He's the only one alive who can put me in a trance and unlock the secret. He holds the key. Even if I'd told Stengel I'd been hypnotized, even if he'd somehow known the signal-phrase, it wouldn't have helped him at all.'

'You expect me to *believe* this? It's too fantastic.'

Emilia let out a sardonic titter. 'And here's the man who claims he saw me in a dream, who knows a phrase he couldn't possibly have known. There's much more in this world than is dreamed of in our philosophy, Captain . . . whatever your name is.'

'Caine,' Caine said sourly. 'Tom Caine.'

'Yes. Caine –'

'All right.' He cut her off. 'For whatever reason, we have to get your brother. I'll accept that.'

'For whatever reason? You don't believe me?'

Caine bit his lip. Could this be an elaborate excuse to make certain her brother wasn't left behind? It seemed *too* elaborate, though. Emilia could have just dug her heels in and said that she wouldn't go without him. *The hypnotic messenger?* It sounded like claptrap. But there *was* his dream: was that claptrap, too?

'It doesn't matter,' he said. 'I'm ready to help get your brother. Where is he?'

Emilia paused: the amber eyes grew moist. 'Ettore has been arrested by the Krauts for partisan activity. That was his ring I got back from Stengel. He's in detention at Orsini, but they're taking him to Jesi tomorrow. After that he's going to be shot.'

31

Near Jesi, Le Marche, Italy
10 October 1943

It was cramped under the bush: Copeland eased his aching leg-muscles, changed position for the dozenth time. He pulled back his face-veil, inserted the eye-pieces of his binos beneath, focused the lenses again on the gates of the Jesi camp. He'd been in position since before first light, had watched the sun bulge out of its cocoon, seen lightbeams paint sinuous van Gogh brush-strokes across the landscape, seen them expand into whorls of crimson and flame-orange, seen the sunlight drive spikes of fire among the placid evergreen copses of pencil cedar and Aleppo pine. The camp wasn't far, but it stood on a rocky promontory, divided from his observation point by a plunging valley, obscured in places by peninsulas of forest, walled in by undulating green hills.

The camp itself was a set of intersecting rectangles of barbed wire, with watch-towers on stilts, chimneys, wooden hut-blocks, a few permanent buildings. An ash-coloured road ran through an avenue of poplars and telephone poles towards Jesi town, a playset of creamcake oblongs and cubes with ochre roofs peeking up amid forged and rusted foliage on another panhandle a mile or so distant.

Cope scoped the telephone lines, followed them to their vanishing point across the saddle: he let the glasses down, reverted to the naked eye. He had to be wary now the sun was getting up: an alert Jerry in one of those towers might spot the flash, send a party to investigate. Copeland thought he'd seen enough to assess their chances of rushing the camp, though. The distance between there and the town was its Achilles' heel, he reckoned. The main Axis forces were billeted in Jesi: judging by the size of the prison, he doubted that more than a company was stationed there – third-rate, rear-echelon troops, probably. A jeep-borne SAS patrol might deal with a company, might just get away with a surprise assault as long as no back-up arrived from the town: the telephone wires would have to be cut as a matter of course.

It would still be hazardous, though. Only one way in, and those watch-towers with their spotlights and Spandaus. Then you'd have to find Caine among thousands of milling prisoners, all of them wanting to jump on the jeeps with you.

Cope let his forehead drop into his hands, cushioned it with his face-veil. In a frontal assault, the best they could get away with would be 50 per cent casualties. That was a lot for one man, even if the man was Tom Caine. He knew Caine had been taken to Jesi, but how could he be sure he was still there? Breaking Jesi open would be a propaganda victory for the Allies, but would it be worth the sacrifice? No, not even Caine would want that. Cope had come here to get Tom out: he wasn't going back without him, but there had to be a better way.

He looked up, caught the sparkle of sunlight on vehicle windscreens at the gates. He lifted his glasses, observed a convoy of lorries emerging from the camp, outridden by Jerry troops in motorcycle combinations. Copeland focused on the convoy as it came out: six – no – seven lorries, with passengers packed in like herrings. Their faces were blurred, but they were mostly men in uniform, without headgear or weapons: some wore grey prison overalls: there was a handful of civilians in mufti, even some women. He noticed that the last lorry in the convoy was piled with wheelbarrows, sacks and digging tools.

Cope suddenly remembered that Cavanaugh had talked about working parties . . . *doing maintenance on the roads. That might be a better bet than trying to bump the prison-camp* . . . It seemed likely they were taken out every morning at this time. He had no idea where they worked, but Lombard could probably find out . . . Cope swallowed, remembered that Lombard wouldn't be doing any intelligence-gathering – not any more. They'd had to leave his body in Santa Lucia – the village in Abruzzo where they'd shot up the Hun. He wasn't the only casualty of the past few days, either. Cavanaugh's patrol had been shot up near Fabriano, by Fascist militia, in a dispute over a checkpoint. They'd ploughed on through with their Vickers rattling, but Cavanaugh had taken a gunshot-wound in the chest: he'd lost a lot of blood, was out of combat. He'd handed operational command of the three-jeep patrol over to Copeland.

They'd managed to cover the distance to Jesi in a night, without bumping into the Hun or Itie militias. They'd found this hill, with a view over the prison camp: the place had good cover on the leeward side: they'd camouflaged the jeeps in trees along a deep valley, well before dawn.

Copeland regretted Lombard's death: he'd been a good man, and his Italian had been useful. He refused to get nostalgic about it, though: war was war, and casualties happened. You had to accept it and live to fight another day. If he were to carry the cross for every man they'd lost, he'd be like Tom Caine.

He shifted his mind back to the convoy. Wherever the wagons were going, it was likely to be outside Jesi, almost certainly the main Ancona–Fabriano road. Attacking a party in the open would be a better option than assaulting the camp: there'd only be a skeleton crew of guards, and it would be easier to find Caine – *if* he was there.

It would have to be in daylight – that was the dicey bit. There was an airfield at Jesi: it wouldn't take Fritz long to put a few kites up. Getting away would be a nightmare, too, on these mountain roads. It wasn't as if you could just belt cross-country like you could in the desert. No, it was going to be a chancey do, whichever way you looked at it.

Chancey do? It's bleedin' oo dares wins, innit, mate?

Cope grinned to himself: he could hear Fred Wallace's voice as clearly as if the big dollop had been standing there. He felt a rush of sadness for Fred and Taff, for the breaking up of their little band of brothers, born of the desert. That had been *real* SAS fighting, he thought: before David Stirling got bagged, before 1st Regiment got turned into a do-or-die stormtrooper mob, which was everything Stirling detested. Some of the desert boys were dead now – Fred and Taff among them, maybe. He'd thought about them a lot since Tunisia: he just couldn't see how they could be alive. Mostly, he told himself that it had been right to leave them: they'd been too badly wounded to move. In any case, it had been Caine's call, not his. Sometimes, though, he felt a pang of guilt: maybe he could have done something: maybe they could have got them out. But that was war, after all: comrades came, comrades went, they got bagged, they got wounded, they died. No good getting misty-eyed about it. *If it's as simple as that, why the hell am I here, busting a gut to find Tom Caine?*

As he watched the wagons disappear into the tunnel of trees and poles, it occurred to him that he might have actually *seen* Caine on the back of one of them.

Don't worry, mate, he said under his breath: *I'm going to get you out.*

As he slid down through the underbrush, he almost ran into Trooper Bill Harris climbing upwards, on time for his stag. Harris was carrying an M1 carbine tight across his chest: his blond hair was concealed by a face-veil as thick as a turban and his face was blacked. Cope paused, passed him the field-glasses.

Harris looped the binos round his neck 'Anything happening, sir?'

'A convoy of seven wagons left the camp about twenty minutes ago, going in the direction of Jesi. Carrying prisoners, military and civilian, and work tools. Working-party by the look of it.'

'They're making the blighters skivvy then.'

'Yep. How's the boss doing?'

'Not looking too chipper.'

'Keep your eyes peeled.'

Copeland pushed on through the scrub, slid down banks among tree-roots, clambered over boulders, dropped into a narrow gully where water trickled beneath a jumble of moss-patinaed blocks, edged by a stand of ropy pines. He pushed through thorny tangles, came out into a wider gorge, dipped into the groves where the jeeps were cammed up.

Most of the patrol were still in their sleeping bags: Sergeant Tony Griffen was on watch, perched on a jerry can near Cavanaugh with a mug of tea in one hand and a Tommy gun across his knees. Cavanaugh was lying under a blanket, his tousled head on a haversack and only his features showing: his face was drawn and bloodless: his lips were blue.

Griffen squinted belligerently at Cope as he sat down.

'How're you doing, sir?' Copeland asked Cavanaugh.

The captain made a sour face: Copeland noticed that he was breathing heavily: beads of sweat trickled down his cheeks.

'Been better,' Cavanaugh muttered. 'Did you get a . . . shufti . . . at the camp?'

'Yep, I did, and –' He broke off as Griffen passed him a mug of milky tea and a ready-lit cigarette.

Copeland sipped the tea, blew on it, took a puff of the fag.

Cavanaugh's eyes, hard and bloodshot, didn't leave Cope's face.

'What are . . . our chances . . . of getting in?'

Copeland let smoke trickle from his nostrils. 'Pretty slim, I'd say. The place is on the edge of a sheer escarpment, with a steep rise up to the gate. We *could* go in all guns firing, but there are towers with spotlights and machine-guns guarding all approaches. Surprise might help us, but we'd still have to get out: I reckon we'd be looking at losing half our chaps.'

Cavanaugh pulled a face. 'That bad? Is there . . . any other way? What about . . . working parties?'

'You were right about that. A convoy left the camp at about 0745 carrying prisoners. Seven lorries, one loaded with tools. Must be a regular thing every day at that time. Like you told Paddy, it'd be a lot simpler to bump them than the camp.'

'Only . . . how do we know . . . Caine will be . . . there?'

Copeland could see that Cavanaugh was straining to keep his eyes open: his breath was coming in pants. 'You all right, sir?' Griffen demanded gruffly: it sounded as though he were swearing at him, Cope thought.

Cavanaugh closed his eyes. Copeland crouched next to him, slid his arms under his shoulders, pulled his torso upright: he jerked the sleeping-bag down. 'I'll take a look at that wound,' he said.

It wasn't good: under the fresh dressing, on the left side of Cavanaugh's chest, was a hole the size of a ha'penny, breathing garish pink fluid. It looked like a sucking pneumothorax. Cope didn't know if the round was still lodged inside but, whatever the case, there wasn't much he could do. He fetched the medical bag from the nearest jeep, cleaned the wound and re-dressed it. Then he gave Cavanaugh a morphia shot.

They sat with him in silence until his eyelids began to flicker: Griffen gave him water from his canteen. Cavanaugh coughed, spluttered, opened his eyes.

'You'll be all right, sir,' Griffen growled. 'Just keep that wound closed.'

'Could do with a fag . . . more than . . . anything else,' Cavanaugh panted. 'Not such a wonderful idea . . . what?'

Griffen gave him a swig of rum instead.

'What were you . . . saying . . . about Caine?' Cavanaugh asked. 'I drifted off a bit there.'

Copeland scratched his cornfield hair.

'I was going to say that we can't be sure Tom Caine's with the working-party. He might not even be at the camp. I think we should just take our chance. At the very least we'll be able to liberate the others.' He stood up. 'Tell you what – why don't we do it now? We could skirt around Jesi, follow the Fabriano road. They've got to be along there somewhere, and it's going to be a daylight job anyway.'

Cavanaugh smiled weakly at him. 'I do . . . appreciate . . . your keenness to pull out your chum, Harry. But I don't think it's wise to rush. No, we'll lay up here till it's dark, move in the early hours. We'll find out where they're working. When they get there tomorrow, guess who'll be waiting for them?'

32

Near Montefalcone, Le Marche, Italy
10 October 1943

There was something familiar about the footprints, Caine thought: not many men had feet that big. He realized he was thinking of Fred Wallace – he'd had the giant's tracks around him constantly in the desert, and there was a certain resemblance – in the length of the stride as well as the shape of the feet. Interestingly, the smaller prints followed at a distance, lagging ever further behind: the outline of a rectangular rim at intervals showed that the laggard had frequently stopped to rest.

Emilia dogged Caine up a slope through a stand of black pines – old trees, bent and distorted, their trunks obscured by many-layered flakes of bark that curled at the edges like reams of blackened paper. They looked like grotesque monuments – totem-poles sprouting leaves, bushy-haired wicker-men with elongated arms and legs. At the top of the rise the going levelled out among ancient beeches with stained and fluted trunks, presenting boughs laden with foliage in bright, metallic colours, like trays of garlands and gaudy fruit. Fallen leaves lay beneath the spreading canopy in deep-pile carpets of red gold.

Caine paused by a big beech, showed Emilia tell-tale disturbances in the leaf-pattern underfoot: men had sat down here. 'They left the jerry cans over there,' he said, pointing. He scrutinized the ground carefully, came up with a tiny twist of burnt paper with a microscopic amount of tobacco-ash inside. He spread it out on his fingers. '*Newspaper*,' he commented. 'If they're rolling fags out of newspaper, they must be hard up.'

'How far ahead are they?'

'These tracks are fresh. Can't be more than an hour.'

Further on, stacks of mossy stones erupted out of the forest floor – trapezoids and oblong blocks, like the relics of a ruined castle. The trees were young and slimmer here: soon they thinned out along a deep grassy bank which gave way to more stands of beech on the far side. Caine crouched behind boulders on the lip of the bank.

'What is it?' Emilia whispered.

He couldn't say exactly. Something wasn't right: maybe it was just a feeling, or maybe he'd heard or seen or felt something that hadn't registered consciously.

Before he could answer, Emilia froze, shoulders hunched, attention riveted like a pointer on something ahead. Caine followed her gaze: a Jerry in field-grey was standing at the base of the bank, on the opposite side, where the trees thickened. A Schmeisser was slung muzzle-forward over his right shoulder: he carried no equipment but a fluted ammo-box on a strap. He wore knee-length boots: his coalscuttle helmet was unbuckled and tilted back: he was smoking a cigarette, but he looked alert. Caine focused on the cigarette: *that was it. I smelt tobacco smoke.*

The soldier turned aside, shouted an order in German. Caine pulled Emilia down next to him. Other men were emerging from the thickets now – a pair of Krauts carrying a casualty between them on a stretcher, another three escorting a couple of civilian captives. The civvies were dressed in rough peasant clothes and broken shoes: their hands were tied behind them with rope, their heads covered with hessian sacks. One of them was short and podgy-looking, the other stood head and shoulders above him – a massive figure with bowsprit shoulders and limbs like telegraph poles.

It didn't take a second glance for Caine to know that he'd found the authors of the tracks they'd followed from the stream: the giant with the size-thirteen shoes: the smaller one who'd lagged behind. They *must* be partisans, he thought: why else would the Hun be taking them in?

The first Jerry gestured to his left: the procession turned away from Caine and Emilia: the Krauts began to make their way along the base of the bank. Caine saw one of the captives – the big man – stumble over a tree root and fall to his knees. The guards jeered, bawled at him, took turns to deliver languid kicks to his body, dragged him up like a pig. The man didn't utter a word, but Caine felt incensed. *There's only half a dozen of them*, he thought. *I could bump them now.*

He hesitated, though: first of all, the fact that this was a small detachment meant there'd be vehicles nearby, with a lot more Krauts: any shooting was likely to bring reinforcements. Then there was his mission: he couldn't deviate from it to liberate partisans from the Hun. *But isn't that my mission now, anyhow? To liberate Emilia's brother – a partisan?* If he and Emilia managed to turn up at the partisan camp having snatched a few of their chaps from Fritz, it wouldn't be a bad start, especially if the Nazi-uniform business came up.

He watched the Jerries, realized his opportunity was slipping away: it was now or never.

He nudged Emilia. 'I'm going to get them,' he said. 'You stay here.'

Emilia poked his arm: Caine noticed that her hair had come loose: it hung around her face in wavy tresses. 'There are six of them,' she said.

'Two are carrying a stretcher.'

Her eyes narrowed. 'If you're going, I'm coming.'

'All right, but we have to move.'

They progressed stealthily through the forest, kept parallel with the path that ran along the foot of the grassy bank. The going would be easier for the Huns, Caine knew, but the stretcher-party would slow them down. At one point they were near enough to the enemy to hear their voices: Caine signalled Emilia to pass on: they hurried ahead until the way was blocked by a stream flowing fast in a shallow gully – dark water streaked with white spume as it scoured the polished basalt chunks that straddled its surface. It wasn't a major obstacle, but the Krauts would have to negotiate it with the stretcher: it was exactly the kind of bottle-neck Caine had been hoping for.

They cut left through the trees to the place where the track crossed the flow, where the grassy bank had become a low step of earth interspersed with mossy stones and protruding roots. They hovered in the trees, shuftied the crossing-point: the torrent was wider here and looked deep: it was edged on their side by water-carved hunks of granite, some smooth, others cushioned with moss, scattered with fallen twigs and stranded leaves like soft magenta stars. Flattish boulders lay in the stream, close enough together to form stepping-stones, giving way to a beach of black gravel, bordered by dense and murky trees on the opposite side. Lichen-crusted branches and forked boughs criss-crossed the watercourse above head-height: the track followed a natural break in the forest that widened as it reached the brook, narrowing on their left to a leafy tunnel through the trees.

They had only just taken up a position behind tangled, denuded beech-roots when the Jerry patrol rounded a bend in the track a hundred yards away. Caine and Emilia ducked: Caine peered through a gap in the roots, dekkoed the approaching squad. The Jerry who'd been smoking was now in the lead: a red-cheeked soldier with brilliant blue eyes and a determined set of jaw, moving warily, Schmeisser ready in both hands. Behind him came the stretcher-party, and behind them the civvies in their blindfold sacks, nudged forward by three Jerry guards.

Caine and Emilia pressed themselves flat as the Krauts passed their position, held their bodies rigid as they moved down to the stream. Caine craned his neck, took in the scene at the crossing-point: the leader had already scrambled across: he was poised on the gravel beach, SMG slung on his back, ready to help the stretcher-bearers: they were struggling to get the casualty across the stepping-stones. The two civilians – Little and Large, Caine had dubbed them – were standing very upright, their heads raised, as if trying to peer through their sacks into the blankness beyond. Two guards stood a little behind them, with a third – a tail-end Charlie – positioned some way to the rear. He was the nearest to Caine: a broad-shouldered soldier with a fat-jowled face and a mouth like a tulip. He was doing his job: facing away from his patrol, rifle at the ready, eyes casting left and right.

Caine took a deep breath, closed his eyes, felt a surge of power rush through him: his heart ramped, his blood steamed: he glimpsed a thousand mirror-images of himself leaping into the open, with his Schmeisser popping. A part of him was dismayed by what he was about to do: there was another part, though, that craved with savage wildness to get it over, to be out there among them, gouging blood. He held on to that wave of feeling, tensed his muscles, ground his teeth. *You ain't Captain Caine. You're the devil.*

He tapped Emilia on the arm, nodded, counted, *one, two, three.* Then he was up, his weapon blattering *tack-tack-tack-tack*. The first burst was fast and accurate: three rounds slammed into the tail-end Charlie's lower abdomen, diverged, ripped through his liver, punctured his bladder, demolished his kidneys. The Jerry staggered, looked mildly indignant, eyebrows raised, tulip mouth puckered. He dropped his rifle, clutched his belly, gazed enraptured at the thick red mashings welling through his fingers, genuflected gracefully and bowed out.

By the time he was down Caine was running: he took in Little and Large in the eternal process of falling prone, saw the two Jerry guards swivel towards him in slow motion, saw them bring up their weapons, saw their faces pass through a sequence of expressions – surprise, fear, fighting resolution. The first Jerry was an oldish man with wide nostrils and pinpoint eyes, carrying a Schmeisser: Caine fired his machine-pistol one-handed on the run, drew Cesare's knife from his belt as he pulled iron. The burst went high: he knew it before he eased metal. Two of the rounds missed Fritz completely: the third struck him spack in the front teeth, sawed a gully across his soft palate, drilled through his brain, exploded from the back of his cranium in a splurge of mincemeat and sparks.

Caine flipped his knife at the other German, a wiry-looking boy with a prominent Adam's apple and eyes like dinner-plates. The throw didn't look much – the merest flick of the wrist – but Caine was a master of ballistic cutlery: the blade flew with deceptive force. The boy already had his rifle at the shoulder when the steel pranged into his neck just above the Adam's apple, severed his windpipe, cut through the nerves in his spinal column. His trigger-finger spasmed: the rifle spat: a shot whinged past Caine's ear.

Caine didn't notice: he was already bracing his weapon towards the stretcher-bearers in midstream and the leader on the other side. The bearers teetered: Caine saw them overbalance, drop the stretcher, saw the bulky casualty tip into the water, saw the stretcher-men crash headlong into the stream. On the far side of the torrent, the leader had gone into a crouch with his SMG poised, about to fire. Caine hit him with a five-round stitcher that drew a track of purple blisters upwards from groin to guts to chest to neck, passed out between his shoulder blades in a flush of mangled crud. The man tottered forward, fell across the gravel: his helmet hit the water, his blood streaked away in the current.

Little and Large were eating dirt: the stretcher-men were floundering waist-deep, trying to bring their weapons to bear. They were too far apart for a single burst. Caine chose the nearest, pulled a crisp double-tap, punched a twin crater into his chest, bulldozed his heart. As the Jerry went down, his comrade came up like a counterweight. Caine saw fight in his dripping face, saw his SMG-muzzle jut forward, pulled iron, felt his working parts thunk on an empty chamber. There was a fraction of a second's hiatus: Caine tensed himself for shots that never came. At that instant a sub-machine gun gavotted behind him: he felt the rounds swarm past on a raft of hot air, saw the Jerry's eye implode, saw the black cavity that appeared like a new eye in the centre of his Kaiser hat, saw gore froth from his nose and mouth. The man was hurled backwards, struck the water with a splash.

Caine glanced over his shoulder, clocked Emilia frozen in an awkward firing stance with a dead soldier's Schmeisser still smoking in her hands: her face was drained, her hair loose and blowing across her shoulders in glossy skeins.

'*Check the civvies!*' Caine snapped. He dashed across the stepping stones, found the Jerry leader, made sure he was dead, relieved him of his Schmeisser and ammo-box. He stood up, turned to survey the water. The stretcher-men had been carried downstream: only the tops of their helmets showed above the surface. Caine saw Emilia getting Little and Large to their feet: he skipped back across the stones towards them, saw the big man stand fully upright, realized for the first time how truly gigantic he was – taller than almost any man Caine had ever known: shoulders wide as a door, a chest like a sheer rock-face, hands like chamber-pots, legs like stone pillars. There was only one man Caine knew with a physique like that: he had left that man in a gunpit in Tunisia, at the mercy of the Hun.

He scrambled over the granite slabs on the opposite side, saw Emilia fumble with the big man's bindings, saw that his shirt cuffs had ridden up, spotted on one of his exposed, hairy forearms the lower part of a tattoo. It was a Sphinx: Caine recognized it at once – the insignia of the Sphinx Battery, Royal Horse Artillery. He knew a giant who'd once served in that unit . . . *but it can't be him. It* can't *be . . .*

'*For Christ's sake, will yer get this bleedin' sack off me 'ead!*'

The voice roared like a foghorn in Caine's ears: he was dreaming, of course: *it's not possible, it can't be.*

He reached up, yanked off the sack: found himself looking at a creased and weathered face: ogre features notched and scarred, a bristle-brush beard, a forehead like a tent-flap, black-pearl eyes set in dark-caverned sockets, a riotous tangle of gypsy hair. The small black eyes met his, the monument of a face sagged in surprise: for an instant they stared at each other. A watery haze whorled in Caine's head. He staggered back: the big man caught him, enveloped him with his great arms, crushed him in a bearhug. '*Tom?* I don't *believe* it. What about this for an 'ow's yer father?'

Caine felt tears in his eyes, felt his hands gripping back-muscles like taut cables. '*Fred?* You're alive? How the hell did you get out of that gunpit?'

'Don't rightly remember . . . woke up in a Kraut stretcher, an' –'

'*Hey come on, boys, lemme loose!*' another voice piped up.

Caine had almost forgotten the other prisoner: he saw Emilia untying the man's bonds, realized that he knew this figure, too: the short, rounded body was leaner than he remembered, but the W/T operator's delicate hands were the same. He broke away from Wallace, pulled the sack off the man's head. '*Taffy Trubman. For Jesus' sake, you're here, too.*'

Trubman blinked dozily, adjusted his glasses: his eyes, magnified by the lenses, were enormous: he fidgeted on his feet, rubbed vigorously at his sore wrists. Caine grasped the signaller's hand in both of his, shook it hard. Trubman gaped at him: rose-madder tints flushed his cheeks. '*Tom?* I heard your voice . . . thought I must be dead. It's really you, skipper? After all this, you're *here*?'

'I never thought I'd see you – either of you – again.'

'Shouldn't we get moving?' Emilia cut in. 'Someone might have heard the shooting.'

Caine remembered Emilia's existence.

'Fred Wallace, Taff Trubman, this is Countess Emilia Falcone. Emilia, these two are old comrades of mine.'

Emilia shook hands hastily, gave her Schmeisser to Wallace. 'You might need this.'

Wallace checked the weapon, ejected a case, cocked the works, set the safety. 'Wot about you?' he growled.

'I'm handier with a rifle – there's at least one spare.'

Wallace gazed around keenly. ''Ere, what about Butterfield? What 'appened to 'im?'

'*Butterfield?*' Caine wasn't sure he'd heard right.

'Yeah, *Major* Butterfield – 2nd SAS, Assistant IO. That was 'im on the stretcher. Where'd 'e get to?'

For an instant, Caine was too dumbfounded to speak.

'He fell in,' Emilia answered for him. 'They dropped the stretcher in the stream.'

Caine was already moving. 'I'll have a dekko,' he said. 'You get those weapons.'

He hurried back to the stepping-stones, scanned the current, spotted the stretcher almost at once: it was caught between sharp rocks downstream, one set of handles protruding, foam tipping it forward and back like a seesaw. Not far away, where the gravel beach gave way to reed-beds, he clocked a dome-shaped bald head on a pair of rounded shoulders. It was Butterfield, and it looked as though he might be alive. Caine crossed the stones, jumped the gap, ran along the gravel beach to the reed-beds: it wasn't until he had crouched down by the globular head that he was certain. *Bunny Butterfeld, large as life.*

He slung his weapon, got his hands under Butterfield's armpits, heaved him out of the water, laid the pear-shaped body on the beach. The major's face was lank and pallid: the pattern of old cuts and bruises stood out on the skin like a dark frieze. If the head-wound he'd sustained had ever been dressed, the dressing was gone now: the graze bulged from his skull in a livid red hogsback. He was certainly alive, though: Caine felt a pulse at his temple, heard ragged stirrings of breath. He was about to turn him over in case his lungs were waterlogged when Butterfield's eyes guttered: he took a whopping breath, launched into a paroxysm of raking coughs: his eyes streamed, his nose ran.

Caine glanced across the stream, signalled the others. He watched Wallace and Trubman troop across the stepping-stones, with Emilia bringing up the rear. His old chums looked business-like now they had Jerry weapons in their hands and ammo-boxes draped across their bodies: he couldn't miss the fact that Wallace dragged one leg slightly, though, or that Trubman hobbled.

They hurried up, knelt down by Butterfield.

'Is he OK?' Wallace boomed.

Before Caine could answer, Butterfield's eyes widened, fixed on his face in horror. '*Don't let him near me!*' he shrieked. He was suddenly up on his elbows, trying to crawl away backwards. '*Caine's a dirty traitor. Sold his soul to the devil. Don't let him near you – he'll kill you all!*'

Emilia shot an anxious glance at Caine. 'Delirious,' she said.

Caine peeked at Wallace, found the big gunner focused on something else: his head raised, a hand cocked to his ear.

'*Dogs*,' he rumbled.

Caine listened, caught a far-off baying, the murmur of voices. 'Not dogs,' he spat. '*One* dog. A tracker.' He glanced back at Butterfield: the major was still shaking his head. 'We'll have to carry him. Come on, let's go.'

33

They struggled through the green passage along the foot of the grassy bank: Wallace and Trubman supported Butterfield between them: he was no lightweight, and it was slow going. Caine knew they didn't stand a chance of evading the dog. It would have been all right if they could have ditched Butterfield, perhaps, but whatever else the major might be, he was Regiment, and the Regiment looked after its own. The best way to confuse the dog would have been to split up, but that was out of the question: he wasn't going to part with Wallace and Trubman now he'd found them: he wasn't going to desert Emilia, either. He still wasn't sure about the hypnotism stuff, but now he'd got her out, she was his responsibility. In any case, he felt he owed her: her encouragement during that horrific moment in the shaft had saved his life.

By the time they'd reached the place where they'd first spotted the Jerries, Wallace was swearing. He shoved Trubman aside, bent his knees, hoisted Butterfield on his shoulder in a power-lift, held him there like a sack. 'That's better,' he declared. 'Just 'ope I don't have to flamin' run.'

Trubman directed them off the track to the old

partisan camp: Caine was astonished to see the scattered equipment, the remains of shelters, the excavated store-pits.

'Don't touch nothink,' Wallace told him. 'Don't go near nothink, neither. Fritz 'as prob'ly booby-trapped the lot.'

'The partisans cleared out pretty sharpish,' Caine commented. 'Must have been tipped off.'

'Yep, but why the 'eck did they leave Butterfield?' Day before yesterday they stick their flamin' necks out to snatch 'im: today they drop 'im without so much as a by yer leave.'

'What about *us*, then?' Trubman cut in. 'Why did Savarin send us to get water an hour away when we could have gone to the stream where the skipper bumped the Jerries? Don't tell me he didn't know it was there.'

'I was thinkin' that meself,' Wallace agreed. 'It's almost like 'e wanted us out of the way.'

'But why?' Emilia asked.

'I dunno, but we *did* get nabbed by the Krauts, di'n't we?'

'You're not saying it was deliberate?'

'I'm not sayin' nothink. Fishy though, *innit*?'

Wallace paused, listening: they heard the yapping of a dog, not too far distant. 'Fritz is on to us,' he croaked.

They boxed hastily around the camp, cut out into the forest, plunged through galleries of changing light, through broad sprays of sunbeams like spills of golden liquid. Emilia and Wallace went ahead with Butterfield still balanced on the giant's battering-ram shoulders, while Caine and Trubman struck out at acute angles, circled round, retraced their steps, laid false trails to confuse the dog. 'It won't stop it,' Caine said. 'But it might slow the handler down.'

The forest opened into broad avenues of beeches where the trees stood like the warped and fluted grey pillars of lost temples, with roots like giants' down-covered feet and great lateral boughs that hooked around each other to form a canopy like a timbered roof. Sunlight slatted through the branches in glittering tumbles. Wallace stopped suddenly, cast around him. ''Ere, Taff,' he said. 'I recognize this . . .'

'You're right, boy,' Trubman said. 'This is near where they scragged the lads.'

'Us too, nearly. I came through 'ere on the run.'

Caine stared at Wallace. 'Of course, it was *you*, wasn't it? Butterfield said there were two men from 1st Regiment, captured in Tunisia, sent for special handling with his own crew. I thought about you, but then dismissed it as impossible.' *Five sacred ibises in the forest: five, not seven.* 'So it's true about the 2nd Regiment lads, then? They're all dead?'

'As flamin' doornails, mate. They was –'

Emilia screamed shrilly. 'There's a *foot* here. A man's *foot*.'

Caine hurried over to her, clocked a place between

two big trees where humus and turf had been disturbed: a human foot, swollen and mould-yellow, protruded from the earth.

Wallace and Trubman mooched over: Wallace let Butterfield down, sat him against a tree-trunk. The major moaned: his eyelids fluttered. Trubman stared at the exposed foot, rubbed his glasses as if he might recognize it. 'It's one of the 2nd Reg. lads,' he said. 'This is where they buried 'em. Shallow grave, see.'

Five dandelion seeds buried in the forest, Caine thought.

'*Bastards*,' Wallace rasped: he shuffled over to Trubman. 'You an' me woulda bin 'ere too, mate, if we 'adn't 'ooked it.'

'We don't have time for this, Fred,' Caine said urgently. 'Fritz is right behind us.'

Wallace's gunbore gaze didn't flinch. 'We got to be sure, skipper. That blinkin' dog is goin' to catch up with us sooner or later, anyway.'

Caine shrugged, knowing he was right. Wallace and Trubman squatted, began to clear away the spoil with their hands. Caine jogged further along the avenue of beeches, with Emilia behind him. They found the second shallow grave not ten paces away: an oblong patch where the bare soil was visible among the grass and dead leaves. The third and fourth graves lay close together by a thicket of thorny bush: the fifth a short distance away. They scouted further, found no more graves. They were about to turn back when Caine noticed a letter cut into the bark of a medium-sized beech tree nearby. From a distance it looked like an 'O', but closer up he saw that it was a 'B', badly carved, recent enough for the white core of the trunk to show through.

'What is it?' Emilia asked.

'The place marked "B",' Caine said uneasily. '*Five dandelion seeds buried in the forest, at the place marked "B".*'

Emilia knotted her brow. '*What?* Did you mention that before . . . ?'

'It was another thing you told me in the dream.'

'*I* told you? But how could I –'

A dog howled. Caine's mouth tightened: it couldn't be more than two hundred yards away. 'They're almost here,' he said. 'Take cover in the trees, I'll –'

'I'm not hiding.' She slapped the rifle slung on her shoulder.

Caine nodded reluctantly.

They legged it back to Wallace and Trubman, found that they had given up on the cadaver's torso, had exposed only the head. They were holding their noses: the smell hit Caine like a mouldering blanket. The corpse's head was bloated, the skin bluish, mottled with discoloured patches, thin as parchment: the eyes were slits – there seemed to be no pupils: the nose was a shapeless carbuncle: the mouth flopped open to reveal blackened stumps of teeth.

Caine pulled them both well away from the corpse. 'You identify him, then?'

'Buggers stripped 'im, didn't they?' Wallace rumbled.

'But I recognized 'im anyway. It's Bob Cameron.' His tone was reverent: he stood up straighter, as if giving the dead man a mental salute. 'Sergeant Robert Cameron, 2nd SAS Regiment: Black Watch was 'is parent unit. I knew 'im for a month at Jesi. Good bloke 'e was. Married. 'Ad a kid.'

'It's Bob all right,' Trubman nodded. 'I saw them shoot him . . . In the guts . . .' He lowered the chub-shaped head, gagged, spat saliva.

The howl came again, much louder this time. As if in answer, Butterfield let out a wail: Emilia shrieked. Caine wheeled round, clocked a huge animal belting towards them out of the trees – a beast so wild and savage-looking that for an instant he was sure it was a wolf. It was a German shepherd, of course: an enormous black-and-tan animal with an ebony face, eyes pale as glass, ears up like daggers, teeth bared in a vicious snarl, feet pattering the turf in leaping bounds. Trubman gasped, fell flat. Caine unslung his Schmeisser: Wallace beat him to it, planted his SMG-stock in his belly, leaned forward, aligned the barrel. He fired three crisp single shots: *Boommffff. Boommffff. Boommffff.* The dog's yelp sounded almost human: Caine saw crimson bloom on its chest, saw gore streak dark fur, saw it lose its footing, saw it crash to the earth, roll over.

'Good shooting, mate.'

'*Christ!*' Wallace swore. 'Had to be a poor, dumb beast. I'd rather 'ave shot a Kraut.'

'Not so dumb as all that.'

A salvo of automatic fire wefted out: *racka-tacka-tack*. Rounds flicked out of the undergrowth, tattered leaves, squibbed up tiny explosions of smoke and humus, went *splick* off trunks.

'*Take cover!*' Caine yelled.

Field-grey men were visible now, working through the underbrush towards them. Trubman had his rifle at the shoulder: he let rip with a controlled volley: *booom-mffff, booommffff, booommffff, booommffff*. 'Go on, boys. I'll hold 'em.'

Caine slid out his last stick-grenade, laid it beside the Welshman.

'Two minutes, Taff. Then pull the string in the handle, lob it, run like the devil. More than five seconds, you're batshit.'

'Got it, skipper.'

Bayowww. Bayowww. Wheeeuuuuuww. Hun fire was dropping closer: Caine ducked, felt a ricochet frazzle air. Trubman pulled iron, fired measured shots. *Booom-mffff. Booommffff. Booommffff*.

Caine slapped Wallace's arm, jerked his chin towards Butterfield. They ran over to him: the major was conscious, his eyes rolling like hollowed-out marbles. When he clocked Caine his mouth contorted with fear. '*Stay away*,' he spluttered.

'It's 'im or the Nazis, sir,' Wallace blared. 'Come on, get up, you great bloop.'

They hoisted him up between them: he shivered but didn't resist. A deafening *bashaaaawww* from nearby seared Caine's eardrums: he clocked Emilia crouching behind a rifle three yards away, her face veiled by the morass of her dark hair falling around the stock. '*Come on!*' he bawled at her. 'Trubman's covering.'

They moved fast into the denser brush beyond the great beech avenues, pulling Butterfield between them so that only his toe-caps dragged. Emilia followed close behind. Caine counted off the seconds, heard Hun weapons rump and spattle, heard Trubman's steady crunch of covering fire. *Come on, Taff. Hit 'em with the spudmasher.* They stumbled down a leafy bank, collapsed in a heap at the bottom: Emilia slid after them. Caine disentangled himself from Butterfield, monkey-ran back up the slope, paused at the top. '*Where the heck is –*'

BABOOOOOOMMMMFFFF.

He heard the detonation, felt hot air blow, felt the earth rumble, heard the blast damp itself out. For a moment there was silence: Caine lay very still, listening. There was a sudden whiplash of rifle-shots and the stuttering stitch of sub-machine-gun fire. Then he heard the soft pad of footfalls in the humus, the whisper of leaves, undergrowth bristling as a body heaved through it. A moment later Taff Trubman came into view, hunched over, breathless, sweating, rifle braced against his arm on a coiled sling. He was heading in the wrong direction. Caine stood up, signalled to him: the Welshman changed course, hobbled through the scrub towards him. They slipped down the bank: Trubman sat panting between Wallace and Emilia, his pudgy face paste-coloured, his pupils dark commas behind thick lenses. 'I chucked the grenade,' he told them, 'but Fritz is still shooting, see. They'll be after us.'

'They'll be cautious, though,' Caine said. 'It'll slow them down . . .'

'Yep.' Wallace winked. 'An' they ain't got no tracker-dog with 'em this time, 'ave they?'

34

By late afternoon Caine reckoned they'd outrun the enemy. Above the forest canopy the sky had clouded over, shrouding the sun, cutting off the rills of rainbow colours, filling the woods with grey shadows and sepulchral gloom. The trees were old here, with knots and bulbous growths bulging from their trunks, some so eaten out by fungi they reminded Caine of grotesquely distorted faces. They'd been pushing through the woods for hours, it seemed: they were hungry and tired. On the upside, Butterfield had recovered enough to walk some of the way, although so slowly it was hardly an advantage. A change had come over him: he crept along in his grey flannel suit and down-at-heel shoes, with his hands wrapped around his belly, head down, great dewlaps hanging over his shirt-collar, teeth clamped, lips tight. He didn't speak to anyone, answered in grunts, remained so quiet that sometimes Caine almost forgot he was there.

They came to a streamlet: black water running like molasses over molar-shaped rocks. Caine called a halt. They took turns to drink: Butterfield slumped against a tree. Emilia drank first, sat down next to Caine. She'd tried to tie her hair back again, but it had caught in branches and thorn-bush: it looked almost as unkempt as Wallace's Gypsy mop. 'Are we still heading west?' she asked.

Caine nodded. He'd been using the sun and shadows to navigate: as long as there was light he could keep them going straight, ever deeper into the Appenines. Their destination was the partisan camp, though, and they had no idea where, or how far away, that was.

Caine watched Wallace kneeling at the stream, slurping water from his hand, splashing it on his face. He watched Trubman waiting his turn, watched Butterfield leaning against his tree with his eyes closed, the livid scar standing out like a red crest on his cupola of a head. Suddenly he had a feeling that someone else was there, watching them. He dismissed the sensation as paranoia, but it refused to go away: it grew stronger. He groped for his weapon, scanned the forest around him, studied the pillars of shadow, the grey knotted undergrowth, the thorn thickets beneath the colossal leaning columns of the trees. He saw nothing, but the feeling remained. He rose on his haunches, brought the Schmeisser across his knees. At that moment he became aware that a man was standing opposite him, pointing a rifle at his chest.

'*Don't move, any of you!*' the man said.

For a moment Emilia looked petrified: Wallace stopped splashing water: Trubman turned to look: Butterfield's eyes snapped open.

The man had moved into the open as silently as a

ghost: he must have been standing in the shadows for some time, Caine thought. He didn't seem to be a Jerry: he'd spoken with a British accent. The only thing vaguely German about him was his knee-length jackboots. Apart from that, he was dressed like an English country squire, in corduroys, a waxed olive-drab shooting-jacket and a plaid scarf. He was dark: his skin was almost the same milk-coffee shade as Emilia's. He was loosely built, with a square face, a prominent jaw, slabbed cheeks, heavy eyebrows, long, thin lips and a high-arched nose. His hair was dark and long, but oiled and combed: his eyes were narrow incisions in a clean-shaven face.

Emilia rose to her feet. '*Savarin?*' she gasped.

The man blinked at her. '*Salve*, Countess.'

'If it ain't our favourite "A" Force operator,' Wallace boomed. He stood upright, turned to face the newcomer. 'Ain't seen you since you sent us to get water at sparrowfart this mornin' –'

'Yeah. We got back to camp and found Fritz there,' Trubman cut in.

'A warnin' would 'ave been nice,' Wallace growled. He jutted his doorstep chin at Butterfield, who was staring at Savarin with a quizzical expression. 'Seems like you left somebody else in the lurch, too.'

Savarin frowned, nodded to Butterfield. 'Major.'

He jerked his lip at Caine. 'Who's this?'

'A British officer,' Emilia said.

'Captain Tom Caine, our old boss,' Wallace said.

'Liberated us from Fritz, din' 'e? 'Im an' the Countess 'ere bumped off half-a-dozen of the blighters.'

Savarin didn't look impressed, neither did he let the rifle drop. 'That means the Krauts will be looking for you. Have you brought them here?

'We lost them,' Caine said.

'Really? I hope you're right. We've had to move camp twice in the last few days.'

'Why don't you lower the gun?' Emilia suggested. 'There are no enemies here.'

Savarin didn't budge. 'I'm not so sure, Countess. Someone ran away from our ambush two days ago, in Kraut uniform. A British traitor, they said: one of Amray's men. Well, Amray got his: the partisans cut his throat. That fellow who ran, though – I'd like to know where he is now.'

Caine glanced at Butterfield, wondering if he would say anything: the major avoided his gaze, kept his mouth shut. Caine traileyed Emilia. *She knows I escaped from the convoy. I didn't mention the Nazi uniform, but she can put two and two together.* She didn't glance back at him, kept her eyes fixed on Savarin. Caine breathed easier: he would have to face the music sooner or later, but he didn't want to go into it now, certainly not while the 'A' Force man had a weapon pointed at him.

'We can vouch for Tom,' Wallace croaked.

Savarin cocked a pipe-brush eyebrow. 'Really? Isn't Caine the one who left you behind in Tunisia?'

There was a heavy silence. Caine stared at Wallace:

a knot of cartilage in the giant's throat trembled: for a moment the ballbearing eyes glinted at him.

It was Emilia who broke the silence. 'Tom risked his life to get me out of the villa,' she said. 'I saw him kill five Germans, and I know he killed more. I don't think you'll get a better character reference than that. Look, it'll soon be dark. You know me, and you know these other guys. Are we going to stand here exchanging accusations all night?'

Savarin grimaced, sighed, let his rifle drop. He gave a piercing whistle. Instantly, half a dozen partisans appeared out of the brush, formed a rough circle around Caine's group, moved forward to shake hands. They were mostly young men with keen, dark-shadowed faces in tattered peasant garb and cloth caps, hefting a crazy assortment of rifles, pistols, sub-machine guns. One of them looked about fifteen, Caine thought: an ivory-faced lad, so thin he was almost emaciated, with clean, girlish features, an angular nose, watchful eyes, jug-handle ears that waggled slightly when he spoke. He carried a double-barrelled shotgun that looked out of place in his long, tapering fingers. Savarin introduced the boy as *Furetto* – Ferret: 'He's the youngest in the band,' he told them. He did look like a ferret, Caine thought – an apologetic one. Furetto's handshake was surprisingly strong: he retained Caine's scarred and swollen hand for an instant longer than necessary, caught his eye, nodded towards Savarin, who was busy introducing the other partisans. His jug ears joggled. '*Later, we talk*,' he said.

By the time they'd reached the camp, the forest stood in leaden twilight, with only a net of smoky shafts like cobwebs to give any contrast to the dimness under the trees. They were challenged once by an unseen sentry: Savarin replied in a harsh whisper, led them forward into an area where the trees were big-boled and widely spaced, where human faces were shards and spangles of reflected light, where there was the murmur of low voices around cooking fires, where the air was heavy with woodsmoke and the savoury smell of cooking stew. There was an excited stir as Savarin's party entered: yells, greetings, enquiries. Men got up to slap Wallace and Trubman on the back: women rose to kiss and shake hands with Emilia.

Savarin led them to a makeshift tent – a large canvas sheet draped over low beech-boughs, pegged down at the corners and back. The place was spacious inside, lit by candles stuck in wine-bottles, lined with straw mattresses. Savarin ordered food brought in on trays. It was a simple meal – fresh bread, goat stew, red wine – but Caine couldn't remember eating better in his life. Afterwards, Savarin took Butterfield off to have his wound dressed: Emilia was claimed by a bevy of ladies, and disappeared with them.

Caine, Wallace and Trubman sat on mattresses, smoked the cigarettes Savarin had distributed: Caine and Wallace passed a flagon of wine between them: Trubman drank tea. Caine smoked, stared at his friends. The events of the day seemed unreal, even fantastic – no more solid than his dream. He'd known some remarkable coincidences in his life, but never in a million years would he have expected to run into Wallace and Trubman in a forest behind enemy lines.

'I thought you'd both bought it,' he told them. 'You were never listed as POWs by the War Box. They officially posted you missing in action, believed killed.'

Trubman swallowed tea from a huge enamel mug, wiped his mouth with the back of his hand. 'Fritz must've had us down for special handling from the start, skipper. That's why they never gave our names to the Red Cross. They spent six months fattening us up like pigs for the slaughter.'

''Ardly worth their while, were it?' Wallace chortled.

'It's a miracle you survived that action in Tunisia,' Caine said. 'You were both so badly wounded, at the time it seemed impossible for us to get you out. Afterwards, I felt bloody terrible that we hadn't even made an attempt. It's been torturing me ever since . . .'

For an instant his voice faltered.

Wallace studied the flagon, raised it with a hand like a T-bone steak sprouting fingers. He drank wine in noisy gulps, offered the flagon to Trubman, who shook his head, held up his mug of tea. The big man took a drag of his cigarette, grinned at Caine through teeth like broken kerbstones. 'I take it that's yer apology, skipper. If it is, it ain't necessary. We always 'ad this thing about gettin' the wounded out, even though it were against SOPs: I know yer feel bad 'cause you think you broke yer promise. Now, to tell yer the truth, what 'appened in that gunpit is all a bit 'azy to me. I remember me an' Jizzard knocked out a couple of Jerry AFVs – at least, I think we did. After that, it's all muddled till I come round on a Jerry stretcher. Then some bastard of a *Totenkopf* warrant officer – head like a blinkin' potato – starts proddin' me wound with me own flamin' shotgun . . .' For a moment the grizzled face became wistful. 'Where's Purdey now, I wonder? I'll bet Potato-Head snaffled 'er. Lohmann, 'is name were, *SS-Sturmschaftführer* Lohmann.'

'He's dead,' Caine cut in abruptly. 'The *SS-Sturmschaftführer* long since departed this world.'

Wallace shook his great head in surprise. ''Ow d'you know? D'you kill 'im, then?'

'Nah. He caught an infection.'

The big man's deep-recessed eyes widened: Caine laughed. 'A long story, mate, but that's for another time. Your beloved Purdey's safe, though. It's in the regimental armoury, waiting for collection.'

The big man looked flabbergasted. '*What?* 'Ow d'you ger er back?'

'Found it in Lohmann's car, abandoned.'

Wallace was beaming. 'I owe you, skipper.'

'You don't owe me a damn' thing, mate: I dumped both of you in the desert.'

'Well, like I said, I'm a bit 'azy about what went on, but there's two things I *do* remember. One is tellin' you an' 'Arry Copeland to fuck off out of it. I called you a bloody great pansy, and threatened to get up and kick yer soggy arse.'

Caine chuckled. 'That you did. You were half bleeding to death at the time, mind you.'

Trubman set his mug down, studied Caine seriously. 'Listen, skipper, it wasn't humanly possible for you to get us out, see. If you'd tried it, none of us would have lived to tell the tale. It was the right decision. We survived. We're all here, aren't we?'

'Except for Cope.'

'What d'yer mean?' Wallace looked alarmed. ''Arry ain't dead is 'e?'

'Not the last I heard. He was with me up till just before I was captured – that's what? Five days ago . . . six? You know he's Acting Adjutant now?'

'*What?* That wanker? 'Ow the flamin' 'eck did 'e manage it?'

'Shortage of admin officers. The regiment's been reorganized: we're only at squadron strength.'

'I 'eard. Commando squadron under Paddy Mayne, innit? It don't sound like progress.'

'It isn't, believe me. We became just what David Stirling wanted us not to be. Let's hope things improve when we get back to Blighty.' He paused. 'You said you remembered *two* things, Fred. What was the other one?'

Wallace took another loud swig from the flagon, passed it to Caine.

'I remember Jizzard tellin' yer that Betty Nolan were alive. Was that true or just his baloney? Did you ever find 'er?'

Caine studied the flagon, weighed it in both hands. 'I found her,' he said at last. 'Not in time though. She took a gunshot wound in the head: she never recovered.'

'*Jesus . . .*'

'Oh, she's alive – I get letters from her sister every so often – but she's a vegetable: she never regained consciousness.'

'What a *bugger*.'

'Yep.'

'What about the countess?' Trubman enquired. 'How did you get mixed up with her?'

Caine hesitated, mustered his thoughts, described the action at the Senarca bridge, his capture, his encounter with Butterfield, his escape from the convoy, his one-man assault on the villa: he excluded any mention of Amray or the British Free Corps. When he'd finished, his mates exchanged embarrassed glances.

'That stuff Butterfield come out with,' Wallace began. 'I mean, 'e said you was a traitor, Tom. Now don't get me wrong: 'e told us that before the Krauts nabbed us, before we even knew it was you 'e meant. 'E said you joined Amray's lot, swore loyalty to the Führer an' all that bollocks. Says you was wearin' SS uniform when you 'ooked it. We just wanna know if it's true.'

Caine went very still. He'd held it back deliberately, but he couldn't avoid the question for ever. He didn't want to start off with his two friends by lying to them: not after six months, not after they'd returned from the dead,

'All right,' he said. 'Yes, I was wearing Nazi uniform when I escaped from the convoy. And yes, I did join Amray's Free Corps. That's all I can say. You'll have to trust that my intentions were honourable.'

'That's all very good, skipper,' Trubman gabbled, 'but whatever your intentions were, they could still get you for treason –'

'– That bastard Amray leaned on us to join 'is bleedin' Free Corps at Jesi,' Wallace cut in. 'Said we'd get scragged if we didn't. We told 'im where 'e could stick it.'

'Good for you.'

Wallace sniffed. 'Look, Tom, I know you must of 'ad a reason, but it ain't us you've got to convince. You saw 'ow cagey Savarin was? 'E *knows* it were you as run away. If Butterfield told us, 'e prob'ly told '*im*, too.'

Caine lowered his voice. 'I didn't like the way Savarin talked about the partisans cutting Amray's throat. All right, Amray deserved it, but it sounded like a threat. I'm not sure I trust him. 'Who is he? What do you know about him?'

''E's an Itie,' Wallace said.

'No, he isn't,' Trubman objected. 'Father's British: he went to school in Blighty. His name isn't Savarin, either. He worked for Marconi in Britain, then in Italy before the war, see. Mussolini's lot nabbed him, gave him the choice of jankers or joining the Italian army as a signals officer. He joined up, but deserted at the first opportunity, got back to Blighty, joined my old mob – the Royal Signals. They took him on as a Phantom operator, promoted him captain, posted him to "A" Force on account of his fluent Italian. They dropped him in here as liaison officer with the Resistance.'

'What I want to know,' Caine said, 'is who snitched on Butterfield's drop, I mean –'

'*Shhh!*' Wallace hissed.

Low voices were approaching the tent. A moment later, Savarin slipped into the candle-light, his long face grave. 'We have to talk,' he said.

35

They found Emilia sitting with Butterfield on the ground by a moribund fire. They were deep in conversation: Caine wondered if she'd told him about Ettore and the *hypnotic messenger* stuff. Most of the partisans had gone: four or five men with weapons were walking prowler-guard. The night was as cloudy as the afternoon had been, with washed-out stars hanging above the highest branches, lodged like flakes of dirty ice on seams of lambent grey. Butterfield wore a clean dressing: he looked comfortable, seated primly, nursing his stomach, with a cigarette in his mouth and a mug of wine in his hand. Emilia poked at the embers, turned them over with a twig.

They settled around the fire with their weapons on their knees: Savarin sat bolt upright, peered at each of them in turn as if trying to make out their features in the darkness. Emilia went down on her hands and knees: Caine couldn't help glancing at her – the willowy figure, the gracious curve of her backside and back, the way her wayward tresses fell forward, shrouding her features. She smoothed her hair away from her face, blew into the fire, coaxed up a flame. She added some dry tinder, fanned it with a piece of stiff cardboard: the twigs blazed up, illuminated their faces with a terracotta glow.

Savarin lit a cigarette, inhaled deeply. He blew out smoke in a long stream, glanced at Caine. 'I appreciate that you pushed the boat out to liberate the countess and your comrades, Captain Caine,' he said. 'What you don't understand is that, whenever something like this happens, there are repercussions: the Krauts execute civilians, or they launch another comb-out for partisans. That's why we have a policy that all actions against them in this area are coordinated through us.'

Caine squinted at him. 'I'll bear it in mind next time.'

Wallace tittered: Savarin ignored them both, took another long draw on his cigarette. 'Your assault on the villa, for instance, was so reckless as to be virtually suicidal. From what the countess has told me, you only got away by the skin of your teeth. We could have helped you. Why did you run away from my people at the ambush?'

Caine felt a sudden tightness in his throat. 'I was in the crossfire. I only had a split second, and I decided not to chance it. I had a mission to carry out – a mission given to me in Jesi, by Major Butterfield here.' He peeked at Butterfield. 'Isn't that correct, Major?'

Butterfield looked up as if startled: his dewlaps quivered. 'Er yes, I suppose it is.' He shot a shifty glance at Savarin. 'I asked Captain Caine to complete the mission my crew and I had failed to carry out. As I've told you, the idea was to snatch the countess from the Villa

Montefalcone and locate the *Codex Aesinias*. I didn't ask Caine to liberate these other two men, but I imagine that was a spontaneous act –'

'– that might easily have brought the Krauts down on us,' Savarin grated.

'*Brought the Krauts down on us?*' Wallace repeated venomously. He leaned forward, blinked with righteous anger. 'That's a good one, that is. If you'd of sent us a warning, we wouldn't of *been* prisoners in the first place, would we? We'd 'ave known to steer clear of the camp, wouldn't we?'

'That's right,' Trubman weighed in. 'And why did you send us to the far ends of the earth to get water? We could have got it much nearer, see.'

'Yeah, an' if yer knew Jerry were comin',' Wallace boomed, 'why did yer ditch the major? Your boys boost 'im from Fritz one day, you drop 'im the next? It don't make sense.'

Savarin's face was owlish, flushed red ochre in the firelight: he stubbed his cigarette out unfinished. 'I had no time to send you a warning,' he said. 'We only got the tip-off minutes ahead of the Krauts. I didn't send you to the nearer place because it wasn't secure, that's all. It's close to the road and the first place the Krauts would look for tracks.' He paused, turned back to Butterfield. 'As for you, Major, I must apologize. You were barely conscious, and we had to split up quickly. I thought someone else had taken care of you, and they thought I had. I'm sorry: it was an oversight.'

Butterfield licked his bruised lips. 'A rather serious oversight, Captain: it could have proved fatal for me.' He waved his hand feebly at Wallace and Trubman. 'For these men too. You're aware that the Hun are in the habit of executing captured SAS personnel?'

Savarin made a sound in his throat. 'Come now, Major, surely you're not persisting with that claim? Granted, they may have used it as a ruse to put pressure on you, but it's against the Geneva Convention to execute prisoners of war.'

'You wanna go take a shufti in the forest about twelve klicks due east of 'ere,' Wallace told him scathingly. 'Five shaller graves, marked with the letter "B", carved in a tree. You know, *five*? Like the number of men in the major's team, who was carted off with us from Jesi?'

'We was *there*, see,' Trubman added. 'I *saw* the Krauts slaughter Howard and the others with my own eyes. I told you: you didn't believe it.'

'Where'd you think we come from, then?' Wallace chortled. 'Fell off a flamin' moonbeam?'

Savarin glanced at Emilia. 'Is this true, Countess? About the graves, I mean. Did you see them?'

She nodded. 'Five graves, just like the man said. We didn't have time to look at them all – the Cabbage-Heads were after us – but these guys identified one corpse as a man who'd been with them in the Jesi camp – a Sergeant Cameron, wasn't it?'

'It was Bob Cameron all right,' Wallace said.

'Poor Bob, ' Butterfield moaned. 'A very good man.'

Savarin retained his composure. 'I'll have it checked,' he said, 'but there must be some other explanation. The Krauts don't just bump off POWs.'

'Like hell they don't,' Wallace swore.

'*All right!*' Savarin stuck his lip out: he sounded slightly rattled now. 'This doesn't excuse the fact that Caine was wearing Nazi uniform when he ran away from the ambush.' He fixed Butterfield with an accusing glare, his eyes were hot needles. 'Didn't you call Caine a traitor, Major? Didn't you tell me he'd gone over to the Krauts? Even swore an oath to the Führer, you said . . .'

'Well, maybe I . . . was a little hasty, old boy,' Butterfield stammered. 'I was half delirious, you see: didn't quite click what was going on. Being escorted to your own execution can do that to you. I mean, yes, Caine was wearing Nazi get-up, and he was acting as a trustee, like that swine Amray. When I first saw him in Waffen-SS togs, I'll admit I was horrified: even at the ford, there, I was too shaken to click that he'd just liberated me by killing half-a-dozen Krauts. No, I'm sure he was faking it. I'd asked him to liberate the countess *if he managed to escape*. I assume it was the only ploy he could think of to get out of the place. He knew or guessed that the Hun intended to take me off somewhere, and saw his opportunity. He was only doing what I'd asked him to do: and, after all, it *worked*.'

Savarin narrowed his eyes at Caine. 'Is that the case,

Captain? You pretended to desert to the Krauts in order to free the major and carry out your mission?'

Once again, Caine tried to remember how he'd come to put on that uniform. He couldn't recall having agreed to do so, not even as a ruse. He wasn't certain, though: the easiest course was to agree with Savarin. 'That's about the size of it,' he said.

Savarin heard his hesitation. 'The point is that we'll never know, will we?' Maybe it was a deliberate ploy to escape. Or maybe it was a convenience, and when you found yourself on the receiving end of a successful partisan attack, you decided it would be more convenient to change sides again.'

'This is dumb, Savarin,' Emilia chirped up. 'Captain Caine put his life on the line for me. He also rescued the major and these two guys. How are those the actions of a traitor?'

'*Yeah*,' Wallace stormed in. 'Tom Caine 'ere 'as been decorated for bravery: DCM *and* DSO. Promoted from the ranks *twice*. You think a bloke . . . I mean, an officer . . . like that, would betray his country?'

'I don't know why we're even wasting time on it,' Emilia said. 'Ettore is being transferred from Orsini to Jesi tomorrow. It's our only chance to get him out. Otherwise Stengel will have him shot.'

'We need the boy to find the Codex,' Butterfield added. 'That's a major priority. Don't forget, five of our men have already died for it.' For almost the first time,

Butterfield seemed animated. 'It would be an insult to their memory not to carry out the mission.'

'That's right, Major,' Caine agreed. 'We need to plan an ambush on that convoy. Do we know what time they're leaving Orsini?'

'Stengel said in the morning,' Emilia replied.

'That doesn't give us much time to get things organized. How many partisans can you spare us, Captain?'

Savarin shook his head. 'I can't help you.'

'*What?*' Emilia sounded incredulous. 'But it's not just Ettore. There may be other partisans on that convoy. *Your* men. Are you telling us that you won't lift a finger to save them? They're going to be *executed*, for God's sake.'

Savarin tilted his head to one side. 'My sources say that all the others have been taken away, probably executed. As for Ettore, I regret it very much, but the Krauts are already stirred up by the escape of you SAS-men and the attack on the convoy the other day. Next time, they'll shoot the entire male population of Orsini. In any case, can you imagine how well guarded that convoy will be, after what happened on Thursday? We don't have the capacity to take on a target like that. Thirdly, I can't commit the partisans to assist an operation at the behest of an officer whose loyalty is suspect. Whatever you say, Caine, we can't be certain of your motives, or what you would have done, for instance, if the ambush had failed. On your own admission, you put on SS uniform, agreed to join the Krauts, swore an oath of allegience to Hitler. Those are acts of treason, and you know it. If this were a conventional unit, you'd be court-martialled.'

'But the Codex?' Butterfield complained. 'How are we going to find it without the boy?'

'That's not my responsibility. I agreed only to coordinate your drop and –'

'Which somebody bubbled to the Krauts,' Wallace chimed in.

'We don't know how they knew,' Savarin said: a note of protest had crept into his voice. 'The Germans have excellent signals counter-intelligence: they may have picked it up in a transmission.' He stood up suddenly, slung his rifle over his shoulder. 'I'm sorry about your brother, Countess, I really am. But we have to weigh his life against our chances of success, and against the lives of dozens of civilians. In war, you have to make hard decisions, and this is mine. I'm not going to take disciplinary action against you, Captain Caine, but I advise Major Butterfield to report the matter to your command when you get back.'

Caine rose to his feet, faced him. 'I'm going to snatch Ettore *and* find the Codex. If you're not with us, we'll do it without you.'

Wallace stood, drew himself up to full height beside Caine, an enormous, bear-shaped block of mahogany shadow. 'We're SAS, mate,' he said. 'Who needs you, anyway?'

36

Caine awoke, knew at once that his inbuilt alarm had kicked in: stealthy footsteps were approaching from the outside. He put his right hand on the Schmeisser under his blanket: with his left he eased Cesare's knife out of his waistband. Two sets of footsteps, he thought: light – *women*? *Emilia?* Wallace and Trubman were snoring peacefully: Caine wondered if he should wake them, decided to wait. He got up silently, glad he still had his boots on. He slung the SMG, swapped the knife into his right hand, positioned himself next to the tent flap just as a thin figure pushed through. He seized the intruder's neck in the crook of his elbow, lodged the tip of his blade against the scrawny spine, heard a suppressed squawk, felt a wiry, strong hand clutch at him, felt nails dig into his skin. '*Tom*,' a woman's voice whispered. '*Lay off him, for God's sake*.' Emilia stood poised in the entrance, bleached teeth and eyeballs in a dark-swathed face. 'It's Furetto. He wants to talk to you.'

Caine let go, dekkoed the almost girlishly slender form of the young partisan he'd shaken hands with when Savarin had first confronted them – the boy who'd told him he needed to talk. He hadn't given it much thought at the time: in fact, he'd forgotten about it. The lad hovered in front of him, panting slightly, clutching his shotgun under his arm: his apologetic face was faintly illuminated by the starlight through the open flap. He put a finger to his lips, bent forward, almost touching Caine's head with his own. 'Savarin plan to take you prisoner. You and your men must go.'

This is a trap, Caine thought. He shot a questioning glance at Emilia. 'Trust him, Tom,' she said. 'We have to get out while there's still time.'

''Ere, what's this?' Wallace was already on his knees with an SMG in his hands: Trubman surfaced bleary-eyed from under his blanket, dug for his glasses.

Caine scanned Furetto's face again, came to a decision.

'We're moving out,' he whispered: he glanced around at Emilia. 'What about Butterfield?'

'He's not coming,' she said. 'Doesn't feel up to it.'

Furetto covered them with his shotgun as they filtered out, crouched outside the tent, watched for prowler-guards. A minute later they were following him through the woods behind the camp, trawling through dense underbrush at a snail's pace, placing their feet carefully to avoid rustling branches and snapping twigs. The night-clouds had passed: the moon was up like a white hole in the cosmos, spilling deep-blue milk-light through the trees, dressing the tangled foliage in silver draperies. Furetto led them to an animal-track, a narrow piste that wove through the trees, meandered around dense groves and deep thickets.

The track led them to a small clearing where jagged rocks pressed like dark teeth out of a lawn of moss and ankle-high grass. Furetto called a halt: Caine signalled Wallace and Trubman to clear the area. They split up, circled the woods, gave the all-clear. They sat together around the mossy stones. Furetto laid his shotgun in the grass, folded his insect limbs: his face was a dim indigo glow in the darkness. 'Savarin don't want you to ambush that convoy,' he said. 'He want to stop you, take you prisoner.'

Caine squinted at him in the darkness: when they'd first met, Furetto had seemed like an adolescent boy: now Caine had the impression of a maturity and a decisiveness that belied his youthful appearance.

'You mean Savarin's a Jerry stool pigeon?' he said.

Furetto wagged his slender head. 'He play his own game: he don't like parachutists: he think you cause trouble for *Giappisti* – partisans.'

'Then why did he order an ambush on Butterfield's convoy?' Caine objected.

'He don't order it. Is me.'

'You? But . . . who *are* you?'

'My name is Bruno Abruzzi: I am nineteen years old. I am *not* youngest in the band, like Savarin say. Ettore is much younger than me. Is me who bring news of your convoy to *Giappisti*. Savarin refuse to attack: he say it is *troppo pericoloso* . . . how you say in *Inglezi* . . . ?'

'Too dangerous,' Emilia said.

'Yes, too dangerous. So we set up ambush without

him. After, when we bring the fat major back, Savarin say is all right, but the next day the Krauts come for our camp. How they know where it is, huh? Savarin leave fat major for Cabbage-Heads to find: he make sure these men –' he nodded at Wallace and Trubman – 'are far away from camp so, when they get back, the *tedeschi* take them. This way, he is finish with parachutists. He don't expect you, Captain. He don't expect you to rescue them: he don't expect *la contessa*. Now he afraid you cause more trouble if you attack convoy from Orsini.'

'But the convoy's carrying Ettore,' Emilia argued. 'If we don't stop that convoy, he'll be killed.'

Furetto sighed. 'That's what we say, but he say, no, is too dangerous. Convoy is too heavy guarded. We be killed or captured.'

'All right,' Caine said, 'but why stop *us*? We've plenty of experience with this kind of stunt.'

'Savarin say it bring Krauts down on civilians. He say that even if attack don't work, they shoot many people in Orsini.'

He paused, regarded Caine with his soft doe eyes. 'He say you cannot be trusted, Captain. You run from our attack in uniform of Krauts: you betray your own side. I say, no, you are pretend to join them, so you find chance to escape: you make yourself a trustee, like Lucia –'

'*Lucia?*' Caine gasped. 'I met a girl called Lucia in Jesi – a trustee.'

'My sister,' the boy told him: he puffed out his sparrow chest and Caine heard pride in his voice. 'I know what they do to her in Jesi, but she is brave. She pretend to help them, and find out the *informazione* for us. She pass it to me by a man who bring meat to the camp. I say you are no more traitor than *mia sorella*: you are pretend, like her.'

Caine started to speak: the memory of Lucia's naked body in bed in Amray's room stopped him. *You can do what you like with her, old man.* But he hadn't, had he? He thought of Cesare, who had helped him: that man must be Furetto's father. There wasn't time to go into it, though: the boy's revelations about Savarin opened up a whole new Pandora's box . . . if they were true, of course. But he'd nursed suspicions about Savarin from the time Emilia had told him that only she and the 'A' Force man had known about Butterfield's drop. That drop had been compromised, had resulted ultimately in the killing of five SAS-men. If Savarin had informed the Jerries, it meant he was responsible for those deaths. That could explain why he'd professed not to believe that Wallace and Trubman had escaped from an execution, or even that there was such a thing as special handling.

'I knew it,' Wallace grumped. 'That sod's as bent as a bucket of frogs.'

'What about Butterfield?' Trubman asked. 'If Savarin tried to get rid of him once, he'll try it again.'

'I say we march right back there,' Wallace declared, 'snatch Butterfield and scrag that slimy, two-faced bastard.'

'The major, he safe for now,' Furetto said. '*Ho paura* . . . I am afraid . . . *solamente* that the Krauts find out you attack Orsini convoy.'

'You mean Savarin'll dob us in to the enemy?' Wallace demanded.

'*Chi sa?*' Furetto brought his watch up to his eyes. 'Is almost five thirty. The convoy leave Orsini at eight thirty. It give us only three hours.'

'Forget it, boys.' Trubman sniggered. 'We can't march it in that time. We may be SAS, but we aren't supermen.'

'You don't march,' Furetto said. 'Is car hidden in forest. Very good car – Alfa Romeo. I have keys. We take her.'

'Good,' Caine nodded. 'You're coming with us then?'

The boy picked up his shotgun, raised his thin chest again. 'Why not? I am good fighter.'

'All right, but can't you get a few more partisans to join us?'

The youth shook his head. 'They afraid they get blame if Cabbage-Heads kill civilians. Also many think ambush is not possible. But Ettore is my friend: I go with you. If we go now, we get to Orsini before full light.'

He broke off, spoke to Emilia in Italian. The countess

scoffed suddenly, made a curt answer, stared at Caine with wide eyes. 'He had the cheek to tell me I ought to stay here because I'm a girl.'

'And what did you tell him?'

'I said Ettore might be his friend, but he's *my* brother: I don't care what happens, I'm not missing this.'

37

Jesi, Le Marche, Italy
10 October 1943

At sunset, Karl Grolsch met *Reichsgeschäftsführer* Wolfram Stengel at a café in Jesi. They sat at a table outside: it was risky, but this wasn't a time for displaying a lack of confidence. In any case, Grolsch had made sure that the square was well seeded with guards from his Sipo-SD. He couldn't help grinning when he stood up to greet the Ahnenerbe chief – Stengel looked in a worse state than himself: he wore a dressing on his head and his bearded face was speckled with lacerations from flying shrapnel flakes: his eyes were bloodshot: he moved painfully from the severe bruising on his arms and legs.

Grolsch felt as bad as Stengel looked: his right arm in a sling, a bandage round his shoulder, his movements clumsy and restricted. He'd been damn' lucky, he thought: one of the partisans' bullets had missed, the other had glanced off his collar-bone. *Probably because it was a woman. Women can't shoot straight.* Had it been an inch or two lower, it would have shattered his heart. His narrow escape, when almost all the other troops in the escort-party had been slaughtered, was a near-miracle: ever since, he'd been experiencing bursts of euphoria.

Of course, on another level, he was exasperated that the partisans had managed to stage such an elaborate decoy and that he'd been stupid enough to fall for it. He felt bad about the men he'd lost: he was incensed that Amray had been killed and that Caine and Butterfield had got away. What with that, and the escape of the two other SAS-men – Fishface and the Giant – the other day, things were getting out of hand. Confidence that Germany would win the war was *de rigueur* amongst SS officers: any converse suggestion amounted to treason. Grolsch couldn't help asking himself, though, what would happen if they didn't win. *I'm a soldier carrying out orders, like any other, but the enemy won't see it that way. If we lose the war and those witnesses are still around, I could be executed as a war-criminal.*

Still, it might have been worse, and he was grateful to God that he'd survived. Yes, he had to admit it: this was the closest he'd come to death, and in the two days since the ambush – somewhat to his own dismay – he'd felt a faint stirring of long-forgotten religious feelings. *Someone up there is looking after me, and I don't mean Adolf Hitler.*

The café stood at one corner of the cobblestone square, blocked in on all sides by the town-houses the Italians called *palazzi* – austere façades, balconies with wrought-iron railings, shuttered windows. The square was coddled in long shadows: the hard nickel sky above was rolling itself up in swells of dove-grey surf, streaked with strawberry ripples.

The waiter, a pot-bellied man in a soiled white shirt with grease-slicked hair and blue jowls, brought them espresso and schnapps. Stengel drank his schnapps in a gulp, let out a sigh. His codfish eyes were haunted, Grolsch thought: a muscle in his pock-marked face jiggered. Grolsch sat straight-backed, lifted his glass with his good hand, took a tentative sip. 'I'm glad to see you up and about, *Reichsgeschäftsführer*,' he said. 'I heard they had confined you to the hospital-wing.'

'I was very fortunate: the countess didn't hit me very hard with the bottle, and when Caine pushed me down the stairs, I fell behind the stairwell: the main blast went the other way. Four men dead: the whole squad wounded.'

'So I understand.'

'Caine killed seven men in his assault on the villa. I underestimated these SAS people: they are utterly ruthless. That is why we must be ruthless in dealing with them. I regret that I have wasted two days in hospital when I could have been directing the search for the Falcone girl and that British traitor.'

The word *traitor* brought a smile to Grolsch's lips. He felt affronted, too, though: hunting escapees was a Sipo-SD job – his responsibility, not Stengel's.

Stengel lifted his empty glass stiffly to the waiter. '*Mi da la bottiglia*,' he said. The pot-bellied man scurried out with the bottle on a tray, topped up Stengel's glass, left the bottle on the table. Stengel raised the glass. '*Heil Hitler!*' he said.

He drank half the schnapps, set the glass down: his eyes were shifty. 'You used to be a priest, eh, *Sturmbannführer*?'

Grolsch wondered what was coming. 'As I have told you, sir. I suppose you could say I'm *unfrocked*.' He chuckled: Stengel's face darkened.

'Did you ever have dealings with demons?'

'*Demons?*' Grolsch's mouth crinkled. 'Not personally, no. Not a big interest in demons in the church these days. There's an exorcism rite, of course, but it's rarely used. Why do you ask?'

Stengel seized his glass, drank down the rest of the schnapps. He slammed the glass back on the table, filled it from the bottle. Grolsch noticed that his hand was shaking. He threw it back in a single swallow.

'I see shadows,' he said in a rush. 'I see faces behind me when I look in the mirror. I hear footsteps: I see eyes watching me. I hear voices in the night.'

Grolsch shook his head. 'That's strain, *Reichsgeschäftsführer*. You've been wounded: I imagine you're also under considerable pressure from Herr Himmler to find the Codex.'

Stengel filled his glass again, motioned the bottle at Grolsch, who shook his head. He studied the clear liquid. 'Do you know what a Jew-Bolshevik commisar is, *Sturmbannführer*?'

'Not exactly, no.'

'A Jew-Bolshevik commissar is a Soviet Yid Communist Party official. We rounded up hundreds of them during the invasion of Russia. They've been in prison-camps in Germany ever since.'

'I see.'

'One hundred and five of them are now dead specimens in the Anatomical Institute of Strasbourg. *One hundred and five.* How do you suppose they got there?'

Grolsch shot Stengel a hard glance. 'I have no idea. It's not my business, is it, sir?'

'Perhaps not, but that is what they look like.'

'Who?'

'The demons. They look like Jew-Bolshevik commissars.'

Grolsch finished his schnapps, put his glass down. He picked up the doll-sized coffee cup, grasped the tiny handle awkwardly between finger and thumb. 'Sir, you've been hit on the head with a bottle, wounded in a grenade-attack, which you were fortunate enough to survive.' He nodded at his arm-sling. 'I was lucky, too, but I know it's a shock to the system. My head hasn't been right since the ambush. You discharged yourself too early, perhaps?'

Stengel ignored the comment. 'Do you know that *what is sought lies in a room with no doors or windows*?'

Grolsch swallowed: Stengel seemed determined to wander beyond the limits of the rational.

'How could anything be found in a room with no

doors or windows?' he said. 'What *is* it that's sought anyway?'

'It was something the countess said when I . . . interrogated . . . her. At first I thought it was nonsense, but now I'm not so sure. What is sought is the Codex: this phrase is the key to its hiding place. If I could find the girl, I could discover what the rest means, but I've wasted too much time. Her trail will be cold by now.'

Stengel hadn't heard the latest reports, Grolsch realized: he wasn't going to be pleased to hear about the casualties they'd sustained. He paused to finish his coffee, set the cup back carefully on its miniature saucer. His shoulder was troubling him: even raising and lowering a doll's-house cup with his left hand was painful.

'There have been several contacts with the partisans in the past couple of days,' he said. 'My men found their camp following a tip-off. Unfortunately, they had skipped only minutes before we arrived.'

Stengel looked annoyed. 'Why didn't your men pursue them?'

'It was a small squad. The i/c left six men at the camp, went back with the rest for reinforcements and a tracker-dog. While he was away there was some sort of counter-attack: all six men were found dead at a ford not far from the camp. The other squad followed their trail with the dog, caught up with a party near the place where we executed the saboteurs. The partisans managed to kill the dog and elude pursuit, *but* –'

Stengel looked disgusted. 'You mean they let them get *away*?'

'*But*,' Grolsch insisted, 'there was a girl with them, my men were certain of that – slim, long dark hair.'

'That covers half the *Fräulein* in Italy.'

'Perhaps, *Reichsgeschäftsführer*, but I'd say that the countess is still in the locality, with the partisans. I'd hazard a guess that she won't leave without her brother.'

A look of interest came over Stengel's face. 'The brother is still locked up in Orsini, no?'

'Yes, but he's due to be transferred here tomorrow: the convoy leaves Orsini at 0830 hours.'

Stengel leaned forward. 'Why is this important?'

'Because I have just received information that the partisans are planning to attack that convoy. If we want to find your countess, and my escaped SAS-men, I suggest we should be ready for them.'

38

Near Montefalcone, Le Marche, Italy
11 October 1943

The car had been run off the road into a thicket and camouflaged with leaves and branches, among several other vehicles belonging to the partisans. She was certainly an Alfa Romeo – a black 1938 Pescara, low, sleek, powerful. Caine had done some work on this model before the war, knew she had a 2300cc engine, a double carburettor and was capable of ninety miles an hour. A tribute to Italian engineering, he thought: it seemed almost a pity to waste her on a military stunt. The bodywork was already battered in places: Furetto told him that the engine had been kept carefully tuned. Caine checked tyres and petrol, had a shufti under the bonnet: the motor was clean and in perfect order. Before they got in, Furetto showed them what was in the boot: blankets, bottles of water, boxes of spare 9mm ammunition, some packets of .303 rifle rounds, spare weapons, including a Breda M37 light machine-gun, and a box of Mills grenades. 'Wot, no mortar?' Wallace grumped.

The big man dipped a hand like a shovel-blade into the boot, picked up the Breda, shucked the mag, cocked the works: it was similar to the Bren, but a tad lighter, fitted with a vertical magazine. 'Now this is my kind of pea-shooter,' he growled.

'Watch it,' Trubman told him. 'Those Bredas have a slow rate of fire.'

'All the more accurate then, *innit*?'

'Yep, but they're prone to jamming, see.'

'I'll take me chances, mate.'

Furetto placed his shotgun in the boot, selected a Beretta sub-machine gun – a 9mm weapon with a slim magazine and a carved wooden stock. 'Is better for job,' he told them. 'Better than Schmeisser. Even Krauts like it.'

Before they got in, Caine broke open the box of grenades, doled out a brace of No. 38s to each of them. 'Make sure you arm 'em,' he told the others. 'Or it'll spoil the effect.'

Furetto threw the pile of blankets into the back seat of the car. '*Allora, andiamo!*' he said.

Caine drove: Furetto sat in the passenger seat to direct him. The others crammed into the back, Wallace and Trubman on the sides, Emilia in the middle. The Alfa Romeo was right-hand drive, but Caine had driven plenty of Itie vehicles in the desert: to start with he toddled her along at snail's pace, bumping along a road that was no more than a cart-track, with parallel grooves and a ridge running dead centre. It was still dark: the limbs of the forest reared like vast undersea reefs on either side, slashed through above by a delta of deep midnight blue, strewn with stars like tarnished silver studs.

When they came to the main Jesi road Caine switched on the headlights: if the Krauts clocked them driving without, it would look suspicious. He changed down, pushed the speed up, kept the beams dipped, followed the green and bronze line of the verge with its thick scattering of russet-hued leaves. Furetto pointed out the turn-off that led to the Villa Montefalcone and, further on, the place where the partisans had staged the ambush. The boy opened the window, leaned out, scanned the area keenly. It looked quite different in darkness: of the overturned cart and the dead horse there was no trace, but Caine clocked the debris of the burnt-out motorcycle-combo strewn along the side of the road.

Furetto wound up his window. 'You know horse and cart is my idea,' he told Caine proudly. 'Is good trick, no?'

'Original,' Caine agreed. He shot a sideways glance at the boy. 'How did a boy like you get mixed up with the partisans?'

'I am not boy,' Furetto bristled. 'I look . . . *giovane* . . . but I am university student. I study law at University of Bologna. My father is poor – a peasant: he save money to help me go there. When I am student, my professor, Stefano Minotti, is socialist. I join socialist party, write articles for Stefano's newspaper against Mussolini and *Fascisti*. I don't use my name – I sign only *Furetto*. Then one day *squadristi* – Blackshirts – they visit Stefano. *Who is Furetto?* they say. *Furetto is furry animal, very fierce*, he tell them. *Is small but have big teeth*. They don't like. *What is his real name?* they say. Stefano don't tell them, so they beat him bad. They leave him in pool of blood, but he is OK: he run away from Bologna. Before, though, he tell me to run, too. I come back to Le Marche, work as school-teacher in Ancona. When they kick out Mussolini, I want to join *Giappisti*, but they say I am not strong. *I am strong and clever*, I tell them, *I prove it*. I plan for them bomb operation at hotel in Ancona: three Krauts killed. They trust me after that.'

'Are all the partisans socialists?' Caine asked.

Furetto shrugged beanpole shoulders. '*Giappisti* are everything: socialist, Marxist, Christian – even Fascist. Is fighting between partisan bands, fighting against Krauts, fighting against fascist militia, fighting among families, fighting everyone against everyone. *Mamma mia!* Italy is in a big mess.'

Within minutes they were descending from the plateau on a series of hairpins: Caine switched to full beam: tree-trunks sprang out at him in galleries of slim grey pillars, like a breakwater, holding back the wild oceanic tide of the forest. At the foot of the pass, Caine clocked the signpost to the villa he remembered from his journey out. He changed gear, was about to press down on the gas when a red light bloomed dimly out of the darkness ahead. He eased off the accelerator. 'What the hell's that?' he asked.

Furetto swore in Italian. 'Is Kraut checkpoint. They use red light. Is new – not here before.'

'Just what we didn't need,' Caine said grimly. 'Is there any way we can turn off?'

'No other road here.'

'Too late, anyway,' Trubman chimed in from the back seat. 'They'll already've clocked our headlights. If we turn off, they'll be on us like flies on cowturds.'

'Crash through, skipper,' Wallace said. 'We'll draw fire, but we've got a good chance.'

'Krauts use oildrums filled with concrete for checkpoints,' Furetto said. 'No way to crash through.'

'We're stuck then, boys,' Trubman said.

'We ain't stuck while I've got this here Breda,' Wallace rumbled.

Caine took a deep breath. 'We either dump the car and hoof it,' he said, 'or we fight it out. Which is it going to be?'

'Don't ask,' Wallace gurned. 'We're SAS, ain't we?'

'If we have a contact, the Krauts'll be alerted all the way to Ancona,' said Trubman. 'It'll be like driving up a blind alley with no exit, see.'

Wallace snorted. 'Oo dares wins, mate, *innit*? Stirlin' an' Mayne once drove right into Benghazi, lay up in a derelict house for a whole day under the noses of the Hun. *And* they got away with it.'

'This isn't Libya, boy: you can't vanish into the desert here.'

'Yeah, an' this ain't Benghazi, it's just a checkpoint.'

'I think we should risk it,' Emilia cut in. 'Or we'll never make Ettore's convoy.'

'All right,' Caine said. 'We're going for it. Keep those weapons out of sight.' He checked that his Schmeisser was across his knees, reached down, slipped the safety catch. He glanced at Furetto, saw that the boy was composed and ready, both hands on the Beretta SMG in his lap. 'Don't anybody get out of the car unless I say so,' he said. 'If it comes to a firefight, take your own arcs: don't be shooting over anyone's shoulder. And if I yell *run*, I want everyone out of the car like greased lightning: OK?'

The checkpoint consisted of a 3-ton lorry and a *Kubelwagen*, plus a gaggle of Jerries hovering like wraiths around two oildrums in the road. A red lamp was set on top of one the drums: both German vehicles were on their side of the barrier, the car on the right, the truck on the left. Caine slowed down as he approached, flipped to sidelights. He pulled up a good fifteen yards from the oildrums, waited for the enemy to approach them.

A Kraut flashed a torch at the car, started walking towards them. Caine scanned the area for armaments or hidden sentries, clocked a wireless antenna rising like a whip from the back of the lorry. *That'll have to go.*

'Pity we don't have that night-sight we had on *Sandhog*, eh?' Trubman whispered.

'Nowt wrong with the Mark 1 SAS eyeball,' Wallace scoffed. He peered over Furetto's shoulder. 'There, skipper, to yer right: there's a machine-gun mounted on the *Kubelwagen* – M42, I reckon. One gunner on stag.'

Caine strained to see it: he could just about make out the protruding muzzle of the Spandau in the greyness – if it *was* a Spandau: Fred Wallace was as keen-eyed as a kite, but Caine found it hard to believe that even he could tell the gun's make at this distance.

He watched the Jerry mooch towards them: he was fully in the sidelights now – a bony soldier with a yellow face, a black gash for a mouth, dark smudges for eyes. He moved loosely, his Schmeisser slung under-arm in the easy-access position, a torch in his left hand. As he approached, Caine saw two more figures detach themselves from the shadows, move in their direction.

'Here comes backup,' he said, 'and there're another two Krauts at the barrier. Furetto, you kill that Spandau – it's on your side.'

'*Si, si, va bene.*'

'Fred, you do the lorry: there's a wireless in there.'

'Got it, mate.'

'Taffy, loft a grenade at the *Kubelwagen*. We'll deal with the other Krauts between us.'

'Right you are, skipper.'

'Wait till I scrag Mr Nosey Parker, though.'

Caine watched the Jerry's torch-beam flit as he inspected the car, no doubt taking in its quality, wondering at its battered and muddied chassis. Caine began to wind his window down. 'He'll come right, to me,' he murmured. 'Wind your windows down: make sure those grenades are handy.'

'Oh *shite*,' Wallace groused. 'I forgot to arm 'em.'

'You great turnip,' Trubman smirked. 'Here, have one of mine.'

The beam of the Jerry's torch fell directly on Caine's face: he blinked. *That's my night-vision gone.* The Jerry had paused at the bonnet: he was probing the car's interior with the torch-beam: a cold slug slithered down Caine's spine. The Jerry cut the light, sidled towards the open window. Caine braced his feet, pressed his back tight against the seat: he got a glimpse of a headless grey-blue torso, a glint of metal. Even before Fritz bent down to look inside, Caine's hand was on his weapon. He saw the yellow face framed in the window, took in knotted brows, skinned-grape eyes, teeth like a gobful of blue light, heard the words. '*Wo gehst du hin?*', lifted the Schmeisser, punched two rounds point-blank into the Kraut's mouth.

The crash creased Caine's eardrums: the Jerry's face swelled out of shape, split apart like a mashed water-melon, burst into a mush of wet red tissue and curlicues of shattered teeth. The soldier slumped backwards: gore snaked in long threads from a mouth like a rad-dled red tunnel, splatted Caine's face.

'*Go. Go. Go!*' Furetto bawled.

Caine hit the accelerator: the car lurched forward, took them abreast of the two Jerry vehicles. Furetto leaned out of his window, boosted a long burst at the

Kubelwagen: Caine felt the deep-bellied *crompa-crompa-cromp* of the Beretta, clocked a blag of fire like a blunt orange bludgeon, felt the tearing squeal of metal as the rounds chomped the wagon's chassis, saw the ghost of the Kraut gunner jig like a dancing puppet. They were almost past the vehicle when Trubman lobbed his grenade: Caine heard the fuse pop, heard the pause, heard the bomb rip out in a spray of shrapnel, felt the air bend, traileyed the gorgeous fireball of flame and smoke that wrapped the *Kubelwagen* like a gush of molten lava, felt the gut-churning *kaaathwompppp* as the jeep's tank blew.

On the left, Wallace had hurled his grenade at almost the same instant. The detonation kicked in as a delayed backslam, just as the other dampened itself out: *baaaaawwuuummmpppphhhh*. Caine felt the car rock on her springs, felt the blast whack his chest like a heavy board, felt a hot vacuum suck at his lungs: he shuftied the mirror, saw a monstrous mountain of fire leap into the night, open out like a vast apricot-coloured flower, snap back with the spastic jerk of cramped red-black fingers.

The car was plunging towards the oildrums in a headlong rush: Caine saw the two trailing Krauts turn and run: saw the other pair at the barrier crouch down in firing positions, saw sharp cones of fire sprout from their weapons, heard rounds rack and tweeter, scorch air, piffle dust, prong hub-caps. Caine's fingers closed on the stock of his Schmeisser: before he could raise it, big Wallace had laid the muzzle of his Breda across the back of his seat, pulled iron: a single shot shattered the windscreen, sent glass chips riffling. Night air slapped Caine's face: Wallace triggered a long spread *chacka-chacka-chacka-chack*: Caine saw the tracer weave a basket of light in front of him, saw the two Jerries crouching by the oildrums buckle and roll, grope air, twist and fly. His ears had gone numb: his eyes were watering from glass-flecks and gun-gas: the car swerved, tyres shrieked. Caine righted her, homed in on the oildrums, saw the two Kraut runners proned out in the shadows on the verge. He gripped the steering wheel with his right hand, lifted his SMG with his left, let fly through the broken windscreen at full arm-extension, heard the mechanism crank like a rotor, heard rounds blister air, *tack-tack-tack-tack*.

He didn't have time to see if his shots struck home: the barrier was only feet away. He stabbed hard on the brakes, felt the tyres quiver, felt the car slew, come to rest left side on to the oil barrels.

'*Shift those drums, Fred!*' he yodelled: his voice sounded muffled and distant to his own ears.

The big man was already out of the door, taking seven-league strides to the barrier: Caine saw his great lateen-rig shoulders strain against the weight of the first drum, saw him lift it, toss it aside like a skittle. The giant had turned towards the second when a Kraut came pounding out of the darkness, a lump of a man, almost as big as Wallace himself, hefting a pistol so small it looked comical in his plate-sized mitt. It might have been, if he hadn't fired point-blank at Wallace's wild-fuzzed capstone of a head. The bullet took the top off the big gunner's left ear. Wallace roared, but his Schmeisser was already braced. *Bommfff.* One shot: the round went in at the base of the Jerry's nose, made his face crumple inwards like a burst balloon. As he went down, thrashing like a sperm-whale, Wallace shot him in the head. Then, with blood from his damaged ear soaking his tattered peasant's shirt, he heaved the other oildrum out of the way: the car was already moving when he hopped into the back.

39

Caine drove fast, followed a pale ribbon of road that twisted through relict copses of forest, climbed low hill-crests, descended through straight stretches along tangled hedgerows, past vineyards and fields. When he could no longer see the fires behind him, he pulled up in a gateway among hedges and pencil-cedars.

'Five minutes,' he said. 'Get a dressing on that ear, Fred.'

Wallace had been holding a piece of rag to his ear, but the bleeding hadn't stopped: his clothes – and Emilia's – were soaked with gore.

'Let me out,' Emilia wailed.

Wallace had hardly scrambled through the blood-streaked door than she pushed past him, clutching her mouth, making retching noises. Caine got out stiffly, stretched, brushed spent cases and glass-chips off his seat. Furetto opened the boot, brought them bottles of water.

Caine's throat was like parchment: he took the bottle thankfully, drank in slow gulps. Wallace sank down on his haunches, pulled at a cigarette while Trubman strapped a field-dressing over his ear with surgical tape.

'Most useless part of yer body,' he guttered, 'and yer bleed like a stuck pig.'

Furetto smoked jauntily, his eyes alive with excitement, his big ears waggling. 'Is good, yes? We blow Kraut vehicles . . . *bwommffff* . . . We kill all Krauts.'

'Won't make any difference,' Trubman mouthed. 'When they don't answer their wireless-check, their base'll despatch a squad to find out what's going on. Might be on their way now.'

The others stared at him: Furetto nodded gravely. 'Is true,' he said.

Emilia appeared out of the bushes, head bowed, wiping her mouth with a handkerchief: she looked shaken. Caine gave her water. 'You all right?' he asked.

She took bird-like sips, spat, drank more. She became aware of Wallace's blood on her trousers, made a feeble attempt to wipe it off with her handkerchief.

'Fred's blood is enough to make anyone throw up,' Caine said.

'It's not just the blood. Seeing a guy shot in the face close-up like that . . . it was awful. I know it had to be done, but that doesn't make it easier. I can't believe that I've shot men. Before the war, I never shot anything but partridges and hares.'

Caine felt suddenly weary. 'It's when you start enjoying it that you've got to watch out,' he said: his words sounded empty to his own ears.

'There's gonna be more of it,' Wallace grunted. He picked up his weapon, rose to full height, pushed a lock of stiffwire hair away from the dressing on his ear. 'The Krauts ain't gonna hand yer brother to us on a plate with chips. Just think about it.'

'But isn't there a way we could do it without all this . . . butchery?' Emilia persisted. 'There's been too much of it lately.' She shivered: *If Stengel were in front of me now, would I kill him? Maybe. I don't know.*

'What's that they say about omelettes and crackin' eggs?' Wallace chortled.

'*No, no, la contessa ha ragione*,' Furetto cut in. 'Is right. We only five: Krauts many more.' He tapped a tapered forefinger against his fragile-looking skull. 'Is better to be clever – *usa il cervello, no?*'

'Out of the mouths of babes, skipper,' Trubman said. 'We can't take on big battalions.'

'Why not?' Wallace argued. 'We did it at el-Fayya, didn't we?'

'At el-Fayya we had a good defensive position,' Trubman countered. 'But slogging it out till one of you falls down – that isn't SAS, is it?'

'*Stealth if possible*.' Caine nodded. 'Force only if there's no other way.'

They were quiet for a moment. Suddenly, Furetto wagged his ears. 'Is a way,' he said. He dropped his fag-end in the dirt, ground it out under his heel, dug in his knapsack, came out with a torch, a field-pad with a pencil attached. He handed the torch to Emilia, nodded to her, leaned across the bonnet of the car, started drawing frantically: the others gathered round, huddled close in the torchlight. 'Road from Orsini come down hill on our left, like this,' he said. 'Very steep. At bottom is Kraut checkpoint, but small: three men, maybe four, with motorcycles . . . and wireless.'

Caine remembered seeing the post on the journey out with Butterfield.

'Wait a minute,' he said. 'I get it. We take over the checkpoint.'

'Is only three, four men. Is easy, no?'

'We wait for the convoy. When they halt at the checkpoint, we bump them.'

'*Bump* them?' Emilia said. 'Doesn't that mean you're going to shoot them?'

Caine shook his head. 'Not necessarily: it depends on how they react. But if we have to kill them to save your brother, we will.'

Furetto touched his arm suddenly. '*You hear?*'

Caine cocked his ears, caught the distant drumming of engines coming from the direction of Orsini: he shuftied the dark road to his left, picked up the faintest drift of headlight-beams.

'It's the Hun,' Wallace growled. 'Got to be.'

'Get in the car,' Caine ordered.

He had the vehicle moving before the doors were shut, switched on the headlights, changed gear, accelerated steadily up to forty-five mph: the stream of air through the gaping windscreen was cold, but a degree warmer than it had been, Caine thought. 'Keep your weapons hidden,' he said. 'As far as the Krauts are concerned, we're a car-load of peasants.'

'In an *Alfa Romeo*?' Emilia giggled. 'Isn't the broken windscreen a bit obvious?'

'Never mind. We'll be past them before they know it.'

He scanned the road ahead: the headlight-glow was nearer now, but the oncoming vehicles weren't in line of sight. A moment later, though, they veered round a bend: lights blazed out at them like burning white eyes. For an instant Caine was blinded: he slowed down, tried to navigate from the verge, switched his own lights to dipped.

A moment later, the leading vehicle dipped. '*Danke schön, Kamerad*,' Caine muttered. He increased speed a little, focused on the ribbon of the road ahead, forced himself not to look at the approaching motors. His fingers gripped the steering-wheel: he was aware only of the splash of light across the road, the dark-humped mass of the vehicles behind it. A second later the lights whisked past in the corner of his eye: he kept the Alfa Romeo going steadily, glanced in the mirror, watched the lights recede into the night.

'Kraut patrol,' Wallace rasped. 'One 3-tonner, one *Kubelwagen*.'

'Dozy buggers,' Trubman said.

'*Diciamo grazie a Dio*,' Coniglio said. 'We say thanks to God.'

'Yep,' Caine agreed. 'Let's just hope there's no more where they came from.'

40

Orsini, Le Marche, Italy
11 October 1943

The *carabinieri* station in Orsini was a wing of rain-blackened stone attached to the dilapidated fortress that stood on the cobbled square in front of the San Giuseppe church. It was eight thirty sharp when they marched Ettore Falcone out of the arched doorway to the waiting transport: Stengel watched from some distance away, behind the wheel of his Horch staff-car. Parked directly behind him were a *Kubelwagen* and two lorries with machine-guns mounted on their cabs. Karl Grolsch was sitting in the *Kubelwagen*: the lorries carried a heavily armed Sipo-SD platoon and what was left of Kaltenbraun's Waffen-SS detachment, withdrawn from the Villa Montefalcone.

Kaltenbraun was to escort the prisoner in a separate *Kubelwagen*, which would go on ahead. Stengel's convoy would follow five minutes behind, staying just out of sight: Grolsch's informer hadn't told them where the ambush was to take place, but they would be close enough to slap down any attack with overwhelming force.

The guards manhandled Ettore into the back of Kaltenbraun's *Kubelwagen*, sandwiched him between two burly SS guards. His hands were cuffed in front of him: he felt drained and dizzy, made an effort to stay alert. He was under no illusions about what was happening: they were taking him to Jesi to be shot. If there were any chance of escape it had to be between here and the camp. Once through those gates, there would be no coming back.

On the one hand, Ettore told himself, he was ready to face death. He was the last male heir of the Falconi – a family whose history stretched back to ancient Rome. There was Emilia, of course – she was tomboy enough to be called an honorary man. The name would die with him, though: his death would be remembered.

On the other, he was aware that this was self-dramatizing bravado: he was a kid, and he was terrified. If he was able to face the idea of execution at all, it was only because he didn't really believe it was going to come to that: it was all a bad dream. He was only *sixteen*, for God's sake: he had his whole life in front of him. Even the Krauts didn't execute kids. Then he remembered the five youths who'd been arrested with him: they'd all quietly disappeared over the past couple of days. He might find them in Jesi camp, but he wouldn't have wanted to bet money on it.

He forced himself to concentrate on what was going on around him. The guards on either side were big men who sat poised and silent with their Schmeissers across their knees, gazing straight ahead. The passenger seat in front was occupied by the foxy-looking young officer called *SS-Hauptsturmführer* Kaltenbraun. The driver next to him was a stout corporal with a face like undercooked meat. There was a Spandau machine-gun mounted on the bonnet in front of Kaltenbraun's seat.

Ettore understood German pretty well: he knew that Kaltenbraun was in charge of the SS-squad sent to escort him. What he couldn't understand, though, was what the other two Nazi big bananas were doing here – the bearded creep with the fish-eyes and the blond-haired, balding *SS-Sturmbannführer* who'd first identified him as Ettore Falcone. He'd recognized them even though their vehicles had been parked some way off: they looked terrible – the guy with the beard had a badly bruised and scarred face and wore a dressing on his head: the bald guy had his arm in a sling. Was he, Ettore Falcone, so special that these officers had come to oversee his transfer personally? Why the two lorries, armed with machine-guns, packed with troops? Only a VIP would need such an escort – unless they were expecting trouble, of course.

Kaltenbraun gave an order: the car started, jounced across the cobbled square. Ettore noted that Stengel's convoy wasn't moving. *Perhaps they aren't escorting me at all.*

The road into the valley followed a winding pass – a configuration of sharply twisting switchbacks running out along grassy spurs. The driver decreased speed to negotiate them. The landscape spread out below –

sparse scrubland in explosive colours – dazzling orange, canary yellow, shocking pink – copses like green islands, strips of dun and pinkish earth raked with tight furrows, and in the far distance the gunmetal greyness of the mountains, merging into a pale sky painted with clouds like fine white eyebrows, flurries, fractured hoops.

The car rounded a tight bend: Ettore glimpsed a group of vehicles on a limb above them. It was only for a second, but he knew it was Stengel's column: the shiny black Horch in the lead was too distinctive to mistake. *They're coming with us after all. Why are they lingering behind, out of sight?* The answer hit him almost at once. *It's a trap. They send a single car ahead unprotected: the main escort follows at a distance, ready to close in when the bait is taken.* If the Germans were expecting an attack, it had to be from the partisans. *I bet Emilia's behind it. She'd never let me go without a fight.*

Ever since their parents had been killed in the aircrash, Emilia had been his sole caretaker. She was only six years older than him, and he knew it had been hard on her, coming to terms with her loss and having to be both mother and father to him when she was hardly out of adolescence herself. She'd been tough on him, too, he thought: no playing hookey from school, no skimping on homework. Sometimes they'd quarrelled: he'd called her names, threatened to leave, but he'd always known that she was there for him when he needed her.

Ettore had been happy in New York: he'd loved the movies and the music – swing was his passion: he'd started to learn jazz clarinet in emulation of his hero, Benny Goodman. Goodman's Carnegie Hall concert had been one of the most poignant events of his life. That had been the last occasion on which the four of them had been out together as a family: the crash had occurred a few days later.

Ettore had never accepted that it was an accident: his father had been flying the Piper Cub himself, and he'd been an excellent pilot. He remembered with a shiver how he and Emilia had sat up for hours in the apartment that night, waiting for their parents to come home: how it had dawned on him slowly that he would never see them again, how one part of him, even now, refused to believe it.

His father, Count Giuseppe, had been a physicist who had worked with Nobel prizewinner Enrico Fermi in Italy, and in the USA: Fermi and his wife, Laura, had stayed frequently at their New York apartment. Ettore was convinced that his father had been too smart to make the pilot error they'd attributed to him. The fact was that the count had *known* something was going to happen: he'd dropped hints about the dangers of the research he was engaged in. Then there'd been the business of the Codex – the elaborate process his father had gone through to make sure that its hiding place was secure and that no one would be able to find it without Ettore and his sister. The hypnosis idea had come from one of the count's scientist-friends: Ettore had never understood why the Codex was so important, but he'd accepted the hypnotism process: it had seemed like a game at the time. He'd only remembered later that his father had insisted it was necessary *in case anything happens to me.*

Ettore's only grudge against his sister was the fact that she'd made him return to Italy, a primitive country whose sole advantage was that they played *real* football – not the nonsense that passed for football in the States. Running off to join the partisans had been his most defiant act of rebellion: Emilia hadn't liked it, but she hadn't been able to stop him either. Exactly why he'd done it, he didn't know, only that he'd felt at home with the *Giappisti*, and that the operations he'd taken part in had been a thrill – especially the time he and his friend had rescued the giant British parachutist and machine-gunned a pair of Krauts.

Now he was paying the price of his stupidity in wearing the Falconi signet ring on his foray to Orsini: it had been a giveaway, although judging by what he suspected had happened to his friends, his fate would have been sealed whatever. What really puzzled him was how the Krauts had known they were going to be there: it smacked of betrayal, he thought.

The road curved gracefully through avenues of trees like blazing fire-beacons, exploding in candy-apple red and chartreuse, dripping burnished leaves that lay across the gravel in burnt-orange drifts. The driver increased speed as the land flattened out through fields of sun-browned grass: the vast panorama of the valley unfolded, descending gracefully, rising up through galleries of woods like angry wounds in ox-blood and plasma yellow, up to a wavy line of peaks draped in purple shadow. The sky was poised and fuming: great rifts of grey cloud were in the process of throttling a golden effervescence which burst forth momentarily in spokes of brilliant light.

There was a checkpoint at the junction where the Orsini road met the main road from Ancona to Fabriano. Over Kaltenbraun's shoulder, Ettore saw that there were oildrums across the road, barring their way. The checkpoint stood in a circle of sparse trees that cast poles of shadow across the road: beyond it, along the main thoroughfare, stood tangled evergreen hedges taller than a man. A couple of motorcycle combinations were drawn up under the trees: a German soldier with a sub-machine gun observed them placidly from the shadows nearby.

Kaltenbraun swore: the driver pulled up in front of the oildrums. The *Hauptsturmführer* stood up, gripped the dashboard, gesticulated at the guard, who sidled reluctantly towards the car. '*Warum haben Sie den Kontrollpunkt nicht geöffnet?*' the officer bawled. 'Why haven't you opened the barrier? I sent an alert before we left Orsini.'

The soldier halted a few yards away: at first, Ettore noticed only that he was unusually lean for a Kraut: his tunic hung loose from his shoulders like a tent. His helmet, too, was two sizes too large: it drooped forward across his eyes, shadowing a face that was as thin as a handle, as white and hairless as a child's.

The soldier shifted slightly on his feet, gripped his weapon: Ettore noticed that it was a Beretta submachine gun. Kaltenbraun cursed again, flung open the car door. '*Salutieren Sie nicht vor einem Offizier?* Come on, you oaf – we haven't got all day.'

The guard flipped back the rim of his helmet with long-tapered fingers: Ettore clocked eyes like sparklers, a pointed nose, keen ferret features, an overcurved mouth twisted in a sardonic grin. For a split second their eyes met: recognition hit him like a thunderbolt. *Furetto. In Kraut uniform.* The crazy idea that his partisan friend had somehow joined the enemy was just forming in his mind when two things happened in quick succession: Kaltenbraun jumped down from the car, and Furetto shot him with a brisk double *tack-tack*. The shots snapped like whipcracks: Ettore smelt burnt air and cordite, heard lead jackets thump flesh, saw the *Hauptsturmführer* hurled backwards with the aggravated look still on his face, felt his body slump against the car's chassis, saw twin buboes blister his chest, saw gore erupt like the clutchings of tiny red fingers. The Jerry driver snatched at the SMG in the dashboard-brace, was jerked back by an arm like a ship's-hawser attached to a shock-haired mountain of a man who seemed to have appeared out of the bushes on the right. It was the same giant British parachutist Ettore had helped snatch from the Krauts, in the same ragged clothes, now covered in blood. Ettore saw a blade glitter, clocked a scorpion-sting movement, saw the steel pierce the base of the Jerry's neck, saw arterial blood jag, saw the giant stab the blade down again and again, plunging it in so deeply that it looked as if he were smashing the Kraut with a fist the size of a baked ham.

The guard to Ettore's right cocked his Schmeisser, brought it to bear on the big man. Ettore threw himself on the Jerry, swung his manacled hands, knocked him off balance. The Kraut's SMG stuttered: rounds spivvied up gravel, ricocheted off the road with indignant shrieks. The giant leaned forward, snatched the weapon out of the Jerry's hands, pointed it at him. The mouth under the bristling black beard crinkled, displayed a graveyard of broken teeth. 'How do yer say *put 'em up* in Jerry?' he chortled. He jabbed the guard in the belly with the SMG-muzzle. '*Put 'em up, Kamerad!*' he roared.

Ettore had half turned towards the second guard when something that felt like a cannon-ball smacked into the side of his head. His world receded down a dim corridor full of tweetering descants and the brilliant fulminations of dying stars.

When he came round he was sitting against a tree: his head felt like it had been trapped in a door: warm blood was trickling down his cheek. Emilia was crouching over him, dabbing at his head with a bloody handkerchief. His handcuffs were gone: Furetto, no longer wearing his Kraut uniform, stood a little behind his sister, grinning through his teeth.

'*Ettore*.' Emilia swept her flowing locks out of her eyes: tears ran down her cheeks, but she looked relieved. Over her shoulder he saw two men in peasant dress hustling a Kraut into the bushes. One of them was the tubby, trout-faced British parachutist they'd found wandering in the woods: the other he didn't know – a man with blunt, freckled features and a weight-lifter's torso. They made the German lie down among the trees, tied his legs with cord. Ettore glimpsed other field-grey bodies lying prone in the trees. Kaltenbraun was gone: only a smear of blood on the road remained where he'd fallen: the dead driver and the other guard had also been moved. The giant was at the barrier, rolling aside the concrete-lined oildrums.

Emilia tried to throw her arms round him: he fended her off. '*How long was I out?*' he gasped.

'Only a few minutes. One of the guards hit you on the head by accident.'

Ettore staggered to his feet, cast an edgy glance back up the Orsini road, grabbed his sister's arm. '*More Krauts are coming. It's a trap. It's a trap*.'

At the same moment there came a brutal swatting sound like a boxing-glove hitting a punch-bag, an accelerating drone, an ear-bending crescendo of tortured air.

'*Take cover!*' someone screamed.

41

The bomb kerauned into the road twenty-five paces short of them with a blinding flash and a seething reflux of firegold and black. Caine, sprawled in the road with his arms around his head, felt the air keedle, felt the earth shimmy, felt his guts convulse. A woft of dust and grit blew over him. *Not in range yet. Next one will be.* He jumped up, clutched his weapon, shuftied along the Orsini road, clocked smoke-spume lufting from the mortar-shell, saw another *Kubelwagen* rolling behind it, saw a platoon of Kraut infantry dodging in and out of cover, advancing in fits and starts along the verge.

Caine had planned to take Kaltenbraun's car: Wallace was already clambering into the driving-seat. He felt a raging certainty, though, that the Krauts would drop the next mortar-round right on her.

'*Leave it Fred!*' he bawled. '*Go for the Alfa.*'

'*Gotcher, mate.*'

Trubman was helping Emilia to her feet: she looked pallid and dazed, but unhurt: Ettore and Furetto were picking themselves up. Caine grabbed the guard's discarded SMG, thrust it at Ettore, put his arm round Emilia's shoulders. '*Run!*' he yelled.

The Alfa Romeo was camouflaged behind one of the

tall hedges near the main road, no further away than the length of a football field. They ran in a staggered bunch, Furetto and Ettore leading, Wallace jogging along at the rear. They had hardly cleared the barrier when Caine heard the mortar go *thwommpppp*, heard air scrape, heard the round plop out of the sky with a caustic drone. He dragged Emilia down, hit the deck almost on top of her, saw Wallace and Trubman bite dust a few yards behind. He felt the road rock like an unsteady boat, clocked glitter and flash, heard a squeal of metal, saw the Jerry wagon come apart in a gush of steel spines and white-cored fire, saw her rear end tip as if kicked by a giant foot, saw her crash down, saw black smoke gutter, saw orange flame-tongues lick, felt scorched air blast.

Before the explosion had played out, a Spandau started going *bomp-bomp-bompa-bomp*: a pattern of tracer fell through the rising smoke-trails, branched into splits of curved lightning that clawed air, chewed up the road surface in ragged bites. Wallace was on his feet, hoisting Trubman with an arm like a gantry, lofting off a spurt of nine milly through the veil of dust and smoke. The enemy gun jabbered in answer, *bompa-bompa-bomp*. Caine saw Wallace stagger, saw the ribbon of crimson that whipped from his thigh, saw him clutch at it frantically with a box-sized hand, saw him go down on one knee. '*Oh shit! Christ!*' the big man bellowed. Trubman swivelled, fired his rifle from the waist, tried to haul Wallace up: Caine saw the Welshman knocked off his feet in a cross-hatched updraught of Spandau fire.

Caine's ears rang: his jaw worked, no words came. He drew Emilia to her feet, saw Ettore and Furetto crouching, staring about in confusion. '*Go. Go,*' he croaked.

He dashed back to help Wallace and Trubman, splittered a burst left-handed, dug a grenade out of his pocket, pinned it with his teeth, squeezed the handle tight in his palm. He hunkered down by Trubman, saw that the signaller had copped a wound in the shoulder, saw him getting up. Indeterminate shapes bobbed behind the blazing hulk of the *Kubelwagen* thirty paces away: Jerry small-arms crashed and clattered, rounds flitted past Caine like angry fireflies, stobbed up grit and dust. He lobbed the grenade overarm, heard the fuse click as the handle fell, heard the bomb hit dirt with a metallic *clink*, heard it detonate with a deep-gut rumble, saw blue-black smoke vortex, saw firedark and burnt-ochre particles spliff. He helped Trubman to his feet, grasped big Wallace's arm.

They had run only a few yards when another mortar-shell craunched over their heads with an accelerating groan, struck earth in the field to their right, exploded in a brilliant nebula of light, shocked up a beach-comber of earth-sods, blazing bushes, powdered dust. The next one sailed in an instant later, creased a hot furrow over them, fishtailed into the hedge behind which the Alfa Romeo was cammed up: Caine heard the shell ramp, heard the howl of ripping iron, clocked the reverse-cone blast of flame and smoke that flexed like a gnarled fist from the hidden vehicle, saw steel shards and glass-specks blow.

An icy tentacle squirmed down his back: his heart sank. He saw Ettore and Furetto pull Emilia to her feet, saw her thick swale of hair flap like a dark flag, glimpsed a scarlet sliver of blood on her face. *She's hit*, he thought. The three of them hesitated in the road for an instant, gaped about them, took in the whorling halos of oily firecloud that pulsated from the wrecked Alfa Romeo like smoke-signals. The Spandau bomped: Jerry sub-machine guns spat and crackled, rounds pitter-pattered along the gravel. *The car's gone. No way of escape.* Caine remembered the ditch on the side of the road opposite the junction: they'd reccied it on the way in. It was their only refuge now.

'*The ditch!*' he bawled at them. '*Get in the ditch!*'

Wallace and Trubman were weaving left and right, dodging and ducking: Caine saw Emilia and the others vanish into cover. Jerry rounds beamed past his ears, gouged tiny craters in the gravel. He zig-zagged, dropped, rolled, came up shooting, bliffed double-taps: *Ba-bamm. Ba-bamm.* They were running across the main road now: Caine saw Furetto's head pop up over the side of the ditch, then Ettore's, saw bright trapezoids of fire bloom from their weapons, heard the burp and chitter of rounds, hoped they could shoot straight.

Wallace and Trubman plunged into the ditch: Caine tumbled in after them. It was wide and grassy, deep enough to conceal a kneeling person: Emilia was helping

Wallace strap the field-dressing from his ear on to the wound in his thigh. The bandage was already soggy with gore, but the wound wasn't spurting: the bullet had missed the artery, Caine thought. Emilia was as white as paper, her big brown eyes stood out like wet carnelians on porcelain features: a thin ribble of blood ran down her cheek from a graze on her temple. Trubman was gasping for breath, trying to stem the bleeding from his shoulder with a piece of four-by-two: sweat dribbled off his forehead in diamond drops. Ettore and Furetto were still leaning over the parapet, packing off short bursts at the enemy. Caine beckoned to them: they ducked down.

'Listen to me,' he growled. 'Emilia, you, Ettore and Furetto – you're civilians. I'm going to give you a chance to escape. I'll count to three – you get out of here. Try and find your way back to the partisan camp –'

'How far do you think we'd get?' Ettore broke in. 'The Krauts will stop us, torture the secret of the Codex out of us, then kill us. I'm staying here.'

'I not go anywhere,' Furetto piped up: his eyeballs were wide: his outsized ears waggled. 'I stay and fight.'

Emilia looked up from Wallace's wound: her face was strained, her sleepy eye almost closed: she swept back her hair, dabbed at her head-wound with her soiled handkerchief. 'Give me a gun,' she said tensely. 'If this is it, I may as well fight, too.'

Caine handed her the spare Schmeisser: his throat felt like pasteboard, but there was no water. There was no spare ammunition either: it had all gone up with the car. He was so parched he'd have killed for a swig of liquid. 'They're going to rush us,' he croaked. 'They know we're only six, with no heavy weapons and no transport. They outnumber us five to one, and they've got mortars and machine-guns. We could surrender, but we're under a death-sentence anyway.' He swallowed hard, realized there wasn't much more to say. *I'm back where I started: in a ditch facing the Hun. The Krauts will already have reinforcements on the way.*

He glanced at Emilia: with her trim figure, her head cocked to one side, her dark, blood-speckled hair falling over one shoulder in a single swathe, her heavy-lidded eyes glittering like jewels, she looked like some beautiful, slender, hunted deer, he thought. He experienced a pang of regret that the life of this young woman should be cut short, should end here in a hole on the side of the road in her native country, a stone's throw from where she was born. What about her brother, Ettore? He was still a kid. *It's not right*, he thought.

He forced the thought aside. '*Come on*,' he said, half to himself. 'We're not dead yet.'

'Fuck 'em,' Wallace boomed.

'All right,' Caine said. 'Check your ammo. If you've got grenades left, pin 'em. When I give the word, everybody at the parapet. On my order, chuck your grenades and start shooting.'

They still had the advantage, he thought: no matter how many Krauts there were, they had no choice but to advance to contact, and they'd take casualties. Their mortars wouldn't be any good when their own men were in range: if enough of them went down they might withdraw.

'I've only got ten rounds,' Trubman chuntered.

'Fifteen,' Wallace gurned, clacking his mag back in place.

Caine had twelve: none of them had a full magazine. 'Make every round count,' he told them. He cocked his weapon, slid the handle forward: the Schmeisser was a good weapon, but he missed the feel of his Tommy-gun. He wondered if Copeland still had it, what would happen to it if he didn't come back. Where was Copeland now? Probably on his way to Algeria with the SRS. He was glad to have Wallace and Trubman with him, blamed himself for getting them mixed up in an op that wasn't their problem. They'd done their time behind the wire: they should have been on their way back to Allied lines by now.

Hun rounds went *gooompah* along the side of the ditch, cut loose grass tufts and soil, scissored air, buzzed like hornets. A round slapped turf by Caine's head, spun off with a piercing shriek. He ducked, cocked his Schmeisser, eyed the others grimly. '*Go!*' he bawled

They came up to the parapet, kept their heads low, dipped behind stones and clumps of grass. Furetto and Ettore were on the left: Caine positioned himself between Emilia and Trubman, with Wallace on the far right. He clocked the twisted frame of the Alfa Romeo half-lodged in a burning hedge, saw smouldering tyres and engine-parts strewn across the road. The enemy was only fifty paces away: the *Kubelwagen* had halted just short of the junction: the gunner was training his M42, about to give covering fire: Jerry troops were running along the sides of the road, shooting as they came.

Caine watched them spread out into a staggered line abreast: there couldn't have been more than two dozen of them, but there seemed to be hundreds. The Spandau on the *Kubelwagen* clattered like a mangle: rounds blasted dirt, crackled on stones along the edge of the ditch. '*Here they come*,' Caine hissed. '*Wait for it*.'

The Jerries rushed across the road in bunches, yipped and roared, weapons going *tack-tack-tack*, counterpointing the the nasal clank of the M42.

Caine's last grenade was in his hand: he gripped the cool, segmented metal, hooked out the pin, squeezed the handle, watched the hurtling Krauts: slugs charred air, lashed dust, went *wheeeuuuwww* off the parapet. He felt as if a catapult were being tightened in his head, cranked by a handle whose turns grew tighter and tighter until the tension was almost unbearable. Krauts were so near he could see the details of their kit – an open pouch, an unbuttoned pocket, a wobbling ammo-box. An ice-ball melted in his chest: the catapult in his head went *snap*. '*Grenades!*' he yelled.

He pitched the Mills bomb, traileyed flexing arms, fingers snapping open, saw bombs fly, heard detonators pop: for a moment the scene hung suspended – Jerries frozen in the act of charging, grenades dangling in the air, defying gravity. Caine forced himself to watch the bombs fall, dipped his head. *BabooommMMM*, *baww-roommppp*, *BAA-ROWWMMFFF*, *beeeeyowwwwmmm*. A chain of echoes swooped and back-eddied: the ground tipped, grit spattered, dust-haze soughed: the air shrilled with birdhouse racket, howls of shock, agonized shrieks.

Caine popped up, saw Kraut bodies littered across the road like dead ninepins, glimpsed a Jerry dry-swimming on bloody stumps, another gouging at a shrapnel wound in the face, a third trying to claw himself up on a red mess of a knee with jagged bone-ends protruding. He saw Jerries blundering aimlessly, saw raw black faces, eyebrows gone, skin hanging in curled-up shreds, saw other Krauts stagger to their feet, shaken but unscathed: some crouched in the road, some started shooting. Muzzles sparked, belched smoke: slugs droned, welted earth in front of the ditch, shivered stones, spouted rock chips and red earth.

A spent case clipped Caine's ear: he flinched, became suddenly aware of the din around him, heard his comrades triphammer fire. He saw Krauts skid, stumble, go down, saw a straw-haired soldier raise a spudmasher: he pulled iron, triggered a burst, felt his rounds spoing the Jerry's gut, straddle flesh, trawl viscera, crush bone. The Jerry fell like a plumb weight, dropped the grenade: his nearest comrade grabbed it, tried to throw it away, was stopped short by a numbing *whaaackck*, a quatrefoil starflash of shimmering white light that ripped his arm from its socket, demolished his head and chest in a shower of tissue and viscous spatters of gore.

Caine ticker-tacked drumfire through wefts of oily blackness, steamdrilled rounds at a squat, bacon-faced Kraut who came reaming at him through the haze with bayonet fixed: Caine saw the rounds strike high in the Jerry's chest, saw him vault up in the air with arms spread, saw blood-gouts flush. A grenade dropped short of the ditch to his left, crumped apart with a piledriver slam, a forked-lightning flash, a halo of ruddy glare: he heard Furetto's coarse shriek, saw him jerk backwards, collapse into the ditch. He saw Ettore duck, saw a Jerry roar out of the smoke at him, saw the boy's Schmeisser jump, saw a splodge of fire-opal kick at the Jerry's throat, saw him falter, saw blood rain down in hosepipe spurts.

Caine traileyed Emilia on his left, saw her struggle with a jammed weapon, saw blades dance in her eyes, saw her teeth grind, saw her tongue lick at the dried blood on her lips. He turned to help: heard a round tweet, felt a tug on his bicep, felt warmth ooze down his arm, saw his sleeve drenched in blood. He swore, sucked air, felt hot wind slam, heard Emilia squeak, saw her knocked back by a richochet that skimmed her neck, whinged off into space. He saw her drop the Schmeisser, saw her slide down with glazed eyes.

His blood went cold: a glacier spread up his legs and arms. The pain from his wound started up abruptly – a steel band clinching his flesh. A Kraut reeled over him – a bandy-legged trooper with ditchwater eyes and a mouth like a tunnel: the Jerry's SMG tacker-tacked, shots leapt and spun: Caine stonked him with a duck-and-drake tap that gouged out an eye, mashed his nose to shreds.

Big Wallace loosed a tremor of fire at a blade-faced Jerry who'd already been hit in the leg and was firing from his knees: Wallace's rounds tore open his stomach, sent him spinning on to his back, gurgling incoherently, drooling gore. The giant heard a Spandau go *blatta-blatta-blatta-blat*, peered through dust-roils, saw that the *Kubelwagen* was rolling out in support, her M42 blabbering. He heard a second Spandau kick in like a low echo, *lob-lob-lob-lob-lob*, saw a lazy curve of tracer float towards him, saw it luft tight in the air, shatter into red wires that lashed and burned. He heard a round hit the stock of Trubman's rifle with an audible *whop*, niffed sulphur, saw the weapon knocked out of the Welshman's hands. He saw Trubman scrabble for it, his hand dripping blood, saw agony written on his face, saw gore-smears on his glasses.

The giant clocked the 3-tonner that was rolling steadily up behind the *Kubelwagen*, saw the Spandau mounted on her cab, saw another lorry and a black civilian car moving behind her, saw a second field-grey squad galloping down the Orsini road. '*Bloody hell!*' he spat.

Huns rushed him, weapons going *tick-tack-tick*: he plastered a long burst at them, felt his working parts prong. He ducked behind the parapet, released his mag, checked it: it was empty. Rounds bleated: a Jerry reared over him. Wallace hurled the useless SMG at his legs: the Jerry jumped, hashed rounds that divebombed Wallace's ears like demented wasps. He grabbed the nearest stone in his huge fist, turned to look down the muzzle of an SMG. *That's it then*, a small voice told him.

The Jerry was swept off his feet by a blast of fire that seemed to come from nowhere: Wallace gaped, saw the Kraut sprawl over the edge of the ditch on top of Trubman, heard an ear-crushing surge of noise, realized that an immense volume of fire was falling on the road: machine-gun volleys bent air, tracer-rounds skimmed and dipped, squealed off gravel, shrieked off stones, beamed into the oncoming Jerries. Wallace saw Huns scatter, fall back, saw a Jerry hit by a round that plunged into his backside, drilled through his pelvis, blew out his groin in a hash of mangled flesh and grey cloth, saw another clutch at a face become mincemeat, saw a third go down with a gaping protrusion of bone and teeth where his jaw had been. He saw the gunner on the *Kubelwagen* traverse the Spandau to his left, saw a spread of tracer drop on the car like a swarm of bright bees, saw both gunner and driver thrash, saw crimson gules welt from field-grey chests, saw rounds chunk bodywork, chomp steel, saw the car leap inches off the ground, heard the *keeeeraaaakkkk*, saw the vehicle dissolve in a swell of lava and smoke, belch spirals of metal slivers, maimed iron, molten flesh. Wallace saw retreating Jerry troops bowled over by the blast, lifted off their feet, dashed to the ground: he saw a Kraut hit by a spindling chunk of steel that knocked his head off, drew cables of gore from his gaping neck.

The Huns were running for it, breaking ranks, diving for cover. Wallace heard the grind and whirr of motors, dekkoed right, saw a wedge of three vehicles poling down the main road in tactical formation: one up, two back, gears grating, mounted guns racking *rat-tat-tat, rat-tat-tat-tat-tat*. His eyes widened: the vehicles were Willy's Bantam jeeps and the tone of the guns was as familiar to him as his own voice: *twin-Vickers 'K's*.

For a moment he thought he must be dreaming: *SAS jeeps. SAS weapons. Here?* He cast a glance at Caine, saw him tending Emilia, who was crouching next to him with her hands around her neck, blood welling through her fingers: he saw Ettore on all fours in the ditch-bed, with Furetto, who was bleeding from the head and throat and looked badly hurt. Wallace shifted the dead Jerry off Trubman, yanked his mate clear, saw the graze on his wrist, dribbling blood. His pupils were dilated behind his gore-daubed lenses, his skin taut. 'You all right, mate?'

'Dandy,' Trubman grimaced. 'What's going on?'

The volume of fire reached a crescendo: rounds squibbed and clittered.

Wallace's rough-cut chunk of a forehead furrowed. '*The bleedin' cavalry, innit.*'

A jeep skidded to a halt in front of the ditch, machine

guns smoking: Caine clocked three men in British Army battledress, features hidden under face-veils. He saw the front-seat gunner swivel the twin Vickers almost ninety degrees, tackhammer tracer across the bonnet, heard the *thunka-thunka-thunk*, heard spent cases plink, whiffed cordite. Before the soldier had eased the trigger, another Vickers, pintle-mounted in the back, took up the refrain: ammo-pans rattled, twin muzzles gnashed spears of crimson flame, wofts of blue smoke. The rear-gunner leaned into his shooting, adjusted the double barrels minutely: Caine clocked SAS wings on his left sleeve. For a split second he was mesmerized – the white parachute, the black-and-white feathers of a sacred ibis. *The procession of sacred ibises in my dream. Why didn't I see the connection?* He recalled the severed head immersed in the fish-tank. *Whoever kills a sacred ibis shall die.* A warm flush touched his cheeks: he'd never before felt so grateful to see that badge.

Another jeep yawed in so close behind the other that they almost bumped: Caine saw a driver and two gunners, a man lying in a stretcher strapped across the back. The front-gunner of this jeep wore SAS wings on his chest in 1st Regiment manner. The man let go the machine-gun, peered through his face-veil at Caine. '*What're you waiting for? Christmas?*'

The voice – and the phrase – were strangely familiar: Caine, already out of the ditch, was helping Emilia up: he stopped in his tracks.

'Do I know you?'

The gunner chuckled, pushed back his face-veil. Caine found himself gawking at a lean face, a kedge-shaped nose, eyes like glittering blue crystals, bogbrush blond hair. Harry Copeland let his mouth twitch at the corners. '*Doctor Livingstone, I presume?*'

42

The junction looked like a slaughter-house hit by a firestorm: 3-tonners blazing in the road, smouldering frames of two *Kubelwagens* and a civilian car: dead, wounded, maimed SS soldiers littering the road and verges, blood everywhere. A miasma of stinking smoke and butcher-shop smells hung over the scene. The only wireless had been in Kaltenbraun's car: it had gone up with the vehicle. Grolsch had sent off a messenger to Jesi in one of the motorcycle combinations that had somehow survived the attack. He had requested a spotter-plane, given instructions that all posts and checkpoints be alerted, and expected a relief column within the hour. He supervised the medical orderlies, told them to move the wounded into the trees, left them to do their work. He lurched back to the Horch staff-car, found Stengel examining the vehicle carefully, whistling the 'Radetzky March' under his breath. 'Six bullet-holes,' the *Reichsgeschäftsführer* said.

Grolsch couldn't help chortling: it had been his idea to park the Horch out of sight in the bush: that it had been hit by a few stray rounds was the least of their worries. He was holding a gore-soaked pad against his cheek, grazed when he'd run out to help the wounded lorry-crews. His face was the colour of pasta: he'd lost his sling in the firefight, and the wound he'd taken a few days earlier had reopened, stained his tunic dark purple at the shoulder. He felt light-headed and heavy-legged but was grateful he'd escaped with only a scratch. He muttered a prayer of thanks to God before he even realized he was doing it. *I shouldn't have killed that priest*, he thought. *Shouldn't have ordered the execution of those SAS-men either, or those partisans at Orsini. I know I was following orders, but that doesn't make it right.*

He opened the door on the passenger side, slumped sideways in the seat with his legs out. Stengel got into the driver's place, hunched over the wheel, pounded it with the side of his fist. '*Jene verdammte Fallschirmspringer wieder*,' he cursed. 'How did they get so deep behind our lines?'

Grolsch pouted, stuck a cigarette in his mouth, tried to summon the strength to light it. 'Not by parachute, I think.'

'Three jeeps, did you see that?'

'Certainly, *Reichsgeschäftsführer*.'

Grolsch lit the cigarette with a lighter, drew in a lung-scorching drag of smoke. He was still in shock: the tables had turned so fast. He tried to replay the sequence of events: the enemy had evidently taken over the checkpoint, had overpowered the Sipo-SD guards, dumped them in the trees. It was an audacious move, he had to admit – one he hadn't anticipated. They'd stopped the *Kubelwagen* carrying Ettore Falcone, shot Kaltenbraun and the driver, captured the others. At that point Grolsch himself had heard shooting, spotted the activity at the barrier: he'd ordered his troops to debus, instructed the mortar crew to open fire. They'd blitzed the barrier, hit the *Kubelwagen*, put the enemy to flight – the Falcone boy and five others in civilian dress, including a woman.

'It was the countess,' Stengel grunted, as if reading his thoughts. 'Caine, too, dressed as a civilian.' His lip curled. *That bitch hit me with a bottle. Caine would have killed me with those grenades.*

'My absconders were there,' Grolsch said. 'Fishface and the Giant. They were wearing civilian clothes also, but you couldn't mistake that big gorilla.'

'*Scheisse!*' Stengel rapped the steering wheel again.

Grolsch smoked grimly. It was during the assault on the ditch that things had gone awry: the *verdammte Fallschirmspringer* had come out of nowhere, rolled in on a hurricane of fire. He'd been thunderstruck by the power of those little cars – that combination of quick-firing machine guns and powerful engines was ingenious and effective. Not only had they mowed down half his men, they'd also demolished the *Kubelwagen* and the lorries: while two jeeps had stopped to pick up the others, another had gone after the 3-tonners, skirted the wreck of the first *Kubelwagen*, steamed in behind a firewall. Grolsch shivered: the attack had been short, sharp and devastating: it was a wonder that any of them was still alive. He'd fired off a clip from his pistol, but the Tommies had manoeuvred the jeeps so fast he doubted he'd hit anything.

'Those men are good,' he croaked.

'They are dangerous,' Stengel corrected him. 'The *Führer* was right to declare no quarter for them. In any case, it's the Codex that concerns me.'

Grolsch held his cigarette with one hand, patted his bloody cheek with the other. Half of his Sipo-SD platoon were dead or wounded: he'd seen the body of one of his corporals, *SS-Rottenführer* Böttcher, from Cologne, whose head had been knocked clean off his shoulders by a lump of flying shrapnel. Of the Waffen-SS men Stengel had brought with him, only a handful remained. Yet all the *Reichsgeschäftsführer* could think about was his blasted Codex and the bullet-holes in his car. Was a damn' book worth all this carnage, no matter how badly Himmler wanted it? He was filled with a surge of loathing for Stengel: his whistling, his muttering, his furtive backward glances. He wasn't a soldier but a bureaucratic toady, a martinet to whom subordinates were expendable. Grolsch retched: he felt decidedly sick, hoped he wouldn't vomit.

He took another lungful of smoke, coughed. 'Do you think they plan to take the Codex?' he asked in a croupy voice.

Stengel's cod-eyes bulged. 'Why else would Caine have snatched the countess? Butterfield and his men were sent for the manuscript, I'm sure of that. Now Caine has taken over the task.'

Or maybe he has it already, he thought. *Maybe they retrieved it from its hiding place in the villa on their way out. But why put so much effort into snatching Ettore Falcone? He's the countess's brother, of course. Could it have been her condition for revealing the whereabouts of the Codex?*

His fingers gripped the steering-wheel. What if it was the boy, not the countess, who knew where the Codex was? That could explain why the bitch had held out, why she'd insisted that she didn't know. He glanced in the rear-view mirror, saw a knot of dark shadows hovering behind the car: rodent-faced men in prison-grey with big, glittery eyes leering at him through the rear window. He recoiled: a cold flush seeped up his back. *One hundred and five Jew-Bolshevik commissars.* He caught his breath, glanced over his shoulder, saw nothing there.

Grolsch clocked the movement. 'What is it, *Reichsgeschäftsführer*?'

Stengel shuddered. He had a sudden vision of the countess's naked body tied to the bed with strands of her own underwear, of himself crouched over her, raping her with a wine-bottle. '*Behold the ravishing beast*,' he whispered.

Grolsch turned away in disgust, dropped his cigarette-butt, drew his legs into the car.

Stengel had almost forgotten him: he was thinking again about the countess, about what she'd whispered under interrogation. *What is sought lies in a room with no doors or windows. I am the door. Another holds the key.* He'd already worked out that *what is sought* was the Codex. The part about a room with no doors or windows didn't add up, but whatever it was, opening it evidently involved two people. *I am the door. Another holds the key.* Suddenly, Stengel saw it. The secret of the Codex concerned both the countess and her brother: the *door* and the *key*. Maybe there was a kind of code of which each of them knew a part and which made sense only when put together? How this was possible, he didn't know, but he was certain he was on the right track.

'They'll be heading for the partisans,' Grolsch commented.

Stengel remembered his presence. '*What?*'

'The partisan camp. That's where they'll be heading.'

'But where *is* the partisan camp?'

Grolsch shut the car door with a bang. 'I have an informer among the *Giappisti*. It's only a matter of time before we find out.'

43

Le Marche, Italy
11 October 1943

It was late afternoon when they halted in the forest. Since Furetto was badly wounded, Ettore and Emilia had acted as guides, directed them along a tortuous network of cart-tracks and bridle-paths, kept them clear of checkpoints and Kraut patrols. They ran the wagons into a grove of ancient trees with trunks like silos and top-heavy boughs that drooped earthwards to a forest floor carpeted with leaves like rusted metal scabs. They leaguered the jeeps under an incline braided with broomstraw, rising among densely packed conifers in verdant herringbone patterns. No sooner had they debussed than a Fieseler Storch aircraft droned over: Caine peeked up through the canopy, clocked her progress across the tiny patches of blueness that showed through the leaves: she was hunting them, he thought: a few minutes later and they'd have been clocked.

'*Squadron adjutant!*' he heard big Wallace exclaim. 'Talk about scrapin' the barrel. Paddy *musta* bin desperate.'

He looked up to see Wallace, Trubman and Copeland in a triple clinch: Cope had an arm round each of them, hugging them incredulously. 'Who *said* you could go AWOL?' he demanded. 'Some blokes will do *anything* to get out of a scrap.'

Wallace's chortle was like broken glass. 'That's good, that is. If certain parties 'adn't of abandoned us in that flamin' gunpit, I'd of bin a flamin' *colonel* by now.'

Copeland's eyes glittered. 'There's hardly a day gone by that me and Tom haven't thought about it, mate. We let you down: we should have got you out, even if it killed us.'

'The big dollop's pulling your plonker, see,' Trubman cut in. 'If you'd tried to shift us, none of us would be here now. Me, all I remember is lying in that pit with half my back hanging off and a couple of Blenheims going into a bombing run.'

'We never blamed yer, Harry,' Wallace growled. 'You might of made it a bit sooner this mornin', mind. I don't call this much of a taxi service.'

Copeland looked as if he didn't know whether to laugh or cry. 'We'll try to do better next time, *Your Honour*: these 2nd Regiment greenhorns haven't got the hang of it yet.'

'2nd Regiment? Never 'eard of it.'

There was a sudden ripple of applause from the jeep crews. The big gunner looked round, clocked five men of 2nd SAS clapping enthusiastically: he flushed, realized they were applauding him and Trubman. ''Ere, wot's this?' he said.

Tony Griffen stalked up to them, his pugilist's face

set in a scowl as if he intended to punch someone. 'Trooper Fred Wallace, MM and bar, Royal Horse Artillery,' he announced solemnly, 'and Corporal Taff Trubman, double MM, Royal Sigs. You was with the *Nighthawk* patrol in Tunisia. You an' Mr Caine and Mr Copeland 'ere held the bridge at el-Fayya against a Jerry recon battalion for forty-eight hours. You was badly wounded, captured by the Krauts, and 'ere you are, still fightin'.'

The men clapped again: Wallace made an ungainly bow: Trubman's pale cheeks came out in rose-coloured blobs. 'I s'pose the way you 'andled them jeeps this mornin' weren't bad for amachewers,' Wallace said grudgingly. 'Could do with a bit of trainin', mind you.'

The men hooted and tittered: most had been combat vets long before they'd joined 2nd SAS: they knew – and they knew Wallace knew – that they'd put on a sterling performance that morning – won the firefight against a superior force, snatched Caine and his crew from under the noses of the enemy.

Bill Harris called Copeland over to look at Cavanaugh: they unstrapped his stretcher, laid him down on the leaf-strewn forest floor in a burst of yellow sunlight. He looked pale and distant, his eyes standing out on the pewter features like burnished black eggs. His chest-wound didn't seem any worse, but he'd been hit again during the contact: Griffen showed Cope the hole in his upper thigh where a stray round had entered. 'No exit wound,' he growled.

Caine came over to shake hands. 'Honoured,' Cavanaugh whispered. 'Heard a lot about you, Tom. Sorry I'm not in a better state to greet you.'

'You'll be all right,' Caine told him. He didn't believe it, though: the bullet was lodged in Cavanaugh's gut and he was no doubt bleeding internally: he had the resigned look of someone ready to make his peace with dying. 'Hold on,' Caine told him. 'We'll get you out.'

Cavanaugh began to cough blood.

They left him with Griffen: at Emilia's request, they went over to examine Furetto, who was sitting propped against a grassy bank. Emilia and her brother were carefully removing his gore-soaked shirt. The youth looked a fright, his hair singed to a black stubble, his left arm caked with blood from the shrapnel that had pierced it in half-a-dozen places: he had other wounds in the chest and neck. Caine introduced Copeland to the three of them: Furetto mustered a bravado grin, a flash of red-flecked teeth in a face dark with dirt and powder-burns. 'Was good, no?' he rasped. 'We get Ettore, kill Krauts.'

Caine gave him a hatless salute. 'You deserve a medal,' he said. 'You all do.'

Ettore chuckled. 'When I saw you in that Kraut get-up I nearly wet myself laughing. You looked like a military scarecrow tied with string. *Salutieren Sie nicht vor einem Offizier?* That means *don't you salute an officer?* in Kraut.'

'Is OK, I salute him now he dead.'

'How're you feeling?' Cope asked, hunkering down with the medical pack.

The youth's eyes rolled upwards. 'Is like they knock a spike in my back with a hammer.' He hiked a shaky breath. 'Is nothing *pori* – is only scratch.' His grin faded: his bright eyes dimmed.

Caine knelt down beside him, pulled the knife from his belt. 'Your father, Cesare, gave me this,' he said. 'I met him on my way to the villa: he helped me. It's a good knife. It's killed two Jerries, at least: Fred Wallace used it at the checkpoint to stick the driver. Your father is a brave man, and you are a very brave man: your sister, Lucia, is brave too.'

Furetto gawked at the knife, smiled wanly. 'You keep it,' he whispered. 'Is for you.'

While Cope tried to make Furetto more comfortable, Caine took care of Emilia: she had two grazes – a shallow one on the forehead and a slightly deeper one on the neck where the round had tracked the flesh all the way up to the cleft below the ear: by the merest chance, it had spun off before penetrating the jugular vein. It would leave a scar, but she'd survived by the merest luck, he thought. He dusted her wounds with sulphonamide powder: Ettore looked on, his expression alternating between pride and concern. 'You're tougher than any of us,' he told his sister. 'Dad would have been so proud of you.'

'We haven't got the Codex yet,' Emilia said. 'I hope you haven't forgotten the signal-phrase?'

Ettore shook his head. '*What is sought lies in a room with no doors or windows.* You are the door: I am the key.'

Caine glanced at him. 'So it's true, then? The location of the Codex is locked in your sister's memory? And you know how to get it out?'

Ettore nodded. 'Dad had some weird ideas, but yes, it's true.'

Caine wound a bandage gently around Emilia's neck: she searched his face as if looking for something, fluttered delicate eyelids. Now he was near her again he felt the tidal draw of her presence. He regretted that he'd disbelieved her over the Codex. It still seemed fantastic, but he supposed the war had thrown up stranger things than that.

They found Trubman and Wallace sitting with the others around a small fire of deadwood Bill Harris had made: the 2nd Reg. men had their mugs out: a sooty, misshapen kettle was already rattling on three stones. Trubman had superficial wounds in the wrist and throat: the round that had hit Wallace's thigh had torn out a chunk of flesh but missed the major blood-vessels. 'Same flamin' leg as last time,' the big man cursed as Caine spread a fresh field-dressing on it. 'An' the old wound ain't even right yet. *Cor*, would yer believe it?'

Caine had Cope dress the wound in his bicep: it was sore and inflamed, but not serious.

'*Char's up*,' Harris called.

'Ain't got no mug,' grumbled Wallace.

'Don't worry, mate,' Copeland said. 'You can always drink it with your arse.'

As they sat down, chuckling, with the others, Griffen came waltzing across with an armful of brown-paper packages, tossed one to each of them. Wallace caught his with panhandle hands. 'Just like Christmas, *innit*,' he crowed. The parcels contained battledress suits, fresh from the stores.

'Our task was to help escaped POWs,' Griffen explained. 'We brought a dozen sets of BD along in case any of 'em was in rags. No insignia, o' course.'

Wallace held up the khaki blouse and trousers, examined them dubiously, his cliff of a brow furrowed. 'I just 'ope it fits, mate. This looks like sommat out of *Snow White and the Seven Dwarfs*.'

'I got scissors,' Griffen grinned. 'You can cut 'em up if yer want, but they'll charge yer for the damage when you get back.'

Emilia and Ettore joined them, looking worried: the morphine had put Furetto to sleep, but his pulse was high and his breathing shallow.

Griffen found mugs for everyone, slopped out tea. The SAS-men lit pipes, handed round cigarettes. Wallace tasted the tea, spat it out. '*What the 'ell is this?*' he demanded.

'All right, it's dogpiss,' Harris assented. 'After six months in Jerry clink, I'd've thought you'd be used to it.'

'You must be the on'y bloke in the British Army as makes char worse than the Krauts.'

'And that's saying something,' Trubman added.

The men cackled: Wallace drank the rest of his tea with apparent relish.

Harris opened six or seven tins of bully-beef stew, bacon and sausages, tipped their contents into a blackened cooking pot. 'I bet you 'aven't got mess-tins or spoons 'ave you, lads?' he said. 'I've got a few spare but you'll have to sign for 'em in triplicate.'

When the food was ready, they ate ravenously: Caine took mess-tins over to Cavanaugh and Furetto, but came back with them. 'Both out for the count,' he said. 'If Roy doesn't get proper medical attention soon, he's going to be in trouble. The boy's in a bad way, too.'

They finished their meal in silence.

Copeland put down his mess-tin, cleared his throat. 'All right,' he said. 'Programme for the rest of the day. Before we start, though, I just want to be clear about the chain of command –'

Wallace snorted powerfully through nostrils the size of golf-balls.

Copeland ignored him. '– Captain Caine is senior rank but, as I'm acting patrol leader on this mission, I retain command.'

Caine grinned to himself. Cope was correct: the patrol was his responsibility – Caine and the others were technically passengers. He wondered, though, if Copeland was remembering old times, when he'd had to go along with what he called Caine's *impulses*. With his own command, he wouldn't have that problem. *Maybe.*

'We'll go into exfiltration directly,' Cope said. 'Make for Allied lines. I've already thought about the route. If we get moving now, we can be back with our own forces within forty-eight hours.'

'Hold your horses, Harry,' Caine said. 'We've got a mission – at least I have. The countess and Ettore are part of it.'

'We're in, too, mate,' Wallace announced. He glared at Trubman, who winked a wan eye behind thick lenses.

Copeland looked taken aback. 'Escaped POWs don't get tasked for missions,' he protested. 'You're officially non-combatants until you've been debriefed.'

'Same old Harry,' Wallace huffed. 'By the book and as per field-regulations. What did yer think we was doin' in that ditch this mornin' then – playin' Ludo?'

Cope swallowed. 'What *is* this mission?'

For the second time Caine described what had happened to him since he'd last seen Copeland in the dyke near the Senarca bridge – Jesi, Butterfield, the Codex, the partisan ambush, his lone mission to snatch Emilia, their liberation of Wallace and Trubman, how they'd taken over the checkpoint, snatched Ettore from the Hun.

When he'd finished, Copeland seemed deflated: he looked wary, as if wondering if he was going to be asked to bow to yet another of Caine's whims.

''Ow come you just 'appened to appear when we

needed yer, then?' Wallace enquired. 'Surely you musta known we was there?'

Copeland opened his mouth to speak, but it was Griffen who took up the story. 'We set up an OP on the Jesi camp – the original idea was to bump the place, but it were too well guarded. So we decides to go for the workin' parties they send out in the mornin': we reckoned it'd be a pushover.'

'And was it?' Caine asked.

'Weren't nowt to push over. See, we thought they sent out workin' parties every day, but they don't. They 'ave Sunday off.' He paused.

'*Well?*' Wallace interjected.

Griffen's pugnacious features softened: his 'O'-shaped mouth twitched with suppressed mirth. 'Talk about cock-up: we snatches an Itie, who tells us that the Krauts are workin' on the Ancona–Fabriano road, between Jesi and Orsini. The sod don't mention that it's Sunday today, and they don't work Sundays. We drove right along the main road, bold as brass, never found a sniff of 'em. Then we've nearly got to the Orsini junction when we 'ears a reg'lar ding-dong goin' on. Well, it 'ad to be the 'Un against partisans, didn't it? So we wades in with all guns blazin' and lo and behold, we picks up three 1st Regiment wallahs, a countess and two trogs.'

The company burst into hoots of laughter.

'Well, there's one thing, mate,' Wallace snickered. 'You can say that's the best mistake you ever made in yer life.'

'There's something I don't get,' Caine said when the laughter had died down. 'Why were you planning to bump Jesi camp – or even a working-party come to that? You said your mission was to assist escaped POWs, not to liberate them. What *was* your objective?'

Copeland blinked at him: there was a look of embarrassment on his face. 'We were aiming to liberate *you*, mate. Call it a side-mission.'

For a moment, Caine was overawed. He saw it all now. There he was, Lieutenant Harold J. Copeland, no-bullshit, by-the-book subaltern, fresh from OCTU, wanting to make good, and he'd joined a perilous mission behind enemy lines, given up the chance of going back with his squadron, to rescue him, Tom Caine. How did he deserve to have friends like that?

He caught Copeland's eye. 'Thanks, Harry,' he said.

Copeland's prominent Adam's apple bobbed. 'You still owe me a crate of beer for favours done, Tom. I wasn't letting you off the hook that easy.' He paused. 'Oh, and that reminds me, I've got something for you . . .'

He pitched a small shiny object at him: Caine caught it deftly. It was his Zippo lighter – minus its protective condom, but his all right: he found the initials *TEC* – Thomas Edward Caine – on its base. 'The Jerry Airborne took this off me when I was captured,' he said. 'How did you get it?'

'We fought an action against the Airborne on the way: village called Santa Lucia, Abruzzo region. I talked to a wounded Jerry: he gave me that. Roy already suspected they might have taken you to Jesi: this chap confirmed it. That's how we knew you were here.'

Caine flicked open the lighter, thumbed the wheel: a yellow flame sparked and flickered. He remembered the condom he'd taken from the effects of the couple in the forest: he still had it. He blew out the flame, closed the lid, found the rubber in his pocket, inserted the lighter into it. It was a small thing, but he was happy to have it back: the Zippo had saved his life at least once: he considered it a good-luck charm. He put it away, smiling. 'Things are looking up,' he said.

'So what *are* your plans, then?' asked Copeland.

Caine considered it for a moment. 'We have to find the Codex.'

'Well, where is it?'

'That's the problem: it could be anywhere.'

Copeland looked confused, glanced at Emilia. 'You and your brother must know, surely?'

'We do and we don't,' she said. 'I mean, we don't know individually, only together . . .'

She quailed under Copeland's gaze, flashed a plaintive glance at Caine.

He took a deep breath. 'There's no easy way of explaining this,' he said, 'so I'll just say it. Emilia's father planted the location of the Codex in her head while she was under hypnosis: when she came out, she couldn't remember it. It's still there, locked in her memory: it can be unlocked by Ettore, using a signal-phrase. The signal-phrase is no good unless it comes from him: no one else can unlock the secret.'

Copeland looked less surprised that Caine had expected. 'Sounds like Svengali,' he commented. 'I've heard of experiments like that.'

'But why is this flamin' Codex important?' Griffen barged in. 'I mean, it's on'y a book, ain't it?'

'It's a priceless artefact,' Emilia said. 'Something Hitler asked for personally before the war. Mussolini refused to give it up but, now he's gone, the SS are after it. They sent an official – a Dr Wolfram Stengel – to get it. He . . . well, he tried to force me to tell, but I couldn't, obviously . . . anyway, if the Germans get it, it'll be a big propaganda victory for them.'

Copeland nodded slowly. 'You said it could be anywhere. Does that entail gallivanting all over the place behind enemy lines?'

'Wot if it's somewhere 'eavily guarded?' Griffen suggested.

Copeland nodded. 'I can't commit the patrol to this, Tom: if we take casualties, the brass will want to know what we've been playing at.'

There was silence for a moment, then Griffen said, 'Wouldn't it be worth at least findin' out, sir? I mean, at least we'd know what we might be up against.'

Copeland considered it reluctantly, cocked an eyebrow at Emilia.

She cast a look at Ettore, who shrugged. 'We're both here,' he said. 'Why not give it a whirl?'

44

Light showed through the branches in scallopings of firegold, drifting like the sails of burning galleons through a haze of lilac and ethereal blue – a sky shawled with feathers of candy-floss pink, edged along the dark horizon with a wine-coloured band, like hot sealing-wax. The trees had lost their depth now: they stood starkly outlined like black candelabra against the solemn and furious sunset colours.

Emilia and Ettore settled down in a spot among the trees, secluded from the rest of the group, sat facing each other like dark chess-figures in the twilight.

Ettore snorted suddenly, collapsed in a fit of giggling.

'Come on, this is serious, ' Emilia told him. 'Think of Mum and Dad.'

'OK, are you ready?' He started sniggering again.

'Grow up, Ettore.'

'All right. I just hope I can remember the words.'

'Get on with it.'

'OK.' He drew a breath through his nostrils. When he spoke again, his voice was steady. 'I am Ettore Falcone. Father told you that only he and I can hypnotize you. He gave you a signal-phrase. I am going to say that phrase now, and you will pass instantly into deep hypnosis. You will tell me the location of the *Codex Aesinias* manuscript of the *Germania* of Tacitus. Do you understand?'

'Yes, I do.'

'OK. The phrase is, *the moon is clear tonight*.'

It was almost an hour before they returned, and the rest of the company were huddled in deep shadows around the embers of the fire. Emilia and her brother sat down silently.

''Ow did our Svengali do, then?' Wallace chuckled.

They eyed each other, didn't answer.

'What happened?' Caine asked. 'Did you find out where the Codex is?'

'Yes, we did,' Emilia said.

There was a beat of silence.

'Come on then, spit it out,' Wallace huffed. 'Don't keep us 'angin on.'

'Where is it?' asked Cope.

Emilia sighed. 'The Codex is hidden in a secret crypt underneath the chapel at Villa Montefalcone.'

'What?' Caine gasped. 'You sure about that?'

'That's where it is. We didn't even know there *was* a crypt under that chapel – the place is hardly big enough to swing a cat. The entrance is, apparently, under the altar.'

'But, Countess,' Copeland said, 'surely the villa is going to be crawling with Jerries now. It'll be guarded tighter than the Bank of England. Forget it. If we go in now, we'll take a lot of casualties.'

'We can't attempt it right this minute,' said Caine. 'We need to get Furetto and Cavanaugh some serious medical assistance. We have to go back to the partisans' camp –'

'Hold on, skipper,' Trubman said. 'Didn't Savarin want to arrest us last time we were there?'

'What's this?' Copeland demanded.

'Another long story, Harry,' said Caine. 'For now, let's just say there's some doubt about Savarin's security –'

'Yeah, like how did the Krauts know I'd be in Orsini when they picked me up?' Ettore cut in. 'How did they know you were going to ambush my escort? And they *did* know: that's why the convoy lagged behind – it was a trap.'

'Almost came off, too.' Caine nodded.

'Yeah, somebody told the Krauts what you were planning to do.'

'Must of bin quick,' Wallace mused. 'Even *we* didn't know we was doin' it till last night. Then there's the little matter of why Savarin tried to arrange it so as Taff an' me would be nabbed by Fritz, an' why he left Butterfield behind.'

There was quiet for a moment: the men mulled it over. Then Cope said. 'Let's get this straight. You want to go to the partisans' camp, even though you think Savarin's compromised?'

Caine heard the doubt in his voice, guessed that he was already seeing the exfiltration plan he'd worked out being diverted to yet another lost cause.

'I reckon we've got to,' Caine said. 'Like I said, Roy and Furetto need a doctor. Second, we have to pick up Butterfield. If we abandon him, the regiment will never let us forget it.'

Before they mounted the jeeps, Copeland called Caine over and presented him with yet another of his belongings: his Thompson sub-machine gun, cleaned and wrapped in oilcloth, with two hundred rounds of .45 calibre ammunition.

45

Near Montefalcone, Le Marche, Italy
11 October 1943

The partisan camp lay in a bowl of darkness: the trees rose around it like black bones, joined by a crazy weave of shoots, boughs and brambles, sharp-focused against the creamy blueness of the night. The place was without movement except for the last few *Giappisti* rolling up bedding and loading packs. Almost everyone else had left. Word had reached Savarin of the attack near Orsini that morning: Ettore Falcone had been successfully snatched from a Kraut convoy. It was clear to him that Caine's group had been responsible, though there were disturbing reports that other elements had been involved.

Savarin wasn't officially the leader of the partisan *banda* – his role was logistic support and liaison with Allied Forces HQ – but in practice his advice was almost always listened to. He'd pointed out to them that the Germans knew Ettore was a partisan: they would order a new search for the camp.

Savarin left the last few stragglers to sort themselves out, struck out into the forest. The Torn 'e' transmitter was hidden inside a hollow tree-trunk, about ten minutes' walk from the camp. The first thing he did when he got there was to check with his torch for any sign that anyone else had visited the place. He found none: the wireless-set was just as he'd left it, wrapped in oilcloth. He leaned his rifle against a tree, put the heavy box on a moss-covered rock, extended the antenna, attached the battery-unit, Morse key and headphones. The set hummed, began to warm up: he rolled the knob, tuned into the Sipo-SD frequency, watched the needles flicker on their crescent-shaped dials. He fitted the headphones, listened to squibs of static, tapped in 'Q' codes. The Gestapo operator came back at once.

The Nazis didn't know who Savarin was: to them he was an anonymous source who sometimes gave them accurate information. The way Savarin looked at it was that he was using them, giving them judicious tip-offs when he saw a tactical advantage. He was and always had been dedicated to the liberation of Italy, his father's country, but he couldn't stand interference from the Allies. For him, their role was to drop weapons and supplies, keep their noses out. Ever since Mussolini's departure, though, they'd acquired the irritating practice of sending in parachutists and behind-the-lines parties – commandos and saboteurs who knew nothing of the local situation: their blundering and heavy-handed activities drew the Hun's attention to the *Giappisti*, or resulted in atrocities against civilians. That had to be avoided at all costs.

As far as he was concerned, the Codex was irrelevant. Why the British were wasting energy on it, he couldn't fathom: the scheme had stirred up a hornets' nest. He'd thought it would be enough to tip off the Nazis about Butterfield's stick when they'd jumped near Ancona. How was he to know they'd be executed? He'd honestly believed they'd be treated as ordinary POWs.

When Ettore and the other young bloods had brought in Wallace and Trubman, he'd refused to believe they'd escaped from an execution. Even when he'd got word of Butterfield's convoy, he'd tried to persuade the boys to let it go. Much to his chagrin, Furetto and the others had ignored his advice and gone and ambushed the convoy anyway. Then he'd found himself burdened with three SAS soldiers the Germans were looking for. At the last camp, he'd attempted to sacrifice them: it would have been all right if that wild card Caine hadn't shown up.

Partisans sometimes donned Nazi uniforms on their operations, but what Caine had done was different: he'd worn the uniform of a collaborator. Whatever his intentions, he'd created a precedent, given the Hun a propaganda victory. That Savarin's own actions in giving information to Sipo-SD might also be construed as collaboration didn't bother him: he knew his motives were pure.

It was true that he'd also provided the Gestapo with the names of Ettore Falcone and other young partisans when they'd visited Orsini: that had been his way of disposing of the unruly faction in his group. It hadn't worked, though: Furetto and others were still around. Furetto had warned Caine that Savarin planned to stop them snatching Ettore: the youth was too clever for his own good: he'd no doubt facilitated their attack that morning, even allowed them to take the Alfa Romeo, which he wasn't expecting to see again. It was only a matter of time before Sipo-SD started combing the woods for the partisan camp. He'd decided to anticipate them by giving away its location: when they arrived, they'd find no one but Butterfield there. Savarin considered himself a good judge of character, and he didn't trust the fat major: under the bumbling exterior there was something about the man that wasn't kosher.

He finished the transmission, removed the headphones: he was about to wrap up when he heard a rustle in the undergrowth. He swung round, just as a pot-bellied figure stepped out of the darkness: it was Butterfield. Savarin let out a sigh of relief. '*Oh, it's you.*' He placed a hand on his heart. 'You scared the heck out of me. What are you doing, creeping around like that?'

Butterfield didn't smile: there was a stillness to him that Savarin didn't recognize. 'I followed you from the camp, old boy. You see, I can move quietly when I want to. Who were were you sending to? The Krauts?'

Savarin's smile was a mouthful of blue. 'Just business with Allied HQ.'

'Really? That's a German set, isn't it? A Torn "e"?

What's wrong with the wireless you've got back in camp?'

'It's diss: this is a back-up. There's nothing odd about using a German wireless – we use Jerry weapons, too.'

'Always the slick answer, eh, old chap? I suppose you hid it in that tree in case there was an attack on the camp?'

Savarin tossed his long hair. 'Something like that.'

Butterfield took a step closer to the wireless, squinted at the dials on its square face. 'I'd hazard a guess that it's tuned into a Jerry frequency. If I were to key in some "Q" codes right now, isn't that what I'd find?'

'Try it.' Savarin grinned. 'Be my guest.'

Butterfield shifted on his thick legs, made a movement as if to pick up the discarded headphones, thought better of it. In that instant, though, Savarin drew a pistol from under his jacket, stood up, jabbed it in Butterfield's midriff. 'Not so fast, *old boy*,' he said.

Butterfield's eyes widened. 'So, after all that guff about Caine being a traitor, we find out who the traitor really is.'

Savarin glowered. 'I'm no traitor. I've done nothing here that wasn't for the good of the partisans.'

Butterfield made a clucking sound: his eyes were hard black buttons. 'What about divulging the time and place of my drop to the Hun? What about my men, murdered by the Nazis? What about dumping me for the enemy to find, last time you moved camp? Was that for the good of the partisans?'

Savarin bristled: levelled the pistol at Butterfield's dome-shaped skull. 'You damn' SAS,' he spat. 'You drop in, carry out some mad scheme and clear off again, leaving us and the civvies to take the flack.'

'We *are* trying to win a war, old boy.'

'Win a war? Is that *really* why you're here, Major? You don't look much of a fighting man to me. And while we're on the subject of traitors, why did you tell me that Caine had joined the enemy and then do a complete about-face? There's something shifty about you: I can't quite put my finger on it, but it's there.'

Butterfield opened his mouth: Savarin cut him short, pressed the muzzle of the pistol into the flesh below his ear. The major took a step backwards. 'That's it,' Savarin said. 'Go back . . . right back into the bush. I was going to leave you alive for the Hun, but now it occurs to me that you might open your mouth too wide. You know what they say about dead men telling no tales.'

Butterfield's face was shiny in the darkness. 'This is silly, old fellow. I'm your superior officer. Put that weapon down at once.'

Savarin gave him a sad smile. At that moment a dark whirlwind erupted: a figure hurtled out of the bush, moving so fast it seemed a black blur: Butterfield flinched, clocked violent movement, heard the cricket-bat clump of a butt hitting Savarin's head, took in the groping white fingers that closed on the wrist of his shooting hand, shook the pistol free.

Butterfield stared at Savarin's suddenly horizontal body and up into the dark features of Tom Caine. It wasn't until that moment that he started shaking.

Caine let out a low whistle: Copeland and Trubman pushed through the black grid of branches: Ettore and Emilia followed close behind. Copeland produced a hank of parachute-cord: together he and Caine lashed Savarin to a tree. He was still conscious, his eyes flickered irately: there was a bump the size of a carbuncle on his head. Trubman crouched by the Torn 'e' set with Savarin's torch, examined the dials, donned the headphones, listened to the Morse traffic. 'That's it, boys,' he declared. 'Tuned to the Kraut network. He was in comms with the enemy, see.'

'He told them the location of the camp,' Butterfield warbled. 'They'll be here any minute.'

Caine and Copeland exchanged glances, the whites of their eyes like polished pearls in the blue dimness. They'd left Wallace and the rest of the SAS boys with the wagons, leaguered near the place they'd found the Alfa Romeo that morning. They'd moved in silently, using the track Furetto had shown them. Caine, scouting ahead of the others, had picked up wireless-hum, the sound of voices: he'd called the rest of the party to halt, gone to investigate. He'd lingered motionless in the bushes long enough to hear Savarin's virtual confession.

'What about the camp?' Caine asked Butterfield.

'Nobody there. Everyone's gone –'

Somewhere a grenade went *kaa-THOMMPPP*: the night air shuddered. Butterfield jumped: Caine half crouched, gripped his Thompson, heard the pop of Very pistols. He strained to peer up through the leaves, saw flares hanging like green cat's eyes on the night sky.

There was a sudden groan from Savarin. '*Too late. They're here.*'

The forest crackled with gunfire: the *tack-tack-tack* of machine guns, rifle shots like brittle branches being snapped. Another grenade went *kaaa-BOMMFFFF*: Caine heard the rip of blasted metal, smelt oil and smoke fumes. 'One of theirs,' he said. 'That was a No. 36: tell it a mile away.'

'Good old Fred,' Trubman said.

Copeland grabbed Caine's arm, manouevred him out of Savarin's hearing: the others followed, squatted together. A Spandau snickered *tacka-tacka-chack-chack-chack*: a Vickers 'K' answered with a deep-throated *punka-punka-punka-punk*.

'We've got to get back to the leaguer, Tom,' Cope whispered. 'Get our wagons out.'

More flares went up: Caine saw ladders of green light like bottle-rockets arcing across the sky. He turned his face to Emilia, saw her brush wayward strands of hair out of her eyes. 'How long will it take us to get to the villa from here – on foot?'

'On *foot*?' she repeated.

'About twenty minutes,' Ettore cut in. 'There's a short-cut through the forest: the short side of a triangle.'

'You know the way?' Caine asked.

'Sure. I grew up in these woods.'

'OK.' Caine leaned forward. 'Harry, you and Taff go back to the leaguer with Major Butterfield. Get the jeeps out if it's the last thing you do. *When* you do, drive like the clappers to the villa.'

Copeland nodded: Caine could sense his reluctance. He hadn't wanted to get mixed up in Caine's mission, and now he'd got caught – just what he'd been afraid of.

'And what are *you* going to do?' he asked.

'We're going to get the Codex. We'll take the path through the woods to the villa. We'll meet you there.'

'But didn't you agree that the place might be full of Jerries?'

'Maybe. Maybe not. We'll take our chance.'

Copeland was quiet for a moment: his face lay in shadow, his eyeballs stood out whitely. Rifles whomped, machine guns *rack-tacked*: Cope heaved a long breath. 'All right, Tom. But if we're not there in an hour, don't hang about.'

'You'll be there, Harry. I know you will.'

'Now wait a minute, old boy,' Butterfield steamed in. 'I'd rather go with you.' Caine glanced at him: his eyes were dark caverns, his billiard-ball head sheeny with sweat.

'Sorry, Major. We need to move fast on this one.'

'But the Codex is *my* mission: I'm the ranking officer here.'

'You effectively handed command over to me. Now I'm deciding. If you want to report me for insubordination, you can add it to the list.'

Butterfield brooded in silence.

'What about Savarin?' Trubman asked.

'Three choices,' Caine said. 'Leave him there, let him go, or kill him. Whatever you decide, don't take too long.'

There was a spike of gunfire from the direction of the leaguer: Caine heard bullets zing, heard slow ricochets drone like bluebottles.

He cradled his Thompson close. 'Emilia. Ettore. You ready to do this?'

'Why not?' Ettore said. 'I was on my way to be executed this morning, anyway.'

'We *have* to come,' Emilia said. 'The Codex is our business.'

'All right. You got weapons and ammunition?'

'Sure.'

Caine paused for a last glance at Copeland's face, a pale ellipsis in the darkness. 'Thanks for pulling us out, Harry. I owe you another crate of beer.'

Copeland stood up, let his SMLE drop into his hands. 'See you on the ledge, mate.'

'Not if I see you first.'

They didn't shake hands or say goodbye but rose silently, melted like shadows into the darkness of the forest.

46

Villa Montefalcone, Le Marche, Italy
11 October 1943

They approached the villa from the western side, passed the rocky crag where they'd sheltered and the hidden door in the forest. It occurred to Caine that they might use the key, get in that way, until Emilia pointed out that the chapel was built into the old girdle wall of the villa and could only be entered from the outside. He remembered the claustrophobic terror he'd suffered in the shaft, whispered a silent prayer.

The villa stood in silvered moonlight, a dark sprawl like a fallen mountain, under a velour sky swarming with stars. Lying in the trees, with Emilia and Ettore on either side, Caine could make out only a denser zone of darkness, a thicket of towers like ebony columns. They lay there for five minutes, listening with bated breath for the sound of voices, probing the darkness for any sign of movement. The silence was almost sinister: Caine's senses told him the place was deserted, but there was a small voice of warning inside his skull.

'I think they've gone,' Ettore whispered in his ear. 'I'd guess they were withdrawn to guard my transfer.

I speak some German: I heard them talking. That officer Furetto shot – he was in charge of troops at the villa.

'*Kaltenbraun*,' Emilia said. 'You're right – he was the chief here.' She paused. 'Poor guy. He was a Kraut all right, but he stopped his men from touching me. Pity it had to be him who was killed.'

'That's war for you.' Caine sighed. He realized that whatever reservations he might have, they'd have to take a gamble. He cupped a breath. 'You're not obliged to do this,' he said. 'You're both civilians, and –'

'– and I'm just a kid, and my sister's a slip of a girl, is that it?' Ettore cut in harshly.

'*Shhh!*' Caine hissed. 'Not at all. I was your age when I joined the army: some of the best fighters I ever met were girls.'

'Anyway,' Emilia said, 'I doubt if you'd find the Codex on your own.'

Caine nodded in resignation. 'Let's go for it, then.'

They moved around the dark maze of buildings, staying in the trees, jogging across open patches, till they came abreast of the chapel, a low, pitch-roofed stone structure that seemed to grow like a spur out of the dark cliff of the girdle-wall: it stood only twenty yards away, across the gravel drive. They watched and waited: nothing stirred.

'All right,' Caine whispered. 'I'll go in. You cover.'

'No,' Ettore said. 'I'll go in. *You* cover.'

'That's an order,' Caine said. 'Wait two minutes, then

you come.' Before Ettore could reply, he was up and moving silently across the drive, towards the chapel. It took only seconds to make the steps on the front portico: he crouched in the recess of the door, cradled his Tommy-gun, ranged the muzzle of his weapon across the chasm of darkness. He waited for the others, heard the crunch of their feet on the gravel, saw them come out of the shadows, saw the glint of their sub-machine guns amidst grey outlines. They squatted together by the door: Caine rose, pushed the wood tentatively: it creaked open. He stepped inside, shone Cope's torch around the interior. It certainly wasn't big as churches went – low ceiling, peeling stucco walls, solid-looking chairs in short rows either side of the aisle. At the far end, about fifteen paces from the door, standing on what appeared to be a Persian carpet, was an altar draped in white linen, decorated with a silver crucifix and candlesticks.

Emilia and Ettore squeezed past him: carried torchlight on their backs, became giant batwings flitting across the ceiling and walls. They halted by the altar: Caine moved up beside them. 'OK, so what do we do?'

'We'll have to shift the altar,' Emilia said. 'The trap door's underneath.'

The altar was marble, and it was heavy: Emilia and Ettore laid their Schmeissers on the nearest chairs: Caine slung his Tommy across his back. It took maximum effort from all three of them to drag it clear. Caine examined the exposed carpet with his torch, saw circular marks where the legs of the altar had compacted it over years. 'Probably never been opened since your father hid the Codex here,' he said.

Emilia and Ettore rolled up the carpet, revealing a floor of white stone flags. In the very centre, directly below where the altar had stood, was a black rectangle about three feet square, flush with the rest of the floor. '*That's it*,' Ettore crowed. 'All the times we used to come here when we were kids, and we never knew it existed.'

'You remember the stories?' Emilia said. 'A secret cave hidden under the chapel, used by Mithras worshippers in Roman times? It was said that the Christians built the *chiesetta* right on top of it.'

'Dad reckoned it was a myth,' Ettore chuckled. 'In any case, there were enough *known* secret passages to keep a kid going, without legends.'

Emilia knelt down, ran her hand across the smooth black stone. 'How do we open it, though? There's no lock or handle – nothing.'

'Shall I try shifting one of the candlesticks?' Ettore smirked. 'That's what they do in the movies.'

Caine knelt beside them. 'These things usually work on a simple counterweight principle,' he said, 'with some kind of pressure mechanism.'

He stood up, pressed one end of the flagstone with his foot: nothing happened. He shifted to the opposite end of the square, pressed again. The black flagstone didn't move, but the adjacent white one rose a millimetre at the far end. Caine pressed the black flagstone a third time: the white slab rose further, the end flipped up suddenly, like a two-inch-thick seesaw: the entire slab lifted clear of the floor on what looked like a hinged metal arm, came to rest at an eighty-degree angle, with a low click.

'*Yeah!*' Ettore cheered.

'*Sssh!*' Emilia told him. 'Keep your voice down.'

'It wasn't medieval Christians or ancient Romans who put this trap door in,' Caine whispered. 'That's modern precision engineering.'

He shone his torch into the dark space below, noted a narrow flight of steps descending into the darkness. 'A proper Aladdin's cave,' he said. 'And I'm going to be Aladdin.'

'I'm going down too,' Emilia said.

'That's three of us,' added Ettore.

'Someone's got to stay here,' said Caine. 'Keep watch.'

Ettore screwed up his thin mouth. 'OK, but I get to go down later. And, by the way, no smooching my sis in the dark.'

Emilia gave him a token slap.

They descended the steps cautiously, Caine leading, with his torch. The air smelt sharp and sour, the torch-beam showed walls of solid rock. Caine was almost on the lowest step when he stopped abruptly: Emilia stumbled into him. She was about to protest when she saw what had stopped him: the floor of the chamber was littered with dismembered skeletons, skulls, ribcages, pelvic girdles, pile upon pile of yellowed bones from scores of bodies.

'A charnel-house,' Caine said.

He stepped down amongst the bones, kicked at a skull, saw it dissolve into fragments and chalk powder. 'You can't pin this one on the Nazis,' he said. 'Been here donkey's years.'

'Mithras worshippers,' Emilia said: she banged the side of her fist against the rock wall. 'This is a cave, just like the stories say: the chapel must have been built on top of it. These skeletons might have been here since the time of Christ.'

Caine moved forward, crunched on bones, booted them aside. The cavern was about the same size as the chapel above: the walls curved, bulging out at the base in small peninsulas, like tree-roots. The rock itself was curiously fluted, giving the whole aspect an organic feel. At the far end, roughly underneath the chapel door, Caine reckoned, a deep alcove was carved into the rock, arching over a wooden chest bound with iron. Caine examined the big box carefully: it looked like a sea-chest in a pirate story – domed, barrel-like lid strengthened with an iron frame and five steel bands across the top. There were metal handles on both sides, and an iron hasp with a large brass padlock on the front face. 'This has to be it,' he said.

Emilia wove her way through the bone-piles: for a long moment they stood elbow to elbow contemplating the object. 'My father overlooked one thing,' Emilia said. 'The key. How are we going to open it?'

Caine ran his hand along the iron rim of the lid,

yanked at the padlock. He pushed at the chest: it didn't budge an inch. 'Base must be weighted with something,' he said. 'Probably lead.'

'Couldn't you pick the lock?'

Caine thumped the lid with a closed fist. 'Dammit. We haven't got time for lock-picking, even if I had the right tool. The only way to get in is to smash it open.'

He began to hunt around among the bones for a sharp stone, gave up, handed the torch to Emilia. He unslung his Tommy-gun, held the butt poised over the chest. 'I just wish we had a sledgehammer,' he said.

He raised the Thompson, brought the butt down with all his strength, struck the space between two iron bands with a hard crack: the wood didn't break. Caine struck it again and again, panting with frustration.

'Everything all right down there?' It was Ettore's voice, sounding muffled and distant, from the direction of the stairs.

'It's OK,' Emilia called out. 'We've found something.'

She peered at the chest, holding the torch-beam close: where Caine had struck the wood, there was a hairline crack, almost imperceptibly branched. She touched it with her fingertips. 'Look,' she said. 'You've made a start. Try again.'

Caine narrowed his eyes, belted the chest again, put all his force and bodyweight behind the blow. The Tommy-gun struck the lid: the wood splintered, caved in. Caine whacked it over and over in a frenzy of blind resolve, opened a jagged hole that grew wider as he worked at the edges, hiving off slivers and wood-chips. He was breathing hard: sweat ran down his forehead. He lifted the Tommy-gun again: Emilia grabbed his wrist.

'That's enough, Tom. We can get in now.'

Caine let his weapon drop, saw that the aperture he'd hacked out between the iron bands was about a foot and a half square. He stood back, his chest heaving, wiped sweat off his brow. He glanced at Emilia, saw her brush hair away from her face, saw eyes that sparkled like garnets in the torchlight. 'That's it, then,' he breathed. 'You want to do the lucky dip?'

Emilia nodded excitedly, passed the torch back to him, took a deep breath, moved nearer to the chest. She hesitated, then pushed her right arm through the opening, until her shoulder touched the lid. She groped around inside. 'There's nothing here,' she gasped. 'No, wait a minute, what's this?'

She fished around for a moment, let out a moan of effort, withdrew her arm carefully, brought up what looked like a double-size shoebox tied with string. Caine slung his weapon, helped her twist and manoeuvre the box between the iron bands. She laid it on the lid in front of them.

For an instant they stood staring at it. Then Caine pulled out his knife, cut the string. He put the knife away, nodded to Emilia, who leaned across the box next to him. 'Oh God,' she gasped. 'This *better* be it.'

She placed her hands either side of the box, lifted the lid carefully, set it aside. Caine shone the torch-beam inside: they both gaped at the book that lay there like an infant in a cradle, in a bed of white cloth. She lifted the manuscript out gingerly: Caine shone the torch, saw a volume bound in gnarled, faded, purplish-brown calfskin with some motif – vaguely floral – embossed into it. What astonished him was how slim it was: no thicker than a commercial counterbook. 'So this is what all the shouting's about?' he asked incredulously.

'Only twenty-three pages.' Emilia smiled. 'Not a book at all, really. There were several other copies, but they were all lost in the Middle Ages.'

She opened the cover: showed Caine crinkled parchment pages covered in cramped lines of writing: a sprawl of spidery black letters with long tails: he wouldn't even have recognized them as belonging to the alphabet. Emilia pointed to the title-page on the left: the lettering here was in alternating lines of red and black, in capitals that were, at least, legible.

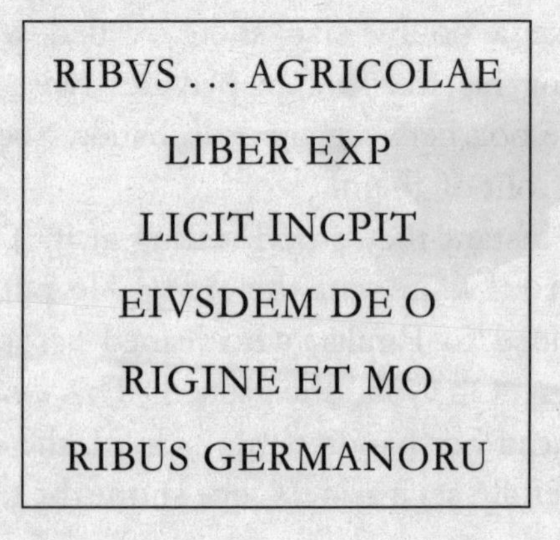

RIBVS . . . AGRICOLAE

LIBER EXP

LICIT INCPIT

EIVSDEM DE O

RIGINE ET MO

RIBUS GERMANORU

'I don't know Dutch,' Caine said. 'Just tell me we got the right book.'

Emilia closed the cover, replaced the manuscript in its box. Suddenly her arms were around him, drawing him to her: he felt her body tight against his, felt yielding, soft breasts, fluid sinew and muscle, felt her thigh against his crotch, felt her breath in his ear.

'*We got it*,' she whispered huskily. '*Thank you*.'

Caine coiled his arms round her waist, touched the lean arc of her back with his left hand: the torch, still in his right, sent rills of brilliance across the stone ceiling. She moved against him: a gush of warmth spread through his blood: tiny pulses swarmed like pins and needles through his limbs. For an instant he forgot the Codex, forgot the Hun, forgot even that they were standing in a charnel-house ankle-deep in bones, forgot everything but the black-haired girl in his arms, with the pillow-soft mouth and the oriental eyes. She turned her face to his: in the deflected torchlight he saw irises like new moons, saw lips part to reveal mother-of-pearl teeth. He bent his head towards her, caressed her lips with his own, sipped the silvery taste of her mouth. She cupped a hand behind his neck, pulled his head gently down, kissed him softly, then much harder. Caine felt the magnetic force of her body dragging him in irresistibly, felt the soft breath from her nostrils on his cheek, buried himself in her. The kiss went on, searching, growing in intensity, an endless moment in which he was utterly and completely lost to the world.

'*How very touching*,' a cold voice said in cracked English.

Caine broke away from Emilia's kiss, went for his knife. '*Stop!*' the voice lashed out. 'Or I will shoot this boy.'

Caine's Thompson was slung vertically across his back: he knew he'd never bring it to bear in time. He turned his head towards the staircase at the opposite end of the chamber, saw two shadowy figures in his torchbeam, standing at the bottom of the stairs. The first was Ettore, his lean face a sick greenish ivory against the inkwashed shadows. Behind him, with a pistol pressed against his spine, he glimpsed the features of Wolfram Stengel: a penumbra of whiskers, sharp devil's eyebrows, eyes of gunpit black.

'Put down the torch,' Stengel snapped.

Caine hesitated: Stengel jabbed Ettore with his pistol.

'All right. All right,' Caine said.

'And your weapons,' Stengel added. 'All of them.'

Caine crouched, laid his torch, Tommy-gun and knife on the rock floor. He stood up slowly: his mouth was dust-dry: a fist clenched tightly in his chest. He was furious with himself. He'd got distracted, forgotten even that he was in a tactical situation. Stengel had overpowered Ettore, forced him down the steps of the crypt at gunpoint, and Caine hadn't even heard them coming: he'd thrown all caution to the wind. It was in such unguarded moments that the enemy got you: it was almost always a fatal mistake.

Stengel switched on a torch, caught Caine and Emilia squarely in its beam. 'The traitor and the countess,' he sneered. 'A fitting match. Did you know that Mr Caine here is a traitor, Countess? Did he tell you that he wore SS uniform and swore an oath of allegiance to the Führer? No? I didn't think so.'

'Fuck you, Stengel,' Emilia spat.

The bearded man chuckled. 'No, but I have fucked *you*. In more than *one* way, eh? Did you know I fucked the countess, Caine? Did she tell you?' He leaned slightly over Ettore's shoulder. 'Did she tell *you*, boy?'

'You'll rot in hell for that, you Nazi bastard,' Ettore spat.

Stengel chuckled. 'In *hell*? I don't think so: we Germans prefer rational alternatives.' He paused. 'For myself, though, I rely a great deal on intuition. For example, I had a . . . what do you say? . . . a *hunch* . . . that you would return to the villa, Countess. I guessed that you needed your brother to find the Codex. *What is sought lies in a place with no doors or windows*, that was the clue. But not this place, not a physical place: a secret locked in your head. You are the door: your brother is the key.'

Caine glanced at Emilia, felt his guts churn: no one could have told Stengel but Ettore, and Caine was sure he hadn't talked. No, Stengel wasn't boasting: he'd worked the whole thing out in a leap of insight. It was clever: Caine had to give him that.

Stengel inched his torchbeam over the iron-bound

chest, halted on the open box. 'And so you have found the Codex,' he said, 'and so it is collection time for me. You can have no idea, any of you, how valuable this manuscript is to the German people. The *Germania* is the only existing record of the loftiness, purity and nobility of our Teutonic ancestors. Long before Rome was even a city, we had an empire that rivalled Alexander's. We are a chosen people: our struggles against our neighbours are legitimate. What was once, shall be again.'

'My father said the *Germania* shows how you Krauts were still eating cabbages and throwing stone clubs at each other when the Romans had reached the pinnacle of civilization,' Emilia said.

Stengel scoffed. 'History is written by the winners, my dear Countess. Your poor father is no longer here to give his opinion. We already have copies of the text: the *Codex Aesinias*, though, is the only extant version of the original – an icon in itself. Herr Himmler has dreamed of obtaining this book for twenty years: he will be most pleased.'

'Bully for Himmler,' Ettore said.

'Yes,' Stengel said sharply: he prodded the boy again with his weapon. 'Now, I want you to throw that box over to me, Countess. Be very careful. If I sense a wrong movement, your brother will be shot. Only when I have the Codex in my hand will I let him go.'

'And then what?' Emilia demanded. 'You're going to kill us all?'

'You killed at least one SS-man: you and Caine tried to kill *me*, and almost succeded. What would you do in these circumstances? To tell you the truth, I have not yet decided. But if you have any ideas of escape, I suggest you forget them. I am not alone: there is a squad of SS-men outside, and they are in no mood to play around with partisans, traitors or saboteurs. Now, throw the Codex to me, please. Make sure it is packed well: I would not want to damage Herr Himmler's present.'

Emilia glanced at Caine: he nodded.

'Don't do it, Emilia,' Ettore croaked. 'Think of Dad. Let him shoot me: it's my fault he got in. I was dozing: I wasn't even holding my weapon.'

Emilia ignored him, turned to the chest, picked up the lid of the cardboard box, fitted it back on with care. She took a couple of paces towards Stengel, swung the box, tossed it in his direction. It fell a little in front of him, landed among the bones with a flat bump, a puff of dust. Stengel shoved Ettore hard towards the others. '*Go. Go!*'

Keeping his pistol pointed at them, he thrust his torch into his armpit, crouched down to pick up the box with his left hand. *Finally*, he thought. *The Reichsführer will never forget this*. His hand froze in mid-flight: he focused with horror on the half-disintegrated skull the box had landed on, the vacant eye-sockets, the gaping, toothless jaw. His eyes shifted left and right: he saw more skulls, spiny ribcages, piles of crumbling bones.

His heart raced: sweat poured down his face: he began to shake. *It's them. The Jew-Bolshevik commissars. They're here.* As he stared, the bones took shape, became whole, started to grow flesh: ribcages sprouted limbs and organs – kidneys, livers, beating hearts. Skulls became faces: boat-hook Jew noses, glittering yellow eyes, rat-like front teeth, paper-thin skin stretched over cheekbones. They rose in a silent squadron, old men, young women, small children in prison-rags: emaciated bodies moving soundlessly towards him, faces leering with wry amusement.

Stengel tried to move, found that his legs were rigid, his feet rooted to the floor. From somewhere came a spine-chilling shriek that seemed to fill his ears, to echo and re-echo off the rock walls. With a new flush of horror, Stengel realized that the scream had come from his own mouth. The echoes were replaced abruptly by rumbling laughter, low at first, but growing in pitch, filling out with bass chuckles and contralto titters, till the crypt was reverberating with noise. Stengel stumbled backwards, dropped his torch, yelled. '*It wasn't me! I was carrying out orders!*'

He raised his pistol, tried to aim with a madly jerking hand: before he could fire, two shots rang out from behind him: a panzer crashed into his back, a supernova exploded inside his head in ear-bending percussion, a gush of putrid gas, shimmering spiderlegs of light. The last thing he saw before he slipped down the long black corridor was one hundred and five Jew-demons gathered around him like vultures, poised on ribbed wings, their hands become sharp claws, their eyes burning red, their mouths full of sharp and bloody teeth.

Caine saw Stengel stagger, saw the mask of terror on his face, saw his torch drop, heard his ear-piercing screams, saw him raise his weapon, heard the *bomff-bomff* of a double tap that crashed and thundered in the chamber, saw Stengel lurch forward, sprawl across the bones. Caine grabbed his Thompson and torch: he crouched with the weapon in one hand, the torch in the other, saw Emilia and Ettore gaping towards the stairs, saw a figure standing framed in the oval stairwell: a dark, protuberant shape like an enormous, bloated chess-pawn – fishbowl head, pear-shaped torso, thick legs, a fat-jowled face that seemed a nebulous mask, the features vague and distorted, like an out-of-focus photograph. Caine remembered his dream, recalled the hooded figure on the endless stairs that came towards him but remained always the same distance away, recalled eyes like diamonds of fire beneath the fine veil of the winding-sheet.

'Didn't know if I could do it, old boy,' a voice panted. 'First time in combat, and all that.'

Caine blinked, recognized the scarred and mottled moonface, the button mouth, the drooping dewlaps: Major Bunny Butterfield. He was poised stolidly on the bottom step, with a haversack slung over his shoulder, a torch clipped to his breast pocket and a pistol in a miniature hand.

'*Major?*' Caine's voice was slightly breathless. 'How did *you* get here?'

Butterfield took a few steps, examined Stengel's body in the light of his torch-beam. 'Followed you, old chap,' he said. 'Sneaked off while the others were debating what to do with Savarin.' He peered around, scanned the chamber. 'My God, look at all these bones. It's a proper graveyard down here.'

He picked up the box containing the Codex. 'Is this it, then? The *Codex Aesinias*? By golly, I've suffered for this.'

Caine and Emilia moved closer to him through the bone-piles: Ettore followed. 'It's a good thing you came,' Emilia said. 'Stengel was going to kill us.'

Butterfield tore his eyes away from the box. 'What on earth was going *on* down here? I heard the most frightful screams.'

Caine nodded at Stengel's body. 'He had some kind of fit. Started bawling and ranting, acted as if he could see something that wasn't there.'

'I hope this manuscript isn't cursed,' Butterfield chuckled. 'Just think how many have died for it. I am so pleased to have it at last: it will be the pride of my collection.'

'*Your* collection?' Ettore snickered. 'In your dreams, bud. The Codex belongs to my family. We're moving it out of the country, not giving it away.'

'I imagine I'm as entitled to it as Himmler. The Codex is worth an absolute mint, but it's not the money:

I'm a collector. I love old things. So much more real than people, don't you think?'

Caine gawked at him in the torchlight. 'You mean you're *stealing* the Codex?'

'I wouldn't *exactly* call it stealing, old boy, more like spoils of war. I put my life on the line. King and country is all very well, but one would like to get something worthwile out of all this. So, if you mean, shall I be handing it in once I get back, no I shan't. It will only end up in the collection of some better-connected gouger. That's the way it goes. Most of the treasures in the BM were nicked from their rightful owners at some time or other. In any case, I've heard about the looting your 1st Regiment chaps have been up to since you first landed in Italy. Why is it any different for me?'

Caine stared at Butterfield, wondered if he'd gone bonkers: he seemed cool and confident, though, as if he was in the process of achieving some great purpose.

'You told me the scheme came down from "A" Force, but it was yours from the beginning, wasn't it?' Caine said. 'The object was always to keep the Codex for yourself?'

Butterfield blew out plump cheeks. 'Start to finish, old chap. Got the notion when I questioned an Itie prisoner, an infantry subaltern captured in Tunisia. Distant relative of yours, Countess: told me all about the Codex, how the Nazis wanted it so badly, how they'd get it now that Musso was out of the picture. Then I found out through int. reports that the SS had dispatched a squad to retrieve it. I had to get it before them: I conceived the scheme, got it approved by the DMI.'

'I don't understand,' Caine said. 'If you wanted it for yourself, why did you give the mission to me?'

'I thought I was for the high-jump at the time. It was an outside chance that I'd escape: I was covering all the angles. Even if they executed me, I didn't want Himmler to get it. Then, when I came round in the partisan camp and realized that I actually *had* escaped, I became even more determined that I wouldn't go back without it.'

'You're off your chump, Major. You must be if you think we're going to let you walk out of here with the Codex: and I'm going to report you the moment we get back.'

Butterfield shifted the box under his free arm, stowed it in his haversack. 'You *are* going to let me walk out of here, Caine. As for reporting me, how many people are going to believe an officer who put on a collaborator's uniform and swore allegiance to Hitler? You're a traitor Caine: whichever way you slice it, you joined the enemy. That's taboo in the British Army, as you well know. Breathe a whisper about the Codex, and I'll shop you, lock, stock and barrel. I'm a major and a staff-officer: I think they'll believe me, don't you?'

'You've certainly changed your tune,' Caine said. 'You told Savarin it was a ruse on my part.'

'Maybe that was your intention, old boy. Maybe you did it because I asked you to break me out. If so, I'm grateful. But I supported you against Savarin because we had to snatch the boy to get the Codex, that's all. I can quite easily change my story.'

'You'll never get out,' Ettore cut in. 'There are Krauts up there.'

'Oh, I think I will, dear boy. There are Jerries around, certainly, making a noise like a herd of elephants: when I arrived they were patrolling the woods. They didn't see me come in, and I doubt they'll see me go out. Our departed friend here left his staff-car conveniently near, *and* he left the keys in it. I thought I might as well do a bunk in style.'

'You're going to leave us here?' Emilia said. 'To the Krauts?'

'I'm sure you'll find a way out. After all, what would you have done if I hadn't come?'

Caine was judging the distance between himself and Butterfield: the major's pistol was pointing at Emilia: Caine had his Thompson under his arm and his torch in one hand. He could drop the torch, bring the weapon up. He readied himself mentally for the move: Emilia suddenly launched herself at the major, hair streaking back, hands flailing, screaming, '*Give it back, you fat bastard!*' Caine jettisoned his torch, grabbed for Butterfield's pistol-hand. His fingers closed around the major's wrist, encountered unexpected resistance: he was aware of Emilia raking at Butterfield's face with her nails, of Ettore closing in behind her with his fists up, of the major trying to twist the pistol away from his grip: suddenly, the pistol went off. Caine felt the shocking impact against his ear-drums, smelt the stiff tang of the bullet, saw the dark rosette that opened up in Emilia's armpit, saw her teeter, saw her slump down into the bone-shards with blood trickling from a wound in her neck. In that instant, Butterfield broke away, seized Ettore by the collar, stuck the pistol into his ribs, backed him away towards the stairs. 'That was your fault, Caine. You tried to grab the pistol and it went off. You're to blame.'

Caine brought up his Thompson: he'd made a head-shot before – he'd once shot Johann Eisner at almost the same range.

'*Shoot, shoot!*' Ettore yelled.

'*He'll die,*' Butterfield quavered: he paused to negotiate the first step. '*I mean it this time.*'

Caine settled the butt of the SMG into his shoulder. His finger was on the trigger: he was about to take first pressure when Ettore stumbled over the steps, wriggled out of Butterfield's grip, drifted right into Caine's sights. Caine shifted his muzzle instantly: in that moment Butterfield fired a single shot: flame speared, gasses tore, Caine ducked, came up into a firing stance: Butterfield had vanished. Ettore was poised to run after him: Caine pulled him back. 'Don't. You're not armed. Look after your sister: try to stop the bleeding.'

He thrust Ettore behind him, was about to mount the stairs when he heard the trap door bang. 'Oh, shit,' he said.

He ran up the steps, heaved his shoulder against the closed slab: the flagstone wouldn't budge. He shifted his attention to the mechanism opposite, humped down on the hinged arm until he felt the counterweights move: the trap door flew open. He emerged cautiously, Tommy-gun ready, found the chapel silent, empty but for its furniture and the two Schmeisser sub-machine guns Ettore and Emilia had left there earlier.

47

Constantine, Algeria
11 November 1943

'*You ain't Captain Caine, you're the devil,*' Caine said.

'What's that?' Blaney asked.

'Something one of the lads came out with after the Murro di Porco raid. Not a mark on him, but he was messed up, half crazy. Said he'd seen me on the battlefield, and that I was the devil. He was right: either that or I've got the devil's curse on me. It was my fault Butterfield shot Emilia. Just like Betty Nolan was my fault. Just like the boys I lost at the Senarca bridge, just like all the other men I've lost through mistakes and impulsive actions.'

Blaney sighed, stared round the cell, glanced at her watch: 0604 hours: it must be almost daybreak up there in the real world. They'd sat up the whole night, and today was supposed to be the day of Caine's court-martial.

She reached across the table, touched his hand. 'I'm sorry about the countess, Tom. It must have been terrible for you after what happened to Betty.'

'You'd think I'd be used to it, all the people I've lost. It doesn't get any easier, though.'

'That's good, Tom: if you can feel that, it means you're still human.'

'At least she's alive.'

He picked up the packet of Gold Flake cigarettes, shook it moodily. There was one fag left.

'Twos up?'

She nodded: Caine lit the cigarette, passed it to Blaney. His eyes had a lost, almost dazed look, she thought.

She blew smoke, handed the fag back to him. 'So, how did you get out in the end?'

Caine let smoke trickle through his nostrils. 'Harry Copeland and his crew broke out of the Jerry cordon: they were a bit late, but they made the RV. Butterfield was long gone, of course. By that stage, I couldn't give a toss about the Codex: I was concerned with Emilia. When I got back down into the crypt, Ettore was with her, trying to staunch the bleeding. She was barely conscious: the round had entered her armpit, come out of the place between shoulder and neck. She was in shock, but at least she was still breathing. We didn't have any field-dressings, so we improvised with strips of torn cloth and the bandage I'd put on her neck earlier. I checked that Stengel was dead: Butterfield's shots had hit him in the upper back, but there was a big exit wound in his chest: it looked as though he'd taken a round through the heart or something. The thing I'll never forget, though, was his face: it was contorted with terror, as if he'd seen all the demons of hell before he died.

'I carried Emilia up to the chapel, laid her on the carpet. For a while I just sat there, knowing there was nothing more I could do, holding her, stroking her hair, listening to her breath. Ettore sat slumped in a corner, shattered. He'd had a pretty rough time that day: started out being transported to his own execution, saw his friend badly wounded, his sister shot, the Codex carried off by a chap who was meant to be an ally. Emilia had been mother and father to him since their parents were killed, and he was terrified of losing her.

'We sat there, half expecting the Jerries to come in, but they never did: we heard their shouts from time to time. Since Stengel's car wasn't there, they probably thought he'd gone, turned their attention elsewhere. Then we heard a firefight start up: the crack and thump of rifles, the *tack-tack* of Schmeissers, the bump of Spandaus, followed by the *pop-pop-pop* of Vickers "K"s and the whack of No. 36 grenades: when I heard that, I knew Harry and the others were there. We'd moved Emilia to the door, ready to carry her into the forest if necessary. A jeep skidded to a halt outside, Wallace on guns, Harry Copeland at the wheel. "*What kept you?*" I said.

'They'd taken casualties: Several of the 2nd Regiment lads had been hit: Bill Harris was the worst – a round had taken off half his jaw. Anyway, the ding-dong was still going on: we loaded Emilia on to a stretcher sharpish, mounted up, took off, ran the gauntlet of Jerry fire with our guns ripping, RV-ed with the other jeeps on the road. We had to keep moving while it was still dark: Cope had worked out a good return route across the mountains: we had no way of knowing which way Butterfield had gone, so we gave up any idea of retrieving the Codex. How he got back, I don't know.

'The bad news was that neither Furetto nor Roy Cavanaugh made it out of the contact. Cavanaugh died from his wounds: Furetto was hit in the crossfire, died instantly. Harry had no choice but to leave their bodies behind. As for Savarin, they just let him go: God only knows where he is now. The good news, though, was that they also acquired a prisoner in the shoot-out – *SS-Sturmbannführer* Karl Grolsch. He was in quite a bad way: he shouldn't even have been in the field. On top of that, he had a new gunshot wound in the face which Fred Wallace had given him before he and Copeland snatched him from under Hun noses. They stuck him in the front jeep with a weapon to his head, yelled at the Jerries that they'd snuff him if they didn't let them through. That was how they got out. Grolsch wasn't in much of a state to talk, and we weren't in much of a mood to question him. We could have shot him, but as a Waffen-SS *Feldkommandant*, we thought he might be useful to Intelligence: as a war criminal, responsible for the execution of British POWs, we reckoned he should be put on trial. We patched him up and kept him going.'

Blaney pricked up her ears. 'So Grolsch survived? Where is he now?'

'All I know is that they brought him here to Constantine. Why?'

'Because he's the only witness to your recruitment to the BFC. He should have been asked for a deposition.'

'It won't make any difference, Celia. I *am* a traitor, just as Stengel said. I put on that uniform of my own free will: I'm pleading guilty.'

Blaney smoked the last of the cigarette, stubbed it out in an ashtray made of a tin-lid already brimful of ash and dog-ends.

'How do you know you did it of your own free will?' she asked bluntly. 'You said you can't remember what happened. You recall walking through a mirror, which is impossible for most mortals, and coming to in a room with a naked girl in your bed, whom Amray claimed you had . . . made *love* to . . . although you have no memory of it. Assuming you're telling the truth – and I'm sure you are – that seems strange. You've got a good memory for detail, but you don't remember *that*? Doesn't it strike you as odd?'

'Maybe I just don't *want* to remember. The fact is that I *did* swear an oath to Hitler, and I *did* put on that uniform. Those are acts of treason, irrespective of why I did it.'

'I'm your advocate, Tom: don't condemn yourself to me. What I need is a defence.'

Caine watched her steadily. 'I can't give you one,

Celia. I'm sorry. Don't think I'm not grateful for your help, but the fact is that I should never have done it. I'm a decorated SAS soldier: me just putting on a collaborator's uniform was a victory for the Hun.'

Blaney sighed: she couldn't deny the truth in that. 'All right,' she said. 'Tell me what happened when you got back to the forward-base.'

Caine thought about it: it had been a confusing time. They'd got back to the 2nd SAS forward operating-base at Bari after forty-eight hours motoring across Italy: lying up in the woods by day, travelling at night. They'd avoided checkpoints, hadn't been challenged: they'd crossed through their own lines without mishap. 'My first priority was to get Emilia to a field hospital,' Caine said. 'The journey had been rough on her: she was still only half-conscious, but I thought she'd be all right. I didn't see her again – the last I heard she'd been sent to a hospital here in Constantine. We handed Grolsch over to the MPs – he was also sent for medical treatment. Wallace and Trubman had to report in as escaped POWs: I should have done too, but I went to the DMI's office instead, intending to tell them about Butterfield, the Codex, special handling, Savarin – the lot.'

'What happened?'

'Butterfield had got there before me, that's what. He must have realized I'd shop him despite his threats; he'd gone right in and given them a statement about me and the BFC. They didn't even give me a chance to speak. Next thing I know, I'm sandwiched between two gigantic Redcaps, being marched to the guardhouse on a charge of treason. Butterfield was right, of course: they believed him rather than me – he's an Int. Corps officer.'

'He's a disgrace to the badge,' Celia said. 'We're not all like that.'

'Granted.'

'Major Butterfield is in town, and he'll be in court – he's the main witness for the prosecution. I haven't spoken to him, but I did get my Field Security colleagues to do some checking. His main job as Assistant IO of 2nd SAS is collecting valuable Italian paintings and *objets d'art*, mostly from Itie churches.'

'I know: he told me.'

'Seems there's already some dark cloud about missing art treasures hanging over him. Nothing proved, of course. He told the DMI that the operation to retrieve the Codex had failed, that he never got the manuscript out.'

Caine remembered the excitement in Emilia's face when they'd found the chest, when she'd opened the box, found the Codex inside. 'There are witnesses,' he said.

'I know, but even by your own testimony, apart from you, only Emilia actually saw it: Ettore didn't get the chance. Ettore will be in court, but I'm told Emilia's not currently able to testify.'

'Are you going to talk to Butterfield?'

Blaney shook her head. 'What I'd really like to do is

have Field Security search that hut he keeps his official art-treasures in. Never know what might turn up.'

Caine scratched his chin. 'What about Harry Copeland and the others? Have you seen them?'

'No, but I know they're around. Lieutenant Copeland is at the 2nd SAS base. Wallace and Corporal Trubman are in a transit camp. Your squadron's gone back to Blighty, anyway, but as escaped POWs they can't be posted straight back to their unit – they have to go through some vetting first.'

'Why? In case they joined the Hun secretly?'

'It's standard procedure, Tom.'

'I know. Doesn't seem right, though. It's as if their loyalty's being questioned.'

Blaney shuftied her watch again. 'I'd better be going. I've got a much better picture of what we're up against now.' She sat back, ran a hand through her flaming curls, surveyed him with soft, dove-coloured eyes. 'The first thing to do, Tom, is to stop feeling guilty about everything. You didn't start the war: none of us can help being here. If men have been killed under your command, it wasn't your fault. It was the dangerous missions you were given that put their lives at risk: some were going to be killed whatever happened. Ditto Betty Nolan and the Countess Emilia. You did your best, and that was damn' good: Hitler may be the devil incarnate, but you're not, Tom. You're a good man: the war can't change that – not unless you let it.'

Caine felt his cheeks flush. 'I still put on that Nazi

uniform, Celia. I still swore loyalty to Hitler. Nothing can change that, either.'

Blaney leaned forward, laid both her hands on his. 'Tell me something, Tom: I want you to be completely honest.'

'What?'

'Do you remember *at any time* making a conscious decision to join the British Free Corps, or to swear allegiance to Hitler – even with an ulterior motive?'

Caine considered it for a moment. 'No,' he said. 'I don't remember. But I know I was wearing the uniform, so I must have done.'

Blaney's lips parted slightly. 'It doesn't necessarily follow. The fact is that you *don't* recall having made a conscious decision to join the enemy, or even to *pretend* to join the enemy. That's the point to hold on to: maybe you never *did* make a conscious decision.'

Caine felt confused. 'How is that possible?'

'I don't know. It's just a feeling.'

She started gathering her things, put them away, stood up, picked up her chip-bag cap. Caine stood facing her, watched her smooth her red curls, pin her cap in place with elegant movements.

'So what time do I stand before the beak?' he asked.

She shook her head. 'Not today, Tom. I'm going straight up to the judge advocate's office now, to ask for a one-day postponement.'

Caine swallowed. 'On what grounds?'

'On the grounds that we have no deposition from a key witness: *Sturmbannführer* Karl Grolsch.'

'*Grolsch?* Even if you find him, how can you be sure he'll talk?'

'He's responsible for the execution of prisoners of war: that's a capital crime under British military law. He also murdered a priest with his own hands. He's an ex-priest himself, you said: he might feel that, with the prospect of the big reckoning looming up, he wants to make amends.'

Caine stepped clear of the table, put his arms around her, kissed her: despite all he'd revealed about himself, all he'd said about Emilia, Blaney's lips were still tender and yielding: she closed her eyes, touched him lightly on the back of the neck with her fingertips. 'Get some rest, Tom,' she said finally. 'If I'm not back today, I'll see you at the hearing. Meanwhile, I want your agreement that we change your plea from guilty to not guilty.'

Caine's face dropped. 'But Celia, how can I? I've spent the whole night explaining why I'm guilty.'

Blaney gave him a melting smile.

'Trust me,' she said.

48

Constantine, Algeria
13 November 1943

'Do you solemnly swear by Almighty God that the testimony you will give to this field general court-martial will be the truth, the whole truth, and nothing but the truth?'

'I do,' Caine said.

Blaney took back the Bible, laid it on the battered school desk she was using as her defence stand: it was littered with papers piled untidily around a package the size of a large cake-box, covered in brown paper. She wore a freshly pressed BD blouse and trousers: officially, she was improperly dressed for a court-martial, but her uniform seemed to provoke nothing but interest from the all-male company. Her burst of curly, flame-coloured hair reminded Caine of the fiery colours of the Italian woods, blazing like a bonfire in the drabness of the disused classroom: bare floorboards, broken easels in a corner, motionless fans drooping from the ceiling like soft propellers, glassless windows that let in far-off street sounds and sunlight in wide blocks.

The president of the board, a full colonel called

Benson, sat behind a rickety trestle-table opposite: he was a staff judge-advocate, but the rainbow of medal ribbons on his chest showed that he'd seen his fair share of combat. He had a long lantern jaw and a cap of wispy white hair: under half-moon spectacles, his eyes were watery blue, but sharp. He was flanked by a lean, sallow captain and a beef-faced major. To one side stood the court usher, a ramrod-straight MP sergeant with a red sash and mirror-like boots.

'You may remove your headgear, Captain,' Blaney said.

Caine's BD suit, complete with rank insignia, medal ribbons and SAS wings, had been supplied by Regimental HQ: his boots were polished: he was wearing his sand-coloured beret for the first time in months. As he slipped it off, he realized how proud of it he still was. He remembered Paddy Mayne's penchant for wearing his beret in combat: it was an amulet of a kind, imbued with symbolic power, earned, not given.

When the provost guard had marched him in, he'd been surprised to find Mayne there, sitting at the back, huge, glowering, perched precariously on a flimsy school chair: around him, crowded together like a rugby-scrum, were Copeland, Wallace, Trubman, officers from the 1st SAS office, other ranks from 2nd SAS. Ettore sat a little distance away, dressed in a dark suit: he looked tired and withdrawn. Caine felt a twinge of disappointment that Emilia wasn't with him: Blaney had told him she was still in hospital, but somehow he'd hoped to find her there.

'Would you state your name, rank and current posting please, sir,' Blaney said.

'Captain Thomas Edward Caine, 1st Special Raiding Squadron, 1st SAS Regiment. My current status is returned prisoner of war.'

'Thank you, Captain. You may sit down.'

Caine sat, glanced at the table to his right where Butterfield was seated next to the prosecuting officer. It was the first time Caine had seen the major since he'd run off from the chapel, and it looked as if he'd put on weight. His BD suit was tight and, until sworn in, he'd been wearing an emperor-sized SAS beret that sat like a pancake on his globe-shaped head. He studiously avoided looking at Caine.

Minutes earlier, the major had sat down with a satisfied expression on his face: the court had heard him deliver his testimony in brief, eloquent sentences – how Caine had donned the uniform of the British Free Corps, a unit recruited from British deserters, how he'd admitted swearing an oath to Hitler, how he had worked for the enemy as a trustee, one of two such collaborators who'd escorted him on a transfer convoy.

Blaney had cross-examined Butterfield, but it hadn't begun well. 'Isn't it true that, while sharing a cell with Captain Caine at the Jesi prison camp, you asked him to help you escape?' she'd demanded.

Butterfield licked his thick lips. 'Yes, it's true.'

'And isn't it also true that, when your convoy was ambushed by partisans, Captain Caine *did* try to help you escape? Didn't he dispense with the Waffen-SS uniform at the first opportunity and take part in offensive operations against the Germans?'

'Whether he helped me or not, I can't remember: I was wounded in the head and lost consciousness. Yes, he later appeared without the SS uniform, in civilian clothes, and took part in operations against the enemy.'

'Isn't it possible, therefore, that Captain Caine pretended to join the so-called British Free Corps, in order to carry out your request?'

'*Objection*, sir.' It was the prosecuting officer, a swag-bellied captain named Ferguson with horn-rimmed glasses and a bullet head. He was on his feet, glaring at Blaney. 'We can't be sure what Caine's motives were. For all we know, it might have been pure opportunism – a bid to obtain more favourable conditions for himself. The essential point is that he joined enemy forces as a collaborator and put on their uniform. That in itself is an act of treason, whatever the motive.'

The president whipped off his glasses. 'That's quite correct, Captain Ferguson. This court-martial must distinguish between a legitimate ruse and a forbidden act of perfidy. A military operation, for instance, in which it might be expedient to deceive the enemy by wearing his uniform, would be a legitimate ruse. Swearing allegiance to the enemy and putting on the uniform of a collaborator, however, is a forbidden act of perfidy *per se*, even if the accused considered it a ruse at the time.'

He replaced his glasses impatiently, peered at Caine. 'Captain Caine, did you or did you not appear in public wearing the uniform of the Waffen-SS, or, more specifically, the uniform of a unit raised from deserters of His Majesty's forces?'

'Yes,' Caine said, 'but I don't –'

'Did you or did you not carry out orders given to you by an enemy, or by another collaborator, to guard a fellow officer and prevent his escape – an act inimical to His Majesty's forces?'

'Yes, I did, but –'

'Did you or did you not swear an oath of allegiance to Adolf Hitler?'

'I don't know –'

'You don't *know*? Come now, Captain, you surely wouldn't forget a thing like that? Did you or did you not swear loyalty to Hitler?'

'All right, maybe I did.'

'Then there's little more to be said, is there? Why you did it need not concern the court. The fact is that you *did* do it: you're guilty. I'm astonished that an officer of your calibre should be capable of such poor judgement, but I must remind you that treason is a very grave charge under British military law, and may be punishable by death.'

There was absolute silence in the court: for a moment, even Blaney looked stunned.

The president stared at her. 'I know you're an amateur here, Lieutenant,' he said. 'But I fail to see the logic in the accused changing his plea from guilty to not guilty when he openly admits his guilt. I'm not wasting any more of this court-martial's time. It's regrettable to see a decorated officer fallen from grace, but in the circumstances I have no option but to call for the full penalty of –'

'Just a moment, sir,' Blaney's voice was small but steady.

Benson stopped in mid-sentence, glowered at her ferociously. He seemed about to plough on regardless when she interrupted him again. 'Captain Caine has not admitted guilt in this case.'

The president raised his eyebrows. 'I may be old, Lieutenant, but I'm not deaf.' He exchanged looks with the other members of the board. 'I think we all heard the accused admit his guilt.'

'Mr Caine has admitted putting on an enemy uniform and collaborating with the enemy, but those in themselves are not acts of treason.'

'*Really*, Lieutenant? Now you *are* telling me my job.'

'That's not my intention, sir, but it is the case that to constitute treason such acts must be carried out with *deliberate intention* on the part of the accused.'

'Intention is implied, Lieutenant. If he carried out those acts he must have had the intention to do so.'

'Not necessarily, sir. People may be coerced into actions they had no intention of doing. If you will allow me to complete my cross-examination, I hope to show that there *was* no such intention.'

'Sir,' Ferguson cut in. 'This woman is squandering the court's time.'

'This *woman* is an officer of the Intelligence Corps,' Blaney responded acidly. 'You may address me as *Lieutenant* or *Miss Blaney*. Thank you, sir.'

The president suppressed a smile, glanced at his watch, sighed. 'All right then, Lieutenant, but make it snappy. We haven't got all day.'

Blaney stood in front of Caine, feet apart, hands clasped behind her back like a stage-lawyer. 'Captain Caine, could you explain to this court-martial why you changed your plea from guilty to not guilty?'

Caine looked into the soft grey eyes. 'Yes. Because I have no recollection of making a conscious decision to join the enemy, even as a ruse.'

There was a scoff from the other table: Ferguson was on his feet again. '*Objection*, sir. It would be most convenient if we could all forget our compromising decisions. We have no way of knowing whether he's telling the truth.'

Blaney bit her lip. 'Captain Caine, I remind you that you are under oath. Do you wish to change your testimony?'

'No. I don't remember making any such decision.'

The president was about to speak when Blaney held up a sheaf of typewritten papers. 'I have a deposition here from the only known witness of Captain Caine's alleged acts of treason. I think it's highly pertinent and I'd like the court to read it. It was dictated to me by *SS-Sturmbannführer* Karl Grolsch, Waffen-SS, a German officer captured behind enemy lines by the same SAS patrol that brought back Captain Caine. *SS-Sturmbannführer* Grolsch was instrumental to, and a witness of, Captain Caine's actions, which are the subject of deliberation of this court-martial. Do I have permission to submit this statement as evidence?'

'*Objection*, sir.' Ferguson was up yet again, scowling at Blaney. 'We should have been shown this testimony earlier. In any case, is the deposition of an enemy officer admissible as evidence?'

The president paused. 'Why is it so late, Lieutenant?'

'I only discovered where the prisoner was yesterday, sir. I had to persuade him to tell the truth. It seems he was troubled about some of his own actions, particularly the killing of a Roman Catholic priest. As an SS officer, he'd been obliged to carry out some duties he now considers wrong.'

'How convenient,' Ferguson commented. 'Now he's a prisoner of war.'

'The point is that it gives him a reason for telling the truth,' Blaney said fiercely. She held up the typed pages. 'Read this and you'll see what I mean.'

The president peered at her over his half-moon lenses. 'Very well,' he said. 'I'm accepting the evidence. Let me see that.'

Blaney handed copies of the typed document to

the three board members, to the prosecution, to Butterfield: finally, she laid a copy down in front of Caine. 'Read it,' she whispered. 'I think you'll find it interesting.'

Caine read:

Statement by *SS-Sturmbannführer* Karl Grolsch, Waffen-SS, currently a prisoner of war of the Allied Forces, Algeria, formerly Field Kommandant, Gestapo Troops (Sipo-SD), Le Marche Region, Italy. Made this day, 12 November 1943, at HQ Allied Forces, Constantine, Algeria.

I, Karl Grolsch, make this statement of my own free will, and under oath that it is the truth, the whole truth, and nothing but the truth. I make it, to the best of my ability, in the English language, as dictated to Lieutenant C. Blaney, No. 2 Field Security Section, Intelligence Corps.

Capt. T. E. Caine, 1st SAS Regiment, was brought into the Jesi prison-camp on 4 October 1943, having been captured by our Airborne Division at the Senarca bridge, near Termoli. From the beginning, it was realized that, as a special service officer of field rank, Capt. Caine might be a valuable asset to our propaganda effort. It was proposed that he should be recruited to the British Free Corps, a unit under the aegis of the Waffen-SS, being raised from British prisoners of war by *SS-Hauptsturmführer* John Amray, a former officer of the New Zealand Army, now deceased.

Hauptsturmführer Amray felt that Capt. Caine might make a good subject for turning, and proposed that he join the British Free Corps. Caine refused point blank, saying that he remained staunchly loyal to his country. Amray still felt that he might be turned, however, using a technique the Gestapo (Sipo-SD) had been experimenting with – a method whose aim was to prove that, by a combination of powerful drugs and hypnosis, an individual could be made to carry out actions contrary to his basic moral principles.

On the evening of 7 October, Amray introduced 3cc of a drug called Citodan into Capt. Caine's food. Caine fell into a trance and was moved to another room, where I was present. He was asked to stare into the lamp of an opthalmoscope, and given certain suggestions – that he would join the British Free Corps, swear allegiance to the Führer, work as a trustee for Sipo-SD, and fight on behalf of the Third Reich. When he woke from the trance, he would have no memory of being hypnotized.

Capt. Caine reacted physically to these suggestions. His breathing became faster, his heart-rate jumped to 120: he clenched his teeth, screwed up his face, shouted. He was again instructed to stare into the opthalmoscope: the suggestions were repeated. He was then told that, when instructed, he would go into a deep sleep: when he woke the following morning, he would believe that he had joined the British Free Corps of his own choice, and would have memories of swearing an oath of allegiance to the Führer. He would also be led to believe that he had had sex with a young Italian girl as a 'reward' for his turning, which, it was believed, would help reinforce the post-hypnotic suggestions.

When Capt. Caine awoke on 8 October, he found himself in different surroundings, wearing SS uniform, with a naked girl in his bed, whom, he was led to believe, he had had sex with. He seemed to have accepted the hypnotic conditioning, to the extent that he agreed – or believed he had already agreed – to escort Major Butterfield, as a trustee, on a convoy transporting him to another destination. The convoy was subsequently ambushed by partisans. I was myself wounded in the attack, but I discovered later that, rather than fighting off the attackers in defence of his supposed 'new comrades', Capt. Caine actually killed several of my men, tried to help Major Butterfield escape, then ran off himself.

I believe that subsequent events show our hypnotic technique to have been flawed. Despite its powerful effect, Capt. Caine retained a strong resistance, and a deep sense of himself. In my opinion, he nursed that resistance quietly until he found a chance to escape. I can state categorically that Capt. Caine never actually took part in a ceremony swearing allegiance to our Führer, nor did he verbally accept the idea of joining the BFC. I have no more access to another's thoughts than anyone else, but I do not believe that he made a conscious decision to carry out any action that might be interpreted as betraying his country. He was coerced by a process that he had not been trained to resist.

Caine read the statement with breathless incredulity: his first thought was that Blaney had made it up. He read it again, his heart bumping. This time, though, it rang true. *The missing day*, he thought. *I woke up with the memory of a day that never was. I couldn't work out why it was still only* 8 *October.* He looked up into Blaney's rose-and-ivory features. 'How did you know?' he whispered.

'I knew you couldn't have done it voluntarily,' she said softly, 'not even as a ruse. I guessed they'd coerced you in some way, but it was strange that you couldn't remember, and I was sure you weren't lying. Then you talked about hypnotic suggestion. It set me thinking. It was just a hunch, but I wondered –'

'*This is preposterous*,' the prosecuting officer boomed. 'Are we supposed to believe this nonsense?Hypnosis, trance-inducing drugs . . . a fantasy concocted by a Nazi war-criminal whose only object is to show himself in a good light?'

Blaney smiled sweetly at him. 'But it *doesn't* show him in a good light, sir. Experimenting on POWs is a war-crime under the Geneva Convention.'

A buzz of voices built up behind them. '*What the 'ell's goin' on, 'ere?*' Caine heard Wallace growl.

The president banged the table with his gavel. '*Quiet!*' he ordered.

The babble died down: the room fell silent. The

judge-advocate adjusted his glasses. 'This is a remarkable document,' he said. 'It not only suggests a fascinating new concept of warfare, but, if true, it also exonerates Captain Caine from the charge of treason. I see no reason to disbelieve the statement simply because it was made by a German officer, especially, as Lt. Blaney says, as he has little to gain by it. I need to discuss it with my colleagues, but I am going to suggest that Captain Caine be acquitted –'

'Excuse me, sir,' Blaney cut in. 'There is still the matter of why Major Butterfield should have accused Captain Caine in the first place.'

The president frowned. 'I don't believe that is relevant to this court-martial, Lieutenant.'

Blaney shook rust-coloured curls. 'With all due respect, sir, I believe it is. A crime has been committed, not by Captain Caine, but by someone else, and I believe it's the duty of this court to ascertain the nature of that crime.' She turned, stared at Butterfield, her face serious now. He had gone pale and was drumming his puppet's fingers on the table: his eyes bulged at her as if unable to tear himself away from her gaze.

'Major Butterfield was sent on a mission of his own devising,' Blaney announced, 'to retrieve a medieval manuscript – the *Codex Aesinias* – the property of an Italian family. The Codex is not only a valuable instrument of German propaganda, it's also worth a fortune. It was the major's intention to steal it for himself –'

The room erupted with a new clamour of voices:

Ferguson was on his feet, trying to catch the president's attention, wiping his head with a handkerchief: Butterfield was white-faced: his eyes darted, his loose lips worked soundlessly.

'. . . He requested Captain Caine to take over the mission from him, and when Mr Caine subsequently found the Codex, Major Butterfield stole it at gunpoint, wounding a civilian woman in the process. The relevant part, sir, is this: that Major Butterfield decided to expose Captain Caine as a traitor in order to discredit him and cover up his theft of the Codex. It worked. Mr Caine's report was discounted, and he was arrested on the major's testimony.'

'*It's true, Your Honour*,' a voice cut in. Blaney glanced round: Ettore was on his feet, his hand raised like a schoolboy asking a question, his eggshell-coloured cheeks flushed. '*I was there. That was my sister the fat guy shot . . .*'

The president banged his gavel again: this time no one took any notice. The court usher roared, '*Silence in the court-martial!*' His words were all but lost under the avalanche of noise.

'*If this is true, where is this so-called Codex now?*' Ferguson bawled.

The noise reached a crescendo: Blaney moved back to her table, a faint smile on her lips. She picked up the brown-paper package, undid the paper, brought out a cardboard box. Caine knew he'd seen the box before. *The box the Codex was in when we found it.*

Blaney laid the box back on the table, slid the lid off with a showman's deliberation. She held up a slim volume covered in gnarled leather, blinking self-deprecatingly, as if she'd just brought a rabbit out of a hat but hadn't expected to find it there.

'Where is the Codex? It's here. Right here in front of you. How did it get here? At first light this morning, my Field Security colleagues raided Major Butterfield's store at the 2nd SAS base at Philippeville: they found the Codex hidden under the floorboards, together with several other art treasures that have been reported missing.'

The clamour rose to a riptide. The president stopped banging his gavel for quiet, whipped off his glasses, stared fixedly at the Codex. Butterfield pushed past the prosecuting officer, took a couple of lumbering steps towards the board's table. There were jeers from the audience: Butterfield froze, cast around him in bewilderment as if trying to pinpoint the hecklers: with his beady eyes, his domed head and his sweeping dewlaps, he looked like a cornered turkey, Caine thought.

'*Stop!*' the president snapped. 'The witness has not been given permission to leave his seat.'

'But come on, old boy,' Butterfield gobbled. 'What kind of a court-martial is this? It's not me who's on trial here.'

'You're accused of a serious offence. You have the right to remain silent. Any statement you do make may be used against you in a court-martial.' The president signalled to the MPs at the back of the court. 'Guard the prisoner,' he ordered.

The MPs were like mountains: wedged between them, Butterfield was a deflated balloon. His bead-like eyes were pinned on Caine. 'This is your doing,' he wailed. 'I risked my life to get that Codex.'

'You're a brave man, Major,' Caine said. 'You *did* risk your life, and you faced execution without batting an eyelid. I salute you for that. But you also risked the lives of others – the countess, Ettore, Lieutenant Howard and the 2nd SAS lads. What are you going to tell their families when they ask why their sons were sacrificed? So that you could spend the rest of your life gloating over some old book?'

Butterfield shook his head. 'A man like you would never understand, Caine.'

Caine rose slowly to his feet, replaced his sand-coloured beret, jerked the flap down over his right temple. He stood up straight, looked Butterfield in the eye. 'You're right, Major,' he said. 'I wouldn't.'

49

After the cheers and backslapping, Caine separated himself from the crowd, found Celia Blaney standing forlorn in the gravel driveway. She had her hands in her pockets and was taking in the view of the sea, a seam of scintillating blue-green stained glass set against minarets and stucco buildings. She turned to face him: a soft breeze ruffled her fiery hair.

'I just wanted to thank you,' Caine said. 'You were magnificent.'

Blaney's grey satin eyes were wary: she didn't take her hands out of her pockets.

'What now, Tom?' she asked: there was a tremor in her voice that he'd never heard before. 'What are you going to do?'

Caine wavered, not sure what she meant: after the brilliant, assured performance she'd put on in court, she seemed subdued, even hostile.

'I don't have a unit to go back to.' He shrugged. 'The SRS is back home: it's due for disbandment, anyway. I can't go back to the Regiment right this minute, but Paddy confirmed that the SAS is due to be expanded into a brigade, with two British regiments, two French, one Belgian. It's going to be training in Britain for the invasion of Europe. He said he'd be looking for troop and squadron leaders: he wants to get all the old desert boys together for the final crack. So I suppose it's back to Blighty for me.'

Blaney gave him a bleak smile. 'So you haven't given up, Tom?'

'Nah, I suppose I'll see the war out, if Fritz doesn't get me first. Haven't really got much choice, have I?'

'It's going to be tough on special troops – this *Commando Order* business. From now on, SAS soldiers will be shot on sight.'

Caine scowled. 'I talked to Paddy about that, too. He says the DMI won't accept there's any such thing as the *Commando Order*. They say it's just enemy propaganda.'

Blaney didn't look surprised. 'They want to suppress it, Tom. They know it's true, but they think that, if it's made public, it'll affect morale. The DMI asked me to get rid of any reference to special handling in Grolsch's statement or the court-martial. Grolsch isn't even going to be tried as a war criminal.'

Caine nodded grimly. 'Is that the deal you did with him to get his statement?'

'No.' Blaney frowned. 'Maybe Grolsch thinks it is, but there's no statute of limitations on war-crimes. He'll get his when the war's over.'

Yes, Caine thought. *Whoever kills a sacred ibis shall die.*

At that moment Ettore bustled past them, carrying the Codex under his arm in its cardboard box.

'Isn't it risky carrying that thing around?' Blaney

asked him. 'Quite a few people have died, or nearly died, for it already.'

Ettore gave her a thin-lipped smile. 'I guess we'll put it in safe-keeping somewhere until the war's over, then we'll donate it to the National Museum of Italy – if it still exists.' He lifted the box, weighed it in both hands. 'It seems kind of lightweight, considering all the lives it's cost. I'm tempted just to throw it into the sea.'

'That would be a mistake,' Blaney told him. 'You know what Milton said: *he who destroys a good book destroys reason itself.*'

'Except that it isn't a good book.' The youth rolled his shoulders. 'It's one of the most dangerous books ever written.' He glanced at the box, stuck it back under his arm resolutely. 'I'm off to see Emilia. Want to come?'

'Perhaps later,' Caine said.

They watched him lope off towards the gate: there was silence between them.

'*No. 6 Military Hospital*,' Blaney blurted out.

'*What?*'

'That's where she is. If you hurry you can catch up with him.'

Caine turned to her, took in the large, moist eyes, the rose-and-vanilla features, the flaming hair, the soft face full of sadness.

'You want to see her, don't you?' she said in a small voice.

Suddenly Caine understood: she was afraid that, now the court-martial was over, he would go back to Emilia and forget her. How could he? She'd saved his life. It was true that Emilia had also saved his life: it was true that in Italy he'd felt attracted to her: he could still taste that startling kiss in the most unexpected of places. He laid a hand on Blaney's arm, pulled on it gently until she withdrew her fingers from her pocket. He linked the arm through his, clasped it firmly, felt no resistance.

'Come on,' he said. 'We'll go together.'

Emilia had been a good companion in the field, but Blaney had waited for him, rescued him, been there for him. Emilia was beautiful and vivacious and a countess, but, after all, Blaney was . . . well, Blaney.